Rudyard Kipling (1865–1936) ⁣⁣⁣⁣⁣⁣⁣⁣⁣⁣⁣⁣ educated in England for some years at the ⁣⁣⁣⁣⁣⁣vices College, Westward Ho, Bideford. Returning to India in 1882, he worked as a newspaper reporter and a part-time writer and this helped him to gain a rich experience of colonial life, which he later presented in his stories and poems. In 1886 he published his first volume of poetry, *Departmental Ditties*, and between 1887 and 1889 he published six volumes of short stories set in and concerned with the India he had come to know and love so well. In 1894 appeared his *Jungle Book*, which became a children's classic all over the world, and *Kim* (1901), the story of Kimball O'Hara and his adventures in the Himalayas, which is perhaps his best-known work. Kipling's works include *Plain Tales from the Hills* (1888), *Under the Deodars* (1888), *Life's Handicap* (1891), *The Second Jungle Book* (1895), *The Seven Seas* (1896), *Captains Courageous* (1897), *The Day's Work* (1898), *Stalky & Co.* (1899), *Just So Stories* (1902), *Trafficks and Discoveries* (1904), *Puck of Pook's Hill* (1906), *Actions and Reactions* (1909), *Land and Sea Tales for Scouts and Guides* (1923), *Debits and Credits* (1926), *Thy Servant a Dog* (1930) and *Limits and Renewals* (1932). In 1907 Kipling won the Nobel Prize in literature and in 1926 the Gold Medal of the Royal Society of Literature. His autobiography, *Something of Myself*, was written in 1936, the last year of his life, and was published posthumously.

*

Sudhakar Marathe is Professor, Department of English, University of Hyderabad. He is the author of *T.S. Eliot's Shakespeare Criticism* and *Read First, Criticize Afterwards*.

STORIES OF INDIA

RUDYARD KIPLING

Edited by Sudhakar Marathe

PENGUIN BOOKS

PENGUIN BOOKS
Published by the Penguin Group
Penguin Books India Pvt. Ltd, 11 Community Centre, Panchsheel Park, New Delhi 110 017, India
Penguin Group (USA) Inc., 375 Hudson Street, New York, New York 10014, USA
Penguin Group (Canada), 90 Eglinton Avenue East, Suite 700, Toronto, Ontario, M4P 2Y3, Canada (a division of Pearson Penguin Canada Inc.)
Penguin Books Ltd, 80 Strand, London WC2R 0RL, England
Penguin Ireland, 25 St Stephen's Green, Dublin 2, Ireland (a division of Penguin Books Ltd)
Penguin Group (Australia), 250 Camberwell Road, Camberwell, Victoria 3124, Australia (a division of Pearson Australia Group Pty Ltd)
Penguin Group (NZ), 67 Apollo Drive, Rosedale, North Shore 0632, New Zealand (a division of Pearson New Zealand Ltd)
Penguin Group (South Africa) (Pty) Ltd, 24 Sturdee Avenue, Rosebank, Johannesburg 2196, South Africa

Penguin Books Ltd, Registered Offices: 80 Strand, London WC2R 0RL, England

First published by Penguin Books India 2003

Copyright © Penguin Books India 2003
Introduction copyright © Sudhakar Marathe 2003

Typeset in Sabon by Mantra Virtual Services, New Delhi
Printed at Anubha Printers, Noida

CONTENTS

Acknowledgements	*vii*
Editor's Note	*ix*
Introduction	*xi*
Preface (from *Life's Handicap*)	1
Little Tobrah	6
Lispeth	9
Watches of the Night	14
Tods' Amendment	20
A Bank Fraud	26
Beyond the Pale	33
Pig	39
The Bronckhorst Divorce-Case	46
The Mark of the Beast	52
His Chance in Life	65
The Bride's Progress	71
An Unqualified Pilot	78
At the Pit's Mouth	88
A Wayside Comedy	94
The Tomb of His Ancestors	105
Consequences	136
The Finances of the Gods	141
William the Conqueror	146
Miss Youghal's Sais	178
Thrown Away	184
The Son of His Father	192

Interchapter 211

The Enlightenments of Pagett, M.P. 213

Georgie Porgie 241

In the Pride of His Youth 250

The Arrest of Lieutenant Golightly 256

The Story of Muhammad Din 261

The Miracle of Purun Bhagat 265

EDITOR'S NOTE

The stories presented in this volume have been selected from nine different collections of Rudyard Kipling, all published in the space of twelve years. That is now well over a hundred years ago. Born in Bombay, he had spent the first six years of his life in India. It is worth knowing that when he returned to India after ten years of school in England Kipling was a young cub reporter of only seventeen. In 1888, when he was only twenty-three years old, *Plain Tales from the Hills* was published. The stories in this volume had already appeared in newspaper columns, which also explains why they are so short. When the last of the volumes represented here was published, he was still only twenty-nine years old. Still one sees an astonishing range of experience in his stories and in his sensitive portrayal of the people and conditions of India.

The stories in this volume were selected for their variety—of characters and situations—and for their reaction to Anglo-Indian encounters. They were also selected for sympathetic and sensitive representation of both British and Indian characters—a feature of Kipling's work many readers do not know. And most importantly, they were selected because they are first-rate examples of the art of storytelling. The volumes from which stories have been taken for the present collection are *Plain Tales from the Hills*; *Under the Deodars*; *Wee Willie Winkie, etc.*; *Life's Handicap*; *From Sea to Sea and Other Stories*; *Land and Sea Tales*; *The Day's Work*; *Many Inventions*; and *The Jungle Book*.

ACKNOWLEDGEMENTS

It was only appropriate that I finished work on this volume on Mother's Day 2002. For I must here acknowledge gratitude to my mother, who was for a long time the only one who believed in me. I owe a great debt also to Meera, who took over the job from my mother; to Kaumudi and Sameer, who think I am somebody special; to Jerry and Beth Bentley, who encouraged me in numerous ways in my association with challenging reading; and V.K. Karthika at Penguin Books India, who was once a student who encouraged me, for recognizing the fact that a substantial volume of Kipling's stories was long overdue by way of restoration and as exciting reading. I particularly acknowledge Ankita Mukherji's meticulous and sensitive work in preparing the manuscript for publication.

ACKNOWLEDGMENTS

It was while a postgraduate that I embarked upon my first attempt at [...] [...] 2005. For many I [...] people [...] a number of people who have been important and that I [...] [...] press. My thanks go to [...] Allison, [...] Jackson, [...] for her [...] and [...] [...] and suggestions that [...] possible. I am [...] my [...] to her and [...] publisher [...] [...] in [...] [...] [...] my special thanks [...] the [...] reviewing [...] descriptions [...] for the [...] thanks to [...] too [...] workers involved in [...] in [...] [...] manner [...] [...] families, friends and [...] [...] [...] Transylvania, [...] whose [...] this book a [...] [...] [...] the [...] of [...].

INTRODUCTION

The stories and sketches of Rudyard Kipling (1865-1936) brought together in this volume are all set in Kipling's India, or to use the appropriate term 'Anglo-India'. They will surprise you with descriptions of India available nowhere in such immediate, vivid and graphic terms. They will surprise you by the range of Indian places and situations in them. They provide a wealth of historical information about what India was a century ago as cannot be found in the work of any other author, Indian or British.

They will make available not only a historical view of India we rarely meet in writings on the subject but also a frighteningly real, almost contemporary and, alas, relevant picture of an India which is still around us, in Ayodhya and Gujarat and numerous other places, and which we can no longer pass off as 'colonial distortion'. They will make us wonder about the fundamental human values we say we cherish.

These stories present a vast picture gallery of Anglo-Indian or colonial British characters unparalleled in the work of any other author. It is a gallery complete with rogues and fools and misguided people, soldiers and civil servants, policemen, wives and sons and daughters—characters who cannot distinguish between what matters and what does not. The gallery includes characters who endear themselves to us because they seem to know and care for India even better than most Indians, and characters who definitely do not endear themselves to us by their insensitivity to India and Indians, by their ignorance of the land they were supposed to govern, serve and 'civilize'.

There are among them people from all walks of Anglo-Indian life who are dramatically presented in an often humorous and frequently critical light—bankers and missionaries, young people and old, honest dealers and cheats, people whom India fascinates and entices with its mysteries and challenges, and people whom it utterly defeats. There are characters here who engage in social work that we wish to do even today, and others who come from outside in total ignorance and yet presumptuously provide unasked-for advice to those who know how to do their work.

And there are children—many children—who reveal astonishing truths about the Imperial government, its machinery and its officials. As in the work of many other Victorian writers, in Kipling's writing you will find both works written for children, such as *Just So Stories*, and child characters in grown-up stories, such as the toddler in 'The Finances of the Gods'. Like other writers of his age such as Charles Kingsley and Charles Dickens, Kipling understood children uncannily well.

The pieces in this volume represent the stage on which India and Anglo-India met, and reveal the limits to their relations and boundaries between their distinct communities. In 'Tods' Amendment' and 'Beyond the Pale' we see the benefits and tragic consequences of transgressing these boundaries. 'Pig' and 'The Bank Fraud', on the other hand, bring before us a foolish Englishman and a right-minded Englishman respectively. Many others like 'A Wayside Story' and 'At the Pit's Mouth' probe the shoddy relations among members of Anglo-Indian communities and the circumstances in which they spawned.

And as in the work of his Victorian contemporaries, in Kipling's adult stories the dramatically real juvenile characters also perform a serious function. They hold the mirror up to grown-up follies, immaturities, misreadings and pettinesses. In 'Tods' Amendment' a crucial government bill is significantly improved by the intervention of a small British boy who only speaks the street language of Simla bazars. Just as interesting is the case of Strickland, a police officer who knows India better than any other Anglo-Indian and, in disguise, can become a very credible fakir or a mullah at will. Kipling clearly approves of Strickland. Yet in 'The Son of His Father' his very young son teaches him a lesson for being presumptuous about India.

His women characters, too, have the ability to criticize Anglo-Indian society, especially men in their public as well as private lives. In Kipling's stories we may meet more men than women, and more Anglo-Indian women than Indian women.

That is only natural, because he mainly inhabited the world of men, and these men were British. But of the many women we do meet only a few are flat characters even when they are sketchily drawn. More often than not they are real women, often suffering women, limited in presentation only because they inhabit the world of very short stories.

Take the story of 'The Bronckhorst Divorce-Case' in which Bronckhorst treats his wife with vile insensitivity even in company. Kipling says that a woman would rather take an occasional blow than be subjected to such heartlessness. While Bronckhorst *is* punished at the end of the story, for Kipling a crucial question still remains: 'What I want to know is, "How do women like Mrs Bronckhorst come to marry men like Bronckhorst?" And my conundrum is . . . unanswerable.' On the other hand, some of Kipling's other male characters could only provoke admiration in our own era of corrupt politicians and corrupt officials.

Many of the stories included in this volume introduce us to fascinating women characters, wives, mothers, sisters and daughters. They are far more fairly represented here than in most writers. Indeed, Kipling demonstrates in 'The Enlightenments of Pagett, M.P.', 'Georgie Porgie', 'A Wayside Comedy', 'William the Conqueror' and 'The Bronckhorst Divorce-Case' his deep understanding of colonial memsahibs as well as the long-suffering women of India. In a virtual epigram at the beginning of his sadly neglected first Indian novel, *The Naulakha*, he shows how very well he knew his subject: 'A hard life is always hardest for the women'.

Rudyard Kipling belonged to the great age of the short story in English, writing in the same era as Thomas Hardy, Joseph Conrad, Robert Louis Stevenson and H.G. Wells. He wrote the stories presented here well over a hundred years ago. Yet they have not been surpassed either as well-told tales or in pithiness, variety of incident, character and methods of narration.

Moreover, his genuinely versatile use of the English language as well as his representation of Indian vernacular (in particular, wonderful English renderings of what we may call 'Hindustani') reveal great resources. Kipling is able to represent great matters with brevity, even with a punch. This is the reason why, while they are genuine in material and incident, we cannot call his stories 'realistic'—for economy and power of vivid description run alongside irony, and at times bitter humour.

Other features of these stories will also reward special attention. Take the epigraphs that come between title and story. Each epigraph very aptly fits the situation in the story or sets up a counter-point worth pondering over. 'Lispeth', the story of Christian missionaries' hypocritical treatment of an orphan Pahari girl, has a biting, hard-hitting epigraph that criticizes the 'cold Christ and the Tangled Trinities' of British missionaries who forgot that Indians were human beings. It is no wonder that, before leaving the mission for ever, Lispeth tells the Chaplain's wife, 'You are all liars, you English.'

Many of these stories also have a fable-like quality, using only generic names for characters such as 'The Boy' as in 'Thrown Away' and 'The Tertium Quid' or the third party in a love-triangle in 'At the Pit's Mouth'. There can be no question that Kipling applied rigorous moral standards of judgement to his characters. Similarly, he applied common sense standards to judge what an officer, or the Imperial government itself, ought to do. 'Pig', 'Consequences', 'Tods' Amendment' and 'William the Conqueror' illustrate this forcefully. Kipling does not tolerate insensitivity to India or Indians either, as we see in stories like 'His Chance in Life', 'The Mark of the Beast' and 'The Bride's Progress'.

The stories have an uncanny knack of hitting the nail on the head while representing human minds, hearts, behaviour, weaknesses, strengths, understanding and sympathy on both sides of the divide between the East and the West. Of course it was and remains even today a real divide for most Indians as for most Westerners. But it is also an apparent divide, because it is capable of being meaningfully bridged. Kipling shows in numerous ways how 'the twain *shall* meet' and under what circumstances. An Indian would be proud to be able to write stories like 'The Finances of the Gods' and 'The Miracle of Purun Bhagat'. For they are so thoroughly, authentically Indian in circumstance and feeling that, had they been written in an Indian language, no one would have suspected Kipling was their author.

Whatever Kipling believed by way of British superiority over India, scores of his stories of British India create a very different picture. For in them he looks at Anglo-Indian characters with a combination of ruthless criticism and sympathy that is rare in any literature. No other writer has criticized as many foibles of the British as Kipling has in these stories; no other writer has presented to us so many types of involvement and encounter between Anglo-Indians and India as he has. No one with the deliberate design of writing a 'human comedy' could have managed to depict such a variety with a constant touch of irony that checks sentimentality and a humour that pricks the balloon of superior feeling and attitude in the British characters.

Historically Kipling's Indian stories are particularly important for us to read for the priceless knowledge they provide of both our India and the colonial British India of a bygone era that is not really available to us elsewhere in the immediate and human terms in which these stories are written. At the same time, no other group of stories will make us look harder at ourselves, or ask us how critically we examine our own aspirations and our own behaviour towards each other even today. For in them Indian society is mirrored with the same degree of honesty of observation and opinion as is British colonial society—even when, on occasion, we may feel Kipling happens to be wrong.

Anyone can go wrong, especially if he likes a land, and Kipling loved India. Anyone can go wrong concerning complicated matters such as the thoughts, feelings, social relations and political or spiritual aspirations of people. We all know this better today than ever before. But if we assume that because Kipling was an Anglo-Indian writer he must be wrong, we do so at our own risk. For far too often he is close to the bone in his observations, as the stories in this volume will demonstrate if we read them without prejudgement. They will reward a second, at times even a third reading. Like all worthwhile literature, these stories also play with the reader, test his ability to put two and two together on the basis of the evidence presented.

Now, in our reading if we come across something we do not like or immediately believe to be wrong, we conclude that the writer *must* be wrong. And obviously we judge even more severely an author who ventures to judge 'us'.

Neither his British nor his Indian readers have, apparently, liked his assessments and his powerful expression of them in his Indian stories. Neither readership today knows the circumstances of the time except through hearsay. And Kipling encourages some of his treatment by his view that imperialism was justified, just as at times he seems to encourage us to treat his humour at face value, even when it is only the carrier of a serious message. Consequently, readers on both sides tend to treat him dismissively. Having read only a few frequently anthologized stories and poems, or what is mistakenly considered to be his only Indian novel *Kim*, they have for long years refused to read more of his work.

Millions of people have read his work over the past hundred and ten years or so. After all, his work sold very well and was even pirated in the United States as soon as it was published. And still in a significant sense he remains 'un'-read by readers on both sides of the colonial divide, because they have shied away from acknowledging his criticism of characters on both sides. You will find the stories in the present volume full of unexpected insight and criticism, even though they come from the pen of a colonial writer.

Of course Kipling was one of the community that colonized India, that believed that India needed a midwife to assist her birth into modern civilization and assumed that the British were the people to take on this difficult role. And, like thousands of his compatriots, he was wrong in this assumption, as all those who colonize are wrong. But at the same time we treat Kipling as an 'outsider' to India at our own cost—because not only did he thoroughly know and genuinely love India, he *was* an Indian in many important senses.

He was born and initially brought up in India and spent two-thirds of his life as an Indian writer in an India he knew very well indeed. And he despised those who trotted about the globe and treated India as a 'mere incident' in their wanderings. Look at his poem 'Pagett, M.P.' and the story of 'The Bride's Progress' through Benares. He never hesitated to reveal where Anglo-Indians went wrong, particularly where they failed as human beings by being insensitive. Both British and Indian readers are today far removed from the reality of that time and in reading his stories they will need to make allowances for Kipling's context.

Many of us these days criticize writers from previous eras for their attitudes, taking their work merely at face value. For instance, it has been said that Kipling attempted to foster the male ideal in his writings, citing works like *Stalky & Co.*, a collection of stories set in a military preparatory school, as examples. But it is poor judgement on our part to forget that most of the world at that time, including India, fostered male ideals and hero worship, and unfortunately does so even today. But many of us make this criticism without reading the numerous stories that mercilessly puncture both the British and the Indian male ideal.

The story titled 'His Chance in Life' presents a Eurasian character who is obliged to fire on a rioting 'communal' mob and kills one person, and (unlike a real sahib) would never perform such an act again. Not only is the description of the rioting perfectly realistic (for comparison, read any newspaper report of rioting from Gujarat during March and April 2002), but also worth noting is Kipling's assessment of how far someone like him can understand India and Indians like the hero Michele D'Cruz. This is what he has to say about Eurasians (today called Anglo-Indians):

> One of these days, this people...will turn out a writer or a poet; and then we shall know how they live and what they feel. *In the meantime, any stories about them cannot be absolutely correct in fact or inference.*

Naturally you will find in these stories numerous critical as well as sympathetic and highly perceptive remarks about India and Indians, expressed with such effective economy and use of the writer's craft as very few can muster today. When you read these stories you will come to the conclusion that, while Kipling was certainly one of the colonizers, he was hardly an outsider, that at worst he was a deeply involved 'insider-outsider', like so many of us today. Kipling is no 'Georgie Porgie' who kissed an Indian girl and made her cry (see the story called 'Georgie

Porgie'). In fact, reading these stories will be a serious test of our own understanding and knowledge of India then and India today, of our own ability to examine objectively and honestly our deep and persistent problems and perverseness of thought and social behaviour. It will certainly test our knowledge of the India of the late-nineteenth century.

Kipling himself said, very early in his career and very perceptively, that a writer runs the risk of both his craft and his intentions being suspected by his readers. In the same place, in his Preface to *Life's Handicap*, he also put his finger on the gulf that quite naturally separated Anglo-Indians and Indians: 'the English do not think as natives do. They brood over matters that a native would dismiss till a fitting occasion; and what they would not think twice about a native will brood over till a fitting occasion. *Then* native and English stare at each other hopelessly across great gulfs of miscomprehension.'

This Preface begins the present volume. That is appropriate, because it is a story about making stories. And it also provides a touching example of how an Anglo-Indian writer 'sahib' and an Indian sadhu *do* meet and commune sensitively with each other, with mutual respect and honour. The same happens to be the real case with the misread and maligned poems 'The Ballad of East and West' and 'Gunga Din'. And there are other stories like 'Beyond the Pale' and 'The Story of Muhammad Din' in which the twain *do* meet, as long as we are willing to allow, in our reading, for the possibility. For example, describing the sadhu Gobind in his Preface to *Life's Handicap*, Kipling says: 'When we grew to know each other well, Gobind would tell me tales *in a voice most like the rumbling of heavy guns over a wooden bridge*.' It is necessary to appreciate that the characterization of Gobind's voice is a *compliment*, not a criticism.

Indeed, anyone who can see himself clearly, and laugh at himself, is well worth encountering. That ability indicates a sense of proportion, besides a kind of humour which is a rare commodity today. Kipling's frequently witty, ironic, even vitriolic criticism of Anglo-Indians at times also includes himself, as in the bitterly tragic story titled 'Thrown Away'. For another example, notice that many people today consider his poem 'The White Man's Burden' deeply colonial. However, in 1912 Kipling himself wrote to his young son a letter ('*O Beloved Kids*') describing a day he spent at Eton: 'I might have gone to attend speeches in the Great Hall but as the first piece *spouted* was "The White Man's Burden" by *R.K.*—I did not.'

The stories in the present volume may also test us in other ways, in places at which, reading carelessly, we may misunderstand Kipling. The likeliest error is failing to understand that certain remarks concern only Anglo-India, not our India. For instance, in 'Thrown Away', which puts the price tag of tragic death on young British colonials' failure to maintain a sense of proportion, we encounter this sentence: 'Now India is a place beyond all others where one must not take things too seriously—the mid-day sun always excepted.' The description that follows is worth reading because it lists a dozen ways in which *British*, not Indian, people tended to pompously and immaturely overrate themselves or exaggerate their difficulties.

And in 'Lispeth' we come across this heavily ironic remark: 'It takes a great deal of Christianity to wipe out *uncivilized* instincts, such as falling in love at first sight.' Our first reaction may be to read it as criticism of 'native' sentiment. But in fact it voices the thought of a Missionary Chaplain's hypocritical wife whose gross insensitivity to Lispeth is reflected in twenty other places in the story as well. It is hardly too much to ask readers to notice what Kipling actually says and whom he really criticizes. Meeting Kipling half-way in the stories in this volume will reveal his relentless criticism of fellow Anglo-Indians and his tremendous sympathy for India and Indians.

The best criticism of literature comes from open-minded readers, not from designated critics. In any case, we need to read criticism with great caution. For example, contrary to expectations, there is very little to learn from what George Orwell has to say about Kipling's writing—one wonders in fact whether he had read much Kipling, for he treats Kipling with little consciousness of the complexity of his personality or his work. In contrast, an accomplished practitioner of the short story like W. Somerset Maugham teaches us, with justified sympathy, a good deal about the virtues and failures of Kipling's work. Yet he too thought Kipling's Anglo-Indian writing lacked variety. There are many more stories apart from those anthologized in the present volume—yet even in the present selection you will find extraordinary variety of character and circumstance and treatment of both. And, in a serious sense, Kipling saw himself as an *Indian* writer, with a feeling and a kind of knowledge other British people did not share. When we have read these stories, *we* can ourselves decide what they accomplish.

The heat and dust of the last colonial rule in India have settled now. We have little reason to avoid reading stories that light up both the Indian and the colonial sides of that period of our history. Indeed, there are good reasons why we should read about an important period of history. The stories in this volume colourfully encourage us to do so, just as by and large they very fairly represent the historical situation. In reading them, therefore, we have the opportunity not only to criticize a colonial writer but also to rediscover British colonial India and the India we believe she was back then but about whom we know very little. In both cases we are bound to come away with enjoyment and profit—we will be both touched and instructed, and to do so remains the chief purpose of literature despite all our modern theories, just as to acknowledge truth remains the main purpose of history.

May 2002   Sudhakar Marathe

PREFACE
(from *Life's Handicap*)

IN NORTHERN INDIA stood a monastery called The *Chubara* of Dhunni Bhagat. No one remembered who or what Dhunni Bhagat had been. He had lived his life, made a little money, and spent it all, as every good Hindu should do, on a work of piety—the *Chubara*. That was full of brick cells, gaily painted with figures of Gods and kings and elephants, where worn-out priests could sit and meditate on the latter end of things: the paths were brick paved, and the naked feet of thousands had worn them into gutters. Clumps of mangoes sprouted from between the bricks; great pipal trees overhung the well-windlass that whined all day; and hosts of parrots tore through the trees. Crows and squirrels were tame in that place, for they knew that never a priest would touch them.

The wandering mendicants, charm-sellers, and holy vagabonds of a hundred miles round used to make the *Chubara* their place of call and rest. Mohammedan, Sikh, and Hindu mixed equally under the trees. They were old men, and when man has come to the turnstile of Night all the creeds in the world seem to him wonderfully alike and colourless.

Gobind the one-eyed told me this. He was a holy man who lived on an island in the middle of a river and fed the fishes with little bread pellets twice a day. In flood-time, when swollen corpses stranded themselves at the foot of the island, Gobind would cause them to be piously burned, for the sake of the honour of mankind, and having regard to his own account with God hereafter. But when two-thirds of the island was torn away in a spate, Gobind came across the river to Dhunni Bhagat's *Chubara*, he and his brass drinking-vessel with the well-cord round the neck, his short arm-rest crutch studded with brass nails, his roll of bedding, his big pipe, his umbrella, and his sugar-loaf hat with the nodding peacock feathers in it. He wrapped himself up in his patched quilt made of every colour and material in the world, sat down in a sunny corner of the very quiet *Chubara*, and, resting his arm on his short-handled crutch, waited for death. The people brought him food and little clumps of marigold flowers, and he gave his blessing in return. He was nearly blind, and his face was seamed and lined and wrinkled beyond belief, for he had lived in his time, which was before the English came within five hundred miles of Dhunni Bhagat's *Chubara*.

When we grew to know each other well, Gobind would tell me tales in a voice most like the rumbling of heavy guns over a wooden bridge. His tales were true, but not one in twenty could be printed in an English book, because the English do not think as natives do. They brood over matters that a native would dismiss till a fitting occasion; and what they would not think twice about a native will brood over till a fitting occasion. Then native and English stare at each other hopelessly across great gulfs of miscomprehension.

'And what,' said Gobind one Sunday evening, 'is your honoured craft, and by what manner of means earn you your daily bread?'

'I am,' said I, 'a *kerani*—one who writes with a pen upon paper, not being in the service of the Government.'

'Then what do you write?' said Gobind. 'Come nearer, for I cannot see your countenance, and the light fails.'

'I write of all matters that lie within my understanding, and of many that do not. But chiefly I write of Life and Death, and men and women, and Love and Fate according to the measure of my ability, telling the tale through the mouths of one, two, or more people. Then by the favour of God the tales are sold and money accrues to me that I may keep alive.'

'Even so,' said Gobind. 'That is the work of the bazar story-teller; but he speaks straight to men and women and does not write anything at all. Only when the tale has aroused expectation, and calamities are about to befall the virtuous, he stops suddenly and demands payment ere he continues the narration. Is it so in your craft, my son?'

'I have heard of such things when a tale is of great length, and is sold, as a cucumber, in small pieces.'

'Ay, I was once a famed teller of stories when I was begging on the road between Koshin and Etra; before the last pilgrimage that ever I took to Orissa. I told many tales and heard many more at the rest-houses in the evening when we were merry at the end of the march. It is in my heart that grown men are but as little children in the matter of tales, and the oldest tale is the most beloved.'

'With your people that is truth,' said I. 'But in regard to our people they desire new tales, and when all is written they rise up and declare that the tale were better told in such-and-such a manner, and doubt either the truth or the invention thereof.'

'But what folly is theirs!' said Gobind, throwing out his knotted hand. 'A tale that is told is a true tale as long as the telling lasts. And of their talk upon it—you know how Bilas Khan, that was the prince of tale-tellers, said to one who mocked him in the great rest-house on the Jhelum road: "Go on, my brother, and finish that I have begun," and he who mocked took up the tale, but having neither voice nor manner for the task came to a standstill, and the pilgrims at supper made him eat abuse and stick half that night.'

'Nay, but with our people, money having passed, it is their right; as we should turn against a shoeseller in regard to shoes if those wore out. If ever I make a book you shall see and judge.'

'And the parrot said to the falling tree, "Wait, brother, till I fetch a prop!"' said Gobind with a grim chuckle. 'God has given me eighty years, and it may be some over. I cannot look for more than day granted by day and as a favour at this tide. Be swift.'

'In what manner is it best to set about the task,' said I, 'O chiefest of those who string pearls with their tongue?'

'How do I know? Yet'—he thought for a little—'how should I not know? God has made very many heads, but there is only one heart in all the world among your people or my people. They are children in the matter of tales.'

'But none are so terrible as the little ones, if a man misplace a word, or in a second telling vary events by so much as a small devil.'

'Ay, I also have told tales to the little ones, but do thou this——'. His eyes fell on the gaudy paintings of the wall, the blue-and-red dome, and the flames of the poinsettias beyond. 'Tell them first of those things that thou hast seen and they have seen together. Thus their knowledge will piece out thy imperfections. Tell them of what thou alone hast seen, then what thou hast heard, and since they be children tell them of battles and kings, horses, devils, elephants, and angels, but omit not to tell them of love and such-like. All the earth is full of tales to him who listens and does not drive away the poor from his door. The poor are the best tale-tellers; for they must lay their ear to the ground every night.'

After this conversation the idea grew in my head, and Gobind was pressing in his inquiries as to the health of the book.

Later, when we had been parted for months, it happened that I was to go away and far off, and I came to bid Gobind good-bye.

'It is farewell between us now, for I go a very long journey.'

'And I also. A longer one than thou. But what of the book?' said he.

'It will be born in due season if it is so ordained.'

'I would I could see it,' said the old man, huddling beneath his quilt. 'But that will not be. I die three days hence, in the night, a little before the dawn. The term of my years is accomplished.'

In nine cases out of ten a native makes no miscalculation as to the day of his death. He has the foreknowledge of the beasts in this respect.

'Then thou wilt depart in peace, and it is good talk, for thou hast said that life is no delight to thee.'

'But it is a pity that our book is not born. How shall I know that there is any record of my name?'

'Because I promise, in the forepart of the book, preceding everything else, that it shall be written, Gobind, *sadhu*, of the island in the river and awaiting God in Dhunni Bhagat's *Chubara*, first spoke of the book,' said I.

'And gave counsel—an old man's counsel. Gobind, son of Gobind of the Chumi village in the Karaon tehsil, in the district of Mooltan. Will that be written also?'

'That will be written also.'

'And the book will go across the Black Water to the houses of your people, and all the Sahibs will know of me who am eighty years old?'

'All who read the book shall know. I cannot promise for the rest.'

'That is good talk. Call aloud to all who are in the monastery, and I will tell them this thing.'

They trooped up, *fakirs*, *sadhus*, *sannyasis*, *bairagis*, *nihangs*, and *mullahs*, priests of all faiths and every degree of raggedness, and Gobind, leaning upon his crutch, spoke so that they were visibly filled with envy, and a white-haired senior bade Gobind think of his latter end instead of transitory repute in the mouths of strangers. Then Gobind gave me his blessing and I came away.

These tales have been collected from all places, and all sorts of people, from priests in the *Chubara*, from Ala Yar the carver, Jiwun Singh the carpenter, nameless men on steamers and trains round the world, women spinning outside their cottages in the twilight, officers and gentlemen now dead and buried; and a few, but these are the very best, my Father gave me. The greater part of them have been published in magazines and newspapers, to whose editors I am indebted; but some are new on this side of the water, and some have not seen the light before.

The most remarkable stories are, of course, those which do not appear—for obvious reasons.

LITTLE TOBRAH

'PRISONER'S HEAD did not reach to the top of the dock', as the English newspapers say. This case, however, was not reported because nobody cared by so much as a hempen rope for the life or death of Little Tobrah. The assessors in the red courthouse sat upon him all through the long hot afternoon, and whenever they asked him a question he salaamed and whined. Their verdict was that the evidence was inconclusive, and the Judge concurred. It was true that the dead body of Little Tobrah's sister had been found at the bottom of the well, and Little Tobrah was the only human being within a half-mile radius at the time; but the child might have fallen in by accident. Therefore Little Tobrah was acquitted, and told to go where he pleased. This permission was not so generous as it sounds, for he had nowhere to go, nothing in particular to eat, and nothing whatever to wear.

He trotted into the court-compound, and sat upon the well-kerb, wondering whether an unsuccessful dive into the black water would end in a forced voyage across the other Black Water. A groom put down an emptied nose-bag on the bricks, and Little Tobrah, being hungry, set himself to scrape out what wet grain the horse had overlooked.

'O Thief—and but newly set free from the terror of the Law! Come along!' said the groom, and Little Tobrah was led by the ear to a large and fat Englishman, who heard the tale of the theft.

'Hah!' said the Englishman three times (only he said a stronger word). 'Put him into the net and take him home.' So Little Tobrah was thrown into the net of the cart, and, nothing doubting that he should be stuck like a pig, was driven to the Englishman's house. 'Hah!' said the Englishman as before. 'Wet grain, by Jove! Feed the little beggar, some of you, and we'll make a riding-boy of him! See? Wet grain, good Lord!'

'Give an account of yourself,' said the Head of the Grooms to Little Tobrah after the meal had been eaten, and the servants lay at ease in their quarters behind the house. 'You are not of the groom caste, unless it be for the stomach's sake. How came you into the court, and why? Answer, little devil's spawn!'

'There was not enough to eat,' said Little Tobrah calmly. 'This is a good place.'

'Talk straight talk,' said the Head Groom, 'or I will make you clean out the stable of that large red stallion who bites like a camel.'

'We be *Telis*, oil-pressers,' said Little Tobrah, scratching his toes in the dust. 'We were *Telis*—my father, my mother, my brother, the elder by four years, myself, and the sister.'

'She who was found dead in the well?' said one who had heard something of the trial.

'Even so,' said Little Tobrah gravely. 'She who was found dead in the well. It befell upon a time, which is not in my memory, that the sickness came to the village where our oil-press stood, and first my sister was smitten as to her eyes, and went without sight, for it was *mata*—the smallpox. Thereafter, my father and my mother died of the same sickness, so we were alone—my brother who had twelve years, I who had eight, and the sister who could not see. Yet were there the bullock and the oil-press remaining, and we made shift to press the oil as before. But Surjun Dass, the grain-seller, cheated us in his dealings; and it was always a stubborn bullock to drive. We put marigold flowers for the Gods upon the neck of the bullock, and upon the great grinding-beam that rose through the roof; but we gained nothing thereby, and Surjun Dass was a hard man.'

'*Bapri-bap*,' muttered the grooms' wives, 'to cheat a child so! But *we* know what the *bunnia*-folk are, sisters.'

'The press was an old press, and we were not strong men—my brother and I; nor could we fix the neck of the beam firmly in the shackle.'

'Nay, indeed,' said the gorgeously-clad wife of the Head Groom, joining the circle. 'That is a strong man's work. When I was a maid in my father's house——'

'Peace, woman!' said the Head Groom. 'Go on, boy.'

'It is nothing,' said Little Tobrah. 'The big beam tore down the roof upon a day which is not in my memory, and with the roof fell much of the hinder wall, and both together upon our bullock, whose back was broken. Thus we had neither home, nor press, nor bullock—my brother, myself, and the sister who was blind. We went crying away from that place, hand-in-hand across the fields; and our money was seven annas and six pies. There was a famine in the land. So, on a night when we were sleeping, my brother took the five annas that remained to us and ran away. I do not know whither he went. The curse of my father be upon him! But I and the sister begged food in the villages, and there was none to give. Only all men said, "Go to the Englishmen and they will give." I did not know what the Englishmen were; but they said that they were white, living in tents. I went forward; but I cannot say whither I went, and there was no more food for myself or the sister. And upon a hot night, she weeping and calling for food, we came to a well, and I bade her sit upon the kerb, and thrust her in, for, in truth, she could not see; and it is better to die than to starve.'

'*Ai*! *Ahi*!' wailed the grooms' wives in chorus; 'he thrust her in, for it is better to die than to starve!'

'I would have thrown myself in also, but that she was not dead and called to me from the bottom of the well, and I was afraid and ran. And one came out of the crops saying that I had killed her and defiled the well, and they took me before an Englishman, white and terrible, living in a tent, and me he sent here. But there were no witnesses, and it is better to die than to starve. She, furthermore, could not see with her eyes, and was but a little child.'

'Was but a little child,' echoed the Head Groom's wife. 'But who art thou, weak as a fowl and small as a day-old colt, what art *thou*?'

'I who was empty am now full,' said Little Tobrah, stretching himself upon the dust. 'And I would sleep.'

The groom's wife spread a cloth over him while Little Tobrah slept the sleep of the just.

LISPETH

Look, you have cast out Love! What Gods are these
You bid me please?
The Three in One, the One in Three? Not so!
To my own Gods I go.
It may be they shall give me greater ease
Than your cold Christ and tangled Trinities.

The Convert

SHE WAS THE DAUGHTER of Sonoo, a Hill-man of the Himalayas, and Jadeh his wife. One year their maize failed, and two bears spent the night in their only opium poppy-field just above the Sutlej Valley on the Kotgarh side; so, next season, they turned Christian, and brought their baby to the Mission to be baptized. The Kotgarh Chaplain christened her Elizabeth, and 'Lispeth' is the Hill or *pahari* pronunciation.

Later, cholera came into the Kotgarh Valley and carried off Sonoo and Jadeh, and Lispeth became half servant, half companion, to the wife of the then Chaplain of Kotgarh. This was after the reign of the Moravian missionaries in that place, but before Kotgarh had quite forgotten her title of 'Mistress of the Northern Hills.'

Whether Christianity improved Lispeth, or whether the Gods of her own people would have done as much for her under any circumstances, I do not know; but she grew very lovely. When a Hill-girl grows lovely, she is worth travelling fifty miles over bad ground to look upon. Lispeth had a Greek face—one of those faces people paint so often and see so seldom. She was of a pale, ivory colour, and, for her race, extremely tall. Also, she possessed eyes that were wonderful and, had she not been dressed in the abominable print-cloths affected by the Missions, you would, meeting her on the hillside unexpectedly, have thought her the original Diana of the Romans going out to slay.

Lispeth took to Christianity readily, and did not abandon it when she reached womanhood, as do some Hill-girls. Her own people hated her because she had, they said, become a white woman and washed herself daily; and the Chaplain's wife did not know what to do with her. One cannot ask a stately goddess, five feet ten in her shoes, to clean plates and dishes. She played with the Chaplain's children and took classes in the Sunday School, and read all the books in the house and grew more and more beautiful, like the Princesses in fairy tales. The Chaplain's wife said that the girl ought to take service in Simla as a nurse or something 'genteel.' But Lispeth did not want to take service. She was very happy where she was.

When travellers—there were not many in those years—came in to Kotgarh, Lispeth used to lock herself into her own room for fear they might take her away to Simla, or out into the unknown world.

One day, a few months after she was seventeen years old, Lispeth went out for a walk. She did not walk in the manner of English ladies—a mile and a half out with a carriage-ride back again. She covered between twenty and thirty miles in her little constitutionals, all about and about, between Kotgarh and Narkanda. This time she came back at full dusk, stepping down the breakneck descent into Kotgarh with something heavy in her arms. The Chaplain's wife was dozing in the drawing-room when Lispeth came in breathing heavily and very exhausted with her burden. Lispeth put it down on the sofa, and said simply, 'This is my husband. I found him on the Bagi road. He has hurt himself. We will nurse him, and when he is well your husband shall marry him to me.'

This was the first mention Lispeth had ever made of her matrimonial views, and the Chaplain's wife shrieked with horror. However, the man on the sofa needed attention first. He was a young Englishman, and his head had been cut to the bone by something jagged. Lispeth said she had found him down the hillside, and had brought him in. He was breathing queerly and was unconscious.

He was put to bed and tended by the Chaplain, who knew something of medicine, and Lispeth waited outside the door in case she could be useful. She explained to the Chaplain that this was the man she meant to marry, and the Chaplain and his wife lectured her severely on the impropriety of her conduct. Lispeth listened quietly, and repeated her first proposition. It takes a great deal of Christianity to wipe out uncivilized instincts, such as falling in love at first sight. Lispeth, having found the man she worshipped, did not see why she should keep silent as to her choice. She had no intention of being sent away, either. She was going to nurse that Englishman until he was well enough to marry her. That was her programme.

After a fortnight of slight fever and inflammation, the Englishman recovered coherence and thanked the Chaplain and his wife, and Lispeth—especially Lispeth—for their kindness. He was a traveller in the East, he said—they never talked about 'globe-trotters' in those days, when the P. & O. fleet was young and small—and had come from Dehra Dun to hunt for plants and butterflies among the Simla hills. No one at Simla, therefore, knew anything about him. He fancied that he must have fallen over the cliff while reaching out for a fern on a rotten tree-trunk, and that his coolies must have stolen his baggage and fled. He thought he would go back to Simla when he was a little stronger. He desired no more mountaineering.

He made small haste to go away, and recovered his strength slowly. Lispeth objected to being advised either by the Chaplain or his wife. Therefore the latter spoke to the Englishman, and told him how matters stood in Lispeth's heart. He laughed a good deal, and said it was very pretty and romantic, but, as he was engaged to a girl at Home, he fancied that nothing would happen. Certainly he would behave with discretion. He did that. Still, he found it very pleasant to talk to Lispeth, and walk with Lispeth, and say nice things to her, and call her pet names while he was getting strong enough to go away. It meant nothing at all to him, and everything in the world to Lispeth. She was very happy while the fortnight lasted, because she had found a man to love.

Being a savage by birth, she took no trouble to hide her feelings, and the Englishman was amused. When he went away, Lispeth walked with him up the Hill as far as Narkanda, very troubled and very miserable. The Chaplain's wife, being a good

Christian and disliking anything in the shape of fuss or scandal—Lispeth was beyond her management entirely—had told the Englishman to tell Lispeth that he was coming back to marry her. 'She is but a child, you know, and, I fear, at heart a heathen,' said the Chaplain's wife. So all the twelve miles up the Hill the Englishman, with his arm round Lispeth's waist, was assuring the girl that he would come back and marry her; and Lispeth made him promise over and over again. She wept on the Narkanda Ridge until he had passed out of sight along the Muttiani path.

Then she dried her tears and went in to Kotgarh again, and said to the Chaplain's wife, 'He will come back and marry me. He has gone to his own people to tell them so.' And the Chaplain's wife soothed Lispeth and said, 'He will come back.' At the end of two months Lispeth grew impatient, and was told that the Englishman had gone over the seas to England. She knew where England was, because she had read little geography primers; but, of course, she had no conception of the nature of the sea, being a Hill-girl. There was an old puzzle-map of the World in the house. Lispeth had played with it when she was a child. She unearthed it again, and put it together of evenings, and cried to herself, and tried to imagine where her Englishman was. As she had no ideas of distance or steamboats her notions were somewhat wild. It would not have made the least difference had she been perfectly correct, for the Englishman had no intention of coming back to marry a Hill-girl. He forgot all about her by the time he was butterfly-hunting in Assam. He wrote a book on the East afterwards. Lispeth's name did not appear there.

At the end of three months Lispeth made daily pilgrimage to Narkanda to see if her Englishman was coming along the road. It gave her comfort, and the Chaplain's wife finding her happier thought that she was getting over her 'barbarous and most indelicate folly'. A little later the walks ceased to help Lispeth, and her temper grew very bad. The Chaplain's wife thought this a profitable time to let her know the real state of affairs—that the Englishman had only promised his love to keep her quiet—that he had never meant anything, and that it was wrong and improper of Lispeth to think of marriage with an

Englishman, who was of a superior clay, besides being promised in marriage to a girl of his own people. Lispeth said that all this was clearly impossible because he had said he loved her, and the Chaplain's wife had, with her own lips, asserted that the Englishman was coming back.

'How can what he said and you said be untrue?' asked Lispeth.

'We said it as an excuse to keep you quiet, child,' said the Chaplain's wife.

'Then you have lied to me,' said Lispeth, 'you and he?'

The Chaplain's wife bowed her head, and said nothing. Lispeth went silent too for a little time; then she went out down the valley, and returned in the dress of a Hill-girl—infamously dirty, but without the nose-stud and ear-rings. She had her hair braided into the long pigtail, helped out with black thread, that Hill-women wear.

'I am going back to my own people,' said she. 'You have killed Lispeth. There is only left old Jadeh's daughter—the daughter of a *pahari* and the servant of Tarka Devi. You are all liars, you English.'

By the time that the Chaplain's wife had recovered from the shock of the announcement that Lispeth had 'verted to her mother's Gods the girl had gone; and she never came back.

She took to her own unclean people savagely, as if to make up the arrears of the life she had stepped out of; and, in a little time, she married a wood-cutter who beat her after the manner of *paharis*, and her beauty faded soon.

'There is no law whereby you can account for the vagaries of the heathen,' said the Chaplain's wife, 'and I believe that Lispeth was always at heart an infidel.' Seeing she had been taken into the Church of England at the mature age of five weeks, this statement does not do credit to the Chaplain's wife.

Lispeth was a very old woman when she died. She had always a perfect command of English, and when she was sufficiently drunk could sometimes be induced to tell the story of her first love-affair.

It was hard then to realise that the bleared, wrinkled creature, exactly like a wisp of charred rag, could ever have been 'Lispeth of the Kotgarh Mission'.

13

WATCHES OF THE NIGHT

> *What is in the Brahmin's books, that is in the
> Brahmin's heart.
> Neither you nor I knew there was so much evil
> in the world.*
>
> Hindu Proverb

THIS BEGAN IN a practical joke; but it has gone far enough now, and is getting serious.

Platte, the Subaltern, being poor, had a Waterbury watch and a plain leather guard.

The Colonel had a Waterbury watch also, and, for guard, the lip-strap of a curb-chain. Lip-straps make the best watch-guards. They are also strong and short. Between a lip-strap and an ordinary leather guard there is no great difference. Between one Waterbury watch and another none at all. Every one in the station knew the Colonel's lip-strap. He was not a horsy man, but he liked people to believe he had been once; and he wove fantastic stories of the hunting bridle to which this particular lip-strap had belonged. Otherwise he was painfully religious.

Platte and the Colonel were dressing at the Club—both late for their engagements, and both in a hurry. That was *Kismet*. The two watches were on a shelf below the looking-glass—guards hanging down. That was carelessness. Platte changed first, snatched a watch, looked in the glass, settled his tie, and ran. Forty seconds later the Colonel did exactly the same thing, each man taking the other's watch.

You may have noticed that many religious people are deeply suspicious. They seem—for purely religious purposes, of course—to know more about iniquity than the unregenerate. Perhaps they were specially bad before they became converted! At any rate, in the imputation of things evil, and in putting the worst construction on things innocent, a certain type of good people may be trusted to surpass all others. The Colonel and his Wife were of that type. But the Colonel's Wife was the worst. She manufactured the station scandal, and—talked to her *ayah*! Nothing more need be said. The Colonel's Wife broke up the Laplaces' home. The Colonel's Wife stopped the Ferris-Haughtrey engagement. The Colonel's Wife induced young Buxton to keep his wife down in the Plains through the first year of the marriage. Wherefore little Mrs. Buxton died, and the baby with her. These things will be remembered against the Colonel's Wife so long as there is a regiment in the country.

But to come back to the Colonel and Platte. They went their several ways from the dressing-room. The Colonel dined with two Chaplains, while Platte went to a bachelor party, and whist to follow.

Mark how things happen! If Platte's groom had put the new saddle-pad on the mare, the butts of the territs would not have worked through the worn leather and the old pad into the mare's withers, when she was coming home at two o'clock in the morning. She would not have reared, bolted, fallen into a ditch, upset the cart, and sent Platte flying over an aloe-hedge on to Mrs. Larkyn's well-kept lawn; and this tale would never have been written. But the mare did all these things, and while Platte was rolling over and over on the turf, like a shot rabbit, the watch and guard flew from his waistcoat—as an Infantry Major's sword hops out of the scabbard when they are firing a *feu-de-joie*—and rolled and rolled in the moonlight, till it stopped under a window.

Platte stuffed his handkerchief under the pad, put the cart straight, and went home.

Mark again how *Kismet* works! This would not arrive once in a hundred years. Towards the end of his dinner with the two Chaplains, the Colonel let out his waistcoat and leaned over the table to look at some Mission Reports. The bar of the watch-guard worked through the button-hole, and the watch—Platte's watch—slid quietly on to the carpet; where the bearer found it the next morning and kept it.

Then the Colonel went home to the wife of his bosom; but the driver of the carriage was drunk and lost his way. So the

Colonel returned at an unseemly hour and his excuses were not accepted. If the Colonel's Wife had been an ordinary Vessel of Wrath appointed for destruction, she would have known that when a man stays on purpose, his excuse is always sound and original. The very baldness of the Colonel's explanation proved its truth.

See once more the workings of *Kismet*! The Colonel's watch which came with Platte hurriedly on to Mrs. Larkyn's lawn, chose to stop just under Mrs. Larkyn's window, where she saw it early in the morning, recognised it, and picked it up. She had heard the crash of Platte's cart at two o'clock that morning, and his voice calling the mare names. She knew Platte and liked him. That day she showed him the watch and heard his story. He put his head on one side, winked and said, 'How disgusting! Shocking old man! With his religious training, too! I should send the watch to the Colonel's Wife and ask for explanations.'

Mrs. Larkyn thought for a minute of the Laplaces—whom she had known when Laplace and his wife believed in each other—and answered, 'I will send it. I think it will do her good. But, remember, we must *never* tell her the truth.'

Platte guessed that his own watch was in the Colonel's possession, and thought that the return of the lip-strapped Waterbury with a soothing note from Mrs. Larkyn would merely create a small trouble for a few minutes. Mrs. Larkyn knew better. She knew that any poison dropped would find good holding-ground in the heart of the Colonel's Wife.

The packet, and a note containing a few remarks on the Colonel's calling hours, were sent over to the Colonel's Wife, who wept in her own room and took counsel with herself.

If there was one woman under heaven whom the Colonel's Wife hated with holy fervour, it was Mrs. Larkyn. Mrs. Larkyn was a frivolous lady, and called the Colonel's Wife 'old cat'. The Colonel's Wife said that someone in Revelation was remarkably like Mrs. Larkyn. She mentioned other Scripture people as well: from the Old Testament. But the Colonel's Wife was the only person who cared or dared to say anything against Mrs. Larkyn. Every one else accepted her as an amusing, honest little body. Wherefore, to believe that her husband had been shedding watches under that 'Thing's' window at ungodly hours, coupled with the fact of his late arrival on the previous night, was . . .

At this point she rose up and sought her husband. He denied everything except the ownership of the watch. She besought him, for his Soul's sake, to speak the truth. He denied afresh, with two bad words. Then a stony silence held the Colonel's Wife, while a man could draw his breath five times.

The speech that followed is no affair of mine or yours. It was made up of wifely and womanly jealousy; knowledge of old age and sunk cheeks; deep mistrust born of the text that says even little babies' hearts are as bad as they make them; rancorous hatred of Mrs. Larkyn, and the tenets of the creed of the Colonel's Wife's upbringing.

Over and above all was the damning lip-strapped Waterbury, ticking away in the palm of her shaking, withered hand. At that hour, I think, the Colonel's Wife realised a little of the restless suspicion she had injected into old Laplace's mind; a little of poor Miss Haughtrey's misery; and some of the canker that ate into Buxton's heart as he watched his wife dying before his eyes. The Colonel stammered and tried to explain. Then he remembered that his watch had disappeared; and the misery grew greater. The Colonel's Wife talked and prayed by turns till she was tired, and went away to devise means for chastening the stubborn heart of her husband. Which, translated, means, in our slang, 'tail-twisting'.

Being deeply impressed with the doctrine of Original Sin, she could not believe in the face of appearances. She knew too much, and jumped to the wildest conclusions.

But it was good for her. It spoilt her life, as she had spoilt the life of the Laplaces. She had lost her faith in the Colonel, and—here the creed-suspicion came in—he might, she argued, have erred many times, before a merciful Providence, at the hands of so unworthy an instrument as Mrs. Larkyn, had established his guilt. He was a bad, wicked, grey-haired profligate. This may sound too sudden a revulsion for a long-wedded wife; but it is a venerable fact that, if a man or woman makes a practice of, and takes a delight in, believing and spreading evil of people indifferent to him or her, he or she will end in believing evil of folk very near and dear. You may think, also, that the mere incident of the watch was too small and trivial to raise this misunderstanding. It is another aged fact, in life as well as racing, that all the worst accidents happen at little ditches and cut-down fences. In the same way, you sometimes see a woman who would have made a Joan of Arc in another century and climate, threshing herself to pieces over all the mean worry of housekeeping . . . But that is another story.

Her belief only made the Colonel's Wife more wretched, because it insisted on the villainy of men. Remembering what she had done, it was pleasant to watch her unhappiness, and the penny-farthing attempts she made to hide it from the station. But the station knew and laughed heartlessly; for they had heard the story of the watch, with much dramatic gesture, from Mrs. Larkyn's lips.

Once or twice Platte said to Mrs. Larkyn, seeing that the Colonel had not cleared himself, 'This thing has gone far enough. I move we tell the Colonel's Wife how it happened.' Mrs. Larkyn shut her lips and shook her head, and vowed that the Colonel's Wife must bear her punishment as best she could. Now Mrs. Larkyn was a frivolous woman, in whom none would have suspected deep hate. So Platte took no action, and came to believe gradually, from the Colonel's silence, that the Colonel must have run off the line somewhere that night, and, therefore, preferred to stand sentence on the lesser count of rambling into other people's compounds out of calling-hours. Platte forgot about the watch business after a while, and moved down-country with his regiment. Mrs. Larkyn went home when her husband's tour of Indian service expired. She never forgot.

But Platte was quite right when he said that the joke had gone too far. The mistrust and the tragedy of it—which we outsiders cannot see and do not believe in—are killing the Colonel's Wife, and are making the Colonel wretched. If either of them read this story, they can depend upon its being a fairly true account of the case, and can kiss and make friends.

Shakespeare alludes to the pleasure of watching an Engineer being shelled by his own Battery. Now this shows that poets should not write about what they do not understand. Any one could have told him that Sappers and Gunners are perfectly different branches of the Service.

But, if you correct the sentence, and substitute Gunner for Sapper, the moral comes just the same.

TODS' AMENDMENT

The World hath set its heavy yoke
Upon the old white-bearded folk
Who strive to please the King.
God's mercy is upon the young,
God's wisdom in the baby tongue
That fears not anything.

The Parable of Chajju Bhagat

NOW TODS' MAMMA was a singularly charming woman, and every one in Simla knew that. Most men had saved him from death on occasions. He was beyond his *ayah's* control altogether, and perilled his life daily to find out what would happen if you pulled a Mountain Battery mule's tail. He was an utterly fearless young pagan, about six years old, and the only baby who ever broke the holy calm of the Supreme Legislative Council.

It happened this way: Tods' pet kid got loose, and fled up the hill, off the Boileaugunge road, Tods after it, until it burst in to the Viceregal lawn, then attached to Peterhof. The Council were sitting at the time, and the windows were open because it was warm. The Red Lancer in the porch told Tods to go away; but Tods knew the Red Lancer and most of the Members of Council personally. Moreover, he had firm hold of the kid's collar, and was being dragged all across the flower beds. 'Give my *salaam* to the long Councillor Sahib, and ask him to help me take Moti back!' gasped Tods. The Council heard the noise through the open windows; and, after an interval, was seen the shocking spectacle of a Legal Member and Lieutenant-Governor helping, under the direct patronage of a Commander-in-Chief and a Viceroy, one small and very dirty boy, in a sailor's suit and a tangle of brown hair, to coerce a lively and rebellious kid. They headed it off down the path to the Mall, and Tods went home in triumph and told his Mamma that *all* the Councillor Sahibs had been helping him to catch Moti. Whereat his mamma smacked Tods for interfering with the administration of the Empire; but Tods met the Legal Member the next day and told him in confidence that if the Legal Member ever wanted to catch a goat, he, Tods, would give him all the help in his power. 'Thank you, Tods,' said the Legal Member.

Tods was the idol of some eighty *jhampanis*, and half as many *saises*. He saluted them all as 'O Brother'. It never entered his head that any living human being could disobey his orders; and he was the buffer between the servants and his Mamma's wrath. The working of that household turned on Tods, who was adored by every one from the *dhobi* to the dog-boy. Even Futteh Khan, the villainous loafer *khit* from Mussoorie, shirked risking Tods' displeasure for fear his co-mates should look down on him.

So Tods had honour in the land from Boileaugunge to Chota Simla, and ruled justly according to his lights. Of course, he spoke Urdu, but he had also mastered many queer side-speeches like the *chotee bolee* of the women, and held grave converse with shopkeepers and Hill-coolies alike. He was precocious for his age, and his mixing with natives had taught him some of the more bitter truths of life: the meanness and sordidness of it. He used, over his bread and milk, to deliver solemn and serious aphorisms, translated from the vernacular into English, that made his Mamma jump and vow that Tods *must* go home next hot weather.

Just when Tods was in the bloom of his power, the Supreme Legislature were hacking out a Bill for the Sub-Montane Tracts, a revision of the then Act, smaller than the Punjab Land Bill, but affecting a few hundred thousand people none the less. The Legal Member had built, and bolstered, and embroidered, and emended that Bill till it looked beautiful on paper. Then the Council began to settle what they called the 'minor details.' As if any Englishman legislating for natives knows enough to know which are the minor and which are the major points, from the native point of view, of any measure! That Bill was a triumph of 'safeguarding the interests of the tenant'. One clause provided that land should not be leased on longer terms than five years at a stretch; because, if the landlord had a tenant bound down for, say, twenty years, he would squeeze the very life out of him. The notion was to keep up a stream of independent cultivators in the Sub-Montane Tracts; and ethnologically and politically the notion was correct. The only drawback was that it was altogether wrong. A native's life in India implies the life of his son. Wherefore, you cannot legislate for one generation at a time.

You must consider the next from the native point of view. Curiously enough, the native now and then, and in Northern India more particularly, hates being over-protected against himself. There was a Naga village once, where they lived on dead *and* buried Commissariat mules . . . But that is another story.

For many reasons, to be explained later, the people concerned objected to the Bill. The Native member of Council knew as much about Punjabis as he knew about Charing Cross. He had said in Calcutta that 'the Bill was entirely in accord with the desires of that large and important class, the cultivators'; and so on, and so on. The Legal Member's knowledge of natives was limited to English-speaking Durbaris, and his own red *chaprassis*; the Sub-Montane Tracts concerned no one in particular; the Deputy-Commissioners were a good deal too driven to make representations, and the measure was one which dealt with small landholders only. Nevertheless, the Legal Member prayed that it might be correct, for he was a nervously conscientious man. He did not know that no man can tell what natives think unless he mixes with them with the varnish off. And not always then. But he did the best he knew. So the measure came up to the Supreme Council for the final touches, while Tods patrolled the Burra Simla Bazar in his morning rides, and played with the monkey belonging to Ditta Mull, the *bunnia*, and listened, as a child listens, to all the stray talk about this new freak of the Lat Sahib's.

One day there was a dinner-party at the house of Tods'· Mamma, and the Legal Member came. Tods was in bed, but he kept awake till he heard the bursts of laughter from the men over the coffee. Then he paddled out in his little red flannel dressing-gown and his night-suit, and took refuge by the side of his father knowing that he would not be sent back. 'See the miseries of having a family!' said Tods' father, giving Tods three prunes, some water in a glass that had been used for claret, and telling him to sit still. Tods sucked the prunes slowly, knowing that he would have to go when they were finished, and sipped the pink water like a man of the world, as he listened to the conversation. Presently, the Legal Member, talking 'shop' to the Head of a Department, mentioned his Bill by its full name—'The Sub-Montane Tracts *Ryotwari* Revised Enactment.' Tods caught the one native word, and lifting up his small voice said:—

'Oh, I know *all* about that! Has it been *murramutted* yet, Councillor Sahib?'

'How much?' said the Legal Member.

'*Murramutted—mended.*—Put *theek*, you know—made nice to please Ditta Mull!'

The Legal Member left his place and moved up next to Tods.

'What do you know about *ryotwari*, little man?' he said.

'I'm not a little man—I'm Tods—and I know *all* about it. Ditta Mull, and Chota Lall, and Amir Nath, and—oh, *lakhs* of my friends tell me about it in the bazars when I talk to them.'

'Oh, they do—do they? What do they say, Tods?'

Tods tucked his feet under his red flannel dressing-gown and said, 'I must *fink*.'

The Legal Member waited patiently. Then Tods, with infinite compassion:—

'You don't speak my talk, do you, Councillor Sahib?'

'No; I am sorry to say I do not,' said the Legal Member.

'Very well,' said Tods, 'I must *fink* in English.'

He spent a minute putting his ideas in order, and began very slowly, translating in his mind from the vernacular to English, as many Anglo-Indian children do. You must remember that the Legal Member helped him on by questions when he halted, and Tods was not equal to the sustained flight of oratory that follows.

'Ditta Mull says, "This thing is the talk of a child, and was made up by fools." But *I* don't think you are a fool, Councillor

23

Sahib,' said Tods hastily. 'You caught my goat. This is what Ditta Mull says:—"I am not a fool, and why should the Sirkar say I am a child? *I* can see if the land is good and if the landlord is good. If I am a fool, the sin is upon my own head. For five years I take my ground for which I have saved money, and a wife I take too, and a little son is born." Ditta Mull has one daughter now, but he *says* he will have a son, soon. And he says, "At the end of five years, by this new *bundobust*, I must go. If I do not go, I must get fresh seals and *takkus*-stamps on the papers, perhaps in the middle of the harvest, and go to the law-courts once is wisdom, but to go twice is *jehannum*." That is *quite* true,' explained Tods gravely. 'All my friends say so. And Ditta Mull says, "Always fresh *takkus* and paying money to Vakils and *chaprassis* and law-courts every five years, or else the landlord makes me go. Why do I want to go? Am I a fool? If I am a fool and do not know, after forty years, good land when I see it, let me die! But if the *bundobust* says for *fifteen* years, that is good and wise. My little son is a man, and I am burnt, and he takes the ground, or another ground, paying only once for the *takkus*-stamps on the papers, and his little son is born, and at the end of fifteen years is a man too. But what profit is there in five years and fresh papers? Nothing but *dikh*—trouble—*dikh*. We are not young men who take these lands, but old ones—not farmers, but tradesmen with a little money—and for fifteen years we shall have peace. Nor are we children that the Sirkar should treat us so".'

Here Tods stopped short, for the whole table were listening. The Legal Member said to Tods, 'Is that all?'

'All I can remember,' said Tods. 'But you should see Ditta Mull's big monkey. It's just like a Councillor Sahib.'

'Tods! Go to bed,' said his father.

Tods gathered up his dressing-gown tail and departed.

The Legal Member brought his hand down on the table with a crash. 'By Jove!' said the Legal Member, 'I believe the boy is right. The short tenure *is* the weak point.'

He left early, thinking over what Tods had said. Now, it was obviously impossible for the Legal Member to play with a *bunnia*'s monkey, by way of getting understanding; but he did better. He made inquiries, always bearing in mind the fact that the real native—not the hybrid, University-trained mule—is as timid as a colt, and, little by little, he coaxed some of the men whom the measure concerned most intimately to give in their views, which squared very closely with Tods' evidence.

So the Bill was amended in that clause; and the Legal Member was filled with an uneasy suspicion that Native members represent very little except the Orders they carry on their bosoms. But he put the thought from him as illiberal. He was a most Liberal man.

After a time, the news spread through the bazars that Tods had got the Bill recast in the tenure-clause, and if Tods' Mamma had not interfered, Tods would have made himself sick on the baskets of fruit and pistachio nuts and Kabuli grapes and almonds that crowded his veranda. Till he went Home, Tods ranked some few degrees before the Viceroy in popular estimation. But for the little life of him Tods could not understand why.

In the Legal Member's private-paper-box still lies the rough draft of the Sub-Montane Tracts *Ryotwari* Revised Enactment; and opposite the twenty-second clause, pencilled in blue chalk, and signed by the Legal Member, are the words *'Tods' Amendment'*.

A BANK FRAUD

He drank strong waters and his speech was coarse;
He purchased raiment and forbore to pay;
He stuck a trusting junior with a horse,
And won gymkhanas in a doubtful way.
Then, 'twixt a vice and folly, turned aside
To do good deeds—and straight to cloak them, lied.
                                                    The Mess-Room

IF REGGIE BURKE were in India now he would resent this tale
being told; but as he is in Hong Kong and won't see it, the
telling is safe. He was the man who worked the big fraud on the
Sind and Sialkot Bank. He was manager of an up-country
Branch, and a sound practical man with a large experience of
native loan and insurance work. He could combine the frivolities
of ordinary life with his work, and yet do well. Reggie Burke
rode anything that would let him get up, danced as neatly as he
rode, and was wanted for every sort of amusement in the station.

As he said himself, and as many men found out rather to
their surprise, there were two Burkes, both very much at your
service. 'Reggie Burke' between four and ten, ready for anything
from a hot-weather gymkhana to a riding-picnic, and, between
ten and four, 'Mr. Reginald Burke, Manager of the Sind and
Sialkot Branch Bank'. You might play polo with him one
afternoon and hear him express his opinions when a man crossed;
and you might call on him next morning to raise a two-thousand
rupee loan on a five-hundred-pound insurance policy, eighty
pounds paid in premiums. He would recognise you; but you
might have some trouble in recognising him.

The Directors of the Bank—it had its headquarters in
Calcutta, and its General Manager's word carried weight with
the Government—picked their men well. They had tested Reggie

up to a fairly severe breaking-strain. They trusted him just as much as Directors ever trust Managers. You must see for yourself whether their trust was misplaced.

Reggie's Branch was in a big station, and worked with the usual staff—one Manager, one Accountant, both English, a Cashier, and a horde of native clerks; besides the police patrol at nights outside. The bulk of its work, for it was in a thriving District, was *hoondi* and accommodation of all kinds. A fool has no grip of this sort of business; and a clever man who does not go about among his clients, and know more than a little of their affairs, is worse than a fool. Reggie was young-looking, clean-shaved, with a twinkle in his eye, and a head that nothing short of a gallon of the Gunners' Madeira could make any impression on.

One day at a big dinner, he announced casually that the Directors had shifted on to him a Natural Curiosity, from England, in the Accountant line. He was perfectly correct. Mr. Silas Riley, Accountant, was a most curious animal—a long, gawky, rawboned Yorkshireman, full of the savage self-conceit that blossoms only in the best county in England. Arrogance was a mild word for the mental attitude of Mr. S. Riley. He had worked himself up, after seven years, to a Cashier's position in a Huddersfield Bank; and all his experience lay among the factories of the North. Perhaps he would have done better on the Bombay side, where they are happy with one-half per cent profits, and money is cheap. He was useless to Upper India and a wheat Province, where a man wants a large head and a touch of imagination if he is to turn out satisfactory balance-sheets.

He was wonderfully narrow-minded in business, and, being new to the country, had no notion that Indian banking is totally distinct from Home work. Like most clever self-made men, he had much simplicity in his nature; and, somehow or other, had constructed the ordinarily polite terms of his letter of engagement into a belief that the Directors had chosen him on account of his special and brilliant talents, and that they set great store by him. This notion grew and crystallised; thus adding to his natural North-country conceit. Further, he was delicate, suffered from some trouble in his chest, and was short in his temper.

You will admit that Reggie had reason to call his new

Accountant a Natural Curiosity. The two men failed to hit it off at all. Riley considered Reggie a wild, feather-headed idiot, given to Heaven only knew what dissipation in low places called 'Messes', and totally unfit for the serious and solemn vocation of banking. He could never get over Reggie's look of youth and 'you-be-damned' air; and he couldn't understand Reggie's friends—clean-built, careless men in the Army—who rode over to big Sunday breakfasts at the Bank, and told sultry stories till Riley got up and left the room. Riley was always showing Reggie how the business ought to be conducted, and Reggie had more than once to remind him that seven years' limited experience between Huddersfield and Beverley did not qualify a man to steer a big up-country business. Then Riley sulked, and referred to himself as a pillar of the Bank and a cherished friend of the Directors, and Reggie tore his hair. If a man's English subordinates fail him in India, he comes to a hard time indeed; for native help has strict limitations. In the winter Riley went sick for weeks at a time with his lung complaint, and this threw more work on Reggie. But he preferred it to the everlasting friction when Riley was well.

One of the Travelling Inspectors of the Bank discovered these collapses and reported them to the Directors. Now, Riley had been foisted on the bank by an M.P., who wanted the support of Riley's father, who, again, was anxious to get his son out to a warmer climate because of those lungs. The M.P. had an interest in the Bank; but one of the Directors wanted to advance a nominee of his own; and, after Riley's father had died, he made the rest of the Board see that an Accountant who was sick for half the year had better give place to a healthy man. If Riley had known the real story of his appointment, he might have behaved better; but, knowing nothing, his stretches of sickness alternated with restless, persistent, meddling irritation of Reggie, and all the hundred ways in which conceit in a subordinate situation can find play. Reggie used to call him striking and hair-curling names behind his back as a relief to his own feelings; but he never abused him to his face, because he said, 'Riley is such a frail beast that half of his loathsome conceit is due to pains in the chest.'

Late one April, Riley went very sick indeed. The Doctor

punched him and thumped him, and told him he would be better before long. Then the Doctor went to Reggie and said, 'Do you know how sick your Accountant is?'—'No!' said Reggie; 'the worse the better, confound him! He's a clacking nuisance when he is well. I'll let you take away the Bank Safe if you can drug him silent for this hot weather.'

But the Doctor did not laugh. 'Man, I'm not joking,' he said. 'I'll give him another three months in his bed and a week or so more to die in. On my honour and reputation, that's all the grace he has in the world. Consumption has hold of him to the marrow.'

Reggie's face changed at once into the face of 'Mr. Reginald Burke,' and he answered, 'What can I do?'—'Nothing,' said the Doctor; 'for all practical purposes the man is dead already. Keep him quiet and cheerful, and tell him he is going to recover. That's all. I'll look after him to the end, of course.'

The Doctor went away, and Reggie sat down to open the evening mail. His first letter was one from the Directors, intimating for his information that Mr. Riley was to resign, under a month's notice, by the terms of his agreement, telling Reggie that their letter to Riley would follow, and advising Reggie of the coming of a new Accountant, a man whom Reggie knew and liked.

Reggie lit a cheroot, and, before he had finished smoking, he had sketched the outline of a fraud. He put away—burked—the Director's letter, and went in to talk to Riley, who was as ungracious as usual, and fretting himself over the way the Bank would run during his illness. He never thought of the extra work on Reggie's shoulders, but solely of the damage to his own prospects of advancement. Then Reggie assured him that everything would be well, and that he, Reggie, would confer with Riley daily on the management of the Bank. Riley was a little soothed, but he hinted in as many words that he did not think much of Reggie's business capacity. Reggie was humble. And he had letters in his desk from the Directors that a Gilbarte or a Hardie might have been proud of!

The day passed in the big darkened house, and the Directors' letter of dismissal to Riley came and was put away by Reggie, who, every evening, brought the books to Riley's room, and showed him what had been going forward, while Riley snarled. Reggie did his best to make statements pleasing to Riley, but the Accountant was sure that the Bank was going to rack and ruin without him. In June, as the lying in bed told on his spirit, he asked whether his absence had been noted by the Directors, and Reggie said that they had written most sympathetic letters, hoping that he would be able to resume his valuable services before long. He showed Riley the letters; and Riley said that the Directors ought to have written to him direct. A few days later, Reggie opened Riley's mail in the half-light of the room, and gave him the sheet—not the envelope—of a letter to Riley from the Directors. Riley said he would thank Reggie knew not to interfere with his private papers, especially as Reggie knew he was too weak to open his own letters. Reggie apologised. Then Riley's mood changed, and he lectured Reggie on his evil ways: his horses and his bad friends. 'Of course, lying here on my back, Mr. Burke, I can't keep you straight; but when I'm well, I *do* hope you'll pay some heed to my words.' Reggie, who had dropped polo, and dinners, and tennis and all, to attend to Riley, said that he was penitent, and settled Riley's head on the pillow, and heard him fret and contradict in hard, dry, hacking whispers, without a sign of impatience. This, at the end of a heavy day's office work, doing double duty, in the latter half of June!

When the new Accountant came, Reggie told him the facts of the case, and announced to Riley that he had a guest staying with him. Riley said that he might have had more consideration than to entertain his 'doubtful friends' at such a time. Reggie made Carron, the new Accountant, sleep at the Club in consequence. Carron's arrival took some of the heavy work off his shoulders, and he had time to attend to Riley's exactions— to explain, soothe, invent, and settle and resettle the poor wretch in bed, and to forge complimentary letters from Calcutta. At the end of the first month Riley wished to send some money home to his mother. Reggie sent the draft. At the end of the second month Riley's salary came in just the same. Reggie paid it out of his own pocket, and, with it, wrote Riley a beautiful letter from the Directors.

Riley was very ill indeed, but the flame of his life burnt unsteadily. Now and then he would be cheerful and confident about the future, sketching plans for going Home and seeing his mother. Reggie listened patiently when the office work was over, and encouraged him.

At other times Riley insisted on Reggie reading the Bible and grim 'Methody' tracts to him. Out of these tracts he pointed morals directed at his Manager. But he always found time to worry Reggie about the working of the Bank, and to show him where the weak point lay.

This indoor, sickroom life and constant strain wore Reggie down a good deal, and shook his nerves, and lowered his billiard-play by forty points. But the business of the Bank, and the business of the sickroom, had to go on, though the glass was 116 in the shade.

At the end of the third month Riley was sinking fast, and had begun to realise that he was very sick. But the conceit that made him worry Reggie kept him from believing the worst. 'He wants some sort of mental stimulant if he is to drag on,' said the Doctor. 'Keep him interested in life if you care about his living.' So Riley, contrary to all the laws of business and finance, received a 25-per-cent rise of salary from the Directors. The 'mental stimulant' succeeded beautifully. Riley was happy and cheerful, and, as is often the case in consumption, healthiest in mind when the body was weakest. He lingered for a full month, snarling and fretting about the Bank, talking of the future, hearing the Bible read, lecturing Reggie on sin, and wondering when he would be able to move abroad.

But at the end of September, one mercilessly hot evening, he rose up in his bed with a little gasp, and said quickly to Reggie: 'Mr. Burke, I'm going to die. I know it in myself. My chest is all hollow inside, and there is nothing to breathe with. To the best of my knowledge I have done nowt'—he was returning to the talk of his boyhood—'to lie heavy on my conscience. God be thanked, I have been preserved from the grosser forms of sin; and I counsel *you*, Mr. Burke . . .'

Here his voice died down, and Reggie stooped over him.

'Send my salary for September to my mother . . . done great things with the Bank if I had been spared . . . mistaken policy . . . no fault of mine . . .'

Then he turned his face to the wall and died.

Reggie drew the sheet over Its face, and went out into the veranda, with his last 'mental stimulant'—a letter of condolence and sympathy from the Directors—unused in his pocket.

'If I'd been only ten minutes earlier,' thought Reggie, 'I might have heartened him up to pull through another day.'

BEYOND THE PALE

Love heeds not caste nor sleep a broken bed.
I went in search of love and lost myself.
                                        Hindu Proverb

A MAN SHOULD, whatever happens, keep to his own caste, race, and breed. Let the White go to the White and the Black to the Black. Then whatever trouble falls is in the ordinary course of things—neither sudden, alien, nor unexpected.

This is the story of a man who wilfully stepped beyond the safe limits of decent everyday society, and paid for it heavily.

He knew too much in the first instance; and he saw too much in the second. He took too deep an interest in native life; but he will never do so again.

Deep away in the heart of the City, behind Jitha Megji's *bustee*, lies Amir Nath's Gully, which ends in a dead-wall pierced by one grated window. At the head of the Gully is a big cow-byre, and the walls on either side of the Gully are without windows. Neither Suchet Singh nor Gaur Chand approve of their women-folk looking into the world. If Durga Charan had been of their opinion he would have been a happier man to-day, and little Bisesa would have been able to knead her own bread. Her room looked out through the grated window into the narrow dark Gully where the sun never came and where the buffaloes wallowed in the blue slime. She was a widow, about fifteen years old, and she prayed to the Gods, day and night, to send her a lover; for she did not approve of living alone.

One day the man—Trejago his name was—came into Amir Nath's Gully on an aimless wandering; and, after he had passed the buffaloes, stumbled over a big heap of cattle-food.

Then he saw that the Gully ended in a trap, and heard a little laugh from behind the grated window. It was a pretty little laugh, and Trejago, knowing that, for all practical purposes, the old *Arabian Nights* are good guides, went forward to the window, and whispered that verse of "The Love Song of Har Dyal" which begins:—

> *Can a man stand upright in the face of the naked Sun; or a Lover in the Presence of his Beloved?*
> *If my feet fail me, O Heart of my own Heart, am I to blame, being blinded by the glimpse of your beauty?*

There came the faint *tchink* of a woman's bracelets from behind the grating, and a little voice went on with the song at the fifth verse:—

> *Alas! Alas! Can the Moon tell the Lotus of her love when the Gate of Heaven is shut and the clouds gather for the rains?*
> *They have taken my Beloved, and driven her with the pack-horses to the North.*
> *There are iron chains on the feet that were set on my heart.*
> *Call to the bowmen to make ready——*

The voice stopped suddenly, and Trejago walked out of Amir Nath's Gully, wondering who in the world could have capped "The Love Song of Har Dyal" so neatly.

Next morning, as he was driving to office, an old woman threw a packet into his dogcart. In the packet was the half of a broken glass bangle, one flower of the blood-red *dhak*, a pinch of *bhusa* or cattle-food, and eleven cardamoms. That packet was a letter—not a clumsy compromising letter, but an innocent, unintelligible lover's epistle.

Trejago knew far too much about these things, as I have said. No Englishman should be able to translate object-letters. But Trejago spread all the trifles on the lid of his office-box and began to puzzle them out.

A broken glass bangle stands for a Hindu widow all India over; because, when a husband dies, a woman's bracelets are broken on her wrists. Trejago saw the meaning of the little bit of glass. The flower of the *dhak* means diversely 'desire,' 'come,' 'write,' or 'danger,' according to the other things with it. One cardamom means 'jealousy'; but when any article is duplicated in an object-letter, it loses its symbolic meaning and stands merely for one of a number indicating time, or, if incense, curds, or saffron be sent also, place. The message ran then: 'A widow— *dhak* flower and *bhusa*,—at eleven o'clock.' The pinch of *bhusa* enlightened Trejago. He saw—this kind of letter leaves much to instinctive knowledge—that the *bhusa* referred to the big heap of cattle-food over which he had fallen in Amir Nath's Gully, and that the message must come from the person behind the grating; she being a widow. So the message ran then: 'A widow, in the Gully in which is the heap of *bhusa*, desires you to come at eleven o'clock.'

Trejago threw all the rubbish into the fireplace and laughed. He knew that men in the East do not make love under windows at eleven in the forenoon, nor do women fix appointments a week in advance. So he went, that very night at eleven, into Amir Nath's Gully, clad in a *boorka*, which cloaks a man as well as a woman. Directly the gongs of the City made the hour, the little voice behind the grating took up "The Love Song of Har Dyal" at the verse where the Panthan girl calls upon Har Dyal to return. The song is really pretty in the vernacular. In English you miss the wail of it. It runs something like this:—

Alone upon the housetops, to the North
 I turn and watch the lightnings in the sky,—
The glamour of thy footsteps in the North.
 Come back to me, Beloved, or I die!

Below my feet the still bazar is laid—
 Far, far below the weary camels lie,—
The camels and the captives of thy raid.
 Come back to me, Beloved, or I die!

My father's wife is old and harsh with years,
 And drudge of all my father's house am I.—
My bread is sorrow and my drink is tears.
 Come back to me, Beloved, or I die!

As the song stopped, Trejago stepped under the grating and whispered, 'I am here.'

Bisesa was good to look upon.

That night was the beginning of many strange things, and of a double life so wild that Trejago to-day sometimes wonders if it were not all a dream. Bisesa, or her old handmaiden who had thrown the object-letter, had detached the heavy grating from the brickwork of the wall; so that the window slid inside, leaving only a square of raw masonry into which an active man might climb.

In the daytime, Trejago drove through his routine of office work, or put on his calling-clothes and called on the ladies of the station, wondering how long they would know him if they knew of poor little Bisesa. At night, when all the City was still, came the walk under the evil-smelling *boorka*, the patrol through Jitha Megji's *bustee*, the quick turn into Amir Nath's Gully between the sleeping cattle and the dead walls, and then, last of all, Bisesa, and the deep, even breathing of the old woman who slept outside the door of the bare little room that Durga Charan allotted to his sister's daughter. Who or what Durga Charan was, Trejago never inquired; and why in the world he was not discovered or knifed never occurred to him till his madness was over, and Bisesa . . . But this comes later.

Bisesa was an endless delight to Trejago. She was as ignorant as a bird; and her distorted versions of the rumours from the outside world that had reached her in her room, amused Trejago almost as much as her lisping attempts to pronounce his name— 'Christopher'. The first syllable was always more than she could manage, and she made funny little gestures with her roseleaf hands, as one throwing the name away, and then, kneeling before Trejago, asked him, exactly as an Englishwoman would do, if he were sure he loved her. Trejago swore that he loved her more than any one else in the world. Which was true.

After a month of this folly, the exigencies of his other life compelled Trejago to be especially attentive to a lady of his acquaintance. You may take it for a fact that anything of this kind is not only noticed and discussed by a man' own race, but by some hundred and fifty natives as well. Trejago had to walk with this lady and talk to her at the Bandstand, and once or twice drive with her; never for an instant dreaming that this would affect his dearer, out-of-the-way life. But the news flew, in the usual mysterious fashion, from mouth to mouth, till Bisesa's duenna heard of it and told Bisesa. The child was so troubled that she did the household work evilly, and was beaten by Durga Charan's wife in consequence.

A week later, Bisesa taxed Trejago with the flirtation. She understood no gradations and spoke openly. Trejago laughed, and Bisesa stamped her little feet—little feet, light as marigold flowers, could lie in the palm of a man's one hand.

Much that is written about Oriental passion and impulsiveness is exaggerated and compiled at second hand; but a little of it is true, and when an Englishman finds that little, it is quite as startling as any passion in his own proper life. Bisesa raged and stormed, and finally threatened to kill herself if Trejago did not at once drop the alien Memsahib who had come between them. Trejago tried to explain, and to show her that she did not understand these things from a Western standpoint. Bisesa drew herself up, and said simply:—

'I do not. I know only this—it is not good that I should have made you dearer than my own heart to me, Sahib. You are an Englishman. I am only a black girl'—she was fairer than bar-gold in the Mint,—'and the widow of a black man.'

Then she sobbed and said: 'But on my soul and my Mother's soul, I love you. There shall no harm come to you, whatever happens to me.'

Trejago argued with the child, and tried to soothe her, but she seemed quite unreasonably disturbed. Nothing would satisfy her save that all relations between them should end. He was to go away at once. And he went. As he dropped out of the window, she kissed his forehead twice, and he walked home wondering.

A week, and then three weeks, passed without a sign from Bisesa. Trejago, thinking that the rupture had lasted quite long enough, went down to Amir Nath's Gully for the fifth time in the three weeks, hoping that his rap at the sill of the shifting grating would be answered. He was not disappointed.

There was a young moon, and one stream of light fell down into Amir Nath's Gully, and struck the grating, which was drawn away as he knocked. From the black dark, Bisesa held out her arms into the moonlight. Both hands had been cut off at the wrists, and the stumps were nearly healed.

Then, as Bisesa bowed her head between her arms and sobbed, some one in the room grunted like a wild beast, and something sharp—knife, sword, or spear,—thrust at Trejago in his *boorka*. The stroke missed his body, but cut into one of the muscles of the groin, and he limped slightly from the wound for the rest of his days.

The grating went into its place. There was no sign whatever from inside the house,—nothing but the moonlight strip on the high wall, and the blackness of Amir Nath's Gully behind.

The next thing Trejago remembers, after raging and shouting like a madman between those pitiless walls, is that he found himself near the river as the dawn was breaking, threw away his *boorka* and went home bareheaded.

What was the tragedy—whether Bisesa had, in a fit of causeless despair, told everything, or the intrigue had been discovered and she tortured to tell; whether Durga Charan knew his name, and what became of Bisesa—Trejago does not know to this day. Something horrible had happened, and the thought of what it must have been comes upon Trejago in the night now and again, and keeps him company till the morning. One special feature of the case is that he does not know where lies the front of Durga Charan's house. It may open on to a courtyard common to two or more houses, or it may lie behind any one of the gates of Jitha Megji's *bustee*. Trejago cannot tell. He cannot get Bisesa—poor little Bisesa—back again. He has lost her in the City where each man's house is as guarded and as unknowable as the grave; and the grating that opens into Amir Nath's Gully has been walled up.

But Trejago pays his calls regularly, and is reckoned a very decent sort of man.

There is nothing peculiar about him, except a slight stiffness, caused by a riding-strain, in the right leg.

PIG

Go, stalk the red deer o'er the heather,
Ride, follow the fox if you can!
But, for pleasure and profit together,
Allow me the hunting of Man—
The chase of the Human, the search for the Soul
To its ruin—the hunting of Man.
                                    The Old Shikarri

I BELIEVE THE difference began in the matter of a horse, with a twist in his temper, whom Pinecoffin sold to Nafferton, and by whom Nafferton was nearly slain. There may have been other causes of offence; the horse was the official stalking-horse. Nafferton was very angry; but Pinecoffin laughed, and said that he had never guaranteed the beast's manners. Nafferton laughed too, though he vowed he would write off his fall against Pinecoffin if he waited five years. Now, a Dalesman from beyond Skipton will forgive an injury when the Strid lets a man live; but a South Devon man is as soft as a Dartmoor bog. You can see from their names that Nafferton had the race-advantage of Pinecoffin. He was a peculiar man, and his notions of humour were cruel. He taught me a new and fascinating form of *shikar*. He hounded Pinecoffin from Mithankot to Jagadri, and from Gurgaon to Abbotabad—up and across the Punjab, a large province, and in places remarkably dry. He said that he had no intention of allowing Assistant Commissioners to 'sell him pups', in the shape of ramping, screaming country breds, without making their lives a burden to them.

Most Assistant Commissioners develop a bent for some special work after their first hot weather in the country. The boys with digestions hope to write their names large on the Frontier, and struggle for dreary places like Bannu and Kohat.

The bilious ones climb into the Secretariat; which is very bad for their liver. Others are bitten with a mania for District work, Ghaznevid coins or Persian poetry; while some, who come of farmers' stock, find that the smell of the earth after the Rains gets into their blood, and calls them to 'develop the resources of the Province'. These men are enthusiasts. Pinecoffin belonged to their class. He knew a great many facts bearing on the cost of bullocks, and temporary wells, and opium-scrapers, and what happens if you burn too much rubbish on a field in the hope of enriching used-up soil. All the Pinecoffins come of a landholding breed, and so the land only took back her own again. Unfortunately—most unfortunately for Pinecoffin—he was a Civilian as well as a farmer. Nafferton watched him, and thought about the horse. Nafferton said, 'See me chase that boy till he drops!' I said, 'You can't get your knife into an Assistant Commissioner.' Nafferton told me that I did not understand the administration of the Province.

Our Government is rather peculiar. It gushes on the agricultural and general information side, and will supply a moderately respectable man with all sorts of 'economic statistics', if he speaks to it prettily. For instance, you are interested in gold-washing in the sands of the Sutlej. You pull the string, and find that it wakes up half-a-dozen Departments, and finally communicates, say, with a friend of yours in the Telegraph, who once wrote some notes on the customs of gold-washers when he was on construction work in their part of the Empire. He may or may not be pleased at being ordered to write out everything he knows for your benefit. This depends on his temperament. The bigger man you are, the more information and the greater trouble can you raise.

Nafferton was not a big man; but he had the reputation of being very 'earnest'. An 'earnest' man can do much with the Government. There was an earnest man once who nearly wrecked . . . But all India knows *that* story. I am not sure what real 'earnestness' is. A very fair imitation can be manufactured by neglecting to dress decently, by mooning about in a dreamy, misty sort of way, by taking office work home, after staying in the office till seven, and by receiving crowds of native gentlemen on Sunday. That is one sort of 'earnestness'.

Nafferton cast about for a peg whereon to hang his earnestness, and for a string that would communicate with Pinecoffin. He found both. They were Pig. Nafferton became an earnest inquirer after Pig. He informed the Government that he had a scheme whereby a very large percentage of the British Army in India could be fed, at a very large saving, on Pig. Then he hinted that Pinecoffin might supply him with the 'varied information necessary to the proper inception of the scheme'. So the Government wrote on the back of the letter, 'Instruct Mr. Pinecoffin to furnish Mr. Nafferton with any information in his power.' Government is very prone to writing things on the backs of letters which, later, lead to trouble and confusion.

Nafferton had no interest in Pig, but he knew that Pinecoffin would flounce into the trap. Pinecoffin was delighted at being consulted about Pig. The Indian Pig is not exactly an important factor in agricultural life; but Nafferton explained to Pinecoffin that there was room for improvement, and corresponded direct with that young man.

You may think that there is not much to be evolved from Pig. It all depends how you set to work. Pinecoffin being a Civilian and wishing to do things thoroughly, began with an essay on the Primitive Pig, the Mythology of the Pig, and the Dravidian Pig. Nafferton filed that information—twenty-seven foolscap sheets—and wanted to know about the distribution of the Pig in the Punjab, and how it stood the Plains in the hot weather. From this point onwards remember that I am giving you only the barest outlines of the affair—the guy-ropes, as it were, of the web that Nafferton spun round Pinecoffin.

Pinecoffin made a coloured Pig-population map, and collected observations on the comparative longevity of Pig (a) in the sub-montane tracts of the Himalayas, and (b) in the Rechna Doab. Nafferton filed that, and asked what sort of people looked after Pig. This started an ethnological excursus on swineherds, and drew from Pinecoffin long tables showing the proportion per thousand of the caste in the Dejarat. Nafferton filed that bundle, and explained that the figures which he wanted referred to the Cis-Sutlej states, where he understood that Pigs were very fine and large, and where he proposed to start a Piggery. By this time Government had quite forgotten their instructions to Mr.

Pinecoffin. They were like gentlemen in Keats' poem, who turned well-oiled wheels to skin other people. But Pinecoffin was just entering into the spirit of the Pig-hunt, as Nafferton well knew he would do. He had a fair amount of work of his own to clear away; but he sat up of nights reducing Pig to five places of decimals for the honour of his Service. He was not going to appear ignorant of so easy a subject as Pig.

Then Government sent him on special duty to Kohat, to 'inquire into' the big, seven-foot, iron-shod spades of that District. People had been killing each other with those peaceful tools; and Government wished to know 'whether a modified form of agricultural implement could not, tentatively and as a temporary measure be introduced among the agricultural population without needlessly or unduly exacerbating the existing religious sentiments of the peasantry.'

Nafferton now began to take up '(a) The Food-supply of the indigenous Pig, with a view to the improvement of its capacities as a flesh-former. (b) The acclimatisation of the exotic Pig, maintaining its distinctive peculiarities.' Pinecoffin replied exhaustively that the exotic Pig would become merged in the indigenous type; and quoted horse-breeding statistics to prove this. This side-issue was debated at great length on Pinecoffin's side, till Nafferton owned that he had been in the wrong, and moved the previous question. When Pinecoffin had quite written himself out about flesh-formers, and fibrins, and glucose, and the nitrogenous constituents of maize and lucerne, Nafferton raised the question of expense. By this time Pinecoffin, who had been transferred from Kohat, had developed a Pig theory of his own, which he stated in thirty-three folio pages—all carefully filed by Nafferton; who asked for more.

These things took ten months, and Pinecoffin's interest in the potential Piggery seemed to die down after he had stated his own views. But Nafferton bombarded him with letters on 'the Imperial aspect of the scheme, as tending to officialise the sale of pork, and thereby calculated to give offence to the Mohammedan population of Upper India.' He guessed that Pinecoffin would want some broad, free-hand work after his niggling, stripling, decimal details. Pinecoffin handled the latest development of the case in masterly style, and proved that no 'popular ebullition of excitement was to be apprehended'. Nafferton said that there was nothing like Civilian insight into matters of this kind, and lured him up a by-path—'the possible profits to accrue to the Government from the sale of hog-bristles.' There is an extensive literature of hog-bristles, and the shoe, brush, and colour-man's trades recognise more varieties of bristles than you would think possible. After Pinecoffin had wondered a little at Nafferton's rage for information, he sent back a monograph, fifty-one pages, on 'Products of the Pig'. This led him, under Nafferton's tender handling, straight to the Cawnpore factories, the trade in hog-skin for saddles—and thence to the tanners. Pinecoffin wrote that pomegranate-seed was the best cure for hog-skin, and suggested—the past fourteen months had wearied him—that Nafferton should 'raise his Pigs before he tanned them.'

Nafferton went back to the second section of his fifth question. How could the exotic Pig be brought to give as much pork as it did in the West and yet 'assume the essentially hirsute characteristics of its Oriental congener'? Pinecoffin felt dazed, for he had forgotten what he had written sixteen months before, and fancied that he was about to reopen the entire question. He was too far involved in the hideous tangle to retreat, and, in a weak moment, he wrote, 'Consult my first letter'; which related to the Dravidian Pig. As a matter of fact, Pinecoffin had still to reach the acclimatisation stage; having gone off on a side-issue on the merging of types.

Then Nafferton really unmasked his batteries! He complained to the Government, in stately language, of 'the paucity of help accorded to me in my earnest attempts to start a potentially remunerative industry, and the flippancy with which my requests for information are treated by a gentleman whose pseudo-scholarly attainments should at least have taught him the primary differences between the Dravidian and the Berkshire variety of the genus *Sus*. If I am to understand that the letter to which he refers me contains his serious views on the acclimatisation of a valuable, though possibly uncleanly, animal, I am reluctantly compelled to believe,' etc. etc.

There was a new man at the head of the Department of Castigation. The wretched Pinecoffin was told that the Service was made for the Country, and not the Country for the Service, and that he had better begin to supply information about Pig.

Pinecoffin answered insanely that he had written everything that could be written about Pig, and that some furlough was due to him.

Nafferton got a copy of that letter, and sent it, with the essay on the Dravidian Pig, to a down-country paper which printed both in full. The essay was rather high-flown; but if the Editor had seen the stacks of paper, in Pinecoffin's handwriting, on Nafferton's table, he would not have been so sarcastic about the 'nebulous discursiveness and blatant self-sufficiency of the modern Competition-wallah, and his utter inability to grasp the practical issues of a practical question.' Many friends cut out these remarks and sent them to Pinecoffin.

I have already stated that Pinecoffin came of a soft stock. This last stroke frightened and shook him. He could not understand it; but he felt that he had been, somehow, shamelessly betrayed by Nafferton. He realised that he had wrapped himself up in the Pigskin without need, and that he could not well set himself right with the Government. All his acquaintances asked after his 'nebulous discursiveness' or his 'blatant self-sufficiency', and this made him miserable.

He took a train and went to Nafferton, whom he had not seen since the Pig business began. He also took the cutting from the paper, and blustered feebly and called Nafferton names, and then died down to a watery, weak protest of the 'I-say-it's-too-bad-you-know' order.

Nafferton was very sympathetic.

'I'm afraid I have given you a good deal of trouble, haven't I?' said he.

'Trouble!' whimpered Pinecoffin; 'I don't mind the trouble so much, though that was bad enough; but what I resent is this showing up in print. It will stick to me like a burr all through my service. And I *did* do my best for your interminable swine. It's too bad of you—on my soul it is!'

'I don't know,' said Nafferton. 'Have you ever been stuck with a horse? It isn't the money I mind, though that is bad enough; but what I resent is that chaff that follows, especially from the boy who stuck me. But I think we'll cry quits now.'

Pinecoffin found nothing to say save bad words; and Nafferton smiled ever so sweetly, and asked him to dinner.

THE BRONCKHORST
DIVORCE-CASE

In the daytime, when she moved about me,
In the night, when she was sleeping at my side,—
I was wearied, I was wearied of her presence,
Day by day and night by night I grew to hate her—
Would God that she or I had died!

Confessions

THERE WAS A man called Bronckhorst—a three-cornered, middle-aged man in the army—grey as a badger, and, some people said, with a touch of country-blood in him. That, however, cannot be proved. Mrs. Bronckhorst was not exactly young, though fifteen years younger than her husband. She was a large, pale, quiet woman, with heavy eyelids over weak eyes, and hair that turned red or yellow as the lights fell on it.

Bronckhorst was not nice in any way. He had no respect for the pretty public and private lies that make life a little less nasty than it is. His manner towards his wife was coarse. There are many things—including actual assault with the clenched fist—that a wife will endure; but seldom a wife can bear—as Mrs. Bronckhorst bore—with a long course of brutal, hard chaff, making light of her weaknesses, her headaches, her small fits of gaiety, her dresses, her queer little attempts to make herself attractive to her husband when she knows that she is not what she has been, and—worst of all—the love that she spends on her children. That particular sort of heavy-handed jest was specially dear to Bronckhorst. I suppose that he had first slipped into it, meaning no harm, in the honeymoon, when folk find their ordinary stock of endearments run short, and so go to the other extreme to express their feelings. A similar impulse makes a man say, '*Hutt*, you old beast!' when a favourite horse nuzzles his coat-front. Unluckily, when the reaction of marriage sets in, the form of speech remains, and, tenderness having died out, hurts the wife more than she cares to say. But Mrs. Bronckhorst was devoted to her 'Teddy' as she called him. Perhaps that was why he objected to her. Perhaps—this is only a theory to account for his infamous behaviour later on—he gave way to the queer, savage feeling that sometimes takes by the throat a husband twenty years married, when he sees, across the table, the same, same face of his wedded wife, and knows that, as he has sat facing it, so must he now continue to sit until the day of its death or his own. Most men and all women know the spasm. It only lasts for three breaths as a rule, must be a 'throw-back' to times when men and women were rather worse than they are now, and is too unpleasant to be discussed.

Dinner at the Bronckhorsts' was an infliction few men cared to undergo. Bronckhorst took a pleasure in saying things that made his wife wince. When their little boy came in at dessert, Bronckhorst used to give him half a glass of wine, and, naturally enough, the poor little mite got first riotous, next miserable, and was removed screaming. Bronckhorst asked if that was the way Teddy usually behaved, and whether Mrs. Bronckhorst could not spare some of her time 'to teach the little beggar decency'. Mrs. Bronckhorst, who loved the boy more than her own life, tried not to cry—her spirit seemed to have been broken by her marriage. Lastly, Bronckhorst used to say, 'There! That'll do, that'll do. For God's sake try to behave like a rational woman. Go into the drawing-room.' Mrs. Bronckhorst would go, trying to carry it all off with a smile; and the guest of the evening would feel angry and uncomfortable.

After three years of this cheerful life—for Mrs. Bronckhorst had no women-friends to talk to—the station was startled by the news that Bronckhorst had instituted proceedings *on the criminal count*, against a man called Biel, who certainly had been rather attentive to Mrs. Bronckhorst whenever she had appeared in public. The utter want of reserve with which Bronckhorst treated his own dishonour helped us to know that the evidence against Biel would be entirely circumstantial and native. There were no letters; but Bronckhorst said openly that he would rack Heaven and Earth until he saw Biel superintending the manufacture of carpets in the Central Jail. Mrs. Bronckhorst kept entirely to her house, and let charitable folks say what they pleased. Opinions were divided. Some two-thirds of the station jumped at once to the conclusion that Biel was guilty; but a dozen men who knew and liked him held by him. Biel was furious and surprised. He denied the whole thing, and vowed that he would thrash Bronckhorst within an inch of his life. No jury, we knew, would convict a man on the criminal count on native evidence in a land where you can buy a murder-charge, including the corpse, all complete for fifty-four rupees; but Biel did not care to scrape through by the benefit of a doubt. He wanted the whole thing cleared; but, as he said one night, 'he can prove anything with servants' evidence, and I've only my bare word.' This was almost a month before the case came on; and beyond agreeing with Biel, we could do little. All that we could be sure of was that the native evidence would be bad enough to blast Biel's character for the rest of his service; for when a native begins perjury he perjures himself thoroughly. He does not boggle over details.

Some genius at the end of the table whereat the affair was being talked over, said, 'Look here! I don't believe lawyers are any good. Get a man to wire to Strickland, and beg him to come down and pull us through.'

Strickland was about a hundred and eighty miles up the line. He had not long been married to Miss Youghal, but he scented in the telegram a chance to return to the old detective work that his soul lusted after, and next night he came in and heard our story. He finished his pipe and said oracularly, 'We must get at the evidence. Oorya bearer, Mussulman *khit* and sweeper *ayah*, I suppose, are the pillars of the charge. I am on in this piece; but I'm afraid I'm going rusty in my talk.'

He rose and went into Biel's bedroom, where his trunk had been put, and shut the door. An hour later, we heard him say, 'I hadn't the heart to part with my old make-ups when I married. Will this do?' There was a loathly *fakir* salaaming in the doorway.

'Now lend me fifty rupees,' said Strickland,' and give me your Words of Honour that you won't tell my wife.'

He got all that he asked for, and left the house while the table drank his health. What he did only himself knows. A *fakir* hung about Bronckhorst's compound for twelve days. Then a sweeper appeared, and when Biel heard of *him*, he said that Strickland was an angel full-fledged. Whether the sweeper made love to Janki, Mrs. Bronckhorst's *ayah*, is a question which concerns Strickland exclusively.

He came back at the end of three weeks, and said quietly, 'You spoke the truth, Biel. The whole business is put up from beginning to end. ''Jove! It almost astonishes *me*! That Bronckhorst beast isn't fit to live.'

There was uproar and shouting, and Biel said, 'How are you going to prove it? You can't say that you've been trespassing on Bronckhorst's compound in disguise!'

'No,' said Strickland. 'Tell your lawyer-fool, whoever he is, to get up something strong about "inherent improbabilities" and "discrepancies of evidence". He won't have to speak, but it will make him happy. *I*'m going to run this business.'

Biel held his tongue, and the other men waited to see what would happen. They trusted Strickland as men trust quiet men. When the case came off the Court was crowded. Strickland hung about in the veranda of the Court, till he met the Mohammedan *khitmutgar*. Then he murmured a *fakir*'s blessing in his ear, and asked him how his second wife did. The man spun round, and, as he looked into the eyes of 'Estreekin Sahib', his jaw dropped. You must remember that before Strickland was married, he was, as I have told you already, a power among the natives. Strickland whispered a rather coarse vernacular proverb to the effect that he was abreast of all that was going on, and went into the Court armed with a gut trainer's-whip.

The Mohammedan was the first witness, and Strickland beamed upon him from the back of the Court. The man moistened his lips with his tongue and, in his abject fear of 'Estreekin Sahib', the *fakir* went back on every detail of his evidence— said he was a poor man, and God was his witness that he had forgotten everything that Bronckhorst Sahib had told him to say. Between his terror of Strickland, the Judge, and Bronckhorst he collapsed weeping.

Then began a panic among the witnesses. Janki, the *ayah*,

49

leering chastely behind her veil, turned grey, and the bearer left the Court. He said that his mamma was dying, and that it was not wholesome for any man to lie unthriftily in the presence of 'Estreekin Sahib.'

Biel said politely to Bronckhorst, 'Your witnesses don't seem to work. Haven't you any forged letters to produce?' But Bronckhorst was swaying to and fro in his chair, and there was a dead pause after Biel had been called to order.

Bronckhorst's Counsel saw the look on his client's face, and without more ado pitched his papers on the little green-baize table, and mumbled something about having been misinformed. The whole court applauded wildly, like soldiers at a theatre, and the Judge began to say what he thought.

Biel came out of the Court, and Strickland dropped a gut trainer's-whip in the veranda. Ten minutes later, Biel was cutting Bronckhorst into ribbons behind the old Court cells, quietly and without scandal. What was left of Bronckhorst was sent home in a carriage; and his wife wept over it and nursed it into a man again.

Later on, Biel had managed to hush up the counter-charge against Bronckhorst of fabricating false evidence, Mrs. Bronckhorst, with her faint, watery smile, said that there had been a mistake, but it wasn't her Teddy's fault altogether. She would wait till her Teddy came back to her. Perhaps he had grown tired of her, or she had tried his patience, and perhaps we wouldn't cut her any more, and perhaps the mothers would let their children play with 'little Teddy' again. He was so lonely. Then the station invited Mrs. Bronckhorst everywhere, until Bronckhorst was fit to appear in public, when he went Home and took his wife with him. According to latest advices, her Teddy did come back to her, and they are moderately happy. Though, of course, he can never forgive her the thrashing that she was the indirect means of getting for him.

What Biel wants to know is, 'Why didn't I press home the charge against the Bronckhorst brute, and have him run in?'

What Mrs. Strickland wants to know is, 'How *did* my husband bring such a lovely, lovely Waler from your station? I know *all* his money affairs; and I'm *certain* he didn't *buy* it.'

What I want to know is, 'How do women like Mrs. Bronckhorst come to marry men like Bronckhorst?'

And my conundrum is the unanswerable of the three.

THE MARK OF THE BEAST

> *Your Gods and my Gods—do you or I know*
> *which are the stronger?*
>
> Native Proverb

EAST OF SUEZ, some hold, the direct control of Providence ceases; Man being there handed over to the power of the Gods and Devils of Asia, and the Church of England Providence only exercising an occasional and modified supervision in the case of Englishmen.

This theory accounts for some of the more unnecessary horrors of life in India; it may be stretched to explain my story.

My friend Strickland of the Police, who knows as much of natives of India as is good for any man, can bear witness to the facts of the case. Dumoise, our doctor, also saw what Strickland and I saw. The inference which he drew from the evidence was entirely incorrect. He is dead now; he died in a rather curious manner, which has been elsewhere described.

When Fleete came to India he owned a little money and some land in the Himalayas, near a place called Dharmsala. Both properties had been left him by an uncle, and he came out to finance them. He was a big, heavy, genial, and inoffensive man. His knowledge of natives was, of course, limited, and he complained of the difficulties of the language.

He rode in from his place in the Hills to spend New Year in the station, and he stayed with Strickland. On New Year's Eve there was a big dinner at the Club, and the night was excusably wet. When men foregather from the uttermost ends of the Empire they have a right to be riotous. The Frontier had sent down a contingent of Catch-'em-Alive-O's who had not seen twenty white faces for a year, and were used to ride fifteen miles to dinner at the next Fort at the risk of a Khyberee bullet where their drinks should lie. They profited by their new security, for they tried to play pool with a curled-up hedgehog found in the garden, and one of them carried the marker round the room in his teeth. Half-a-dozen planters had come in from the South and were talking 'horse' to the Biggest Liar in Asia, who was trying to cap all their stories at once. Everybody was there, and there was a general closing up of ranks and taking stock of our losses in dead or disabled that had fallen during the past year. It was a very wet night, and I remember that we sang 'Auld Lang Syne' with our feet in the Polo Championship Cup, and our heads among the stars, and swore that we were all dear friends. Then some of us went away and annexed Burma, and some tried to open up the Sudan and were opened up by Fuzzies in that cruel scrub outside Suakin, and some found stars and medals, and some were married, which was bad, and some did other things which were worse, and the others of us stayed in our chains and strove to make money on insufficient experiences.

Fleete began the night with sherry and bitters, drank champagne steadily up to dessert, then raw, rasping Capri with all the strength of whisky, took Benedictine with his coffee, four or five whiskies and sodas to improve his pool strokes, beer and bones at half-past two, winding up with old brandy. Consequently, when he came out, at half-past three in the morning, into fourteen degrees of frost, he was very angry with his horse for coughing, and tried to leapfrog into the saddle. The horse broke away and went to his stables; so Strickland and I formed a Guard of Dishonour to take Fleete home.

Our road lay through the bazar, close to a little temple of Hanuman, the Monkey God, who is a leading divinity worthy of respect. All Gods have good points, just as have all priests. Personally, I attach much importance to Hanuman, and am kind to his people—the great grey apes of the Hills. One never knows when one may want a friend.

There was a light in the temple, and as we passed we could hear voices of men chanting hymns. In a native temple the priests rise at all hours of the night to do honour to their god. Before we could stop him, Fleete dashed up the steps, patted two priests on the back, and was gravely grinding the ashes of his cigar-butt into the forehead of the red stone image of Hanuman. Strickland tried to drag him out, but he sat down and said solemnly:—

'Shee that? Mark of the B—beasht! *I* made it. Ishn't it fine?'

In half a minute the temple was alive and noisy, and Strickland, who knew what came of polluting gods, said that things might occur. He, by virtue of his official position, long residence in the country, and weakness for going among the natives, was known to the priests and he felt unhappy. Fleete sat on the ground and refused to move. He said that "good old Hanuman" made a very soft pillow.

Then, without any warning, a Silver Man came out of a recess behind the image of the god. He was perfectly naked in that bitter, bitter cold, and his body shone like frosted silver, for he was what the Bible calls "a leper as white as snow". Also he had no face, because he was a leper of some years' standing, and his disease was heavy upon him. We two stooped to haul Fleete up, and the temple was filling and filling with folk who seemed to spring from the earth, when the Silver Man ran in under our arms, making a noise exactly like the mewing of an otter, caught Fleete round the body and dropped his head on Fleete's breast before we could wrench him away. Then he retired to a corner and sat mewing while the crowd blocked all the doors.

The priests were very angry until the Silver Man touched Fleete. That nuzzling seemed to sober them.

At the end of a few minutes' silence one of the priests came to Strickland and said, in perfect English, 'Take your friend away. He has done with Hanuman, but Hanuman has not done with him.' The crowd gave room and we carried Fleete into the road.

Strickland was very angry. He said that we might all three have been knifed, and that Fleete should thank his stars that he had escaped without injury.

Fleete thanked no one. He said that he wanted to go to bed. He was gorgeously drunk.

We moved on, Strickland silent and wrathful, until Fleete was taken with violent shivering fits and sweating. He said that the smells of the bazar were overpowering, and he wondered why slaughter-houses were permitted so near English residences. 'Can't you smell the blood?' said Fleete.

We put him to bed at last, just as the dawn was breaking, and Strickland invited me to have another whisky and soda. While we were drinking he talked of the trouble in the temple, and admitted that it baffled him completely. Strickland hates being mystified by natives, because his business in life is to overmatch them with their own weapons. He has not yet succeeded in doing this, but in fifteen or twenty years he will have made some small progress.

'They should have mauled us,' he said, 'instead of mewing at us. I wonder what they meant. I don't like it one little bit.'

I said that the Managing Committee of the temple would in all probability bring a criminal action against us for insulting their religion. There was a section of the Indian Penal Code which exactly met Fleete's offence. Strickland said he only hoped and prayed that they would do this. Before I left I looked into Fleete's room, and saw him lying on his right side, scratching his left breast. Then I went to bed, cold, depressed, and unhappy, at seven o'clock in the morning.

At one o'clock I rode over to Strickland's house to inquire after Fleete's head. I imagined that it would be a sore one. Fleete was breakfasting and seemed unwell. His temper was gone, for he was abusing the cook for not supplying him with an underdone chop. A man who can eat raw meat after a wet night is a curiosity. I told Fleete this and he laughed.

'You breed queer mosquitoes in these parts,' he said. 'I've been bitten to pieces, but only in one place.'

'Let's have a look at the bite,' said Strickland. 'It may have gone down since this morning.'

While the chops were being cooked, Fleete opened his shirt and showed us, just over his left breast, a mark, the perfect double of the black rosettes—the five or six irregular blotches arranged in a circle—on a leopard's hide. Strickland looked and said, 'It was only pink this morning. It's grown black now.'

Fleete ran to a glass.

'By Jove!' he said, 'this is nasty. What is it?'

We could not answer. Here the chops came in, all red and juicy, and Fleete bolted three in a most offensive manner. He ate on his right grinders only, and threw his head over his right shoulder as he snapped the meat. When he had finished, it struck him that he had been behaving strangely, for he said apologetically, 'I don't think I ever felt so hungry in my life. I've bolted like an ostrich.'

After breakfast Strickland said to me, 'Don't go. Stay here, and stay for the night.'

Seeing that my house was not three miles from Strickland's, this request was absurd. But Strickland insisted, and was going to say something, when Fleete interrupted by declaring in a shamefaced way that he felt hungry again. Strickland sent a man to my house to fetch over my bedding and a horse, and we three went down to Strickland's stables to pass the hours until it was time to go for a ride. The man who has a weakness for horses never wearies of inspecting them; and when two men are killing time in this way they gather knowledge and lies the one from the other.

There were five horses in the stables, and I shall never forget the scene as we tried to look them over. They seemed to have gone mad. They reared and screamed and nearly tore up their pickets; they sweated and shivered and lathered and were distraught with fear. Strickland's horses used to know him as well as his dogs; which made the matter more curious. We left the stable for fear of the brutes throwing themselves in their panic. Then Strickland turned back and called me. The horses were still frightened, but they let us 'gentle' and make much of them, and put their heads in our bosoms.

'They aren't afraid of *us*,' said Strickland. 'D' you know, I'd give three months' pay if Outrage here could talk.'

But Outrage was dumb, and could only cuddle up to his master and blow out his nostrils, as is the custom of horses when they wish to explain things but can't. Fleete came up when we were in the stalls, and as soon as the horses saw him, their fright broke out afresh. It was all that we could do to escape from the place unkicked.

Strickland said, 'They don't seem to love you, Fleete.'

'Nonsense,' said Fleete; 'my mare will follow me like a dog.' He went to her: she was in a loose-box; but as he slipped the bars she plunged, knocked him down, and broke away into the garden. I laughed, but Strickland was not amused. He took his moustache in both fists and pulled it till it nearly came out.

Fleete, instead of going off to chase his property, yawned, saying that he felt sleepy. He went to the house to lie down, which was a foolish way of spending New Year's Day.

Strickland sat with me in the stables and asked if I had noticed anything peculiar in Fleete's manner. I said that he ate his food like a beast; but that this might have been the result of living alone in the Hills out of the reach of society as refined and elevating as ours for instance. Strickland was not amused. I do not think that he listened to me, for his next sentence referred to the mark on Fleete's breast, and I said that it might have been caused by blister-flies, or that it was possibly a birth-mark newly born and now visible for the first time. We both agreed that it was unpleasant to look at, and Strickland found occasion to say that I was a fool.

'I can't tell you what I think now,' said he, 'because you would call me a madman; but you must stay with me for the next few days, if you can. I want you to watch Fleete, but don't tell me what you think till I have made up my mind.'

'But I am dining out to-night,' I said.

'So am I,' said Strickland, 'and so is Fleete. At least if he doesn't change his mind.'

We walked about the garden smoking, but saying nothing— because we were friends, and talking spoils good tobacco—till our pipes were out. Then we went to wake up Fleete. He was wide awake and fidgeting about his room.

'I say, I want some more chops,' he said. 'Can I get them?'

We laughed and said, 'Go and change. The ponies will be round in a minute.'

'All right,' said Fleete. 'I'll go when I get the chops— underdone ones, mind.'

He seemed to be quite in earnest. It was four o'clock, and we had had breakfast at one; still, for a long time, he demanded those underdone chops. Then he changed into riding clothes and went out into the veranda. His pony—the mare had not been caught—would not let him come near. All three horses were unmanageable—mad with fear—and finally Fleete said that he would stay at home and get something to eat. Strickland and I rode out wondering. As we passed the temple of Hanuman the Silver Man came out and mewed at us.

'He is not one of the regular priests of the temple,' said Strickland. 'I think I should particularly like to lay my hands on him.'

There was no spring in our gallop on the race-course that evening. The horses were stale, and moved as though they had been ridden out.

'The fright after breakfast has been too much for them,' said Strickland.

That was the only remark he made through the remainder of the ride. Once or twice, I think, he swore to himself; but that did not count.

We came back in the dark at seven o'clock, and saw that there were no lights in the bungalow. 'Careless ruffians my servants are!' said Strickland.

My horse reared at something on the carriage-drive, and Fleete stood up under its nose.

'What are you doing, grovelling about the garden?' said Strickland.

But both horses bolted and nearly threw us. We dismounted by the stables and returned to Fleete, who was on his hands and knees under the orange-bushes.

'What the devil's wrong with you?' said Strickland.

'Nothing, nothing in the world,' said Fleete, speaking very quickly and thickly. 'I've been gardening—botanising, you know. The smell of the earth is delightful. I think I'm going for a walk—a long walk—all night.'

Then I saw that there was something excessively out of order somewhere, and I said to Strickland, 'I am not dining out.'

'Bless you!' said Strickland. 'Here, Fleete, get up. You'll catch fever there. Come in to dinner and let's have the lamps lit. We'll all dine at home.'

Fleete stood up unwillingly, and said, 'No lamps—no lamps. It's much nicer here. Let's dine outside and have some more chops—lots of 'em and underdone—bloody ones with gristle.'

Now a December evening in Northern India is bitterly cold, and Fleete's suggestion was that of a maniac.

'Come in,' said Strickland sternly. 'Come in at once.'

Fleete came, and when the lamps were brought, we saw that he was literally plastered with dirt from head to foot. He must have been rolling in the garden. He shrank from the light and went to his room. His eyes were horrible to look at. There was a green light behind them, not in them, if you understand, and the man's lower lip hung down.

Strickland said, 'There's going to be trouble—big trouble—to-night. Don't you change your riding-things.'

We waited and waited for Fleete's reappearance, and ordered dinner in the meantime. We could hear him moving about his own room, but there was no light there.

Presently from the room came the long-drawn howl of a wolf.

People write and talk lightly of blood running cold and hair standing up, and things of that kind. Both sensations are too horrible to be trifled with. My heart stopped as though a knife had been driven through it, and Strickland turned as white as the tablecloth.

The howl was repeated, and was answered by another howl far across the fields.

That set the gilded roof on the horror. Strickland dashed into Fleete's room. I followed, and we saw Fleete getting out of the window. He made beast-noises in the back of his throat. He could not answer us when we shouted at him. He spat.

I don't quite remember what followed, but I think that Strickland must have stunned him with the long boot-jack, or else I should never have been able to sit on his chest. Fleete could not speak, he could only snarl, and his snarls were those of a wolf, not of a man. The human spirit must have been giving way all day and have died out with the twilight. We were dealing with a beast that had once been Fleete.

The affair was beyond any human and rational experience. I tried to say 'Hydrophobia', but the word wouldn't come, because I knew that I was lying.

We bound this beast with leather thongs of the punkah-rope, and tied his thumbs and big toes together, and gagged it with a shoe-horn, which makes a very efficient gag if you know how to arrange it. Then we carried it into the dining-room, and sent a man to Dumoise, the doctor, telling him to come over at once. After we had despatched the messenger and were drawing breath, Strickland said, 'It's no good. This isn't any doctor's work.' I, also, knew that he spoke the truth.

The beast's head was free, and it threw it about from side to side. Any one entering the room would have believed that we were curing a wolf's pelt. That was the most loathsome accessory of all.

Strickland sat with his chin in the heel of his fist, watching the beast as it wiggled on the ground, but saying nothing. The shirt had been torn open in the scuffle and showed the black rosette mark on the left breast. It stood out like a blister.

In the silence of the watching we heard something without mewing like a she-otter. We both rose to our feet, and, I answer for myself, not Strickland, felt sick—actually and physically sick. We told each other, as did the men in *Pinafore*, that it was the cat.

Dumoise arrived, and I never saw a little man so unprofessionally shocked. He said that it was a heart-rending case of hydrophobia, and that nothing could be done. At least any palliative measures would only prolong the agony. The beast was foaming at the mouth. Fleete, as we told Dumoise, had been bitten by dogs once or twice. Any man who keeps half-a-dozen terriers must expect a nip now and again. Dumoise could offer no help. He could only certify that Fleete was dying of hydrophobia. The beast was then howling, for it had managed to spit out the shoe-horn. Dumoise said that he would be ready to certify to the cause of death, and that the end was certain. He was a good little man, and he offered to remain with us; but Strickland refused the kindness. He did not wish to poison Dumoise's New Year. He would only ask him not to give the real cause of Fleete's death to the public.

So Dumoise left, deeply agitated; and as soon as the noise of the cart-wheels had died away, Strickland told me, in a whisper, his suspicions. They were so wildly improbable that he dared not say them out aloud; and I, who entertained all Strickland's beliefs, was so ashamed of owning to them that I pretended to disbelieve.

'Even if the Silver Man had bewitched Fleete for polluting the image of Hanuman, the punishment could not have fallen so quickly.'

As I was whispering this the cry outside the house rose again, and the beast fell into a fresh paroxysm of struggling till we were afraid that the thongs that held it would give way.

'Watch!' said Strickland. 'If this happens six times I shall take the law into my own hands. I order you to help me.'

He went into his room and came out in a few minutes with the barrels of an old shot-gun, a piece of fishing-line, some thick cord, and his heavy wooden bedstead. I reported that the convulsions had followed the cry by two seconds in each case, and the beast seemed perceptibly weaker.

Strickland muttered, 'But he can't take away the life! He can't take away the life!'

I said, though I knew that I was arguing against myself, 'It may be a cat. It must be a cat. If the Silver Man is responsible, why does he dare to come here?'

Strickland arranged the wood on the hearth, put the gun-barrels into the glow of the fire, spread the twine on the table, and broke a walking-stick in two. There was one yard of fishing-line, gut lapped with wire, such as is used for masheer-fishing, and he tied the two ends together in a loop.

Then he said, 'How can we catch him? He must be taken alive and unhurt.'

I said that we must trust to providence, and go out softly with polo-sticks into the shrubbery at the front of the house. The man or animal that made the cry was evidently moving round the house as regularly as a night-watchman. We could wait in the bushes till he came by and knock him over.

Strickland accepted this suggestion, and we slipped out from a bath-room window into the front veranda and then across the carriage-drive into the bushes.

In the moonlight we could see the leper coming round the corner of the house. He was perfectly naked, and from time to time he mewed and stopped to dance with his shadow. It was an unattractive sight, and thinking of poor Fleete, brought to such degradation by so foul a creature, I put away all my doubts and resolved to help Strickland from the heated gun-barrels to the loop of twine—from the loins to the head and back again—with all tortures that might be needful.

The leper halted in the front porch for a moment and we jumped out on him with the sticks. He was wonderfully strong, and we were afraid that he might escape or be fatally hurt before we caught him. We had an idea that lepers were frail creatures, but this proved to be incorrect. Strickland knocked his legs from under him and I put my foot on his neck. He mewed hideously, and even through my riding-boots I could feel his flesh was not the flesh of a clean man.

He struck us with his hand- and feet-stumps. We looped the lash of a dog-whip round him, under the armpits, and dragged him backwards into the hall and so into the dining-room where the beast lay. There we tied him with trunk-straps. He made no attempt to escape, but mewed.

When we confronted him with the beast the scene was beyond description. The beast doubled backwards into a bow as though he had been poisoned with strychnine, and moaned in the most pitiable fashion. Several other things happened also, but they cannot be put down here.

'I think I was right,' said Strickland. 'Now we will ask him to cure this case.'

But the leper only mewed. Strickland wrapped a towel round his hand and took the gun-barrels out of the fire. I put the half of the broken walking-stick through the loop of fishing-line and buckled the leper comfortably to Strickland's bedstead. I understood then how men and women and little children can endure to see a witch burnt alive; for the beast was moaning on the floor, and though the Silver Man had no face, you would see horrible feelings passing through the slab that took its place, exactly as waves of heat play across red-hot iron—gun-barrels, for instance.

Strickland shaded his eyes with his hands for a moment and we got to work. This part is not to be printed.

The dawn was beginning to break when the leper spoke. His mewings had not been satisfactory up to that point. The beast had fainted from exhaustion and the house was very still. We unstrapped the leper and told him to take away the evil spirit. He crawled to the beast and laid his hand upon the left breast. That was all. Then he fell face down and whined, drawing in his breath as he did so.

We watched the face of the beast, and saw the soul of Fleete coming back into his eyes. Then a sweat broke out on the forehead, and the eyes—they were human eyes—closed. We waited for an hour, but Fleete still slept. We carried him to his room and bade the leper go, giving him the bedstead, and the sheet on the bedstead to cover his nakedness, the gloves and the towels with which we had touched him, and the whip that had been hooked round his body. He put the sheet about him and went out into the early morning without speaking or mewing.

Strickland wiped his face and sat down. A night-gong, far away in the city, made seven o'clock.

'Exactly four-and-twenty hours!' said Strickland. 'And I've done enough to ensure my dismissal from the Service, besides permanent quarters in a lunatic asylum. Do you believe that we are awake?'

The red-hot gun-barrel had fallen on the floor and was singeing the carpet. The smell was entirely real.

That morning at eleven we two together went to wake up Fleete. We looked and saw that the black leopard-rosette on his chest had disappeared. He was very drowsy and tired, but as soon as he saw us, he said, 'Oh! Confound you fellows! Happy New Year to you. Never mix your liquors. I'm nearly dead.'

'Thanks for your kindness, but you're over time,' said Strickland. 'To-day is the morning of the second. You've slept the clock round with a vengeance.'

The door opened, and little Dumoise put his head in. He had come on foot, and fancied that we were laying out Fleete.

'I've brought a nurse,' said Dumoise. 'I suppose that she can come in for . . . what is necessary.'

'By all means,' said Fleete cheerily, sitting up in bed. 'Bring on your nurses.'

Dumoise was dumb. Strickland led him out and explained that there must have been a mistake in the diagnosis. Dumoise remained dumb and left the house hastily. He considered that his professional reputation had been injured, and was inclined to make a personal matter of the recovery. Strickland went out too. When he came back, he said that he had been to call on the Temple of Hanuman to offer redress for the pollution of the god, and had been solemnly assured that no white man had ever touched the idol, and that he was an incarnation of all the virtues labouring under a delusion. 'What do you think?' said

Strickland.

I said, ' "There are more things . . .".'

But Strickland hates that quotation. He says that I have worn it threadbare.

One other curious thing happened which frightened me as much as anything in all the night's work. When Fleete was dressed he came into the dining-room and sniffed. He had a quaint trick of moving his nose when he sniffed. 'Horrid doggy smell, here,' said he. 'You should really keep those terriers of yours in better order. Try sulphur, Strick.'

But Strickland did not answer. He caught hold of the back of a chair, and, without warning, went into an amazing fit of hysterics. It is terrible to see a strong man overtaken with hysteria. Then it struck me that we had fought for Fleete's soul with the Silver Man in that room, and had disgraced ourselves as Englishmen for ever, and I laughed and gasped and gurgled as shamefully as Strickland, while Fleete thought that we had both gone mad. We never told him what we had done.

Some years later, when Strickland had married and was a church-going member of society for his wife's sake, we reviewed the incident dispassionately, and Strickland suggested that I should put it before the public.

I cannot myself see that this step is likely to clear up the mystery; because, in the first place, no one will believe a rather unpleasant story, and, in the second, it is well known to every right-minded man that the Gods of the heathen are stone and brass, and any attempt to deal with them otherwise is justly condemned.

HIS CHANCE IN LIFE

Then a pile of heads he laid—
Thirty thousands heaped on high—
All to please the Kafir maid,
Where the Oxus ripples by.
Grimly spake Atulla Khan:—
'Love hath made this thing a Man.'

Oatta's Story

IF YOU GO away from Levees and Government House Lists, past Trades' Balls—far beyond everything and everybody you ever knew in your respectable life—you cross, in time, the Borderline where the last drop of White blood ends and the full tide of Black sets in. It would be easier to talk to a new-made Duchess on the spur of the moment than to the Borderline folk without violating some of their conventions or hurting their feelings. The Black and the White mix very quaintly in their ways. Sometimes the White shows in spurts of fierce, childish pride—which is Pride of Race run crooked—and sometimes the Black in still fiercer abasement and humility, half-heathenish customs and strange, unaccountable impulses to crime. One of these days, this people—understand they are far lower than the class whence Derozio, the man who imitated Byron, sprung—will turn out a writer or a poet; and then we shall know how they live and what they feel. In the meantime, any stories about them cannot be absolutely correct in fact or inference.

Miss Vezzis came from across the Borderline to look after some children who belonged to a lady until a regularly ordained nurse could come out. The lady said Miss Vezzis was a bad, dirty nurse and inattentive. It never struck her that Miss Vezzis had her own life to lead and her own affairs to worry over; or that these affairs were the most important things in the world to

Miss Vezzis. A few mistresses admit this sort of reasoning. Miss Vezzis was as black as a boot, and, to our standard of taste, hideously ugly. She wore cotton-print gowns and bulgy shoes; and when she lost her temper with the children, she abused them in the language of the Borderline—which is part English, part Portuguese, and part Native. She was not attractive; but she had her pride, and she preferred being called 'Miss Vezzis.'

Every Sunday she dressed herself wonderfully and went to ask her Mamma, who lived, for the most part, on an old cane chair in a greasy tussore-silk dressing-gown and a big rabbit-warren of a house full of Vezzises, Pereiras, Ribieras, Lisboas, and Gonsalveses, and a floating population of loafers; besides fragments of the day's market, garlic, stale incense, clothes thrown on the floor, petticoats hung on strings for screens, old bottles, pewter crucifixes, dried *immortelles*, pariah puppies, plaster images of the Virgin, and hats without crowns. Miss Vezzis drew twenty rupees a month for acting as nurse, and she squabbled with her Mamma as to the percentage to be given towards housekeeping. When the quarrel was over, Michele D'Cruze used to shamble across the low mud wall of the compound and make love to Miss Vezzis after the fashion of the Borderline, which is hedged about with much ceremony. Michele was a poor, sickly weed and very black; but he had his pride. He would not be seen smoking a hookah for anything; and he looked down on natives as only a man with seven-eighths native blood in his veins can. The Vezzis family had their pride too. They traced their descent from a mythical platelayer who had worked on the Sone Bridge when railways were new in India, and they valued their English origin. Michele was a Telegraph Signaller on Rs.35 a month. The fact that he was in Government employ made Mrs. Vezzis lenient to the shortcomings of his ancestors.

There was a compromising legend—Dom Anna the tailor brought it from Poonani—that a black Jew of Cochin had once married into the D'Cruze family; while it was an open secret that an uncle of Mrs. D'Cruze was, at that very time, doing menial work, connected with cooking, for a Club in Southern India! He sent Mrs. D'Cruze seven rupees eight annas a month; but she felt the disgrace to the family very keenly all the same.

However, in the course of a few Sundays, Mrs. Vezzis brought herself to overlook these blemishes, and gave her consent to the marriage of her daughter with Michele, on condition that Michele should have at least fifty rupees a month to start married life upon. This wonderful prudence must have been a lingering touch of the mythical platelayer's Yorkshire blood, for across the Borderline people take pride in marrying when they please— not when they can.

Having regard to his Departmental prospects, Mrs. Vezzis might as well have asked Michele to go away and come back with the moon in his pocket. But Michele was deeply in love with Miss Vezzis, and that helped him to endure. He accompanied Miss Vezzis to Mass one Sunday, and after Mass, walking home through the hot stale dust with her hand in his, he swore by several Saints, whose names would not interest you, never to forget Miss Vezzis; and she swore by her Honour and the Saints—the oath runs rather curiously; '*In nomine Sanctissimae*—' (whatever the name of the she-Saint is) and so forth, ending with a kiss on the forehead, a kiss on the left cheek, and a kiss on the mouth—never to forget Michele.

Next week Michele was transferred, and Miss Vezzis dropped tears upon the window-sash of the 'Intermediate' compartment as he left the station.

If you look at the telegraph map of India you will see a long line skirting the coast from Backergunge to Madras. Michele was ordered to Tibasu, a little Sub-office one-third down this line, to send messages on from Behrampur to Chicacola, and to think of Miss Vezzis and his chances of getting fifty rupees a month out of office-hours. He had the noise of the Bay of Bengal and a Bengali Babu for company. Nothing more. He sent foolish letters, with crosses tucked inside the flaps of the envelopes, to Miss Vezzis.

When he had been at Tibasu for nearly three weeks his chance came.

Never forget that unless the outward and visible signs of Our Authority are always before a native he is as incapable as a child of understanding what authority means, or where is the danger of disobeying it. Tibasu was a forgotten little place with a few Orissa Mohammedans in it. These, hearing nothing of the Collector-Sahib for some time, and heartily despising the Hindu Sub-Judge, arranged to start a little Mohurrum riot of their own. But the Hindus turned out and broke their heads; when, finding lawlessness pleasant, Hindus and Mohammedans together raised an aimless sort of Donnybrook just to see how far they could go. They looted each other's shops, and paid off private grudges in the regular way. It was a nasty little riot, but not worth putting in the newspapers.

Michele was working in his office when he heard the sound that a man never forgets all his life—the '*ah-yah*' of an angry crowd. (When that sound drops about three tones, and changes to a thick, droning *ut*, the man who hears it had better go away if he is alone.) The native Police Inspector ran in and told Michele that the town was in an uproar and coming to wreck the Telegraph-office. The Babu put on his cap and quietly dropped out of the window; while the Police Inspector, afraid, but obeying the old race-instinct which recognises a drop of White blood as far as it can be diluted, said, "What orders does the Sahib give?"

The 'Sahib' decided Michele. Though horribly frightened, he felt that, for the hour, he, the man with the Cochin Jew and the menial uncle in his pedigree, was the only representative of English authority in the place. Then he thought of Miss Vezzis and the fifty rupees, and took the situation on himself. There were seven native policemen in Tibasu, and four crazy smooth-bore muskets among them. All the men were grey with fear, but not beyond leading. Michele dropped the key of the telegraph instrument, and went out, at the head of his army, to meet the mob. As the shouting crew came round a corner of the road, he dropped and fired; the men behind him loosing off instinctively at the same time.

The whole crowd—curs to the backbone—yelled and ran, leaving one man dead and another dying in the road. Michele was sweating with fear; but he kept his weakness under, and went down into the town, past the house where the Sub-Judge had barricaded himself. The streets were empty. Tibasu was more frightened than Michele, for the mob had been taken at the right time.

Michele returned to the Telegraph-office, and sent a message to Chicacola asking for help. Before an answer came, he received a deputation of the elders of Tibasu, telling him that the Sub-Judge said his actions generally were 'unconstitutional', and trying to bully him. But the heart of Michele D'Cruze was large and white in his breast, because of his love for Miss Vezzis, the nurse-girl, and because he had tasted for the first time Responsibility and Success. Those two make an intoxicating drink, and have ruined more than ever has Whisky. Michele answered that the Sub-Judge might say what he pleased, but, until the Assistant Collector came, he, the Telegraph Signaller, was the Government of India in Tibasu, and the elders of the town would be held accountable for further rioting. Then they bowed their heads and said, "Show mercy!" or words to that effect, and went back in great fear; each accusing the other of having begun the riot.

Early in the dawn, after a night's patrol with his seven policemen, Michele went down the road, musket in hand, to meet the Assistant Collector who had ridden in to quell Tibasu. But, in the presence of this young Englishman, Michele felt himself slipping back more and more into the native; and the tale of the Tibasu riots ended, with the strain on the teller, in an hysterical outburst of tears, bred by sorrow that he had killed a man, shame that he could not feel as uplifted as he had felt through the night, and childish anger that his tongue could not do justice to his great deeds. It was the White drop in Michele's veins dying out, though he did not know it.

But the Englishman understood; and, after he had schooled those men of Tibasu, and had conferred with the Sub-Judge till that excellent official turned green, he found time to draft an official letter describing the conduct of Michele. Which letter filtered through the proper Channels, and ended in the transfer of Michele up-country once more, on the Imperial Salary of sixty-six rupees a month.

So he and Miss Vezzis were married with great state and ancientry; and now there are several little D'Cruzes sprawling about the verandas of the Central Telegraph Office.

But, if the whole revenue of the Department he serves were to be his reward, Michele could never, never repeat what he did at Tibasu for the sake of Miss Vezzis the nurse-girl.

Which proves that, when a man does good work out of all

proportion to his pay, in seven cases out of nine there is a woman at the back of the virtue.

The two exceptions must have suffered from sunstroke.

THE BRIDE'S PROGRESS

And school-foundations in the act
Of holiday, three files compact,
Shall learn to view thee as a fact
Connected with that zealous tract:
'Rome,—Babylon and Nineveh.'

D. G. Rossetti

IT WOULD HAVE been presumption and weariness deliberately to have described Benares. No man, except he who writes a guide-book, 'does' the Strand or Westminster Abbey. The foreigner—French or American—tells London what to think of herself, as the visitor tells the Anglo-Indian what to think of India. Our neighbour over the way always knows so much more about us than we ourselves. The Bride interpreted Benares as fresh youth and radiant beauty can interpret a city grey and worn with years. Providence had been very good to her, and she repaid Providence by dressing herself to the best advantage— which, if the French speak truth, is all that a fair woman can do toward religion. Generations of untroubled ease and well-being must have builded the dainty figure and rare face, and the untamable arrogance of wealth looked out of the calm eyes. 'India', said The Bride philosophically, 'is an incident only in our trip. We are going on to Australia and China, and then Home by San Francisco and New York. We shall be at Home again before the season is quite ended.' And she patted her bracelets, smiling softly to herself over some thought that had little enough to do with Benares or India—whichever was the 'incident'. She went into the city of Benares. Benares of the Buddhists and the Hindus—of Durga of the Thousand Names— of Two Thousand Temples, and twice two thousand stenches. 'Why does Benares smell so?' demanded The Bride pathetically.

'*Must* we do it, if it smells like this?' The Bridegroom was high-coloured, fair-whiskered, and insistent, as an Englishman should be. 'Of course we must. It would never do to go Home without having seen Benares. Where is a guide?' The streets were alive with them, and the couple chose him who spoke English most fluently. 'Would you like to see where the Hindus are burnt?' said he. They would, though The Bride shuddered as she spoke, for she feared that it would be very horrible. A ray of gracious sunlight touched her hair as she turned, walking cautiously in the middle of the narrow way, into the maze of the byways of Benares.

The sunlight ceased after a few paces, and the horrors of the Holy City gathered round her. Neglected rainbow-hued sewage sprawled across the path, and a bull, rotten with some hideous disease that distorted his head out of all bestial likeness, pushed through the filth. The Bride picked her way carefully, giving the bull the wall. A lean bitch, dying of mange, growled and yelped among her starveling puppies on a threshold that led into the darkness of some unclean temple. The Bride stooped and patted the beast on the head. 'I think she's something like Bessie,' said The Bride, and once again her thoughts wandered far beyond Benares. The lanes grew narrower and the symbols of a brutal cult more numerous. Hanuman, red, shameless, and smeared with oil, leaped and leered upon the walls above stolid, black stone bulls, knee-deep in yellow flowers. The bells clamoured from unseen temples, and half-naked men with evil eyes rushed out of dark places and besought her for money, saying that they were priests—*padres*, like the *padres* of her own Faith. One young man—who knows in what Mission school he had picked up his speech?—told her this in English, and The Bride laughed merrily, shaking her head. 'These men speak English,' she called back to her husband. 'Isn't it funny?'

But the mirth went out of her face when a turn in the lane brought her suddenly above the burning-ghat, where a man was piling logs on some Thing that lay wrapped in a white cloth, near the water of the Ganges. 'We can't see well from this place,' said The Bridegroom stolidly. 'Let us get a little closer.' They moved forward through deep grey dust—white sand of the river and black dust of man blended—till they commanded a full view of the steeply sloping bank and the Thing under the logs. A man was laboriously starting a fire at the river end of the pile; stepping wide now and again to avoid the hot embers of a dying blaze actually on the edge of the water. The Bride's face blanched, and she looked appealingly to her husband, but he had only eyes for the newly lit flame. Slowly, very slowly, a white dog crept on his belly down the bank, toward a heap of ashes among which the water was hissing. A plunge, followed by a yelp of pain, told that he had reached food, and that the food was too hot for him. With a deftness that marked long training, he raked the capture from the ashes on to the dust and slobbered, nosing it tentatively. As it cooled, he settled, with noises of animal delight, to his meal and worried and growled and tore. 'Will!' said The Bride faintly. The Bridegroom was watching the newly lit pyre and could not attend. A log slipped sideways, and through the chink showed the face of the man below, smiling the dull thick smile of death, which is such a smile as a very drunken man wears when he has found in his wide-swimming brain a joke of exquisite savour. The dead man grinned up to the sun and the fair face of The Bride. The flames sputtered and caught and spread. A man waded out knee-deep into the water, which was covered with greasy black embers and an oily scum. He chased the bobbing driftwood with a basket, that it might be saved for another occasion, and threw each take on a mound of such economies or on the back of the unheeding dog deep in the enjoyment of his hot dinner.

Slowly, very slowly, as the flames crackled, the Smiling Dead Man lifted one knee through the light logs. He had just been smitten with the idea of rising from his last couch and confounding the spectators. It was easy to see he was tasting the notion of this novel, this stupendous practical joke, and would presently, always smiling, rise up, and up, and up, and . . .

The fire-shrivelled knee gave way, and with its collapse little flames ran forward and whistled and whispered and fluttered from heel to head. 'Come away, Will,' said The Bride, 'come away! It is too horrible. I'm sorry that I saw it.' They left together, she with her arm in her husband's for a sign to all the world that, though Death be inevitable and awful, Love is still greater, and in its sweet selfishness can set at naught even the horrors of the burning-ghat.

'I never thought what it meant before,' said The Bride, releasing her husband's arm as she recovered herself; 'I see it now.' 'See what?' 'Don't you know?' said The Bride, 'what Edwin Arnold says:—

> *"For all the tears of all the eyes*
> *Have room in Gunga's bed,*
> *And all the sorrow is gone to-morrow*
> *When the white flames have fed."*

I see now. I think it is very, *very* horrible.' Then to the guide, suddenly, with a deep compassion, 'And will you be— will you be burnt in that way, too?' 'Yes, your Ladyship,' said the guide cheerfully, 'we are all burnt that way.' 'Poor wretch!' said The Bride to herself. 'Now show us some more temples.' A second time they dived into Benares City, but it was at least five long minutes before The Bride recovered those buoyant spirits which were hers by right of Youth and Love and Happiness. A very pale and sober little face peered into the filth of the Temple of the Cow, where the odours of Holiness and Humanity are highest. Fearful and wonderful old women, crippled in hands and feet, body and back, crawled round her; some even touching the hem of her dress. And at this she shuddered, for the hands were very foul. The walls dripped filth, the pavement sweated filth, and the contagion of uncleanliness walked among the worshippers. There might have been beauty in the Temple of the Cow; there certainly was horror enough and to spare; but The Bride was conscious only of the filth of the place. She turned to the wisest and best man in the world, asking indignantly, 'Why don't these horrid people clean the place out?' 'I don't know,' said The Bridegroom; 'I suppose their religion forbids it.' Once more they set out on their journey through the city of monstrous creeds—she in front, the pure white hem of her petticoat raised indignantly clear of the mire, and her eyes full of alarm and watchfulness. Closed galleries crossed the narrow way, and the light of day fainted and grew sick ere it could climb down into the abomination of the gullies. A litter of gorgeous red and gold barred the passage to the Golden Temple.

'It is the Maharani of Hazaribagh,' said the guide. 'She coming to pray for a child.' 'Ah!' said The Bride, and turning quickly to her husband, said, 'I wish Mother were with us.' The bridegroom made no answer. Perhaps he was beginning to repent of dragging a young English girl through the iniquities of Benares. He announced his intention of returning to his hotel, and The Bride dutifully followed. At every turn lewd gods grinned and mouthed at her, the air was clogged with thick odours and the reek of rotten marigold flowers, and disease stood blind and naked before the sun. 'Let us get away quickly,' said The Bride; and they escaped to the main street, having honestly accomplished nearly two-thirds of what was written in the little red guide-book. An instinct inherited from a century of cleanly English housewives made The Bride pause before getting into the carriage, and addressing the seething crowd generally, murmur, 'Oh! You horrid people! Shouldn't I like to wash you!'

Yet Benares—which name must certainly be derived from *be*, and *nares*, nostrils—is not entirely a Sacred Midden. Very early in the morning, almost before the light had given promise of the day, a boat pulled out from the ghat and rowed upstream till it stayed in front of the ruined magnificence of Scindia's Ghat—a range of ruined wall and drunken bastion. The Bride and Bridegroom had risen early to catch their last glimpse of the city. There was no one abroad at that hour, and, except for three of four stone-laden boats rolling down from Mirzapur, they were alone upon the river. In the silence a voice thundered far above their heads: '*I bear witness that there is no God but God.*' It was the mullah, proclaiming the Oneness of God in the city of the Million Manifestations. The call rang across the sleeping city and far over the river, and be sure that the Mullah abated nothing of the defiance of his cry for that he looked down upon a sea of temples and smelt the incense of a hundred Hindu shrines. The Bride could make neither head nor tail of the business. 'What is he making that noise for, Will?' she asked. 'Worshipping Vishnu,' was the ready reply; for at the outset of his venture into matrimony a young husband is at the least infallible. The Bride snuggled down under her wraps, keeping her delicate, chill-pinked little nose toward the city. Day broke over Benares, and The Bride stood up and applauded with both her hands. It was finer, she said, than any transformation scene; and so in her gratitude she applauded the earth, the sun, and the everlasting sky. The river turned to a silver flood and the ruled lines of the ghats to red gold. 'How can I describe this to Mother?' she cried, as the wonder grew, and timeless Benares roused to a fresh day. The Bride nestled down in the boat and gazed round-eyed. As water spurts down through a leaky dam, as ants pour out from the invaded nest, so the people of Benares poured down the ghats to the river. Wherever The Bride's eye rested, it saw men and women stepping downwards, always downwards, by rotten wall, worn step, tufted bastion, riven water-gate, and stark, bare, dusty bank, to the water. The hundred priests drifted down to their stations under the large mat-umbrellas that all pictures of Benares represent so faithfully. The Bride's face lighted with joy. 'Will! Do you recollect that pantomime we went to ages and ages ago—before we were engaged—at Brighton? Doesn't it remind you of the scene of the Fairy Mushrooms—just before they all got up and danced, you know? Isn't it splendid?' She leaned forward, her chin in her hand, and watched long and intently; and Nature, who is without doubt a Frenchwoman, so keen is her love for effect, arranged that the shell-like pink of The Bride's cheek should be turned against a dull-red house, in the windows of which sat women in blood-red clothes, letting down crimson turban-cloths for the morning breeze to riot with. From the burning-ghat rose lazily a welt of thick blue smoke, and an eddy of the air blew a wreath across the river. The Bride coughed. 'Will,' she said, 'promise me when I die you won't have me cremated—if cremation is the fashion then.' And 'Will' promised lightly, as a man promises who is looking for long years.

The life of the city went forward. The Bride heard, though she did not understand, the marriage-song, and the chant of prayers, and the wail of the mourners. She looked long and steadfastly at the beating heart of Benares and at the Dead for whom no day had dawned. The place was hers to watch and enjoy if she pleased. Her enjoyment was tempered with some thought of regret; for her eyebrows contracted and she thought. Then the trouble was apparent. 'Will!' she said softly, 'they don't seem to think much of *us*, do they?' Did she expect, then, that the whole city would make obeisance to young Love, robed and crowned in a grey tweed travelling-dress and velvet toque?

The boat drifted downstream, and an hour or so later the Dufferin Bridge bore away The Bride and Bridegroom on their travels, in which India was to be 'only an incident.'

AN UNQUALIFIED PILOT

*This tale is founded on something that happened a good
many years ago in the Port of Calcutta, before wireless
telegraphy was used on ships, and men and boys were
less easy to catch when once they were in a ship. It is not
meant to show that anybody who thinks he would like to
become eminent in his business can do so at a moment's
notice; but it proves the old saying that if you want
anything badly enough and are willing to pay the price
for it, you generally get it. If you don't get what you
want, it is a sign either that you did not seriously want it,
or that you tried to bargain over the price.*

ALMOST ANY PILOT will tell you that his work is much more
difficult than you imagine; but the Pilots of the Hugli know that
they have one hundred miles of the most dangerous river on
earth running through their hands—the Hugli between Calcutta
and the Bay of Bengal—and they say nothing. Their Service is
picked and sifted as carefully as the Bench of the Supreme Court,
for a judge can only hang the wrong man, or pass a bad law;
but a careless pilot can lose a ten-thousand-ton ship with crew
and cargo in less time than it takes to reverse her engines.

There is very little chance of anything getting off again
when once she touches in the furious Hugli current, loaded with
all the fat silt of the fields of Bengal, where the soundings change
two feet between tides, and new channels make and unmake
themselves in one rainy season. Men have fought the Hugli for
two hundred years, till now the river owns a huge building,
with drawing, survey, and telegraph departments, devoted to
its private service, as well as a body of wardens, who are called
the Port Commissioners.

They and their officers govern everything that floats from

the Hugli Bridge to the last buoy at Pilots' Ridge, one hundred and forty miles away, far out in the Bay of Bengal, where the steamers first pick up the pilots from the pilot brig.

A Hugli pilot does not kindly bring papers aboard for the passengers, or scramble up the ship's side by wet, swaying rope-ladders. He arrives in his best clothes, with a native servant or an assistant pilot to wait on him, and he behaves as a man should who can earn two or three thousand pounds a year after twenty years' apprenticeship. He has beautiful rooms in the Port Office at Calcutta, and generally keeps himself to the society of his own profession, for though the telegraph reports the more important soundings of the river daily, there is much to be learned from brother pilots between each trip.

Some million tons of shipping must find their way to and from Calcutta each twelvemonth, and unless the Hugli were watched as closely as his keeper watches an elephant, there is a fear that it might silt up, as it has silted up round the old Dutch and Portuguese ports twenty and thirty miles behind Calcutta.

So the Port Office sounds and scours and dredges the river, and builds spurs and devices for coaxing currents, and labels all the buoys with their proper letters, and attends to the semaphores and the lights and the drum, ball and cone storm signals; and the pilots of the Hugli do the rest; but, in spite of all care and the very best attention, the Hugli swallows her ship or two every year. Even the coming of wireless telegraphy does not spoil her appetite.

When Martin Trevor had waited on the river from his boyhood; when he had risen to be a Senior Pilot, entitled to bring up to Calcutta the very biggest ships; when he had thought and talked of nothing but Hugli pilotage all his life to nobody except Hugli pilots, he was exceedingly surprised and indignant that his only son should decide to follow his father's profession. Mrs. Trevor had died when the boy was a child, and as he grew older, Trevor, in the intervals of his business, noticed that the lad was very often by the river-side—no place, he said, for a nice boy. But, as he was not often at home, and as the aunt who looked after Jim naturally could not follow him to his chosen haunts, and as Jim had not the faintest intention of giving up old friends there, nothing but ineffectual growls came of the remark. Later, when Trevor once asked him if he could make anything out of the shipping on the water, Jim replied by reeling off the list of all the house-flags in sight at the moorings, together with supplementary information about their tonnage and captains.

'You'll come to a bad end, Jim,' said Trevor. 'Boys of your age haven't any business to waste their time on these things.'

'Oh, Pedro at the Sailors' Home says you can't begin too early.'

'At what, please?'

'Piloting. I'm nearly fourteen now, and—and I know where most of the shipping in the river is, and I know what there was yesterday over the Mayapur Bar, and I've been down to Diamond Harbour—of, a hundred times already, and I've—'

'You'll go to school, son, and learn what they teach you, and you'll turn out something better than a pilot,' said his father, who wanted Jim to enter the Subordinate Civil Service. But he might just as well have told a shovel-nosed porpoise of the river to come ashore and begin life as a hen. Jim held his tongue; he noticed that all the best pilots in the Port Office did that; and devoted his young attention and all his spare time to the River he loved. He had seen the nice young gentlemen in the Subordinate Civil Service, and he called them a very rude native name for 'clerks.'

He became as well known as the Bankshall itself; and the Port Police let him inspect their launches, and the tug-boat captains had always a place for him at their tables, and the mates of the big steam-dredgers used to show him how the machinery worked, and there were certain native row-boats which Jim practically owned; and he extended his patronage to the railway that runs to Diamond Harbour, forty miles down the river. In the old days nearly all the East India Company's ships used to discharge at Diamond Harbour, on account of the shoals above, but now ships go straight up to Calcutta, and they have only some moorings for vessels in distress there, and a telegraph service, and a harbour-master, who was one of Jim's most intimate friends.

He would sit in the Office listening to the soundings of the shoals as they were reported every day, and attending to the movements of the steamers up and down (Jim always felt he had lost something irretrievable if a boat got in or out of his River without his knowing about it), and when the big liners with their rows of blazing portholes tied up in Diamond Harbour for the night, Jim would row from one ship to the other through the sticky hot air and the buzzing mosquitoes and listen respectfully as the pilots conferred together about the habits of steamers.

Once, for a treat, his father took him down clear out to the Sandheads and the pilot brig there, and Jim was happily seasick as she tossed and pitched in the Bay. The cream of life, though, was coming up in a tug or a police-boat from Diamond Harbour to Calcutta, over the 'James and Mary', those terrible sands Christened after a royal ship that they sunk two hundred years before. They are made by two rivers that enter the Hugli six miles apart and throw their own silt across the silt of the main stream, so that with each turn of the weather and tide the sands shift and change under water like clouds in the sky. It was here (the tales sound much worse when they are told in the rush and growl of the muddy waters) that the *Countess of Stirling*, fifteen hundred tons, touched and capsized in ten minutes, and a two-thousand-ton steamer in two, and a pilgrim ship in five, and another steamer literally in one instant, holding down her men with the masts and shrouds as she lashed over. When a ship touches on the 'James and Mary', the river knocks her down and buries her, and the sands quiver all around her and reach out under water and take new shapes all over the corpse.

Young Jim would lie up in the bows of the tug and watch the straining buoys kick and choke in the coffee-coloured current, while the semaphores and flags signalled from the bank how much water there was in the channel, till he learned that men who deal with men can afford to be careless, on the chance of their fellows being like them; but men who deal with things dare not relax for an instant. 'And that's the very reason,' old McEwan said to him once, 'that the "James and Mary" is the safest part of the river,' and he shoved the big black *Bandoorah*, that draws twenty-five feet, through the Eastern Gut, with a turban of white foam wrapped around her forefoot and her screw beating as steadily as his own heart.

If Jim could not get away to the river there was always the big, cool Port Office, where the soundings were worked out and the maps drawn; or the Pilots' room, where he could lie in a long chair and listen quietly to the talk about the Hugli. There was the library, too, where if you had money you could buy charts and books of directions against the time that you would actually have to steam over the places themselves. It was exceedingly hard for Jim to hold the list of Jewish Kings in his head, and he was more than uncertain as to the end of the verb *audio* if you followed it far enough down the page, but he could keep the soundings of the three channels distinct in his head, and, what is more confusing, the changes in the buoys from 'Garden Reach' down to Saugor, as well as the greater part of the *Calcutta Telegraph*, the only paper he ever read.

Unluckily, you cannot peruse about the Hugli without money, even though you are the son of the best-known pilot of the river, and as soon as Trevor understood how his son was spending his time, he cut down his pocket-money, of which Jim had a very generous allowance. In his extremity he took counsel with Pedro, the plum-coloured mulatto at the Sailors' Home, and Pedro was a bad, designing man. He introduced Jim to a Chinaman in Muchuatollah, an unpleasing place in itself, and the Chinaman, who answered to the name of Erh-Tze, when he was not smoking opium, talked business in pidgin-English to Jim for an hour. Every bit of that business from first to last was flying in the face of every law on the river, but it interested Jim.

'S'pose you takee. Can do?' Erh-Tze said at last.

Jim considered his chances. A junk, he knew, would draw about eleven feet, and the regular fee for a qualified pilot, outward to the Sandheads, would be two hundred rupees. On the one hand he was not qualified, so he dared not ask more than half. *But*, on the other hand, he was fully certain of the thrashing of his life from his father for piloting without a license, let alone what the Port Authorities might do to him. So he asked one hundred and seventy-five rupees, and Erh-Tze beat him down to a hundred and twenty. The cargo of his junk was worth anything from seventy to a hundred and fifty thousand rupees, some of which he was getting as enormous freight on the coffins of thirty or forty dead Chinamen, whom he was taking to be buried in their native country.

Rich Chinamen will pay fancy prices for this service, and they have a superstition that the iron of steamships is bad for the spiritual health of their dead. Erh-Tze's junk had crept up from Singapore, *via* Penang and Rangoon, to Calcutta, where Erh-Tze had been staggered by the Pilot dues. This time he was going out at a reduction with Jim, who, as Pedro kept telling him, was just as good as a pilot, and a heap cheaper.

Jim knew something of the manners of junks, but he was not prepared, when he went down that night with his charts, for the confusion of cargo and coolies and coffins and clay cooking-places, and other things that littered her decks. He had sense enough to haul the rudder up a few feet, for he knew that a junk's rudder goes far below the bottom, and he allowed a foot extra to Erh-Tze's estimate of the junk's depth. Then they staggered out into midstream very early, and never had the city of his birth looked so beautiful as when he feared he would not come back to see it. Going down 'Garden Reach' he discovered that the junk would answer to her helm if you put it over far enough, and she had a fair, though Chinese, notion of sailing. He took charge of the tiller by stationing three Chinese on each side of it, and standing a little forward, gathered their pigtails into his hands, three right and three left, as though they had been the yoke-lines of a row-boat. Erh-Tze almost smiled at this; he felt he was getting good care for his money; and took a neat little polished bamboo to keep the men attentive, for he said this was no time to teach the crew pidgin-English. The more way they could get on the junk the better would she steer, and as soon as he felt a little confidence in her, Jim ordered the stiff, rustling sails to be hauled up tighter and tighter. He did not know their names—at least any name that would be likely to interest a Chinaman—but Erh-Tze had not banged about the waters of the Malay Archipelago all his life for nothing. He rolled forward with his bamboo, and the sail rose like Eastern incarnations.

Early as they were on the river, a big American oil (but they called it 'kerosene' in those days) ship was ahead of them in tow, and when Jim saw her through the lifted mist he was thankful. She would draw all of her seventeen feet, and if he could steer by her they would be safe. It is easier to scurry up and down the 'James and Mary' in a police-boat that some one else is handling than to cram a hard-mouthed old junk across the same sands alone, with the certainty of a thrashing if you come out alive.

Jim glued his eyes to the American, and saw that at Fultah she dropped her tug and stood down the river under sail. He all but whooped aloud, for he knew that the number of pilots who preferred to work a ship through the "James and Mary' was strictly limited. 'If it isn't Father, it is Dearsley,' said Jim. 'And Dearsley went down yesterday with the *Bancoora*. So it's Father. If I'd gone home last night instead of going to Pedro, I'd have met him. He must have got his ship quick, but—Father *is* a very quick man.' Then Jim reflected that they kept a piece of knotted rope on the pilot brig that stung like a wasp; but this thought he dismissed as beneath the dignity of an officiating pilot, who needed only to nod his head to set Erh-Tze's bamboo to work.

As the American came round, just before the Fultah Sands, Jim raked her with his spy-glass, and saw his father on the poop, an unlighted cigar between his teeth. That cigar, Jim knew, would be smoked on the other side of the 'James and Mary', and Jim felt so entirely safe and happy that he lit a cigar on his own account. This kind of piloting was child's play. His father could not make a mistake if he tried; and Jim, with his six obedient pigtails in his two hands, had leisure to admire the perfect style in which the American was handled—how she would point her bowsprit jeeringly at a hidden bank, as much as to say, 'Not to-day, thank you, dear,' and bow down lovingly to a buoy, as much as to say, '*You*'re a gentleman, at any rate,' and come round sharp on her heel with a flutter and a rustle, and a slow, steady swing like a well-dressed woman staring all round the theatre through opera glasses.

It was hard work to keep the junk near her, though Erh-Tze set everything that was by any means settable, and used his bamboo most generously. When they were nearly under her counter, and a little to her left, Jim, hidden behind a sail, would feel warm and happy all over, thinking of the thousand nautical and piloting things that he knew. When they fell more than half a mile behind, he was cold and miserable thinking of the million things he did not know or was not quite sure of. And so they went down, Jim steering by his father, turn for turn, over the Mayapur Bar, with the semaphores on each bank duly signalling the depth of water, through the Western Gut, and round Makaoputti Lumps, and in and out of twenty places, each more exciting than the last, and Jim nearly pulled the six pigtails out for pure joy when the last of the 'James and Mary' had gone astern, and they were walking through Diamond Harbour.

From there to the mouth of the Hugli things are not so bad—at least, that was what Jim thought, and held on till the swell from the Bay of Bengal made the old junk heave and snort, and the river broadened into an inland sea, with islands only a foot or two high scattered about it.

The American walked away from the junk as soon as they were beyond Kedgeree, and the night came on and the river looked very big and desolate, so Jim promptly anchored somewhere in grey water, with the Saugor Light away off toward the east. He had a great respect for the Hugli to the last yard of her, and had no desire whatever to find himself on the Gaspar Sand or any other little shoal. Erh-Tze and crew highly approved of this piece of seamanship. They set no watch, lit no lights, and at once went to sleep.

Jim lay down between a red-and-black lacquer coffin and a little live pig in a basket. As soon as it was light he began studying his chart of the Hugli mouth, and trying to find out where in the river he might be.

He decided to be on the safe side and wait for another sailing-ship and follow her out. So he made an enormous breakfast of rice and boiled fish, while Erh-Tze lit fire-crackers and burnt gilt paper to the Joss who had saved them so far. Then they heaved up their rough-and-tumble anchor, and made after a big, fat, iron four-masted sailing ship, heavy as a hay-wain.

The junk, which was really a very weatherly boat, and might have begun life as a private pirate in Annam forty years before, followed under easy sail; for the four-master would run no risks. She was in old McEwan's hands, and she waddled about like a broody hen, giving each shoal wide allowances. All this happened near the outer Floating Light, some hundred and twenty miles from Calcutta, and apparently in the open sea.

Jim knew old McEwan's appetite, and often heard him quite pride himself on getting his ship to the pilot brig close upon meal hours, so he argued that if the pilot brig was get-at-able (and Jim himself had not the ghost of a notion where she would lie), McEwan would find her before one o'clock.

It was a blazing hot day, and McEwan fidgeted the four-master down to Pilots' Ridge with what little wind remained, and, sure enough, there lay the pilot brig, and Jim felt shivers up his back as Erh-Tze paid him his hundred and twenty rupees and went overside in the junk's one crazy dinghy. McEwan was leaving the four-master in a long, slashing whale-boat that looked very spruce and pretty, and Jim could see that there was a certain amount of excitement among the pilots on the brig. There was his father too. The ragged Chinese boatmen gave way in a most ragged fashion, and Jim felt very unwashed and disreputable when he heard the click of McEwan's oars alongside, and McEwan saying, 'James Trevor, I'll trouble you to lay alongside me.'

Jim obeyed, and from the corner of one eye watched McEwan's angry whiskers stand up all round his face, which turned purple.

'An' how is it you break the regulations o' the Port o' Calcutta? Are you aware of the penalties and impreesonments ye've laid yourself open to?' McEwan began.

Jim said nothing; there was not very much to say just then; and McEwan roared aloud: 'Man, ye've perrsonated a Hugli pilot, an' that's as much as to say ye've perrsonated *ME*! What did yon heathen give ye for honorarium?'

'Hundred and twenty,' said Jim.

'An' by what manner o' means did ye get through the 'James and Mary'?'

'Father,' was the answer. 'he went down the same tide and I—we—steered by him.'

McEwan whistled and choked, perhaps it was with anger. 'Ye've made a stalkin'-horse o' your father, then? Jim, laddie, he'll make an example o' you.'

The boat hooked on to the brig's chains, and McEwan said, as he set foot on the deck before Jim could speak: 'Yon's an enterprisin' cub o' yours, Trevor. Ye'd better enter him in the regular business, or one o' these fine days he'll be actin' as pilot before he's qualified, and sinkin' junks in the fairway. He fetched yon junk down last night. If ye've no other designs I'm thinkin' I'll take him as my cub, for there's no denyin' he's a resourceful lad—for all he's an unlicked whelp.'

'That,' said Trevor, reaching for Jim's left ear, 'is something we can remedy,' and he led Jim below.

The little knotted rope that they keep for general purposes on the pilot brig did its duty, but when it was all over Jim was unlicked no longer. He was McEwan's property to be registered under the laws of the Port of Calcutta, and a week later, when the *Ellora* came along, he bundled over the pilot brig's side with McEwan's enamelled leather hand-bag and a roll of charts and a little bag of his own, and he dropped into the stern sheets of the pilot gig with a very creditable imitation of McEwan's slow, swaying sit-down and hump of the shoulders.

AT THE PIT'S MOUTH

Men say it was a stolen tide—
The Lord that sent it He knows all,
But in mine ear will aye abide
The message that the bells let fall,
And awesome bells they were to me,
That in the dark rang 'Enderby'.

Jean Ingelow

ONCE UPON A time there was a Man and his Wife and a Tertium Quid.

All three were unwise, but the wife was the unwisest. The Man should have looked after his Wife, who should have avoided the Tertium Quid, who, again, should have married a wife of his own, after clean and open flirtations, to which nobody can possibly object, round Jakko or Observatory Hill. When you see a young man with his pony in a white lather and his hat on the back of his head, flying downhill at fifteen miles an hour to meet a girl who will be properly surprised to meet him, you naturally approve of that young man, and wish him Staff appointments, and take an interest in his welfare, and, as the proper time comes, give them sugar-tongs or side-saddles according to your means and generosity.

The Tertium Quid flew downhill on horseback, but it was to meet the Man's Wife; and when he flew uphill it was for the same end. The Man was in the Plains, earning money for his Wife to spend on dresses and four-hundred-rupee bracelets, and inexpensive luxuries of that kind. He worked very hard, and sent her a letter or a post-card daily. She also wrote to him daily, and said that she was longing for him to come up to Simla. The Tertium Quid used to lean over her shoulder and laugh as she wrote the notes. Then the two would ride to the

Post Office together.

Now, Simla is a strange place and its customs are peculiar; nor is any man who has not spent at least ten seasons there qualified to pass judgment on circumstantial evidence, which is the most untrustworthy in the Courts. For these reasons, and for others which need not appear, I decline to state positively whether there was anything irretrievably wrong in the relations between the Man's Wife and the Tertium Quid. If there was, and hereon you must form your own opinion, it was the Man's Wife's fault. She was kittenish in her manners, wearing generally an air of soft and fluffy innocence. But she was deadlily learned and evil-instructed; and, now and again, when the mask dropped, men saw this, shuddered and—almost drew back. Men are occasionally particular, and the least particular men are always the most exacting.

Simla is eccentric in its fashion of treating friendships. Certain attachments which have set and crystallised through half-a-dozen seasons acquire almost the sanctity of the marriage bond, and are revered as such. Again, certain attachments equally old, and, to all appearances, equally venerable, never seem to win any recognised official status; while a chance-sprung acquaintance, not two months born, steps into the place which by right belongs to the senior. There is no law reducible to print which regulates these affairs.

Some people have a gift which secures them infinite toleration, and others have not. The Man's Wife had not. If she looked over the garden wall, for instance, women taxed her with stealing their husbands. She complained pathetically that she was not allowed to choose her own friends. When she put up her big white muff to her lips, and gazed over it and under her eyebrows at you as she said this thing, you felt that she had been infamously misjudged, and that all the other women's instincts were all wrong. Which was absurd. She was not allowed to own the Tertium Quid in peace; and was so strangely constructed that she would not have enjoyed peace had she been so permitted. She preferred some semblance of intrigue to cloak even her most commonplace actions.

After two months of riding, first round Jakko, then Elysium, then Summer Hill, then Observatory Hill, then under Jutogh, and lastly up and down the Cart Road, as far as the Tara Devi gap in the dusk, she said to the Tertium Quid, 'Frank, people say we are too much together, and people are so horrid.'

The Tertium Quid pulled his moustache, and replied that horrid people were unworthy of the consideration of nice people.

'But they have done more than talk—they have written—written to my hubby—I'm sure of it,' said the Man's Wife, and she pulled a letter from her husband out of her saddle-pocket and gave it to the Tertium Quid.

It was an honest letter, written by an honest man, then stewing in the Plains on two hundred rupees a month (for he allowed his wife eight hundred and fifty), and in a silk singlet and cotton trousers. It said that, perhaps, she had not thought of the unwisdom of allowing her name to be so generally coupled with the Tertium Quid's; that she was too much of a child to understand the dangers of that sort of thing; that he, her husband, was the last man in the world to interfere jealously with her little amusements and interests, but that it would be better were she to drop the Tertium Quid quietly and for her husband's sake. The letter was sweetened with many pretty little pet names, and it amused the Tertium Quid considerably. He and She laughed over it, so that you, fifty yards away, could see their shoulders shaking while the horses slouched along side by side.

Their conversation was not worth reporting. The upshot of it was that, next day, no one saw the Man's Wife and the Tertium Quid together. They had both gone down to the Cemetery, which, as a rule, is only visited officially by the inhabitants of Simla.

A Simla funeral with the clergyman riding, the mourners riding, and the coffin creaking as it swings between the bearers, is one of the most depressing things on this earth, particularly when the procession passes under the wet, dark dip beneath the Rockliffe Hotel, where the sun is shut out, and all the hill streams are wailing and weeping together as they go down the valleys.

Occasionally folk tend the graves, but we in India shift and are transferred so often that, at the end of the second year, the Dead have no friends—only acquaintances who are far too busy amusing themselves up the hill to attend to old partners. The idea of using a Cemetery as a rendezvous is distinctly a feminine one. A man would have said simply, 'Let people talk. We'll go down the Mall.' A woman is made differently, especially if she be such a woman as the Man's Wife. She and the Tertium Quid enjoyed each other's society among the graves of men and women whom they had known and danced with aforetime.

They used to take a big horse-blanket and sit on the grass a little to the left of the lower end, where there is a dip in the ground, and where the occupied graves stop short and the ready-made ones are not ready.

Each well-regulated Indian Cemetery keeps half-a-dozen graves permanently open for contingencies and incidental wear and tear. In the Hills these are more usually baby's size, because children who come up weakened and sick from the Plains often succumb to the effects of the Rains in the Hills or get pneumonia from their *ayahs* taking them through damp pine-woods after the sun has set. In cantonments, of course, the man's size is more in request; these arrangements varying with the climate and population.

One day when the Man's Wife and the Tertium Quid had just arrived in the Cemetery, they saw some coolies breaking ground. They had marked out a full-size grave, and the Tertium Quid asked them whether any Sahib was sick. They said that they did not know; but it was an order that they should dig a Sahib's grave.

'Work away,' said the Tertium Quid, 'and let's see how it's done.'

The coolies worked away, and the Man's Wife and the Tertium Quid watched and talked for a couple of hours while the grave was being deepened. Then a coolie, taking the earth in baskets as it was thrown up, jumped over the grave.

'That's queer,' said the Tertium Quid. 'Where's my ulster?'

'What's queer?' said the man's Wife.

'I have got a chill down my back—just as if a goose had walked over my grave.'

'Why do you look at the thing, then?' said the Man's Wife. 'Let us go.'

The Tertium Quid stood at the head of the grave, and stared without answering for a space. Then he said, dropping a pebble down, 'It is nasty—and cold: horribly cold. I don't think I shall come to the Cemetery any more. I don't think grave-digging is cheerful.'

The two talked and agreed that the Cemetery was depressing. They also arranged for a ride next day out from the Cemetery through the Mashobra Tunnel up to Fagoo and back, because all the world was going to a garden-party at Viceregal Lodge, and all the people of Mashobra would go too.

Coming up the Cemetery road, the Tertium Quid's horse tried to bolt uphill, being tired and standing so long, and managed to strain a back sinew.

'I shall have to take the mare to-morrow,' said the Tertium Quid, 'and she will stand nothing heavier than a snaffle.'

They made their arrangements to meet in the Cemetery, after allowing all the Mashobra people time to pass into Simla. That night it rained heavily, and, next day, when the Tertium Quid came to the trysting-place, he saw that the new grave had a foot of water in it, the ground being a tough and sour clay.

'Jove! That looks beastly,' said the Tertium Quid. 'Fancy being boarded up and dropped into that well!'

They then started off to Fagoo, the mare playing with the snaffle and picking her way as though she were shod with satin, and the sun shining divinely. The road below Mashobra to Fagoo is officially styled the Himalayan-Tibet Road; but in spite of its name it is not much more than six feet wide in most places, and the drop into the valley below may be anything between one and two thousand feet.

'Now we're going to Tibet,' said the Man's Wife merrily, as the horses drew near to Fagoo. She was riding on the cliff side. 'Into Tibet,' said the Tertium Quid, 'ever so far from people who say horrid things, and hubbies who write stupid letters. With you—to the end of the world!'

A coolie carrying a log of wood came round a corner, and the mare went wide to avoid him—forefeet in and haunches out, as a sensible mare should go.

'To the world's end,' said the man's Wife, and looked unspeakable things over her near shoulder at the Tertium Quid.

He was smiling, but, while she looked, the smile froze stiff, as it were, on his face, and changed to a nervous grin—the sort of grin men wear when they are not quite easy in their saddles. The mare seemed to be sinking by the stern, and her nostrils cracked while she was trying to realise what was happening. The rain of the night before had rotted the drop-side of the Himalayan-Tibet Road, and it was giving way under her. 'What are you doing?' said the Man's Wife. The Tertium Quid gave no answer. He grinned nervously and set his spurs into the mare, who rapped with her forefeet on the road, and the struggle began. The Man's Wife screamed, 'Oh, Frank, get off!'

But the Tertium Quid was glued to the saddle—his face blue and white—and he looked into the Man's Wife's eyes. Then the Man's Wife clutched at the mare's head and caught her by the nose instead of the bridle. The brute threw up her head and went down with a scream, the Tertium Quid upon her, and the nervous grin still set on his face.

The Man's Wife heard the tinkle-tinkle of little stones and loose earth falling off the roadway, and the sliding roar of the man and horse going down. Then everything was quiet, and she called on Frank to leave his mare and walk up. But Frank did not answer. He was underneath the mare, nine hundred feet below, spoiling a patch of Indian corn.

As the revellers came back from Viceregal Lodge in the mists of the evening, they met a temporarily insane woman, on a temporarily mad horse, swinging round the corners, with her eyes and her mouth open, and her head like the head of a Medusa. She was stopped by a man at the risk of his life, and taken out of the saddle, a limp heap, and put on the bank to explain herself. This wasted twenty minutes, and then she was sent home in a lady's 'rikshaw, still with her mouth open and her hands picking at her riding-gloves.

She was in bed through the following three days, which were rainy; so she missed attending the funeral of the Tertium Quid, who was lowered into eighteen inches of water, instead of the twelve to which he had objected.

A WAYSIDE COMEDY

Because to every purpose there is time and judgment,
therefore the misery of man is great upon him.

Ecclesiastes VIII.6

FATE AND THE Government of India have turned the Station of Kashima into a prison; and, because there is no help for the poor souls who are now lying there in torment, I write this story, praying that the Government of India may be moved to scatter the European population to the four winds.

Kashima is bounded on all sides by the rock-tipped circle of the Dosehri hills. In spring, it is ablaze with roses. In summer, the roses die and the hot winds blow from the hills. In autumn, the white mists from the *jhils* cover the place as with water, and in winter, the frosts nip everything young and tender to earth-level. There is but one view in Kashima—a stretch of perfectly flat pasture and plough-land, running up to the grey-blue scrub of the Dosehri hills.

There are no amusements, except snipe and tiger shooting; but the tigers have been long since hunted from their lairs in the rock-caves, and the snipe only come once a year. Narkarra—one hundred and forty-three miles by road—is the nearest station to Kashima. But Kashima never goes to Narkarra, where there are at least twelve English people. It stays within the circle of the Dosehri hills.

All Kashima acquits Mrs. Vansuythen of any intention to do harm; but all Kashima knows that she, and she alone, brought about their pain.

Boulte, the Engineer, Mrs. Boulte, and Captain Kurrell know this. They are the English population of Kashima, if we except Major Vansuythen, who is of no importance whatever, and Mrs. Vansuythen, who is the most important of all.

You must remember, though you will not understand, that all laws weaken in a small and hidden community where there is no public opinion. When a man is absolutely alone in a Station he runs a certain risk of falling into evil ways. This risk is multiplied by every addition to the population up to twelve—the Jury-number. After that, fear and consequent restraint begin, and human action becomes less grotesquely jerky.

There was deep peace in Kashina till Mrs. Vansuythen arrived. She was a charming woman, every one said so everywhere; and she charmed every one. In spite of this, or perhaps, because of this, since Fate is so perverse, she cared only for one man, and he was Major Vansuythen. Had she been plain or stupid, this matter would have been intelligible to Kashima. But she was a fair woman, with very still grey eyes, the colour of a lake just before the light of the sun touches it. No man who had seen those eyes could, later on, explain what fashion of woman she was to look upon. The eyes dazzled him. Her own sex said that she was 'not bad-looking, but spoilt by pretending to be so grave.' And yet her gravity was natural. It was not her habit to smile. She merely went through life, looking at those who passed; and the women objected while the men fell down and worshipped.

She knows and is deeply sorry for the evil she has done to Kashima; but Major Vansuythen cannot understand why Mrs. Boulte does not drop in to afternoon tea at least three times a week. 'When there are only two women in one Station, they ought to see a great deal of each other,' says Major Vansuythen.

Long and long before ever Mrs. Vansuythen came out of those far-away places where there is society and amusement, Kurrell had discovered that Mrs. Boulte was the one woman in the world for him and—you dare not blame them. Kashima was as out of the world as Heaven or the Other Place, and the Dosehri hills kept their secret well. Boulte had no concern in the matter. He was in camp for a fortnight at a time. He was a hard, heavy man, and neither Mrs. Boulte nor Kurrell pitied him. They had all Kashima and each other for their very, very own; and Kashima was the Garden of Eden in those days. When Boulte returned from his wanderings he would slap Kurrell between the shoulders and call him 'old fellow', and the three would dine together.

Kashima was happy then when the Judgment of God seemed almost as distant as Narkarra or the railway that ran down to sea. But the Government sent Major Vansuythen to Kashima, and with him came his wife.

The etiquette of Kashima is much the same as that of a desert island. When a stranger is cast away there, all hands go down to the shore to make him welcome. Kashima assembled at the masonry platform close to the Narkarra Road, and spread tea for the Vansuythens. That ceremony was reckoned a formal call, and made them free of the Station, its rights and privileges. When the Vansuythens settled down they gave a tiny house-warming to all Kashima; and that made Kashima free of their house, according to the immemorial usage of the Station.

Then the Rains came, when no one could go into camp, and the Narkarra Road was washed away by the Kasun River, and in the cup-like pastures of Kashima the cattle waded knee-deep. The clouds dropped down from the Dosehri hills and covered everything.

At the end of the Rains Boulte's manner towards his wife changed and became demonstrably affectionate. They had been married twelve years, and the change startled Mrs. Boulte, who hated her husband with the hate of a woman who has met with nothing but kindness from her mate, and, in the teeth of this kindness, has done him a great wrong. Moreover, she had her own trouble to fight with—her watch to keep over her own property, Kurrell. For two months the Rains had hidden the Dosehri hills and many other things besides; but, when they lifted, they showed Mrs. Boulte that her man among men, her Ted—for she called him Ted in the old days when Boulte was out of earshot—was slipping the links of the allegiance.

'The Vansuythen woman has taken him,' Mrs. Boulte said to herself; and when Boulte went away, wept over her belief, in the face of the over-vehement blandishments of Ted. Sorrow in Kashima is as fortunate as Love because there is nothing to weaken it save the flight of Time. Mrs. Boulte had never breathed her suspicion to Kurrell because she was not certain; and her nature led her to be very certain before she took steps in any direction. That is why she behaved as she did.

Boulte came into the house one evening, and leaned against the door-post of the drawing-room, chewing his moustache. Mrs. Boulte was putting some flowers into a vase. There is a pretence of civilisation even in Kashima.

'Little woman,' said Boulte quietly, 'do you care for me?'

'Immensely,' said she, with a laugh. 'Can you ask it?'

'But I'm serious,' said Boulte. '*Do* you care for me?'

Mrs. Boulte dropped the flowers, and round quickly. 'Do you want an honest answer?'

'Ye-es, I've asked for it.'

Mrs. Boulte spoke in a low, even voice for five minutes, very distinctly, that there might be no misunderstanding her meaning. When Samson broke the pillars of Gaza, he did a little thing, and one not to be compared with the deliberate pulling down of a woman's homestead about her own ears. There was no wise female friend to advise Mrs. Boulte, the singularly cautious wife, to hold her hand. She struck at Boulte's heart, because her own was sick with suspicion of Kurrell, and worn out with the long strain of watching alone through the Rains. There was no plan or purpose in her speaking. The sentences made themselves; and Boulte listened, leaning against the doorpost with his hands in his pockets. When all was over, and Mrs. Boulte began to breathe through her nose before breaking into tears, he laughed and stared straight in front of him at the Dosehri hills.

'Is that all?' he said. 'Thanks, I only wanted to know, you know.'

'What are you going to do?'

'Do! Nothing. What should I do? Kill Kurrell, or send you Home, or apply for leave to get a divorce? It's two days' *dak* into Narkarra.' He laughed again and went on: 'I'll tell you what *you* can do. You can ask Kurrell to dinner to-morrow— no, on Thursday, that will allow you time to pack—and you can bolt with him. I give you my word I won't follow.'

He took up his helmet and went out of the room, and Mrs. Boulte sat till the moonlight streaked the floor, thinking and thinking and thinking. She had done her best upon the spur of the moment to pull the house down; but it would not fall. Moreover, she could not understand her husband, and she was afraid. Then the folly of her useless truthfulness struck her, and she was ashamed to write to Kurrell, saying, 'I have gone mad and told everything. My husband says that I am free to elope with you. Get a *dak* for Thursday, and we will fly after dinner.' There was a cold-bloodedness about that procedure which did not appeal to her. So she sat still in her own house and thought.

At dinner-time Boulte came back from his walk, white and worn and haggard, and the woman was touched at his distress. As the evening wore on she muttered some expression of sorrow, something approaching to contrition. Boulte came out of a brown study and said, 'Oh, *that*! I wasn't thinking about that. By the way, what does Kurrell say to the elopement?'

'I haven't seen him,' said Mrs. Boulte. 'Good God, is that all?'

But Boulte was not listening, and her sentence ended in a gulp.

The next day brought no comfort to Mrs. Boulte, for Kurrell did not appear, and the new life that she, in the five minutes' madness of the previous evening, had hoped to build out of the ruins of the old, seemed to be no nearer.

Boulte ate his breakfast, advised her to see her Arab pony fed in the veranda, and went out. The morning wore through, and at mid-day the tension became unendurable. Mrs. Boulte could not cry. She had finished her crying in the night, and now she did not want to be left alone. Perhaps the Vansuythen Woman would talk to her; and, since talking opens the heart, perhaps there might be some comfort to be found in her company. She was the only other woman in the Station.

In Kashima there are no regular calling-hours. Every one can drop in upon every one else at pleasure. Mrs. Boulte put on a big *terai* hat, and walked across to the Vansuythens' house to borrow last week's *Queen*. The two compounds touched, and instead of going up the drive, she crossed through the gap in the cactus-hedge, entering the house from the back. As she passed through the dining-room, she heard, behind the *purdah* that cloaked the drawing-room door, her husband's voice, saying:—

'But on my Honour! On my Soul and Honour, I tell you she doesn't care for me. She told me so last night. I would have told you then if Vansuythen hadn't been with you. If it is for *her* sake that you'll have nothing to say to me, you can make your mind easy. It's Kurrell—'

'What?' said Mrs. Vansuythen, with a hysterical little laugh. 'Oh, it can't be! You two must have made some horrible mistake. Perhaps you—you lost your temper, or misunderstood, or something. Things *can't* be as wrong as you say.'

Mrs. Vansuythen had shifted her defence to avoid the man's pleading, and was desperately trying to keep him to a side-issue.

'There must be some mistake,' she insisted, ' and it can be all put right again.'

Boulte laughed grimly.

'It can't be Captain Kurrell! He told me that he had never taken the least—the least interest in your wife, Mr. Boulte. Oh, *do* listen! He said he had not. He swore he has not,' said Mrs. Vansuythen.

The *purdah* rustled, and the speech was cut short by the entry of a little thin woman, with big rings round her eyes. Mrs. Vansuythen stood up with a gasp.

'What was that you said?' asked Mrs. Boulte. 'Never mind that man. What did Ted say to you? What did he say to you? What did he say to you?'

Mrs. Vansuythen sat down helplessly on the sofa, overborne by the trouble of her questioner.

'He said—I can't remember exactly what he said—but I understood him to say—that is—But, really, Mrs. Boulte, isn't it rather a strange question?'

'*Will* you tell me what he said?' repeated Mrs. Boulte. Even a tiger will fly before a bear robbed of her whelps, and Mrs. Vansuythen was only an ordinarily good woman. She began in a sort of desperation, 'Well, he said that he never cared for you at all, and, of course, there was not the least reason why he should have, and—and—that was all.'

'You said he *swore* he had not cared for me. Was that true?'

'Yes,' said Mrs. Vansuythen very softly.

Mrs. Boulte wavered for an instant where she stood, and then fell forward fainting.

'What did I tell you?' said Boulte, as though the conversation had been unbroken. 'You can see for yourself. She cares for *him.*' The light began to break into his dull mind, and he went on: 'And he—what was *he* saying to you?'

But Mrs. Vansuythen, with no heart for explanations or impassioned protestations, was kneeling over Mrs. Boulte.

'Oh, you brute!' she cried. 'Are *all* men like this? Help me to get her into my room—and her face is cut against the table. Oh, *will* you be quiet, and help me to carry her? I hate you, and I hate Captain Kurrell. Lift her up carefully, and now—go! Go away!'

Boulte carried his wife into Mrs. Vansuythen's bedroom, and departed before the storm of that lady's wrath and disgust, impenitent and burning with jealousy. Kurrell had been making love to Mrs. Vansuythen—would do Vansuythen as great a wrong as he had done Boulte, who caught himself considering whether Mrs. Vansuythen would faint if she discovered that the man she loved had forsworn her.

In the middle of these meditations, Kurrell came cantering along the road and pulled by with a cheery 'Good mornin'. Been mashing Mrs. Vansuythen as usual, eh? Bad thing for a sober, married man, that. What will Mrs. Boulte say?'

Boulte raised his head and said slowly: 'Oh, you liar!' Kurrell's face changed. 'What's that?' he asked quickly.

'Nothing much,' said Boulte. 'Has my wife told you that you two are free to go off whenever you please? She has been good enough to explain the situation to me. You've been a true friend to me, Kurrell—old man—haven't you?'

Kurrell groaned, and tried to frame some sort of idiotic sentence about being willing to give 'satisfaction'. But his interest in the woman was dead, had died out in the Rains, and, mentally, he was abusing her for her amazing indiscretion. It would have been so easy to have broken off the thing gently and by degrees, and now he was saddled with—Boulte's voice recalled him.

'I don't think I should get any satisfaction from killing you, and I'm pretty sure you'd get none from killing me.'

Then in a querulous tone, ludicrously disproportioned to his wrongs, Boulte added:—

'Seems rather a pity that you haven't the decency to keep to the woman, now you've got her. You've been a true friend to *her* too, haven't you?'

Kurrell stared long and gravely. The situation was getting beyond him.

'What do you mean?' he said.

Boulte answered, more to himself than the questioner: 'My wife came over to Mrs. Vansuythen's just now; and it seems you'd been telling Mrs. Vansuythen that you'd never cared for Emma. I suppose you lied, as usual. What had Mrs. Vansuythen to do with you, or you with her? Try to speak the truth for once in a way.'

Kurrell took the double insult without wincing, and replied by another question: 'Go on. What happened?'

'Emma fainted,' said Boulte simply. 'But, look here, what had you been saying to Mrs. Vansuythen?'

Kurrell laughed. Mrs. Boulte had, with unbridled tongue, made havoc of his plans; and he could at least retaliate by hurting the man in whose eyes he was humiliated and shown dishonourable.

'Saying to her? What *does* a man tell a lie like that for? I suppose I said pretty much what you've said, unless I'm a good deal mistaken.'

'I spoke the truth,' said Boulte, again more to himself than Kurrell. 'Emma told me she hated me. She has no right in me.'

'No! I suppose not. You're only her husband, y'know. And what did Mrs. Vansuythen say after you had laid your disengaged heart at her feet?'

Kurrell felt most virtuous as he put the question.

'I don't think that matters,' Boulte replied; 'and it doesn't concern you.'

'But it does! I tell you it does'—began Kurrell shamelessly.

The sentence was cut by a roar of laughter from Boulte's lips. Kurrell was silent for an instant, and then he, too, laughed—laughed long and loudly, rocking in his saddle. It was an unpleasant sound—the mirthless mirth of these men on the long white line of the Narkarra Road. There were no strangers in Kashima, or they might have thought that captivity within the Dosehri hills had driven half the European population mad. The laughter ended abruptly, and Kurrell was the first to speak.

'Well, what are you going to do?'

Boulte looked up the road, and at the hills. 'Nothing,' said he quietly. 'What's the use? It's too ghastly for anything. We must let the old life go on. I can only call you a hound and a liar, and I can't go on calling you names for ever. Besides which, I don't feel that I'm much better. We can't get out of this place. What *is* there to do?'

Kurrell looked round the rat-pit of Kashima and made no reply. The injured husband took up the wondrous tale.

'Ride on, and speak to Emma if you want to. God knows *I* don't care what you do.'

He walked forward, and left Kurrell gazing blankly after him. Kurrell did not ride on either to see Mrs. Boulte or Mrs. Vansuythen. He sat in his saddle and thought, while his pony grazed by the roadside.

The whir of approaching wheels roused him. Mrs. Vansuythen was driving home Mrs. Boulte, white and wan, with a cut on her forehead.

'Stop, please,' said Mrs. Boulte. 'I want to speak to Ted.'

Mrs. Vansuythen obeyed, but as Mrs. Boulte leaned forward, putting her hand upon the splash-board of the dog-cart, Kurrell spoke.

'I've seen your husband, Mrs. Boulte.'

There was no necessity for any further explanation. The man's eyes were fixed, not upon Mrs. Boulte, but her companion. Mrs. Boulte saw the look.

'Speak to him!' she pleaded, turning to the woman at her side. 'Oh, speak to him! Tell him what you told me just now. Tell him you hate him. Tell him you hate him.'

She bent forward and wept bitterly, while the *sais*, impassive, went forward to hold the horse. Mrs. Vansuythen turned scarlet and dropped the reins. She wished to be no party to such unholy explanations.

'I've nothing to do with it,' she began coldly; but Mrs. Boulte's sobs overcame her, and she addressed herself to the man. 'I don't know what I am to say, Captain Kurrell. I don't know what I can call you. I think you've—you've behaved abominably, and she has cut her forehead terribly against the table.'

'It doesn't hurt. It isn't anything,' said Mrs. Boulte feebly, '*That* doesn't matter. Tell him what you told me. Say you don't care for him. Oh, Ted, *won't* you believe her?'

'Mrs. Boulte has made me understand that you were—that you were fond of her once upon a time,' went on Mrs. Vansuythen.

'Well!' said Kurrell brutally. 'It seems to me that Mrs. Boulte had better be fond of her own husband first.'

'Stop!' said Mrs. Vansuythen. 'Hear me first. I don't care—I don't want to know anything about you and Mrs. Boulte; but I want *you* to know that I hate you, that I think you are a cur, and that I'll never, *never* speak to you again. Oh, I don't dare to say what I think of you—man!'

'I want to speak to Ted,' moaned Mrs. Boulte, but the dog-cart rattled on, and Kurrell was left on the road, shamed, and boiling with wrath against Mrs. Boulte.

He waited till Mrs. Vansuythen was driving back to her own house, and, she being freed from the embarrassment of Mrs. Boulte's presence, learned for the second time her opinion of himself and his actions.

In the evenings it was the wont of all Kashima to meet on the platform on the Narkarra Road, to drink tea and discuss the trivialities of the day. Major Vansuythen and his wife found themselves alone at the gathering-place for almost the first time in their remembrance; and the cheery major, in the teeth of his wife's remarkably reasonable suggestion that the rest of the Station might be sick, insisted upon driving round to the two bungalows and unearthing the population.

'Sitting in the twilight!' said he, with great indignation, to the Boultes. 'That'll never do! Hang it all, we're one family here! You *must* come out, and so must Kurrell. I'll make him bring his banjo.'

So great is the power of honest simplicity and a good digestion over guilty consciences that all Kashima did turn out, even down to the banjo; and the Major embraced the company in one expansive grin. As he grinned, Mrs. Vansuythen raised her eyes for an instant and looked at all Kashima. Her meaning was clear. Major Vansuythen would never know anything. He was to be the outsider in that happy family whose cage was the Dosehri hills.

'You're singing villainously out of tune, Kurrell,' said the Major truthfully. 'Pass me that banjo.'

And he sang in excruciating wise till the stars came out and all Kashima went to dinner.

That was the beginning of the New Life of Kashima—the life that Mrs. Boulte made when her tongue was loosened in the twilight.

Mrs. Vansuythen has never told the Major; and since he insists upon keeping up a burdensome geniality, she has been compelled to break her vow of not speaking to Kurrell. This speech, which must of necessity preserve the semblance of politeness and interest, serves admirably to keep alight the flame of jealousy and dull hatred in Boulte's bosom, as it awakens the same passions in his wife's heart. Mrs. Boulte hates Mrs. Vansuythen because she has taken Ted from her, and, in some curious fashion, hates her because Mrs. Vansuythen—and here the wife's eyes see far more clearly than the husband's—detests Ted. And Ted—that gallant Captain and honourable man—knows now that it is possible to hate a woman once loved, to the verge of wishing to silence her for ever with blows. Above all is he shocked that Mrs. Boulte cannot see the error of her ways.

Boulte and he go out tiger-shooting together in all friendship. Boulte has put their relationship on a most satisfactory footing.

'You're a blackguard,' he says to Kurrell, 'and I've lost any self-respect I may have ever had; but when you're with me, I feel certain that you are not with Mrs. Vansuythen, or making Emma miserable.'

Kurrell endures anything that Boulte may say to him. Sometimes they are away for three days together, and then the Major insists upon his wife going over to sit with Mrs. Boulte; although Mrs. Vansuythen has repeatedly declared that she prefers her husband's company to any in the world. From the way in which she clings to him, she would certainly seem to be speaking the truth.

Bu of course, as the Major says, 'In a little Station we must all be friendly.'

THE TOMB OF HIS ANCESTORS

SOME PEOPLE WILL tell you that if there were but a single loaf of bread in all India it would be divided equally between the Plowdens, the Trevors, the Beadons, and the Rivett-Carnacs. That is only one way of saying that certain families serve India generation after generation as dolphins follow in line across the open sea.

Let us take a small and obscure case. There has been at least one representative of the Devonshire Chinns in or near Central India since the days of Lieutenant-Fireworker Humphrey Chinn, of the Bombay European Regiment, who assisted at the capture of Seringapatam in 1799. Alfred Ellis Chinn, Humphrey's younger brother, commanded a regiment of Bombay Grenadiers from 1804 to 1813, when he saw mixed fighting; and in 1834 John Chinn of the same family—we will call him John Chinn the First—came to light as a level-headed administrator in time of trouble at a place called Mundesur. He died young, but left his mark on the new country, and the Honourable Board of Directors of the Honourable the East India Company embodied his virtues in a stately resolution, and paid for the expenses of his tomb among the Satpura hills.

He was succeeded by his son, Lionel Chinn, who left the little old Devonshire home just in time to be severely wounded in the Mutiny. He spent his working life within a hundred and fifty miles of John Chinn's grave, and rose to the command of a regiment of small, wild hill-men, most of whom had known his father. His son John was born in the small thatched-roofed, mud-walled cantonment, which is even to-day eighty miles from the nearest railway, in the heart of a scrubby, tigerish country. Colonel Lionel Chinn served thirty years and retired. In the Canal his steamer passed the outward-bound troopship, carrying his son, John Chinn the Second, eastward to the family duties.

The Chinns are luckier than most folk, because they know exactly what they must do. A clever Chinn passes for the Bombay Civil Service, and gets away to Central India, where everybody is glad to see him. A dull Chinn enters the police Department or the Woods and Forests, and sooner or later he, too, appears in Central India, and that is what gave rise to the saying, 'Central India is inhabited by Bhils, Mairs, and Chinns, all very much alike.' The breed is small-boned, dark, and silent, and the stupidest of them are good shots. John Chinn the Second was rather clever, but as the eldest son he entered the army, according to Chinn tradition. His duty was to abide in his father's regiment for the term of his natural life, though the corps was one which most men would have paid heavily to avoid. They were Irregulars, small, dark, and blackish, clothed in rifle-green with black-leather trimmings; and friends called them the 'Wuddars', which means a race of low-caste people who dig up rats to eat. But the Wuddars did not resent it. They were the only Wuddars, and their points of pride were these:—

Firstly, they had fewer English officers than any native regiment. Secondly, their subalterns were not mounted on parade, as is their general rule, but walked at the head of their men. A man who can hold his own with the Wuddars at their quick-step must be sound in wind and limb. Thirdly, they were the most *pukka shikarris* [out and out hunters] in all India. Fourthly—up to one hundredthly—they were the Wuddars—Chinn's Irregular Bhil Levies of the old days, but now, henceforward and for ever, the Wuddars.

No Englishman entered their Mess except for love or through familiar usage. The officers talked to their soldiers in a tongue not two hundred white folk in India understood; and the men were their children, all drawn from the Bhils, who are, perhaps, the strangest of the many strange races in India. They were, and at heart are, wild men, furtive, shy, full of untold superstitions. The races whom we call natives of the country found the Bhil in possession of the land when they first broke into that part of the world thousands of years ago. The books call them Pre-Aryan, Aboriginal, Dravidian, and so forth; and, in other words, that is what the Bhils call themselves. When a Rajput chief, whose bards can sing his pedigree backwards for twelve hundred years, is set on the throne, his investiture is not complete till he has been marked on the forehead with blood from the veins of a Bhil. The Rajputs say the ceremony has no meaning, but the Bhil knows that it is the last, last shadow of his old rights as the long-ago owner of the soil.

Centuries of oppression and massacre made the Bhil a cruel and half-crazy thief and cattle-rustler, and when the English came he seemed to be almost as open to civilisation as the tigers of his own jungles. But John Chinn the First, father of Lionel, grandfather of our John, went into his country, lived with him, learned his language, shot the deer that stole his poor crops, and won his confidence, so that some Bhils learned to plough and sow, while others were coaxed into the Company's service to police their friends.

When they understood that standing in line did not mean instant execution, they accepted soldiering as a cumbrous but amusing kind of sport, and were zealous to keep the wild Bhils under control. That was the thin end of the wedge. John Chinn the First gave them written promises that, if they were good from a certain date, the Government would overlook previous offences; and since John Chinn was never known to break his word—he promised once to hang a Bhil locally esteemed invulnerable, and hanged him in front of his tribe for seven proved murders—the Bhils settled down as steadily as they knew how. It was slow, unseen work, of the sort that is being done all over India to-day; and though John Chinn's only reward came, as I have said, in the shape of a grave at Government expense, the little people of the hills never forgot him.

Colonel Lionel Chinn knew and loved them too, and they were very fairly civilised, for Bhils, before his service ended. Many of them could hardly be distinguished from low-caste Hindu farmers; but in the south, where John Chinn the First was buried, the wildest still clung to the Satpura ranges, cherishing a legend that some day Jan Chinn, as they called him, would return to his own. In the meantime they mistrusted the white man and his ways. The least excitement would stampede them plundering at random, and now and then killing; but if they were handled discreetly they grieved like children, and promised never to do it again.

The Bhils of the Regiment—the uniformed men—were virtuous in many ways, but they needed humouring. They felt bored and homesick unless taken after tigers as beaters; and their cold-blooded daring—all Wuddars shoot tigers on foot—it is their caste-mark—made even the officers wonder. They would follow up a wounded tiger as unconcernedly as though it were a sparrow with a broken wing; and this through a country full of caves and rifts and pits, where a wild beast could hold a dozen men at his mercy. Now and then some little man was brought to barracks with his head smashed in or his ribs torn away; but his companions never learned caution. They contented themselves with settling the tiger.

Young John Chinn was decanted at the veranda of the Wuddars' lonely Mess-house from the back seat of a two-wheeled cart, his gun-cases cascading all round him. The slender, little, hooky-nosed boy looked forlorn as a strayed goat when he slapped the white dust of his knees, and the cart jolted down the glaring road. But in his heart he was happy. After all, this was the place where he had been born, and things were not much changed since he had been sent to England, a child, fifteen years ago.

There were a few new buildings, but the air and the smell and the sunshine were the same; and the little green men who crossed the parade-ground looked very familiar. Three weeks ago John Chinn would have said he did not remember a word of the Bhil tongue, but at the Mess-door he found his lips moving in sentences that he did not understand—bits of old nursery rhymes, and tail-ends of such orders as his father used to give the men.

The Colonel watched him come up the steps, and laughed.

'Look!' he said to the Major. 'No need to ask the young un's breed. He's a *pukka* Chinn. Might be his father in the 'Fifties over again.'

'Hope he'll shoot as straight!' said the Major. 'He's brought enough ironmongery with him.'

'Wouldn't be a Chinn if he didn't. Watch him blowin' his nose. Regular Chinn beak. Flourishes his handkerchief like his father. It's the second edition—line for line.'

'Fairy tale, by Jove!' said the Major, peering through the slats of the jalousies. 'If he's the lawful heir, he'll . . . Now old Chinn could no more pass that chick without fiddling with it than . . .'

'His son!' said the Colonel, jumping up.

'Well, I'll be blowed!' said the Major. The boy's eye had been caught by a split reed screen that hung on a slew between the veranda pillars, and mechanically he had tweaked the edge to set it level. Old Chinn had sworn three times a day at that screen for many years; he could never get it to his satisfaction. His son entered the ante-room in the middle of a five-fold silence. They made him welcome for his father's sake and, as they took stock of him, for his own. He was ridiculously like the portrait of the Colonel on the wall, and when he had washed a little of the dust from his throat he went to his quarters with the old man's short, noiseless jungle-step.

'So much for heredity,' said the Major. 'That comes of three generations among the Bhils.'

'And the men know it,' said a Wing-Officer. 'They've been waiting for this youth with their tongues hanging out. I am persuaded that, unless he absolutely beats 'em over the head, they'll lie down by companies and worship him.'

'Nothing like having a father before you,' said the Major. 'I'm a parvenu with my chaps. I've only been twenty years in the Regiment, and my revered parent he was a simple squire. There's no getting at the bottom of a Bhil's mind. Now, *why* is the superior bearer that young Chinn brought with him fleeing across country with his bundle?' He stepped into the veranda, and shouted after the man—a typical new-joined subaltern's servant who speaks English and cheats his master.

'What is it?' he called.

'Plenty bad men here. I going, sar,' was his reply. 'Have taken Sahib's keys, and say will shoot.'

'Doocid lucid—doocid convincin'. How those up-country thieves can leg it! He has been badly frightened by some one.' The Major strolled to his quarters to dress for Mess.

Young Chinn, walking like a man in a dream, had fetched a compass round the entire cantonment before going to his own tiny cottage. The Captains' quarters, in which he had been born, delayed him for a little; then he looked at the well on the parade-ground, where he had sat of evenings with his nurse, and at the ten-by-fourteen church, where the officers went to service if a Chaplain of any official creed happened to come along. It seemed very small compared with the gigantic building he used to stare up at, but it was the same place.

From time to time he passed a knot of silent soldiers, who saluted. They might have been the very men who had carried him on their backs when he was in his first knickerbockers. A faint light burned in his room, and, as he entered, hands clasped his feet, and a voice murmured from the floor.

'What is it?' said young Chinn, not knowing that he spoke in the Bhil tongue.

'I bore you in my arms, Sahib, when I was a young man and you were a small one—crying, crying, crying! I am your servant, as I was your father's before you. We are all your servants.'

Young Chinn could not trust himself to reply, and the voice went on:—

'I've taken your keys from that fat foreigner, and sent him away; and the studs are in the shirt for Mess. Who should know, if I do not know? And so the baby has become a man, and forgets his nurse; but my nephew shall make a good servant, or I will beat him twice a day.'

Then there rose up, with a rattle, as straight as a Bhil arrow, a little white-haired wizened ape of a man, with medals and orders on his trunk, stammering, saluting, and trembling. Behind him a young and wiry Bhil, in uniform, was taking the trees out of Chinn's Mess-boots.

Chinn's eyes were full of tears. The old man held out his keys.

'Foreigners are bad people. He will never come back again. We are all servants of your father's son. Has the Sahib forgotten who took him to see the trapped tiger in the village across the river, when his mother was so frightened and he was so brave?'

The scene came back to Chinn in great magic-lantern flashes. 'Bukta!' he cried; and all in a breath: 'You promised nothing should hurt me. *Is* it Bukta?'

The man was at his feet a second time. 'He has not forgotten.

He remembers his own people as his father remembered. Now I can die. But first I will live and show the Sahib how to kill tigers. That *that* yonder is my nephew. If he is not a good servant, beat him and send him to me, and I will surely kill him, for now the Sahib is with his own people. Ai, Jan *baba*— Jan *baba*! My Jan *baba*! I will stay here and see that this does his work well. Take off his boots, fool. Sit down upon the bed, Sahib, and let me look. It *is* Jan *baba*!'

He pushed forward the hilt of his sword as a sign of service, which is an honour paid only to viceroys, governors, generals, or to little children whom one loves dearly. Chinn touched the hilt mechanically with three fingers, muttering he knew not what. It happened to be the old answer of his childhood, when Bukta in jest called him the little General Sahib.

The Major's quarters were opposite Chinn's, and when he heard his servant gasp with surprise he looked across the room. Then the Major sat on the bed and whistled; for the spectacle of the senior native commissioned officer of the Regiment, an 'unmixed' Bhil, a Companion of the Order of British India, with thirty-five years' spotless service in the Army, and a rank among his own people superior to that of many Bengal princelings, valeting the last-joined subaltern, was a little too much for his nerves.

The throaty bugles blew Mess-call that has a long legend behind it. First a few piercing notes like the shrieks of beaters in a far-away cover, and next, large, full. And smooth, the refrain of the wild song: 'And oh, and oh, the green pulse of Mundore— Mundore!'

'All little children were in bed when the Sahib heard that call last,' said Bukta, passing Chinn a clean handkerchief. The call brought back memories of his cot under the mosquito-netting, his mother's kiss, and the sound of footsteps growing fainter as he dropped asleep. So he hooked the dark collar of his new Mess-jacket, and went to dinner like a prince who has newly inherited his father's crown.

Old Bukta swaggered forth curling his whiskers. He knew his own value, and no money and no rank within the gift of the Government would have induced him to put studs in young officers' shirts, or to hand them clean ties. Yet, when he took off his uniform that night, and squatted among his fellows for a quiet smoke, he told them what he had done, and they said that he was entirely right. Thereat Bukta propounded a theory which to a white mind would have seemed raving insanity; but the whispering, level-headed little men of war considered it from every point of view, and thought that there might be a great deal in it.

At Mess under the oil-lamps the talk turned as usual to the unfailing subject of *shikar*—big-game shooting of every kind and under all sorts of conditions. Young Chinn opened his eyes when he understood that each one of his companions had shot several tigers in the Wuddar-style—on foot, that is—making no more of the business than if the brute had been a dog.

'In nine cases out of ten,' said the Major, 'a tiger is almost as dangerous as porcupine. The tenth time you come home feet first.'

That set all talking, and long before midnight Chinn's brain was in a whirl with stories of tigers—man-eaters and cattle-killers each pursuing his own business as methodically as clerks in an office; new tigers that had lately come into such-and-such a district; and old, friendly beasts of great cunning, known by nicknames in the Mess—such as 'Puggy,' who was lazy, with huge paws, and Mrs. Malaprop, who turned up when you never expected her, and made female noises. Then they spoke of Bhil superstitions, a wide and picturesque field, till young Chinn hinted that they must be pulling his leg.

''Deed we aren't,' said a man on his left. 'We know all about you. You're a Chinn and all that, and you've a sort of vested right here; but if you don't believe what we're telling you, what will you do when old Bukta begins his stories? He knows about ghost-tigers, and tigers that go to a hell of their own; and tigers that walk on their hind feet; and your grandpapa's riding-tiger, as well. Odd he hasn't spoken of that yet.'

'You know you've an ancestor buried down Satpura way, don't you?' said the Major, as Chinn smiled irresolutely.

'Of course I do,' said Chinn, who had the chronicle of the Book of Chinn by heart. It lies in a worn old ledger on the Chinese lacquer table behind the piano in the Devonshire home, and the children are allowed to look at it on Sundays.

'Well, I wasn't sure. Your revered ancestor, my boy, according to the Bhils, has a tiger of his own—a saddle-tiger that he rides round the country whenever he feels inclined. *I* don't call it decent in an ex-Collector's ghost; but that is what the Southern Bhils believe. Even our men, who might be called moderately cool, don't care to beat the country if they hear that Jan Chinn is running about on his tiger. It is supposed to be a clouded animal—not stripy, but blotchy, like a tortoise-shell tom-cat.

No end of a brute, it is, and a sure sign of war or pestilence or—something. There's a nice family legend for you.'

'What's the origin of it, d'you suppose?' said Chinn.

'Ask the Satpura Bhils. Old Jan Chinn was a mighty hunter before the Lord. Perhaps it was the tiger's revenge, or perhaps he's huntin' 'em still. You must go to his tomb one of these days and inquire. Bukta will probably attend to that. He was asking me before you came whether by any ill-luck you had already bagged your tiger. If not, he is going to enter you under his own wing. Of course, for you of all men it's imperative. You'll have a first-class time with Bukta.'

The Major was not wrong. Bukta kept an anxious eye on young Chinn at drill, and it was noticeable that the first time the new officer lifted up his voice in an order the whole line quivered. Even the Colonel was taken aback, for it might have been Lionel Chinn returned from Devonshire with a new lease of life. Bukta had continued to develop his peculiar theory among his intimates, and it was accepted as a matter of faith in the lines, since every word and gesture on young Chinn's part so confirmed it.

The old man arranged early that his darling should wipe out the reproach of not having shot a tiger; but he was not content to take the first or any beast that happened to arrive. In his own villages he had dispensed the high, low, and middle justice, and when his people—naked and fluttered—came to him with word of a beast marked down, he bade them send spies to the kills and the watering-places, that he might be sure the quarry was such an one as suited the dignity of such a man.

Three or four times the reckless trackers returned, most truthfully saying that the beast was mangy, undersized—a tigress worn with nursing, or a broken-toothed old male—and Bukta would curb young Chinn's impatience.

At last, a noble animal was marked down—a ten-foot cattle-killer with a huge roll of loose skin along the belly, glossy-hided, full-frilled about the neck, whiskered, frisky, and young. He had slain a man in pure sport, they said.

'Let him be fed,' quoth Bukta, and the villagers dutifully drove out cows to amuse him, that he might lie up nearby.

Princes and potentates have taken ship to India and spent great moneys for the mere glimpse of beasts one-half as fine as this of Bukta's.

'It is not good,' said he to the Colonel, when he asked for shooting-leave, 'that my Colonel's son who may be—that my Colonel's son should lose his maidenhead on any small jungle beast. That may come after. I have waited long for this which is a tiger. He has come in from the Mair country. In seven days we will return with the skin.'

The Mess gnashed their teeth enviously. Bukta, had he chosen, might have invited them all. But he went out alone with Chinn, two days in a shooting-cart and a day on foot, till they came to a rocky, glary valley with a pool of good water in it. It was a parching day, and the boy very naturally stripped and went in for a bathe, leaving Bukta by the clothes. A white skin shows far against brown jungle, and what Bukta beheld on Chinn's back and right shoulder dragged him forward step by step with staring eyeballs.

'I'd forgotten it isn't decent to strip before a man of his position,' thought Chinn, flouncing in the water. 'How the little devil stares! What is it, Bukta?'

'The Mark!' was the whispered answer.

'It is nothing. You know how it is with my people!' Chinn was annoyed. The dull-red birthmark on his shoulder, something like a conventionalised Tartar cloud, had just slipped memory, or he would not have bathed. It occurred, so they said at home, in alternate generations, appearing, curiously enough, eight or nine years after birth, and, save that it was part of the Chinn inheritance, would not be considered pretty. He hurried ashore, dressed again, and went on till they met two or three Bhils, who promptly fell on their faces. 'My people,' grunted Bukta, not

114

condescending to notice them. 'And so your people, Sahib. When I was a young man we were fewer, but not so weak. Now we are many, but poor stock. As may be remembered. How will you shoot him, Sahib? From a tree; from a shelter which my people shall build; by day or by night?'

'On foot and in the daytime,' said young Chinn.

'That was your custom, as I have heard,' said Bukta to himself. 'I will get news of him. Then you and I will go to him. I will carry one gun. You have yours. There is no need of more. What tiger shall stand against *thee*?'

He was marked down by a little water-hole at the head of a ravine, full-gorged and half-asleep in the May sunlight. He was walked up like a partridge, and he turned to do battle for his life. Bukta made no motion to raise his rifle, but kept his eyes on Chinn, who met the shattering roar of the charge with a single shot—it seemed to him hours as he sighted—which tore through the throat, smashing the backbone below the neck and between the shoulders. The brute crouched, choked, and fell, and before Chinn knew well what had happened Bukta bade him stay still while he paced the distance between his feet and the ringing jaws.

'Fifteen,' said Bukta. 'Short paces. No need for a second shot, Sahib. He bleeds cleanly where he lies, and we need not spoil the skin. I said there would be no need of these, but they came—in case.'

Suddenly the sides of the ravine were crowned with the heads of Bukta's people—a force that could have blown the ribs out of the beast had Chinn's shot failed; but their guns were hidden, and they appeared as interested beaters, some five or six, waiting the word to skin. Bukta watched the life fade from the wild eyes, lifted one hand, and turned on his heel.

'No need to show that *we* care,' said he. 'After this, we can kill what we choose. Put out your hand, Sahib.'

Chinn obeyed. It was entirely steady, and Bukta nodded. 'That also was your custom. My men skin quickly. They will carry the skin to cantonments. Will the Sahib come to my poor village for the night and, perhaps, forget that I am his officer?'

'But those men—the beaters. They have worked hard, and perhaps—'

'Oh, if they skin clumsily, we will skin them. They are my people. In the lines I am one thing. Here I am another.'

This was very true. When Bukta doffed uniform and reverted to the fragmentary dress of his own people, he left his civilisation of drill in the next world. That night, after a little talk with his subjects, he devoted to an orgy; and a Bhil orgy is a thing not to be safely written about. Chinn, flushed with triumph, was in the thick of it, but the meaning of the mysteries was hidden. Wild folk came and pressed about his knees with offerings. He gave his flask to the elders of the village. They grew eloquent, and wreathed him about with flowers. Gifts and loans, not all seemly, were thrust upon him, and infernal music rolled and maddened round red fires, while singers sang songs of the ancient times, and danced peculiar dances. The aboriginal liquors are very potent and Chinn was compelled to taste them often, but, unless the stuff had been drugged, how came he fell asleep suddenly, and to waken late the next day—half a march from the village?

'The Sahib was very tired. A little before dawn he went to sleep,' Bukta explained. 'My people carried him here, and now it is time we should go back to cantonments.'

The voice, smooth and deferential, the step, steady and silent, made it very hard to believe that only a few hours before Bukta was yelling and capering with naked fellow-devils of the scrub.

'My people were very pleased to see the Sahib. They will never forget. When next the Sahib goes out recruiting, he will go to my people, and they will give him as many men as we need.'

Chinn kept his own counsel, except as to the shooting of the tiger, and Bukta embroidered that tale with a shameless tongue. The skin was certainly one of the finest ever hung up in the Mess, and the first of many. When Bukta could not accompany his boy on shooting trips, he took care to put him in good hands, and Chinn learned more of the mind and desire of the wild Bhil in his marches and campings, by talks at twilight or at wayside pools, than an uninstructed man could have come at in a lifetime.

Presently his men in the Regiment grew bold to speak of their relatives—mostly in trouble—and to lay cases of tribal custom before him. They would say, squatting in his veranda at twilight, after the easy, confidential style of the Wuddars, that

116

such-and-such a bachelor had run away with such-and-such a wife at a far-off village. Now, how many cows would Chinn Sahib consider a just fine? Or, again, if written order came from the Government that a Bhil was to repair to a walled city of the plains to give evidence in a law-court, would it be wise to disregard that order? On the other hand, if it were obeyed, would the rash voyager return alive?

'But what have I to do with these things?' Chinn demanded of Bukta impatiently. 'I am a soldier. I do not know the Law.'

'Hoo! Law is for fools and white men. Give them thy large and loud order and they will abide by it. Thou art their Law.'

'But wherefore?'

Every trace of expression left Bukta's countenance. The idea might have smitten him for the first time. 'How can I say?' he replied. 'Perhaps it is on account of the name. A Bhil does not love strange things. Give them orders, Sahib—two, three, four words at a time—such as they can carry away in their heads. That is enough.'

Chinn gave orders then, valiantly, not realising that a word spoken in haste before Mess became the dread unappealable law of villages beyond the smoky hills—was, in truth, no less than the Law of Jan Chinn the First, who, so the whispered legend ran, had come back to earth to oversee the third generation in the body and bones of his grandson.

There could be no sort of doubt in this matter. All the Bhils knew that Jan Chinn reincarnated had honoured Bukta's village with his presence after slaying his first—in this life—tiger; that he had eaten and drunk with the people, as he was used; and—Bukta must have drugged Chinn's liquor very deeply—upon his back and right shoulder all men had seen the same angry red Flying Cloud that the high Gods had set on the flesh of Jan Chinn the First when first he came to the Bhil. As concerned the foolish white world which has no eyes, he was a slim and young officer in the Wuddars; but his own people knew he was Jan Chinn, who had made the Bhil a man; and, believing, they hastened to carry his words, careful never to alter them on the way.

Because the savage and the child who plays lonely games have one horror of being laughed at or questioned, the little folk kept their convictions to themselves; and the Colonel, who thought he knew his Regiment, never guessed that each one of the six hundred quick-footed, beady-eyed rank-and-file, at attention beside their rifles, believed serenely and unshakenly that the subaltern on the left flank of their line was a demigod twice born—tutelary deity of their land and people. The Earth-gods themselves had stamped the incarnation, and who would dare to doubt the handiwork of the Earth-gods?

Chinn, being practical above all things, saw that his family name served him well in the lines and in camp. His men gave no trouble—one does not commit Regimental offences with a God in the chair of justice—and he was sure of the best beaters in the district when he needed them. They believed that the protection of Jan Chinn the First cloaked them, and were bold in that belief beyond the utmost daring of excited Bhils.

His quarters began to look like an amateur natural-history museum, in spite of duplicate heads and horns and skulls that he sent home to Devonshire. The people, very humanly, learned the weak side of their God. It was true he was unbribable, but bird-skins, butterflies, beetles, and, above all, news of big game pleased him. In other respects, too, he lived up to the Chinn tradition. He was fever-proof. A night's sitting out over a tethered goat in a damp valley, that would have filled the Major with a month's malaria, had no effect on him. He was, as they said, 'salted before he was born'.

Now in the autumn of his second year's service an uneasy rumour crept out of the earth and ran about among the Bhils. Chinn heard nothing of it till a brother-officer said across the Mess-table: 'Your revered ancestor's on the rampage in the Satpura country. You'd better look him up.'

'I don't want to be disrespectful, but I'm a little sick of my revered ancestor. Bukta talks of nothing else. What's the old boy supposed to be doing now?'

'Riding cross-country by moonlight on his processional tiger. That's the story. He's been seen by about two thousand Bhils, skipping along the tops of the Satpuras, and scaring people to death. They believe it devoutly, and all the Satpura chaps are worshipping away at his shrine—tomb, I mean—like good 'uns. You really ought to go down there. Must be a queer thing to see your grandfather treated as a God.'

'What makes you think there's any truth in the tale?' said Chinn.

'Because all our men deny it. They say they've never heard of Chinn's tiger. Now that's a manifest lie, because every Bhil *has*.'

'There's only one thing you've overlooked,' said the Colonel, thoughtfully. 'When a local God reappears on earth it's always an excuse for trouble of some kind; and those Satpura Bhils are about as wild as your grandfather left them, young 'un. It means something.'

'Meanin' they may go on the war-path?' said Chinn.

'Can't say—as yet. Shouldn't be surprised one little bit.'

'I haven't been told a syllable.'

'Proves it all the more. They are keeping something back.'

'Bukta tells me everything, too, as a rule. Now, why didn't he tell me that?'

Chinn put the question directly to the old man that night, and the answer surprised him.

'Why should I tell what is well known? Yes, the Clouded Tiger is out in the Satpura country.'

'What do the wild Bhils think that it means?'

'They do not know. They wait, Sahib, what *is* coming? Say only one little word, and we will be content.'

'We? What have tales from the south, where the jungly Bhils live, to do with drilled men?'

'When Jan Chinn wakes is time for any Bhil to be quiet.'

'But he has not waked, Bukta.'

'Sahib'—the old man's eyes were full of tender reproof—'if he does not wish to be seen, why does he go abroad in the moonlight? We know he is awake, but we do not know what he desires. Is it a sign for all the Bhils, or one that concerns the Satpura folk alone? Say one little word, Sahib, that I may carry it to the lines, and send on to our villages. Why does Jan Chinn ride out? Who has done wrong? Is it pestilence? Is it murrain? Will our children die? Is it the sword? Remember, Sahib, we are thy people and thy servants, and in this life I bore thee in my arms—not knowing.'

'Bukta has evidently looked on the cup this evening,' Chinn

thought; 'but if I can do anything to soothe the old chap I must. It's like the Mutiny rumours on a small scale.'

He dropped into a deep wicker chair, over which was thrown his first tiger-skin, and his weight on the cushion flapped the clawed paws over his shoulders. He laid hold of them mechanically as he spoke, drawing the painted hide, cloak-fashion, about him.

'Now will I tell the truth, Bukta,' he said, leaning forward, the dried muzzle on his shoulder, to invent a specious lie.

'I see that it is the truth,' was the answer, in a shaking voice.

'Jan Chinn goes abroad among the Satpuras, riding on the Clouded Tiger, ye say? Be it so. Therefore the sign of the wonder is for the Satpura Bhils only, and does not touch the Bhils who plough in the north and east, the Bhils of the Khandesh, or any others, except the Satpura Bhils, who, as we know, are wild and foolish.'

'It is, then, a sign for *them*. Good or bad?'

'Beyond doubt, good. For why should Jan Chinn make evil to those whom he has made men? The nights over yonder are hot; it is ill to lie in one bed over long without turning, and Jan Chinn would look again upon his people. So he rises, whistles his Clouded Tiger, and goes abroad a little to breathe the cool air. If the Satpura Bhils kept to their villages, and did not wander after dark, they would not see him. Indeed, Bukta, it is no more than that he would see the light again in his own country. Send this news south, and say that it is my word.'

Bukta bowed to the floor. 'Good Heavens!' thought Chinn, 'and this blinking pagan is a first-class officer, and as straight as a die! I may as well round it off neatly.' He went on:

'If the Satpura Bhils ask for the meaning of the sign, tell them that Jan Chinn would see how they kept their old promises of good living. Perhaps they have plundered; perhaps they mean to disobey the orders of the Government; perhaps there is a dead man in the jungle; and so Jan Chinn has come to see.'

'Is he, then, angry?'

'Bah! Am *I* ever angry with my Bhils? I say angry words, and threaten many things. *Thou* knowest, Bukta. I have seen thee smile behind thy hand. I know, and thou knowest. The

Bhils are my children. I have said it many times.'

'Ay. We be thy children,' said Bukta.

'And no otherwise is it with Jan Chinn, my father's father. He would see the land he loved and the people once again. It is a good ghost, Bukta. I say it. Go and tell them. And I do hope devoutly,' he added, 'that it will calm 'em down.' Flinging back the tiger-skin, he rose with a long, unguarded yawn that showed his well-kept teeth.

Bukta fled, to be received in the lines by a knot of panting inquirers.

'It is true,' said Bukta. 'He wrapped himself in the skin and spoke from it. He would see his own country again. The sign is not for us; and, indeed, he is a young man. How should he lie idle of nights? He says his bed is too hot and the air is bad. He goes to and fro for the love of night-running. He has said it.'

The grey-whiskered assembly shuddered.

'He says the Bhils are his children. Ye know he does not lie. He has said it to me.'

'But what of the Satpura Bhils? What means the sign for them?'

'Nothing. It is only night-running, as I have said. He rides to see if they obey the Government, as he taught them to do in his first life.'

'And what if they do not?'

'He did not say.'

The light went out in Chinn's quarters.

'Look,' said Bukta. 'Now he goes away. None the less it is a good sign, as he has said. How shall we fear Jan Chinn, who made the Bhil a man? His protection is on us; and ye know Jan Chinn never broke a protection spoken or written on paper. When he is older and has found himself a wife he will lie in his bed till morning.'

A commanding officer is generally aware of the Regimental state of mind a little before the men; and this is why the Colonel said a few days later that some one had been putting the fear of God into the Wuddars. As he was the only person officially entitled to do this, it distressed him to see such unanimous virtue. 'It's too good to last,' he said. 'I only wish I could find out what the little chaps mean.'

The explanation, as it seemed to him, came at the change of the moon, when he received orders to hold himself in readiness to 'allay any possible excitement' among the Satpura Bhils, who were, to put it mildly, uneasy because a paternal Government had sent up against them a Mahratta State-educated vaccinator,' and 'were on the point of neglecting or evading their tribal obligations.'

'That means they are in a blue funk—same as they were at census-time,' said the Colonel; 'and if we stampede them into the hills we'll never catch 'em, in the first place, and, in the second, they'll whoop off plundering till further orders. Wonder who the God-forsaken idiot is who is trying to vaccinate a Bhil. I knew trouble was coming. One good thing is that they'll only use local corps, and we can knock up something we'll call a campaign, and let them down easy. Fancy is not potting our best beaters because they don't want to be vaccinated! They're only crazy with fear.'

'Don't you think, sir,' said Chinn the next day, 'that perhaps you could give me a fortnight's shooting-leave?'

'Desertion in the face of the enemy, by Jove!' the Colonel laughed. 'I might, but I'd have to antedate it a little, because we're warned for service, as you might say. However, we'll assume that you applied for leave three days ago, and are now well on your way south.'

'I'd like to take Bukta with me.'

'Of course, yes. I think that will be the best plan. You have some kind of hereditary influence with the little chaps, and they may listen to you when a glimpse of our uniforms would drive them wild. You've never been in that part of the world before, have you? Take care they don't send you to your family vault in your youth and innocence. I believe you'll be all right if you can get 'em to listen to you.'

'I think so, sir; but if—if they should accidentally put an—make asses of 'emselves—they might, you know—I hope you'll represent that they were only frightened. There isn't an ounce of real vice in 'em, and I should never forgive myself if any one of—of my name get them into trouble.'

The Colonel nodded, but said nothing.

Chinn and Bukta departed at once. Bukta did not say that,

ever since the official vaccinator had been dragged into the hills by indignant Bhils, runner after runner had skulked up to the lines, entreating, with forehead in the dust, that Jan Chinn should come and explain this unknown horror that hung over his people.

The portent of the Clouded Tiger was now too clear. Let Jan Chinn comfort his own, for vain was the help of mortal man. Bukta toned down these beseechings to a simple request for Chinn's presence. Nothing would have pleased the old man better than a rough-and-tumble campaign against the Satpuras, whom he, as an 'unmixed' Bhil, despised; but he had a duty to all his nation as Jan Chinn's interpreter, and he devoutly believed that forty plagues would fall on his village if he tampered with that obligation. Besides, Jan Chinn knew all things, and he rode the Clouded Tiger.

They covered thirty miles a day on foot and pony, raising the blue wall-like line of the Satpuras as swiftly as might be. Bukta was very silent.

They began the stiff climb a little after noon, but it was near sunset ere they reached the stone platform clinging to the side of the rifted, jungle-covered hill, where Jan Chinn the First was laid, as he had desired, that he might overlook his people. All India is full of neglected graves that date from the beginning of the eighteenth century—tombs of forgotten Colonels of corps long since disbanded; mates of East Indiamen who went on shooting expeditions and never came back; factors, agents, writers, and ensigns of the Honourable the East India Company by hundreds and thousands and ten thousands. English folk forget quickly, but natives have long memories, and if a man have done good in his life it is remembered after his death. The weathered marble four-square tomb of Jan Chinn was hung about with wild flowers and nuts, packets of wax and honey, bottles of native spirits, and infamous cigars, with buffalo horns and plumes of dried grass. At one end was a rude clay image of a white man, in the old-fashioned top-hat, riding on a bloated tiger.

Bukta salaamed reverently as they approached. Chinn bared his head and began to pick out the blurred inscription. So far as he could read it ran thus—word for word, and letter for letter:—

To the Memory of John Chinn, Esq.
Late Collector of . . . .
. . . . without Bloodshed or . . . error of Authority
Employ. Only. . eans of Conciliat . . . and Confiden .
Accomplished the . . . tire Subjection . . .

A Lawless and Predatory Peop . . .
. . . . taching them to . . . . ish Government
by a Conque . . over . . . . Minds
The most perma . . . and rational Mode of Do, ini . .
. . . Governor-General and Counc . . . engal
have ordered thi . . . . erected
. . . arted this Life Aug. 19, 184 . Ag . . .

On the other side of the grave were ancient verses, also
very worn. As much as Chinn could decipher said:—

. . . . *the savage band*
Foresook their Haunts and b . . . . is Command
. . . . mended . . rals check a . . . st for spoil
And . s . ing Hamlets prove his gene . . . . toil
Humanit . . . survey . . . . . . ights restore . .
A nation . . ield . . subdued without a Sword.

For some little time he leaned on the tomb thinking of this
dead man of his own blood, and of the house in Devonshire;
then, nodding to the plains: 'Yes; it's a big work—all of it—
even my little share. He must have been worth knowing . . .
Bukta, where are my people?'

'Not here, Sahib. No man comes here except in full sun.
They wait above. Let us climb and see.'

But Chinn, remembering the first law of Oriental Diplomacy,
in an even voice answered: 'I have come this far only because
the Satpura folk are foolish, and dared not visit our lines. Now
bid them wait on me *here*. I am not a servant, but the master of
the Bhils.'

'I go—I go,' clucked the old man. Night was falling, and at
any moment Jan Chinn might whistle up his dreaded steed from
the darkening scrub.

Now for the first time in a long life Bukta disobeyed a lawful command and deserted his leader; for he did not come back, but pressed to the flat table-top of the hill, and called softly. Men stirred all about him—little trembling men with bows and arrows who had watched the two since noon.

'Where is he?' whispered one.

'At his own place. He bids you come,' said Bukta.

'Now?'

'Now.'

'Rather let him loose the Clouded Tiger upon us. We do not go.'

'Nor I, though I bore him in my arms when he was a child in this his life. Wait here till day.'

'But surely he will be angry.'

'He will be very angry, for he has nothing to eat. But he has said to me many times that the Bhils are his children. By sunlight I believe this, but—by moonlight I am not so sure. What folly have ye Satpura pigs compassed that ye should need him at all?'

'One came to us in the name of the Government with little ghost-knives and a magic calf, meaning to turn us into cattle by the cutting off of our arms. We were greatly afraid, but we did not kill the man. He is here, bound—a black man; and we think he comes from the West. He said it was an order to cut us all with knives—especially the women and the children. We did not hear that it was an order, so we were afraid, and kept to our hills. Some of our men have taken ponies and bullocks from the plains, and others pots and cloths and ear-rings.'

'Are any slain?'

'By our men? Not yet. But the young men are blown to and fro by many rumours like flames upon a hill. I sent runners asking for Jan Chinn lest worse should come to us. It was this fear that he foretold by the sign of the Clouded Tiger.'

'He says it is otherwise,' said Bukta, and repeated, with amplifications, all that young Chinn had told him at the conference of the wicker chair.

'Think you,' said the questioner, at last, 'that the Government will lay hands on us?'

'Not I,' Bukta rejoined. 'Jan Chinn will give an order, and

ye will obey. The rest is between the Government and Jan Chinn. I myself know something of the ghost-knives and the scratching. It is a charm against the Smallpox. But how it is done I cannot tell. Nor need that concern you.'

'If he stands by us and before the anger of the Government we will most strictly obey Jan Chinn, except—except we do not go down to that place to-night.'

They could hear young Chinn below them shouting for Bukta; but they cowered and sat still, expecting the Clouded Tiger. The tomb had been holy ground for nearly half a century. If Jan Chinn chose to sleep there, who had better right? But they would not come within eyeshot of the place till broad day.

At first Chinn was exceedingly angry, till it occurred to him that Bukta most probably had a reason (which, indeed, he had), and his own dignity might suffer if he yelled without answer. He propped himself against the foot of the grave, and, alternately dozing and smoking, came through the warm night proud that he was a lawful, legitimate, fever-proof Chinn.

He prepared his plan of action much as his grandfather would have done; and when Bukta appeared in the morning with a most liberal supply of food, said nothing of the overnight desertion. Bukta would have been relieved by an outburst of human anger; but Chinn finished his victuals leisurely, and a cheroot, ere he made any sign.

'They are very much afraid,' said Bukta, who was not too bold himself. 'It remains only to give orders. They say they will obey if thou wilt only stand between them and the Government.'

'That I know,' said Chinn, strolling slowly to the table-land. A few of the elder men stood in an irregular semicircle in an open glade; but the ruck of the people—women and children—were hidden in the thicket. They had no desire to face the first anger of Jan Chinn the First.

Seating himself on a fragment of split rock, he smoked his cheroot to the butt, hearing men breathe hard all about him. Then he cried, so suddenly that they jumped:—

'Bring the man that was bound!'

A scuffle and a cry were followed by the appearance of a Hindu vaccinator, quaking with fear, bound hand and foot, as the Bhils of old were accustomed to bind their human sacrifices.

He was pushed cautiously before his presence; but young Chinn did not look at him.

'I said—the man that *was* bound. Is it a jest to bring me one tied like a buffalo? Since when could the Bhil bind folk at his pleasure? Cut!'

Half-a-dozen hasty knives cut away the thongs, and the man crawled to Chinn, who pocketed his case of lancets and tubes of lymph. Then, sweeping the semi-circle with one comprehensive forefinger, and in the voice of compliment, he said, clearly and distinctly: 'Pigs!'

'Ai!' whispered Bukta. 'Now he speaks. Woe to foolish people!'

'I have come on foot from my house' (the assembly shuddered) 'to make clear a matter which any other than a Satpura Bhil would have seen with both eyes from a distance. Ye know the Smallpox, who pits and scars your children so that they look like waspcombs. It is an order of the Government that whoso is scratched on the arm with these little knives which I hold up is charmed against Her. All Sahibs are thus charmed, and very many Hindus. This is the mark of the charm. Look!'

He rolled back his sleeve to the armpit and showed the white scars of the vaccination-mark on the white skin. 'Come all, and look.'

A few daring spirits came up, and nodded their heads wisely. There was certainly a mark, and they knew well what other dread marks were hidden by the shirt. Merciful was Jan Chinn, that he had then and there proclaimed his godhead.

'Now all these things the man ye bound told you.'

'I did—a hundred times; but they answered with blows,' groaned the operator, chafing his wrists and ankles.

'But, being pigs, ye did not believe; and so came I here to save you, first from Smallpox, next from a great folly of fear, and lastly, it may be, from the rope and the jail. It is no gain to me; it is no pleasure to me; but for the sake of that one who is yonder, who made the Bhil a man'—he pointed down the hill—'I, who am of his blood, the son of his son, come to turn your people. And I speak the truth, as did Jan Chinn.'

The crowd murmured reverently, and men stole out of the thicket by twos and threes to join it. There was no anger in their god's face.

'These are my orders. (Heaven send they'll take 'em , but I seem to have impressed them so far!) I myself will stay among you while this man scratches your arms with knives, after the order of the Government. In three, or it may be five or seven, days, your arms will swell and itch and burn. That is the power of Smallpox fighting in your base blood against the orders of the Government. I will therefore stay among you till I see the Smallpox is conquered, and I will not go away till the men and the women and the little children show me upon their arms such marks as I have even now showed you. I bring with me two very good guns, and a man whose name is known among beasts and men. We will hunt together, I and he, and your young men and the others shall eat and lie still. This is my order.'

There was a long pause while victory hung in the balance. A white-haired old sinner, standing on one uneasy leg, piped up:—

'There are ponies and some few bullocks and other things for which we need a *kowl* [protection]. They were *not* taken in the way of trade.'

The battle was won, and Jan Chinn drew a breath of relief. The young Bhils had been raiding, but if taken swiftly all could be put right.

'I will write a *kowl* as soon as the ponies, the bullocks, and the other things are counted before me and sent back whence they came. But first we will put the Government mark on such as have not been visited by Smallpox.' In an undertone, to the vaccinator: 'If you show you are afraid you'll never see Poona again, my friend.'

'There is not sufficient ample supply of vaccine for all this population,' said the man. 'They destroyed the offeecial calf.'

'They won't know the difference. Scrape 'em all round, and give me a couple of lancets. I'll attend to the elders.'

The aged diplomat who had demanded protection was the first victim. He felt Chinn's hand, and dared not cry out. As soon as he was freed he dragged up a companion, and held him fast, and the crisis became, as it were, a child's sport; for the vaccinated chased the unvaccinated to treatment, vowing that all the tribe must suffer equally. The women shrieked, and the children ran howling; but Chinn laughed, and waved the pink-tipped lancet.

'It is an honour,' he cried. 'Tell them, Bukta, how great an honour it is that I myself should mark them. Nay, I cannot mark every one—the Hindu must also do his work—but I will touch all marks that he makes, so there will be an equal virtue in them. Thus do the Rajputs stick pigs. Ho, brother with one eye! Catch that girl and bring her to me. She need not run away yet, for she is not married, and I do not seek her in marriage. She will not come? Then she shall be shamed by her little brother, a fat boy, a bold boy. He puts out his arm like a soldier. Look! *He* does not flinch at the blood. Some day he shall be in my Regiment. And now, mother of many, we will lightly touch thee, for Smallpox has been before us here. It is a true thing, indeed, that this charm breaks the power of Mata. There will be no more pitted faces among the Satpuras, and so ye can ask many cows for each maid to be wed.'

And so on and so on—quick-poured showman's patter, sauced in the Bhil hunting proverbs and tales of their own brand of coarse humour—till the lancets were blunted and both operators worn out.

But, nature being the same the world over, the unvaccinated grew jealous of their marked comrades, and came near to blows about it. Then Chinn declared himself a court of justice, no longer a medical board, and made formal inquiry into the late robberies.

'We are the thieves of Mahadeo,' said the Bhils simply. 'it is our fate, and we were frightened. When we are frightened we always steal.'

Simply and directly as children, they gave in the tale of the plunder, all but two bullocks and some spirits that had gone a-missing (these Chinn promised to make good out of his own pocket), and ten ring-leaders were despatched to the lowlands with a wonderful document, written on the leaf of a notebook, and addressed to an Assistant District Superintendent of Police. There was warm calamity in that note, as Jan Chinn warned them, but anything was better than loss of liberty.

Armed with this protection, the repentant raiders went downhill. They had no desire whatever to meet Mr. Dundas

Fawne of the Police, aged twenty-two, and of cheerful countenance, nor did they wish to revisit the scene of their robberies. Steering a middle course, they ran into the camp of the one Government Chaplain allowed to various irregular corps through a district of some fifteen thousand square miles, and stood before him in a cloud of dust. He was by way of being a priest, they knew, and, what was more to the point, a good sportsman who paid his beaters generously.

When he read Chinn's note he laughed, which they deemed a lucky omen, till he called up a policeman, who tethered the ponies and the bullocks by the piled house-gear, and laid stern hands upon three of that smiling band of the thieves of Mahadeo. The Chaplain himself addressed them magisterially with a riding whip. That was painful, but Jan Chinn had prophesied it. They submitted, but would not give up the written protection, fearing the jail. On their way back they met Mr. D. Fawne, who had heard about the robberies, and was not pleased.

'Certainly,' said the eldest of the gang, when the second interview was at an end, 'certainly Jan Chinn's protection has saved us our liberty, but it is as though there were many beatings in one small piece of paper. Put it away.'

One climbed into a tree, and stuck the letter into a cleft forty feet from the ground, where it could do no harm. Warmed, sore, but happy, the ten returned to Jan Chinn next day, where he sat among uneasy Bhils, all looking at their right arms, and all bound under terror of their god's disfavour not to scratch.

'It was a good *kowl*,' said the leader. 'First the Chaplain, who laughed, took away our plunder, and beat three of us, as was promised. Next, we met Fawne Sahib, who frowned, and asked for the plunder. We spoke the truth, and so he beat us all, one after another, and called us chosen names. He then gave us these two bundles'—they set down a bottle of whisky and a box of cheroots—'and we came away. The *kowl* is left in a tree, because its virtue is that as soon as we show it to a Sahib we are beaten.'

'But for that *kowl*,' said Jan Chinn, sternly, 'ye would have been marching to jail with a policeman on either side. Ye come now to serve as beaters for me. These people are unhappy, and we will go hunting till they are well. To-night we will make a

130

feast.'

It is written in the chronicles of the Satpura Bhils, together with many other matters not fit for print, that through five days, after the day that he had put his mark upon them, Jan Chinn the First hunted for his people; and on five nights of those days the tribe was gloriously and entirely drunk. Jan Chinn bought country spirits of an awful strength, and slew wild pig and deer beyond counting, so that if any fell sick they might have two good reasons.

Between head- and stomach-aches they found no time to think of their arms, but followed Jan Chinn obediently through the jungles, and with each day's returning confidence men, women, and children stole away to their villages as the little army passed by. They carried news that it was good and right to be scratched with ghost-knives; that Jan Chinn was indeed reincarnated as a god of free food and drink, and that of all nations the Satpura Bhils stood first in his favour, if they would only refrain from scratching. Henceforward that kindly deity would be connected in their minds with great gorgings and the vaccine and lancets of a paternal Government.

'And to-morrow I go back to my home,' said Jan Chinn to his faithful few, whom neither spirits, overeating, nor swollen glands could conquer. It is hard for children and savages to behave reverently at all times to the idols of their make-belief, and they had frolicked excessively with Jan Chinn. But the reference to his home cast a gloom on the people.

'And the Sahib will not come again?' said he who had been vaccinated first.

'That is to be seen,' answered Chinn warily.

'Nay, but come as a white man—come as a young man whom we know and love; for; as thou alone knowest, we are a weak people. If we again saw thy—thy horse—.' They were picking up their courage.

'I have no horse. I came on foot—with Bukta, yonder. What is this?'

'Thou knowest—the Thing which thou hast chosen for night-horse.' The little men squirmed in fear and awe.

'Night-horse? Bukta, what is this last tale of children?'

Bukta had been a silent leader in Chinn's presence since the night of his desertion, and was grateful for a chance-flung question

'They know, Sahib,' he whispered. 'It is the Clouded Tiger. That which comes from the place where thou didst once sleep. It is thy horse—as it has been these three generations.'

'My horse! That was a dream of the Bhils.'

'It is no dream. Do dreams leave the tracks of broad pugs on earth? Why make two faces before thy people? They know of the night-ridings, and they—and they—.'

'Are afraid, and would have them cease.'

Bukta nodded. 'If thou hast no further need of him. He is thy horse.'

'The thing leaves a trail, then?' said Chinn.

'We have seen it. It is like a village road under the tomb.'

'Can ye find and follow it for me?'

'By daylight—if one comes with us, and, above all, stands near by.'

'I will stand close, and we will see to it that Jan Chinn does not rise any more.'

The Bhils shouted the last words again and again.

From Chinn's point of view the stalk was nothing more than an ordinary one—downhill, through split and crannied rocks, unsafe, perhaps, if a man did not keep his wits by him, but no worse than twenty others he had undertaken. Yet his men—they refused absolutely to beat, and would only trail—dripped sweat at every move. They showed the marks of enormous pugs that ran, always downhill, to a few hundred feet below Jan Chinn's tomb, and disappeared in a narrow-mouthed cave. It was an insolently open road, a domestic highway, beaten without thought of concealment.

'The beggar might be paying rents and taxes,' Chinn muttered ere he asked whether his friend's taste ran to cattle or man.

'Cattle,' was the answer. 'Two heifers a week. We drive them for him at the foot of the hill. It is his custom. If we did not, he might seek is.'

'Blackmail and piracy,' said Chinn. 'I can't say I fancy going into that cave after him. What's to be done?'

The Bhils fell back as Chinn lodged himself behind a rock

with his rifle ready. Tigers, he knew, were shy beasts, but one who had been long cattle-fed in this sumptuous style might prove overbold.

'He speaks!' some one whispered from the rear. 'He knows, too.'

'Well, of *all* the infernal cheek!' said Chinn. There was an angry growl from the cave—a direct challenge.

'Come out, then,' Chinn shouted. 'Come out of that! Let's have a look at you.'

The brute knew well enough that there was some connection between brown nude Bhils and his weekly allowance; but the white helmet in the sunlight annoyed him, and he did not approve of the voice that broke his rest. Lazily as a gorged snake he dragged himself out of the cave, and stood yawning and blinking at the entrance. The sunlight fell upon his flat right side, and Chinn wondered. Never had he seen a tiger marked after this fashion. Except for his head, which was staringly barred, he was dappled—not striped, but dappled like a child's rocking-horse in rich shades of smoky black on red gold. That portion of his belly and throat which should have been white was orange, and his tail and paws were black.

He looked leisurely for some ten seconds, and then deliberately lowered his head, his chin dropped and drawn in, staring intently at the man. The effect of this was to throw forward the round arch of his skull, with two broad bands across it, while below the bands glared the unwinking eyes; so that, head-on, as he stood, he showed something like a diabolically scowling pantomime-mask. It was a piece of natural mesmerism that he had practised many times on his quarry, and though Chinn was by no means a terrified heifer, he stood for a while, held by the extraordinary oddity of the attack. The head—the body seemed to have been packed away behind it—the ferocious, skull-like head, crept nearer, to the switching of an angry tail-tip in the grass. Left and right the Bhils had scattered to let Jan Chinn subdue his own horse.

'My word!' he thought. 'He's trying to frighten me!' and fired between the saucer-like eyes, leaping aside upon the shot.

A big coughing mass, reeking of carrion, bounded past him up the hill, and he followed directly. The tiger made no attempt to turn into the jungle; he was hunting for sight and breath—nose up, mouth open, the tremendous fore-legs scattering the gravel in spurts.

'Scuppered!' said John Chinn, watching the flight. 'Now if he was a partridge he'd tower. Lungs must be full of blood.'

The brute had jerked himself over a boulder and fallen out of sight on the other side. John Chinn looked over with a ready barrel. But the red trail led straight as an arrow even to his grandfather's tomb, and there, among the smashed spirit-bottles and fragments of the mud image, the life left with a flurry and a grunt.

'If my worthy ancestor could see that,' said John Chinn, 'he'd have been proud of me. Eyes, lower jaw, and lungs. A very nice shot.' He whistled for Bukta as he drew the tape over the stiffening bulk.

'Ten—six—eight—by Jove! It's nearly eleven—call it eleven. Fore-arm, twenty-four—five—seven and a half. A short tail, too; three feet one. But *what* a skin! Oh, Bukta! Bukta! The men with the knives swiftly.'

'Is he beyond question dead?' said an awe-stricken voice behind a rock.

'That was not the way I killed my first tiger,' said Chinn. 'I did not think that Bukta would run. I had no second gun.'

'It—it is the Clouded Tiger,' said Bukta, unheeding the taunt. 'He is dead.'

Whether all the Bhils, vaccinated and unvaccinated, of the Satpuras had lain by to see the kill, Chinn could not say; but the whole hill's flank rustled with little men, shouting, singing, and stamping. And yet, till he had made the first cut in the splendid skin, not a man would take a knife; and, when the shadows fell, they ran from the red-stained tomb, and no persuasion would bring them back till dawn. So Chinn spent a second night in the open, guarding the carcass from jackals, and thinking about his ancestor.

He returned to the lowlands to the triumphal chant of an escorting army three hundred strong, the Mahratta vaccinator close at his elbow, and the rudely dried skin a trophy before him. When that army suddenly and noiselessly disappeared, as do quail in high corn, he argued he was near civilisation, and a turn in the road brought him upon the camp of a wing of his own corps. He left the skin on a cart-tail for the world to see, and sought the Colonel.

'They're perfectly right,' he explained earnestly. 'There isn't an ounce of vice in 'em. They were only frightened. I've vaccinated the whole boiling, and they like it awfully. What are—what are we doing here, sir?'

'That's what I'm trying to find out,' said the Colonel. 'I don't know yet whether we're a piece of a brigade or a police force. However, I think we'll call ourselves a police force. How did you manage to get a Bhil vaccinated?'

'Well, sir,' said Chinn, 'I've been thinking it over, and, as far as I can make out, I've got a sort of hereditary influence over 'em.'

'So I know, or I wouldn't have sent you; but *what* exactly?'

'It's rather rummy. It seems, from what I can make out, that I'm my grandfather reincarnated, and I've been disturbing the peace of the country by riding a pad-tiger of nights. If I hadn't done that, I don't think they'd have objected to the vaccination; but the two together were more than they could stand. And so, sir, I've vaccinated 'em, and shot my tiger-horse as a sort o' proof of good faith. You never saw such a skin in your life.'

The Colonel tugged his moustache thoughtfully. 'Now, how the deuce,' said he, 'am I to include that in my report?'

Indeed, the official version of the Bhils' anti-vaccination stampede said nothing about Lieutenant John Chinn, his godship. But Bukta knew, and the corps knew, and every Bhil in the Satpura hills knew.

And now Bukta is zealous that John Chinn shall swiftly be wedded and impart his powers to a son; for if the Chinn succession fails, and the little Bhils are left to their own imaginings, there will be fresh trouble in the Satpuras.

CONSEQUENCES

Rosicrucial subtleties
In the Orient had rise;
Ye may find their teachers still
Under Jacatala's Hill.
Seek ye Bombast Paracelsus,
Read what Flood the Seeker tells us
Of the Dominant that runs
Through the Cycles of the Suns—
Read my story last, and see
Luna at her apogee.

THERE ARE YEARLY appointments, and two-yearly appointments, and five-yearly appointments to Simla, and there are, or used to be, permanent appointments, whereon you stayed up for the term of your natural life, and secured red cheeks and a nice income. Of course, you could descend in the cold weather; for Simla is rather dull then.

Tarrion came from goodness knows where—all away and away in some forsaken part of Central India, where they call Pachmari a Sanitarium, and drive behind trotting-bullocks, I believe. He belonged to a Regiment; but what he really wanted to do was to escape from his Regiment and live in Simla for ever and ever. He had no preference for anything in particular, beyond a good horse and a nice partner. He thought he could do everything well; which is a beautiful belief when you hold it with all your heart. He was clever in many ways, and good to look at, and always made people round him comfortable—even in Central India.

So he went up to Simla, and, because he was clever and amusing, he gravitated naturally to Mrs. Hauksbee, who could forgive everything but stupidity. Once he did her great service by changing the date on an invitation-card for a big dance which Mrs. Hauksbee wished to attend, but couldn't, because she had quarrelled with the A.D.C., who took care, being a mean man, to invite her to a small dance on the 6th instead of the big Ball of the 26th. It was a very clever piece of forgery; and when Mrs. Hauksbee showed the A.D.C. her invitation-card, and chaffed him mildly for not better managing his vendettas, he really thought that he had made a mistake; and—which was wise—realised that it was no use to fight with Mrs. Hauksbee. She was grateful to Tarrion, and asked what she could do for him. He said simply, 'I'm a Freelance up here on leave, on the look-out for what I can loot. I haven't a square inch of interest in all Simla. My name isn't known to any man with an appointment in his gift, and I want an appointment—a good, sound one. I believe you can do anything you turn yourself to. Will you help me?' Mrs. Hauksbee thought for a minute, and passed the lash of her riding-whip through her lips, as was her custom when thinking. Then her eyes sparkled and she said, 'I will'; and she shook hands on it. Tarrion, having perfect confidence in this great woman, took no further thought of the business at all, except to wonder what sort of appointment he would win.

Mrs. Hauksbee began calculating the prices of all the Heads of Departments and Members of Council she knew, and the more she thought the more she laughed, because her heart was in the game and it amused her. Then she took a Civil List and ran over a few of the appointments. (There are some beautiful appointments in the Civil List.) Eventually, she decided that, though Tarrion was too good for the Political Department, she had better begin by trying to place him there. Her own plans to this end do not matter in the least, for Luck or Fate played into her hands, and she had nothing to do but to watch the course of events and take the credit of them.

All Viceroys, when they first come out, pass through the Diplomatic Secrecy craze. It wears off in time; but they all catch it in the beginning, because they are new to the country. This particular Viceroy who was suffering from the complaint just then—this was a long time ago, before Lord Dufferin ever came from Canada, or Lord Ripon from the bosom of the English Church—had it very badly; and the result was that men who were new to keeping official secrets went about looking unhappy; and the Viceroy plumed himself on the way in which he had instilled notions of reticence into his staff.

Now, the Supreme Government have a careless custom of committing what they do to printed papers. These papers deal with all sorts of things—from the payment of Rs.200 to a 'Secret Service' native, up to rebukes administered to Vakils and Motamids of Native States, and rather brusque letters to Native Princes, telling them to put their houses in order, to refrain from kidnapping women, or filling offenders with pounded red pepper, and eccentricities of that kind. Of course, these things could never be made public, because Native Princes never err officially, and their States are officially as well administered as Our territories. Also, the private allowances to various queer people are not exactly matters to put into newspapers, though they give quaint reading sometimes. When the Supreme Government is at Simla these papers are presented there, and go round to the people who ought to see them in office-boxes or by post. The principle of secrecy was to that Viceroy quite as important as the practice; and he held that a benevolent despotism like Ours should never allow even little things, such as appointments of subordinate clerks, to leak out till the proper time. He was always remarkable for his principles.

There was a very important batch of papers in preparation at that time. It had to travel from one end of Simla to the other by hand. It was not put into an official envelop, but a large, square, pale pink one; the matter being in MS. on soft crinkly paper. It was addressed to 'The Head Clerk, etc. etc.'. Now, between 'The Head Clerk, etc. etc.' and 'Mrs. Hauksbee' and a flourish, is no very great difference, if the address be written in a very bad hand, as this was. The orderly who took the envelope was not more of an idiot than most orderlies. He merely forgot where this most unofficial cover was to be delivered, and so asked the first Englishman he met, who happened to be a man riding down to Annandale in a great hurry. The Englishman hardly looked at it, said, 'Mrs. Hauksbee', and went on. So did the orderly, because the letter was the last in stock and he wanted to get his work over. There was no book to sign; he thrust the letter into Mrs. Hauksbee's bearer's hands and went off to smoke with a friend. Mrs. Hauksbee was expecting some cut-out pattern things in a flimsy paper from a friend. As soon as she got the big square packet, therefore, she said, 'Oh, the dear creature!' and tore it open with a paper-knife, and all the MS. enclosures tumbled out on the floor.

Mrs. Hauksbee began reading. I have said the batch was rather important. That is quite enough for you to know. It referred to some correspondence, two measures, a peremptory order to a native chief, and two dozen other things. Mrs. Hauksbee gasped as she read, for the first glimpse of the naked machinery of the Great Indian Government, stripped of its casings, and lacquer, and paint, and guard rails, impresses even the most stupid man. And Mrs. Hauksbee was a clever woman. She was a little afraid at first, and felt as if she had taken hold of a lightning-flash by the tail, and did not quite know what to do with it. There were remarks and initials at the side of the papers; and some of the remarks were rather more severe than the papers. The initials belonged to men who are all dead or gone now; but they were great in their day. Mrs. Hauksbee read on and thought calmly as she read. Then the value of her trove struck her, and she cast about for the best method of using it. Then Tarrion dropped in, and they read through all the papers together, and Tarrion, not knowing how she had come by them, vowed that Mrs. Hauksbee was the greatest woman on earth. Which I believe was true or nearly so.

'The honest course is always the best,' said Tarrion, after an hour and a half of study and conversation. 'All things considered, the Intelligence Branch is about my form. Either that or the Foreign Office. I go to lay siege to the High Gods in their Temples.'

He did not seek a little man, or a little big man, or a weak Head of a strong Department, but he called on the biggest and strongest man that the Government owned, and explained that he wanted an appointment at Simla on a good salary. The compound insolence of this amused the Strong Man, and, as he had nothing to do for the moment, he listened to the proposals of the audacious Tarrion. 'You have, I presume, some special qualifications, besides the gift of self-assertion, for the claims you put forward?' said the Strong Man. 'That, sir,' said Tarrion, 'is for you to judge.' Then he began, for he had a good memory, quoting a few of the more important notes in the papers—slowly and one by one as a man drops chlorodyne into a glass. When he had reached the peremptory order—and it was a very peremptory order—the Strong Man was troubled. Tarrion wound up: 'And I fancy that special knowledge of this kind is at least as valuable for, let us say, a berth in the Foreign Office, as the fact of being the nephew of a distinguished officer's wife.' That hit the Strong Man hard, for the last appointment to the Foreign Office had been by black favour, and he knew it.

'I'll see what I can do for you,' said the Strong Man.

'Many thanks,' said Tarrion. Then he left, and the Strong Man departed to see how the appointment was to be blocked.

Followed a pause of eleven days; with thunders and lightnings and much telegraphing. The appointment was not a very important one, carrying only between Rs.500 and Rs.700 a month; but, as the Viceroy said, it was the principle of diplomatic secrecy that had to be maintained, and it was more than likely that a boy so well supplied with special information would be worth translating. So they translated Tarrion. They must have suspected him, though he protested that his information was due to singular talents of his own. Now, much of this story, including the after-history of the missing envelope, you must fill in for yourself, because there are reasons why it cannot be written. If you do not know about things Up Above, you won't understand how to fill in, and you will say it is impossible.

What the Viceroy said when Tarrion was introduced to him was: 'This is the boy who "rushed" the Government of India, is it? Recollect, sir, that is not done twice.' So he must have known something.

What Tarrion said when he saw his appointment gazetted was: 'If Mrs. Hauksbee were twenty years younger, and I her husband, I should be Viceroy of India in fifteen years.'

What Mrs. Hauksbee said when Tarrion thanked her, almost with tears in his eyes, was first: 'I told you so!' and next, to herself: 'What fools men are!'

THE FINANCES OF THE GODS

THE EVENING MEAL was ended in Dhunni Bhagat's *Chubara*, and the old priests were smoking or counting their beads. A little naked child pattered in, with its mouth wide open, a handful of marigold flowers in one hand, and a lump of conserved tobacco in the other. It tried to kneel and make obeisance to Gobind, but it was so fat that it fell forward on its shaven head, and rolled on its side, kicking and gasping, while the marigold flowers tumbled one way and the tobacco the other. Gobind laughed, set it up again, and blessed the marigold flowers as he received the tobacco.

'From my father,' said the child. 'He has the fever, and cannot come. Wilt thou pray for him, father?'

'Surely, littlest; but the smoke is on the ground, and the night-chill is in the air, and it is not good to go abroad naked in the autumn.'

'I have no clothes,' said the child, 'and all to-day I have been carrying cow-dung cakes to the bazar. It was very hot, and I am very tired.' It shivered a little, for the twilight was cool.

Gobind lifted an arm under his vast tattered quilt of many colours, and made an inviting little nest by his side. The child crept in, and Gobind filled his brass-studded leather water-pipe with the new tobacco. When I came to the *Chubara* the shaven head with the tuft atop and the beady black eyes looked out of the folds of the quilt as a squirrel looks from his nest, and Gobind was smiling while the child played with his beard.

I would have said something friendly, but remembered in time that if the child fell ill afterwards I should be credited with the Evil Eye, and that is a horrible possession.

'Sit still, Thumbling,' I said, as it made to get up and run away. 'Where is thy slate, and why has the teacher let such an evil character loose on the streets when there are no police to protect us weaklings? In which ward dost thou try to break thy neck with flying kites from the house-tops?'

'Nay, Sahib, nay,' said the child, burrowing its face into Gobind's beard, and twisting uneasily. 'There was a holiday to-day among the schools, and I do not always fly kites. I play ker-li-kit like the rest.'

Cricket is the national game among the schoolboys of the Punjab, from the naked hedge-school children, who use an old kerosene-tin for wicket, to the B.A.'s of the University, who compete for the Championship belt.

'Thou play kerlikit! Thou art half the height of the bat!' I said.

The child nodded resolutely. 'Yea, I *do* play. *Perlay-ball. Ow-at*! *Ran, ran, ran*! I know it all.'

'But thou must not forget with all this to pray to the Gods according to custom,' said Gobind, who did not altogether approve of cricket and Western innovations.

'I do not forget,' said the child in a hushed voice.

'Also to give reverence to thy teacher, and'—Gobind's voice softened—'to abstain from pulling holy men by the beard, little badling. Eh, eh, eh?'

The child's face was altogether hidden in the great white beard, and it began to whimper till Gobind soothed it as children are soothed all the world over, with the promise of a story.

'I did not think to frighten thee, senseless little one. Look up! Am I angry? *Arre, arre, arre*! Shall I weep too, and of our tears make a great pond and drown us both, and then thy father will never get well, lacking thee to pull his beard? Peace, peace, and I will tell thee of the Gods. Thou hast heard many tales?'

'Very many, father.'

'Now, this is a new one which thou has not heard. Long and long ago when the Gods walked with men as they do to-day, but that we have not faith to see, Shiv, the greatest of Gods, and Parbati his wife, were walking in the garden of a temple.'

'Which temple? That in the Nandgaon ward?' said the child.

'Nay, very far away. May be at Trimbak or Hurdwar, whither thou must make pilgrimage when thou art a man. Now, there was sitting in the garden under the jujube-trees a mendicant that had worshipped Shiv for forty years, and he lived on the offerings of the pious, and meditated holiness night and day.'

'O father, was it thou?' said the child, looking up with large eyes.

'Nay, I have said it was long ago, and, moreover, this mendicant was married.'

'Did they put him on a horse with flowers on his head, and forbid him to go to sleep all night long? Thus the child did to me when they made my wedding,' said the child, who had been married a few months before.

'And what didst thou do?' said I.

'I wept, and they called me evil names, and then I smote *her*, and we wept together.'

'Thus did not the mendicant,' said Gobind; 'for he was a holy man, and very poor. Parbati perceived him sitting naked by the temple steps where all went up and down, and she said to Shiv, "What shall men think of the Gods when the Gods thus scorn their worshippers? For forty years yonder man has prayed to us, and yet there be only a few grains of rice and some broken cowries before him after all. Men's hearts will be hardened by this thing." And Shiv said, "It shall be looked to," and so he called to the temple which was the temple of his son Ganesh of the elephant head, saying, "Son, there is a mendicant without who is very poor. What wilt thou do for him?" Then the great elephant-headed One awoke in the dark and answered, "In three days, if it be thy will, he shall have one lakh rupees." Then Shiv and Parbati went away.

'But there was a money-lender in the garden hidden among the marigolds'—the child looked at the ball of crumpled blossoms in its hands—'ay, among the yellow marigolds, and he heard the Gods talking. He was a covetous man, and of a black heart, and he desired that lakh of rupees for himself. So he went to the mendicant and said, "O brother, how much do the pious give thee daily?" The mendicant said, "I cannot tell. Sometimes a little rice, sometimes a little pulse, and a few cowries and, it has been, pickled mangoes, and dried fish".'

'That is good,' said the child, smacking its lips.

'Then said the money-lender, "Because I have long watched thee, and learned to love thee and thy patience, I will give thee now five rupees for all thy earnings of the three days to come. There is only a bond to sign on the matter." But the mendicant said, "Thou art mad. In two months I do not receive the worth of five rupees," and he told the thing to his wife that evening. She, being a woman, said, "When did a money-lender ever make a bad bargain? The wolf runs through the corn for the sake of the fat deer. Our fate is in the hands of the Gods. Pledge it not even for three days."

'So the mendicant returned to the money-lender, and would not sell. Then the wicked man sat all day before him offering him more and more for those three days' earnings. First, ten, fifty, and a hundred rupees; and then, for he did not know when the Gods would pour down their gifts, rupees by the thousand, till he had offered half a lakh rupees. Upon this sum the mendicant's wife shifted her counsel, and the mendicant signed the bond, and the money was paid in silver; great white bullocks bringing it by the cartload. But saving only all that money, the mendicant received nothing from the Gods at all, and the heart of the money-lender was uneasy on account of expectation. Therefore at noon of the third day the money-lender went into the temple to spy upon the councils of the Gods, and to learn in what manner the gift might arrive. Even as he was making his prayers, a crack between the stones of the floor gaped, and, closing, caught him by the heel. Then he heard the Gods walking in the temple in the darkness of the columns, and Shiv called to his son Ganesh, saying, "Son, what hast thou done in regard to the lakh of rupees for the mendicant?" And Ganesh woke, for the money-lender heard the dry rustle of his trunk uncoiling, and he answered, "Father, one-half of the money has been paid, and the debtor for the other half I hold here fast by the heel".'

The child bubbled with laughter. 'And the money-lender paid the mendicant?' it said.

'Surely, for he whom Gods hold by the heel must pay to the uttermost. The money was paid at evening, all silver, in great carts, and thus Ganesh did his work.'

'Nathu! Ohe, Nathu!'

A woman was calling in the dusk by the door of the courtyard.

The child began to wriggle. 'That is my mother,' it said.

'Go then, littlest,' answered Gobind; 'but stay a moment.'

He ripped a generous yard from his patchwork-quilt, put it over the child's shoulders, and the child ran away.

WILLIAM THE CONQUEROR

PART 1

I have done one braver thing
Than all the Worthies did;
And yet a braver thence doth spring,
Which is, to keep that hid.

'IS IT OFFICIALLY declared yet?'

'They've gone as far as to admit extreme local scarcity, and they've started relief-work in one or two districts, the paper says.'

'That means it will be declared as soon as they can make sure of the men and the rolling-stock. Shouldn't wonder if it were as bad as the Big Famine.'

'Can't be,' said Scott, turning a little in the long cane chair. 'We've had fifteen-anna crops in the north, and Bombay and Bengal report more than they know what to do with. They'll be able to check it before it gets out of hand. It will only be local.'

Martyn picked up the *Pioneer* from the table, read through the telegrams once more, and put up his feet on the chair-rests. It was a hot, dark, breathless evening, heavy with the smell of the newly-watered Mall. The flowers in the Club gardens were dead and black on their stalks, the little lotus-pond was a circle of caked mud, and the tamarisk-trees were white with the dust of days. Most of the men were at the bandstand in the public gardens—from the Club veranda you could hear the native Police band hammering stale waltzes—or on the polo-ground or in the high-walled fives-court, hotter than a Dutch oven. Half-a-dozen grooms, squatted at the heads of their ponies, waited their masters' return. From time to time a man would ride at a foot-pace into the Club compound, and listlessly loaf over to the whitewashed barracks beside the main building. These were supposed to be chambers. Men lived in them, meeting the same faces night after night at dinner, and drawing out their office work till the latest possible hour, that they might escape that doleful company.

'What are you going to do?' said Martyn, with a yawn. 'Let's have a swim before dinner.'

'Water's hot,' said Scott. 'I was at the bath to-day.'

'Play you a game o' billiards—fifty up.'

'It's a hundred and five in the hall now. Sit still and don't be so abominably energetic.'

A grunting camel swung up to the porch, his badged and belted rider fumbling a leather pouch.

'*Kubber-kargaz—ki—yektraa,*' the man whined, handing down the newspaper extra—a slip printed on one side only, and damp from the press. It was pinned on the green-baize board, between notices of ponies for sale and fox-terriers missing.

Martyn rose lazily, read it, and whistled. 'It's declared!' he cried. 'One, two, three—eight Districts go under the operations of the Famine Code *ek dum*. They've put Jimmy Hawkins in charge.'

'Good business!' said Scott, with the first sign of interest he had shown. 'When in doubt hire a Punjabi. I worked under Jimmy when I first came out and he belonged to the Punjab. He has more *bundobust* than most men.'

'Jimmy is a Jubliee Knight now,' said Martyn. 'He was a good chap, even though he is a thrice-born Civilian and went to the Benighted Presidency. What unholy names these Madras Districts rejoice in—all *ungas* or *pillays* or *polliums*.'

A dog-cart drove up, and a man entered, mopping his head. He was editor of the one daily paper at the capital of a Province of twenty-five million natives and a few hundred white men, and as his staff was limited to himself and one assistant, his office hours ran variously from ten to twenty a day.

'Hi, Raines; you're supposed to know everything,' said Martyn, stopping him. 'How's this Madras "scarcity" going to turn out?'

'No one knows yet. There's a message as long as your arm

147

coming in on the telegraph. I've left my cub to fill it out. Madras has owned she can't manage it alone, and Jimmy Arbuthnot's warned to hold himself in readiness.'

' "Badger" Arbuthnot?'

'The Peshawur chap. Yes. And the *Pi* says Ellis and Clay have been moved from the North-West already, and they've taken half-a-dozen Bombay men, too. It's *pukka* famine, by the looks of it.'

'They're nearer the scene of action than we are; but if it comes to indenting on the Punjab this early, there's more in this than meets the eye,' said Martyn.

'Here to-day and gone to-morrow. Didn't come to stay for ever,' said Scott, dropping one of Marryat's novels, and rising to his feet. 'Martyn, your sister's waiting for you.'

A rough grey horse was backing and shifting at the edge of the veranda, where the light of a kerosene lamp fell on a brown calico habit and a white face under a grey hat.

'Right-o!' said Martyn. 'I'm ready. Better come and dine with us if you've nothing to do, Scott. William, is there any dinner in the house?'

'I'll go home first and see,' was the rider's answer. 'You can drive him over—at eight, remember.'

Scott moved leisurely to his room, and changed into the evening-dress of the season and the country; spotless white linen from head to foot, with a broad silk cummerbund. Dinner at the Martyns' was a decided improvement on the goat-mutton, twiney-tough fowl, and tinned entrees of the club. But it was a great pity Martyn could not afford to send his sister to the Hills for the hot weather. As an Acting District Superintendent of Police, Martyn drew the magnificent pay of six hundred depreciated silver rupees a month, and his little four-roomed bungalow said just as much. There were the usual blue-and-white striped jail-made rugs on the uneven floor; the usual glass-studded Amritzar *phulkaris* draped to mails driven into the flaking whitewash of the walls; the usual half-dozen chairs that did not match, picked up at sales of dead men's effects; and the usual streaks of black grease where the leather punkah-thong ran through the wall. It was as though everything had been unpacked the night before to be repacked next morning. Not a door in the house was true on its hinges. The little windows, fifteen feet up, were darkened with wasp-nests, and lizards hunted flies between the beams of the wood-ceiled roof. But all this was part of Scott's life. Thus did people live who had such an income; and in a land where each man's pay, age, and position are printed in a book, that all may read, it is hardly worth while to play at pretences in word of deed. Scott counted eight years' service in the Irrigation Department, and drew eight hundred rupees a month, on the understanding that if he served the State faithfully for another twenty-two years he could retire on a pension of some four hundred rupees a month. His working life, which had been spent chiefly under canvas or in temporary shelters where a man could sleep, eat, and write letters, was bound up with the opening and guarding of irrigation canals, the handling of two or three thousand workmen of all castes and creeds, and the payment of vast sums of coined silver. He had finished that spring, not without credit, the last section of the great Mosuhl Canal, and—much against his will, for he hated office work—had been sent in to serve during the hot weather on the accounts and supply side of the Department, with sole charge of the sweltering sub-office at the capital of the Province. Martyn knew this; William, his sister, knew it; and everybody knew it.

Scott knew, too, as well as the rest of the world, that Miss Martyn had come out to India four years before, to keep house for her brother, who, as every one, again, knew, had borrowed money to pay for her passage, and that she ought, as all the world said, to have married long ago. Instead of this, she had refused some half-a-dozen subalterns, a civilian twenty years her senior, one Major, and a man in the Indian Medical Department. This, too, was common property. She had 'stayed down three hot weathers', as the saying is, because her brother was in debt and could not afford the expense of her keep at even a cheap hill-station. Therefore her face was white as bone, and in the centre of her forehead was a big silvery scar about the size of a shilling—the mark of a Delhi sore, which is the same as a 'Bagdad date'. This comes from drinking bad water, and slowly eats into the flesh till it is ripe enough to be burned out with acids.

None the less William had enjoyed herself hugely in her four years. Twice she had been nearly drowned while fording a river on horseback; once she had run away with on a camel; had witnessed a midnight attack of thieves on her brother's camp; had seen justice administered, with long sticks, in the open under trees; could speak Urdu and even rough Punjabi with a fluency that was envied by her seniors; had altogether fallen out of the habit of writing to her aunts in England, or cutting the pages of the English magazines; had been through a very bad cholera year, seeing sights unfit to be told: and had wound up her experience by six weeks of typhoid fever, during which her head had been shaved; and hoped to keep her twenty-third birthday that September. It is conceivable that her aunts would not have approved of a girl who never set foot on the ground if a horse were within hail; who rode to dances with a shawl thrown over her skirt; who wore her hair cropped and curling all over her head; who answered indifferently to the name of William or Bill; whose speech was heavy with the flowers of the vernacular; who could act in amateur theatricals, play on the banjo, rule eight servants and two horses, their accounts and their diseases, and look men slowly and deliberately between the eyes—yea, after they had proposed to her and had been rejected.

'I like men who do things,' she had confided to a man in the Educational Department, who was teaching the sons of cloth merchants and dyers the beauty of Wordsworth's "Excursion" in annotated cram-books; and when he grew poetical, William explained that she 'didn't understand poetry very much; it made her head ache,' and another broken heart took refuge at the Club. But it was all William's fault. She delighted in hearing men talk of their own work, and that is the most fatal way of bringing a man to your feet.

Scott had known her more or less for some three years, meeting her, as a rule, under canvas when his camp and her brother's joined for a day on the edge of the Indian Desert. He had danced with her several times at the big Christmas gatherings, when as many as five hundred white people came into the Station; and he had always a great respect for her housekeeping and her dinners.

She looked more like a boy than ever when, after their meal, she sat, one foot tucked under her, on the leather camp-sofa, rolling cigarettes for her brother, her low forehead puckered beneath the dark curls as she twiddled the papers. She stuck out her rounded chin when the tobacco stayed in place, and, with a gesture as true as a schoolboy's throwing a stone, tossed the finished article across the room to Martyn, who caught it with one hand, and continued his talk with Scott. It was all 'shop',— canals and the policing of canals; the sins of villagers who stole more water than they had paid for, and the grosser sin of native constables who connived at the thefts; of the transplanting bodily of villages to newly-irrigated ground, and of the coming fight with the desert in the south when the Provincial funds should warrant the opening of the long-surveyed Luni Protective Canal System. And Scott spoke openly of his great desire to be put on one particular section of the work where he knew the land and the people, and Martyn sighed for a billet in the Himalayan foot-hills, and spoke his mind of his superiors, and William rolled cigarettes and said nothing, but smiled gravely on her brother because he was happy.

At ten Scott's horse came to the door, and the evening was ended.

The lights of the two low bungalows in which the daily paper was printed showed bright across the road. It was too early to try to find sleep, and Scott drifted over to the editor. Raines, stripped to the waist like a sailor at a gun, lay in a long chair, waiting for night telegrams. He had a theory that if a man did not stay by his work all day and most of the night he laid himself open to fever; so he ate and slept among his files.

'Can you do it?' he said drowsily. 'I didn't mean to bring you over.'

'About what? I've been dining at the Martyns'.'

'The famine, of course. Martyn's warned for it, too. They're taking men where they can find 'em. I sent a note to you at the Club just now, asking if you could do us a letter once a week from the south—between two and three columns, say. Nothing sensational, of course, but just plain facts about who is doing what, and so forth. Our regular rates—ten rupees a column.'

'Sorry, but it's out of my line,' Scott answered, staring absently at a map of India on the wall. 'It's rough on Martyn—

very. Wonder what he'll do with his sister. Wonder what the deuce they'll do with me? I've no famine experience. This is the first I've heard of it. *Am* I ordered?'

'Oh, yes. Here's the wire. They'll put you on relief-works,' Raines went on, 'with a horde of Madrassis dying like flies; one native apothecary and half a pint of cholera-mixture among the ten thousand of you. It comes of your being idle for the moment. Every man who isn't doing two men's work seems to have been called upon. Hawkins evidently believes in Punjabis. It's going to be quite as bad as anything they have had in the last ten years.'

'It's all in the day's work, worse luck. I suppose I shall get my orders officially some time to-morrow. I'm glad I happened to drop in. Better go and pack my kit now. Who relieves me here—do you know?'

Raines turned over a sheaf of telegrams. 'McEuan,' said he, 'from Murree.'

Scott chuckled. 'He thought he was going to be cool all summer. He'll be sick about this. Well, no good talking. 'Night.'

Two hours later, Scott, with a clear conscience, laid himself down to rest on a string cot in a bare room. The worn bullock-trunks, a leather water-bottle, a tin ice-box, and his pet saddle sewed up in sacking were piled at the door, and the Club secretary's receipt for last month's bill was under his pillow. His orders came next morning, and with them an unofficial telegram from Sir James Hawkins, who did not forget good men, bidding him report himself with all speed at some unpronounceable place fifteen hundred miles to the south, for the famine was sore in the land, and white men were needed.

A pink and fattish youth arrived in the red-hot noonday, whimpering a little at fate and famines, which never allowed any one three months' peace. He was Scott's successor—another cog in the machinery, moved forward behind his fellow, whose services, as the official announcement ran, 'were placed at the disposal of the Madras Government for famine duty until further orders'. Scott handed over the funds in his charge, showed him the coolest corner in the office, warned him against excess of zeal, and, as twilight fell, departed from the Club in a hired carriage with his faithful body-servant, Faiz Ullah, and a mound of disordered baggage atop, to catch the Southern Mail at the loopholed and bastioned railway-station. The heat from the thick brick walls struck him across the face as if it had been a hot towel, and he reflected that there were at least five nights and four days of travel before him. Faiz Ullah, used to the chances of service, plunged into the crowd on the stone platform, while Scott, a black cheroot between his teeth, waited till his compartment should be set away. A dozen native policemen, with their rifles and bundles, shouldered into the press of Punjabi farmers, Sikh craftsmen, and greasy-locked Afridi peddlers, escorting with all pomp Martyn's uniform-case, water-bottles, ice-box, and bedding-roll. They saw Faiz Ullah's lifted hand, and steered for it.

'My Sahib and your Sahib,' said Faiz Ullah to Martyn's man, 'will travel together. Thou and I, O brother, will thus secure the servants' places close by, and because of our masters' authority none will dare to disturb us.'

When Faiz Ullah reported all things ready, Scott settled down coatless and bootless on the broad leather-covered bunk. The heat under the iron-arched roof of the station might have been anything over a hundred degrees. At the last moment Martyn entered, hot and dripping.

'Don't swear,' said Scott lazily. 'It's too late to change your carriage, and we'll divide the ice.'

'What are you doing here?' said the policeman.

'Lent to the Madras Government, same as you. By Jove, it's a bender of a night! Are you taking any of your men down?'

'A dozen. Suppose I'll have to superintend relief distributions. Didn't know you were under orders too.'

'*I* didn't till after I left you last night. Raines had the news first. My orders came this morning. McEuan relieved me at four, and I got off at once. Shouldn't wonder if it wouldn't be a good thing—this famine—if we come through it alive.'

'Jimmy ought to put you and me to work together,' said Martyn; and then, after a pause: 'My sister's here.'

'Good business! said Scott, heartily. 'Going to get off at Umballa, I suppose, and go up to Simla. Who'll she stay with there?'

'No-o; that's just the trouble of it. She's going down with me.'

Scott sat bolt upright under the oil lamp as the train jolted past Tarn-Taran station. 'What! You don't mean you couldn't afford—'

'Oh, I'd have scraped up the money somehow.'

'You might have come to me, to begin with,' said Scott stiffly. 'We aren't altogether strangers.'

'Well, you needn't get stuffy about it. I might, but—you don't know my sister. I've been explaining and exhorting and entreating and commanding and all the rest of it all day—lost my temper since this morning, and haven't got it back yet—but she wouldn't hear of any compromise. A woman's entitled to travel with her husband if she wants to, and William says she's on the same footing. You see, we've been together all our lives, more or less, since my people died. It isn't as if she were an ordinary sister.'

'All the sisters I've heard of would have stayed where they were well off.'

'She's as clever as a man, confound her,' Martyn went on. 'She broke up the bungalow over my head while I was talking at her. Settled the whole *subchiz* in three hours—servants, horses, and all. I didn't get my orders till nine.'

'Jimmy Hawkins won't be pleased,' said Scott. 'A famine's no place for a woman.'

'Mrs. Jim—I mean Lady Jim's in camp with him. At any rate, she says she will look after my sister. William wired down to her on her own responsibility, asking if she could come, and knocked the ground from under me by showing me her answer.'

Scott laughed aloud. 'If she can do that she can take care of herself, and Mrs. Jim won't let her run into mischief. There aren't many women, sisters or wives, who would walk into a famine with their eyes open. It isn't as if she didn't know what these things mean. She was through the Jaloo cholera last year.'

The train stopped at Amritzar, and Scott went back to the ladies' compartment, immediately behind their carriage. William, a cloth riding-cap on her curls, nodded affably.

'Come in and have some tea,' she said. 'Best thing in the world for heat-apoplexy.'

'Do I look as if I were going to have apoplexy?'

'Never can tell,' said William wisely. 'It's best to be ready.'

She had arranged her belongings with the knowledge of an old campaigner. A felt-covered water-bottle hung in the draught of one of the shuttered windows; a tea-set of Russian china, packed in a wadded basket, stood ready on the seat; and a travelling spirit-lamp was clamped against the woodwork above it.

William served them generously, in large cups, hot tea, which saves the veins of the neck from swelling inopportunely on a hot night. It was characteristic of the girl that, her plan of action once settled, she asked for no comments on it. Life with men who had a great deal of work to do, and very little time to do it in, had taught her the wisdom of effacing as well as of fending for herself. She did not by word or deed suggest that she would be useful, comforting, or beautiful in their travels, but continued about her business serenely: put the cups back without clatter when tea was ended, and made cigarettes for her guests.

'This time last night,' said Scott, 'we didn't expect—er—this kind of thing, did we?'

'I've come to expect anything,' said William. 'You know, in our Service, we live at the end of the telegraph; but, of course, this ought to be a good thing for us all, departmentally—if we live.'

'It knocks us out of the running in our own Province,' Scott replied, with equal gravity. 'I hoped to be put on the Luni Protective Works this cold weather; but there's no saying how long the famine may keep us.'

'Hardly beyond October, I should think,' said Martyn. 'It will be ended, one way or the other, then.'

'And we've nearly a week of this,' said William. 'Shan't we be dusty when it's over!'

For a night and a day they knew their surroundings; and for a night and a day, skirting the edge of the great Indian Desert on a narrow-gauge line, they remembered how in the days of their apprenticeship they had come by that road from Bombay. Then the languages in which the names of the stations were written changed, and they launched south into a foreign land, where the very smells were new. Many long and heavily-laden grain trains were in front of them, and they could feel the hand of Jimmy Hawkins from far off. They waited in extemporised sidings blocked by processions of empty trucks returning to the north, and were coupled on to slow, crawling trains, and dropped at midnight, Heaven knew where; but it was furiously hot; and they walked to and fro among sacks, and dogs howled.

Then they came to an India more strange to them than to the untravelled Englishman—the flat, red India of palm-tree, palmyra-palm, and rice, the India of the picture-books, of *Little Henry and His Bearer*—all dead and dry in the baking heat. They had left the incessant passenger-traffic of the North and West far behind them. Here the people crawled to the side of the train, holding their little ones in their arms; and a loaded truck would be left behind, men and women clustering round and above it like ants on spilled honey. Once in the twilight they saw on a dusty plain a regiment of the little brown men, each bearing a body over his shoulder; and when the train stopped to leave yet another truck, they perceived that the burdens were not corpses, but only foodless folk picked up beside their dead oxen by a corps of irregular troops. Now they met more white men, here one and there two, whose tents stood close to the line, and who came armed with written authorities and angry words to cut off a truck. They were too busy to do more than nod at Scott and Martyn, and stare curiously at William, who could do nothing except make tea, and watch how her men staved off the rush of wailing, walking skeletons, putting them down three at a time in heaps; with their own hands uncoupling the marked trucks, or taking receipts from the hollow-eyed, weary white men, who spoke another argot than theirs.

They ran out of ice, out of soda-water, and out of tea; for they were six days and seven nights on the road, and it seemed to them like seven times seven years.

At last, in a dry, hot dawn, in a land of death, lit by long red fires of railway sleepers, where they were burning the dead, they came to their destination, and were met by Jim Hawkins, the Head of the Famine, unshaven, unwashed, but cheery, and entirely in command of affairs.

Martyn, he decreed, then and there, was to live on trains till further orders; was to go back with empty trucks, filling

156

them with starving people as he found them, and dropping them at a famine-camp on the edge of the Eight Districts. He would pick up supplies and return, and his constables would guard the loaded grain-cars, also picking up people, and would drop them at a camp a hundred miles south. Scott—Hawkins was very glad to see Scott again—would, that same hour, take charge of a convoy of bullock-carts, and would go south, feeding as he went, to yet another famine-camp far from the rail, where he would leave his starving—there would be no lack of starving on the route—and wait for orders by telegraph. Generally, Scott, was in all small things to do what he thought best.

William bit her underlip. There was no one in the wide world like her one brother, but Martyn's orders gave him no discretion. She came out, masked with dust from head to foot, a horse-shoe wrinkle on her forehead, put there by much thinking during the past week, but as self-possessed as ever. Mrs. Jim—who should have been Lady Jim, but that no one remembered to call her aright—took possession of her with a little gasp.

'Oh, I'm so glad you're here,' she almost sobbed. 'You oughtn't to, of course, but there—there isn't another woman in the place, and we must help each other, you know; and we've all the wretched people and the little babies they are selling.'

'I've seen some,' said William.

'Isn't it ghastly? I've bought twenty; they're in our camp; but won't you have something to eat first? We've more than ten people can do here; and I've got a horse for you. Oh, I'm so glad you've come! You're a Punjabi too, you know.'

'Steady, Lizzie,' said Hawkins, over his shoulder. 'We'll look after you, Miss Martyn. Sorry I can't ask you to breakfast, Martyn. You'll have to eat as you go. Leave two of your men to help Scott. These poor devils can't stand up to load carts. Saunders' (this to the engine-driver, half-asleep in the cab), 'back down and get those empties away. You've "line clear" to Arundrapillay; they'll give you orders north of that. Scott, load up your carts from that B.P.P. truck, and be off as soon as you can. The Eurasian in the pink shirt is your interpreter and guide. You'll find an apothecary of sorts tied to the yoke of the second wagon. He's been trying to bolt. You'll have to look after him. Lizzie, drive Miss Martyn to camp, and tell them to send the red horse down here for me.'

Scott, with Faiz Ullah and two policemen, was already busy on the carts, backing them up to the truck and unbolting the sideboards quietly, while the others pitched in the bags of millet and wheat. Hawkins watched him for as long as it took to fill a cart.

'That's a good man,' he said. 'If all goes well I shall work him—hard.' This was Jim Hawkins's notion of the highest compliment one human being could pay another.

An hour later Scott was under way; the apothecary threatening him with the penalties of the law for that he, a member of the Subordinate Medical Department, had been coerced and bound against his will and all laws governing the liberty of the subject; the pink-shirted Eurasian begging leave to see his mother, who happened to be dying some three miles away: 'Only verree, verree short leave of absence, and I will presently return, sar——'; the two constables, armed with staves, bringing up the rear; and Faiz Ullah, a Mohammedan's contempt for all Hindus and foreigners in every line of his face, explaining to the drivers that though Scott Sahib was a man to be feared on all fours, he, Faiz Ullah, was Authority itself.

The procession creaked past Hawkins's camp—three stained tents under a clump of dead trees; behind them the famine-shed where a crowd of hopeless ones tossed their arms around the cooking-kettles.

'Wish to Heaven William had kept out of it,' said Scott to himself, after a glance. 'We'll have cholera, sure as a gun, when the Rains come.'

But William seemed to have taken kindly to the operations of the Famine Code, which, when famine is declared, supersede the workings of the ordinary law. Scott saw her, the centre of a mob of weeping women, in a calico riding-habit and a blue-grey felt hat with a gold *pagri*.

'I want fifty rupees, please. I forgot to ask Jack before he went away. Can you lend it me? It's for condensed milk for the babies,' said she.

Scott took the money from his belt, and handed it over without a word. 'For goodness' sake, take care of yourself,' he said.

'Oh, I shall be all right. We ought to get the milk in two days. By the way, the orders are, I was to tell you, that you're to take one of Sir Jim's horses. There's a grey Kabuli here that I thought would be just your style, so I've said you'd take him. Was that right?'

'That's awfully good of you. We can't either of us talk much about style, I'm afraid.'

Scott was in a weather-stained drill shooting-kit, very white at the seams and a little frayed at the wrists. William regarded him thoughtfully, from his pith helmet to his greased ankle-boots. 'You look very nice, I think. Are you sure you've everything you'll need—quinine, chlorodyne, and so on?'

'Think so,' said Scott, patting three or four of his shooting pockets as the horse was led up, and he mounted and rode alongside his convoy.

'Good-bye,' he cried.

'Good-bye, and good luck,' said William. 'I'm awfully obliged for the money.' She turned on a spurred heel and disappeared into the tent, while the carts pushed on past the famine-sheds, past the roaring lines of the thick, fat fires, down to the baked Gehenna of the South.

PART II

So let us melt and make no noise,
No tear-floods nor sigh-tempests move;
'Twere profanation of our joys
To tell the laity our love.

                                        Donne

IT WAS PUNISHING work, even though he travelled by night and camped by day; but within the limits of his vision there was no man whom Scott could call master He was as free as Jimmy Hawkins—freer, in fact, for the Government held the Head of Famine tied neatly to a telegraph-wire, and if Jimmy had ever regarded telegrams seriously, the death-rate of that famine would have been much higher than it was.

At the end of a few days' crawling Scott learned something

of the size of the India which he served; and it astonished him. His carts, as you know, were loaded with wheat, millet, and barley, good food-grains needing only a little grinding. But the people to whom he brought the life-giving stuffs were rice-eaters. They knew how to hull rice in their mortars, but they knew nothing of the heavy stone querns of the North, and less of the material that the white man convoyed so laboriously. They clamoured for rice—unhusked paddy, such as they were accustomed to—and, when they found that there was none, broke away weeping from the sides of the cart. What was the use of these strange hard grains that choked their throats? They would die. And then and there were many who képt their word. Others took their allowance and bartered enough millet to feed a man through a week for a few handfuls of rotten rice saved by some less unfortunate. A few put their shares into the rice-mortars, pounded it, and made a paste with foul water; but they were very few. Scott understood dimly that many people in the India of the South ate rice, as a rule, but he had spent his service in a grain Province, had seldom seen rice in the blade or the ear, and least of all would have believed that, in time of deadly need, men would die at arm's length of plenty, sooner than touch food they did not know. In vain the interpreters interpreted; in vain his two policemen showed by vigorous pantomime what should be done. The starving crept away to their bark and weeds, grubs, leaves, and clay, and left the open sacks untouched. But sometimes the women laid their phantoms of children at Scott's feet, looking back as they staggered away.

Faiz Ullah opined it was the will of God that these foreigners should die, and therefore it remained only to give orders to burn the dead. None the less there was no reason why the Sahib should lack his comforts, and Faiz Ullah, a campaigner of experience, had picked up a few goats and had added them to the procession. That they might give milk for the morning meal, he was feeding them on the good grain that these imbeciles rejected. 'Yes,' said Faiz Ullah; 'if the Sahib thought fit, a little milk might be given to some of the babies'; but, as the Sahib well knew, babies were cheap, and, for his own part, Faiz Ullah held that there was no Government order as to babies. Scott spoke forcefully to Faiz Ullah and the two policemen, and bade them capture goats where they could find them. This they most joyfully did, for it was a recreation, and many ownerless goats were driven in. Once fed, the poor brutes were willing enough to follow the carts, and a few days' good food—food such as human beings for lack of—set them in milk again.

'But I am no goatherd,' said Faiz Ullah. 'It is against my *izzat* [my honour].'

'When we cross the Bias River again we will talk of *izzat*,' Scott replied. 'Till that day thou and the policemen shall be sweepers to the camp, if I give the order.'

'Thus, then, it is done,' grunted Faiz Ullah, 'if the Sahib will have it so'; and he showed how a goat should be milked, while Scott stood over him.

'Now we will feed them,' said Scott. 'Thrice a day we will feed them'; and he bowed his back to the milking, and took a horrible cramp.

When you have to keep connection unbroken between a restless mother of kids and a baby who is at the point of death, you suffer in all your system. But the babies were fed. Morning, noon, and evening Scott would solemnly lift them out one by one from their nest of gunny-bags under the cart-tilts. There were always many who could do no more than breathe, and the milk was dropped into their toothless mouths drop by drop, with due pauses when they choked. Each morning, too, the goats were fed; and since they would straggle without a leader, and since natives were hirelings, Scott was forced to give up riding, and pace slowly at the head of his flocks, accommodating his step to their weaknesses. All this was sufficiently absurd, and he felt the absurdity keenly; but at least he was saving life, and when the women saw that their children did not die, they made shift to eat a little of the strange foods, and crawled after the carts, blessing the master of the goats.

'Give the women something to live for,' said Scott to himself, as he sneezed in the dust of a hundred little feet, 'and they'll hang on somehow. But this beats William's condensed-milk trick all to pieces. I shall never live it down, though.'

He reached his destination very slowly, found that a rice-ship had come in from Burma, and that stores of paddy were available; found also an overworked Englishman in charge of the shed, and, loading the carts, set back to cover the ground he had already passed. He left some of the children and half his goats at the famine-shed. For this he was not thanked by the Englishman, who had already more stray babies than he knew what to do with. Scott's back was suppled to stooping now, and he went on with his wayside ministrations in addition to distributing the paddy. More babies and more goats were added unto him; but now some of the babies wore rags, and beads round their wrists or necks. '*That*,' said the interpreter, as though Scott did not know, 'signifies that their mothers hope in eventual contingency to resume them officially.'

'The sooner the better,' said Scott; but at the same time he marked, with the pride of ownership, how this or that little Ramaswamy was putting on flesh like a bantam. As the paddy-carts were emptied he headed for Hawkins's camp by the railway, timing his arrival to fit in with the dinner-hour, for it was long since he had eaten at a cloth. He had no desire to make any dramatic entry, but an accident of the sunset ordered it that, when he had taken off his helmet to get the evening breeze, the low light should fall across his forehead, and he could not see what was before him; while one waiting at the tent door beheld, with new eyes, a young man, beautiful as Paris, a god in a halo of golden dust, walking slowly at the head of his flocks, while at his knee ran small naked Cupids. But she laughed—William in a slate-coloured blouse laughed consumedly till Scott, putting the best face he could upon the matter, halted his armies and bade her admire the kindergarten. It was an unseemly sight, but the proprieties had been left ages ago, with the tea-party at Amritzar Station, fifteen hundred miles to the northward.

'They're coming on nicely,' said William. 'We've only five-and-twenty here now. The women are beginning to take them away again.'

'Are you in charge of the babies, then?'

'Yes—Mrs. Jim and I. We didn't think of goats, though. We've been trying condensed milk and water.'

'Any losses?'

'More than I care to think of,' said William, with a shudder. 'And you?'

162

Scott said nothing. There had been many little burials along his route—many mothers who had wept when they did not find again the children they had trusted to the care of the Government.

Then Hawkins came out carrying a razor, at which Scott looked hungrily, for he had a beard that he did not love. And when they sat down to dinner in the tent he told his tale in few words, as it might have been an official report. Mrs. Jim snuffled from time to time, and Jim bowed his head judicially; but William's grey eyes were on the clean-shaven face, and it was to her that Scott seemed to speak.

'Good for the Pauper Province!' said William, her chin in her hand, as she leaned forward among the wine-glasses. Her cheeks had fallen in, and the scar on her forehead was more prominent than ever, but the well-turned neck rose roundly as a column from the ruffle of the blouse which was the accepted evening-dress in camp.

'It was awfully absurd at times,' said Scott. 'You see, I didn't know much about milking and babies. They'll chaff my head off, if the tale goes North.'

'Let 'em,' said William haughtily. 'We've all done coolie-work since we came. I know Jack has.' This was to Hawkins's address, and the big man smiled blandly.

'Your brother's a highly efficient officer, William,' said he, 'and I've done him the honour of treating him as he deserves. Remember, I write the confidential reports.'

'Then you must say that William's worth her weight in gold,' said Mrs. Jim. 'I don't know what I should have done without her. She has been everything to us.' She dropped her hand upon William's, which was rough with much handling of reins, and William patted it softly. Jim beamed on the company. Things were going well with his world. Three of his more grossly incompetent men had died, and their places had been filled by their betters. Every day brought the Rains nearer. They had put out the famine in five of the Eight Districts, and, after all, the death-rate had not been too heavy—things considered. He looked Scott over carefully, as an ogre looks over a man, and rejoiced in his thews and iron-hard condition.

'He's just the least bit in the world tucked up,' said Jim to himself, 'but he can do two men.' Then he was aware that Mrs.

Jim was telegraphing to him, and according to the domestic code the message ran: 'A clear case. Look at them!'

He looked and listened. All that William was saying was: 'What can you expect of a country where they call a *bhisti* [water-carrier] a *tunni-cutch*?' and all that Scott answered was: 'I shall be precious glad to get back to the Club. Save me a dance at the Christmas ball, won't you?'

'It's a far cry from here to the Lawrence Hall,' said Jim. 'Better turn in early, Scott. It's paddy-carts to-morrow; you'll begin loading at five.'

'Aren't you going to give Mr. Scott *one* day's rest?'

'Wish I could, Lizzie. 'Fraid I can't. As long as he can stand up we must use him.'

'Well, I've had one Europe evening at least . . . By Jove, I'd nearly forgotten! What do I do about those babies of mine?'

'Leave them here,' said William—'we are in charge of that—and as many goats as you can spare. I must learn how to milk now.'

'If you care to get up early enough to-morrow I'll show you. I have to milk, you see; and, by the way, half of 'em have beads and things round their necks. You must be careful not to take 'em off, in case the mothers turn up.'

'You forget I've had some experience here.'

'I hope to goodness you won't overdo.' Scott's voice was unguarded.

'I'll take care of her,' said Mrs. Jim, telegraphing hundred-word messages as she carried William off, while Jim gave Scott his orders for the coming campaign. It was very late—nearly nine o'clock.

'Jim, you're a brute,' said his wife that night; and the Head of Famine chuckled.

'Not a bit of it, dear. I remember doing the first Jandiala Settlement for the sake of a girl in a crinoline; and she was slender, Lizzie. I've never done as good a piece of work since. *He*'ll work like a demon.'

'But you might have given him one day.'

'And let things come to a head now? No, dear. It's their happiest time.'

'I don't believe either of the dears know what's the matter

with them. Isn't it beautiful? Isn't it lovely?'

'Getting up at three to learn to milk, bless her heart! Ye Gods, why must we grow old and fat?'

'She's a darling. She has done more work under me——'

'Under *you*! The day after she came she was in charge and you were her subordinate, and you've stayed there ever since. She manages you almost as well as she manages me.'

'She doesn't, and that's why I love her. She's as direct as a man—as her brother.'

'Her brother's weaker than she is. He's always coming to me for orders; but he's honest, and a glutton for work. I confess I'm rather fond of William, and I had a daughter——'

The talk ended there. Far away in the Derajat was a child's grave more than twenty years old, and neither Jim nor his wife spoke of it any more.

'All the same, you're responsible,' Jim added, after a moment's silence.

'Bless 'em!' said Mrs. Jim, sleepily.

Before the stars paled, Scott, who slept in an empty cart, waked and went about his work in silence; it seemed at that hour unkind to rouse Faiz Ullah and the interpreter. His head being close to the ground, he did not hear William till she stood over him in the dingy old riding-habit, her eyes still heavy with sleep, a cup of tea and a piece of toast in her hands. There was a baby on the ground, squirming on a piece of blanket, and a six-year-old child peered over Scott's shoulder.

'Hai, you little rip,' said Scott, 'how the deuce do you expect to get your rations if you aren't quiet?'

A cool white hand steadied the brat, who forthwith choked as the milk gurgled into his mouth.

'Mornin',' said the milker. 'You've no notion how these little fellows can wriggle.'

'Oh yes, I have,' she whispered, because the world was asleep. 'Only I feed them with a spoon or a rag. Yours are fatter than mine . . . And you've been doing this day after day, twice a day?' The voice was almost lost.

'Yes! it was absurd. Now you try,' he said, giving place to the girl. 'Look out! A goat's not a cow.'

The girl protested against the amateur, and there was a

scuffle, in which Scott snatched up the baby. Then it was all to do over again, and William laughed softly and merrily. She managed, however, to feed two babies, and a third.

'Don't the little beggars take it well!' said Scott. 'I trained 'em.'

They were very busy and interested, when lo! it was broad daylight, and before they knew, the camp was awake, and they kneeled among the goats, surprised by the day, both flushed to the temples. Yet all the round world rolling up out of the darkness might have heard and seen all that had passed between them.

'Oh,' said William, unsteadily, snatching up the tea and toast. 'I had this made for you. It's stone-cold now. I thought you mightn't have anything ready so early. Better not drink it. It's—it's stone-cold.'

'That's awfully kind of you. It's just right. It's awfully good of you, really. I'll leave my kids and goats with you and Mrs. Jim; and, of course, any one in camp can show you about the milking.'

'Of course,' said William; and she grew pinker and pinker and statelier and more stately, as she strode back to her tent, fanning herself vigorously with the saucer.

There were shrill lamentations through the camp when the elder children saw their nurse move off without them. Faiz Ullah unbent so far as to jest with the policemen, and Scott turned purple with shame because Hawkins, already in the saddle, roared.

A child escaped from the care of Mrs. Jim, and, running like a rabbit, clung to Scott's boot, William pursuing with long, easy strides.

'I will not go—I will not go!' shrieked the child, twining his feet round Scott's ankle. 'They will kill me here. I do not know these people.'

'I say,' said Scott, in broken Tamil, 'I say, she will do you no harm. Go with her and be well fed.'

'Come!' said William, panting, with a watchful glance at Scott, who stood helpless and, as it were, hamstrung.

'Go back,' said Scott quickly to William. 'I'll send the little chap over in a minute.'

The tone of authority had its effect, but in a way Scott did not exactly intend. The boy loosened his grasp, and said with gravity, 'I did not know the woman was thine. I will go.' Then he cried to his companions, a mob of three-, four-, and five-year-olds waiting on the success of his venture ere they stampeded: 'Go back and eat. It is our man's woman. She will obey his orders.'

Jim collapsed where he sat; Faiz Ullah and the two policemen grinned; and Scott's orders to the cartmen flew like hail.

'That is the custom of the Sahibs when truth is told in their presence,' said Faiz Ullah. 'The time comes that I must seek new service. Young wives, especially such as speak our language and have knowledge of the ways of the Police, make great trouble for honest butlers in the matter of weekly accounts.'

What William thought of it all she did not say, but when her brother, ten days later, came to camp for orders, and heard of Scott's performances, he said, laughing: 'Well, that settles it. He'll be *Bakri* Scott to the end of his days' [*Bakri*, in the Northern vernacular, means a goat]. 'What a lark! I'd have given a month's pay to have seen him nursing famine babies. I fed some with *conji* [rice-water], but that was all right.'

'It's perfectly disgusting,' said his sister, with blazing eyes. 'A man does something like—like that—and all you other men think of is to give him an absurd nickname, and then you laugh and think it's funny.'

'Ah,' said Mrs. Jim sympathetically.

'Well, *you* can't talk, William. You christened little Miss Demby the Button-quail last cold weather; you know you did. India's the land of nicknames.'

'That's different,' William replied. 'She was only a girl, and she hadn't done anything except walk like a quail, and she *does*. But it isn't fair to make fun of a man.'

'Scott won't care,' said Martyn. 'You can't get a rise out of old Scotty. I've been trying for eight years, and you've only known him for three. How does he look?'

'He looks very well,' said William, and went away with a flushed cheek. '*Bakri* Scott, indeed!' Then she laughed to herself, for she knew the country of her service. 'But it will be *Bakri* all the same'; and she repeated it under her breath several times slowly, whispering it into favour.

167

When he returned to his duties on the railway, Martyn spread the name far and wide among his associates, so that Scott met it as he led his paddy-carts to war. The natives believed it to be some English title of honour, and the cart-drivers used it in all simplicity till Faiz Ullah, who did not approve of foreign japes, broke their heads. There was very little time for milking now, except at the big camps, where Jim had extended Scott's idea, and was feeding large flocks on the useless northern grains. Enough paddy had come into the Eight Districts to hold the people safe, if it were only distributed quickly; and for that purpose no one was better than the big Canal Officer, who never lost his temper, never gave an unnecessary order, and never questioned an order given. Scott pressed on, saving his cattle, washing their galled necks daily, so that no time should be lost on the road; reported himself with his rice at the minor famine-sheds, unloaded, and went back light by forced night-march to the next distributing centre, to find Hawkins's unvarying telegram: 'Do it again.' And he did it again and again, and yet again, while Jim Hawkins, fifty miles away, marked off on a big map the tracks of his wheels gridironing the stricken lands. Others did well—Hawkins reported at the end that they all did well—but Scott was the most excellent, for he kept good coined rupees by him, and paid for his own cart-repairs on the spot, and ran to meet all sorts of unconsidered extras, trusting to be recouped later. Theoretically, the Government should have paid for every shoe and linchpin, for every hand employed in the loading; but Government vouchers cash themselves slowly, and intelligent and efficient clerks write at great length, contesting unauthorised expenditures of eight annas. The man who wishes to make his work a success must draw on his own bank-account of money and other things as he goes.

'I told you he'd work,' said Jimmy to his wife at the end of six weeks. 'he's been in sole charge of a couple of thousand men up north on the Mosuhl Canal for a year, and he gives one less trouble than young Martyn with his ten constables; and I'm morally certain—only Government doesn't recognize moral obligations—that he's spent about half his pay to grease his wheels. Look at this, Lizzie, for one week's work! Forty miles in two days with twelve carts; two days' halt building a famine-shed for young Rogers (Rogers ought to have built it himself, the idiot!). Then forty miles back again, loading six carts on the way, and distributing all Sunday. Then in the evening he pitches in a twenty-page demi-official to me, saying that the people where he is might be "advantageously employed on relief-work," and suggesting that he put 'em to work on some broken-down old reservoir he's discovered, so as to have a good water-supply when the Rains come. He thinks he can caulk the dam in a fortnight. Look at his marginal sketches—aren't they clear and good? I knew he was *pukka*, but I didn't know he was as *pukka* as this!'

'I must show these to William,' said Mrs. Jim. 'The child's wearing herself out among the babies.'

'Not more than you are, dear. Well, another two months ought to see us out of the wood. I'm sorry it's not in my power to recommend you for a V.C.'

William sat late in her tent that night, reading through page after page of the square handwriting, patting the sketches of proposed repairs to the reservoir, and wrinkling her eyebrows over the columns of figures of estimated water-supply.

'And he finds time to do all this,' she cried to herself, 'and . . . Well, I also was present. I've saved one or two babies.'

She dreamed for the twentieth time of the god in the golden dust, and woke refreshed to feed loathsome black children, scores of them, wastrels picked up by the wayside, their bones almost breaking their skin, terrible and covered with sores.

Scott was not allowed to leave his cart-work, but his letter was duly forwarded to the Government, and he had the consolation, not rare in India, of knowing that another man was reaping where he had sown. That also was discipline profitable to the soul.

'He's much too good to waste on canals,' said Jimmy. 'Any one can oversee coolies. You needn't be angry, William: he can—but I need my pearl among bullock-drivers, and I've transferred him to the Khanda district, where he'll have it all to do over again. He should be marching now.'

'He's *not* a coolie,' said William furiously. 'He ought to be doing his regulation work.'

'He's the best man in his Service, and that's a good deal;

but if you *must* use razors to cut grindstones, why, I prefer the best cutlery.'

'Isn't it almost time we saw him again?' said Mrs. Jim. 'I'm sure the poor boy hasn't had a respectable meal for a month. He probably sits on a cart and eats sardines with his fingers.'

'All in good time, dear. Duty before decency—wasn't it Mr. Chucks said that?'

'No; it was Midshipman Easy,' William laughed. 'I sometimes wonder how it will feel to dance or listen to a band again, or sit under a roof. I can't believe that I ever wore a ball-frock in my life.'

'One minute,' said Mrs. Jim, who was thinking. 'If he goes to Khanda, he passes within five miles of us. Of course he'll ride in.'

'Oh, no, he won't,' said William.

'How do you know, dear?'

'It'll take him off his work. He won't have time.'

'He'll make it,' said Mrs. Jim, with a twinkle.

'It depends on his own judgment. There's absolutely no reason why he shouldn't, if he thinks fit,' said Jim.

'He won't see fit,' William replied, without sorrow or emotion. 'It wouldn't be him if he did.'

'One certainly gets to know people rather well in times like these,' said Jim drily; but William's face was serene as ever, and, as she prophesied, Scott did not appear.

The Rains fell at last, late, but heavily; and the dry, gashed earth was red mud, and servants killed snakes in the camp, where every one was weather-bound for a fortnight—all except Hawkins, who took horse and splashed about in the wet, rejoicing. Now the Government decreed that seed-grain should be distributed to the people as well as advances of money for the purchase of new oxen; and the white men were doubly worked for this new duty, while William skipped from brick to brick laid down on the trampled mud, and dosed her charges with warming medicines that made them rub their little round stomachs; and the milch-goats throve on the rank grass. There was never a word from Scott in the Khanda district, away to the south-east, except the regular telegraphic report to Hawkins. The rude country roads had disappeared; his drivers were half mutinous; one of Martyn's loaned policemen had died of cholera; and Scott was taking thirty grains of quinine a day to fight the fever that comes if one works hard in heavy rain; but those were things he did not consider necessary to report. He was, as usual, working from a base of supplies on a railway line, to cover a circle of fifteen miles radius, and since full loads were impossible, he took quarter-loads, and toiled four times as hard by consequence; for he did not choose to risk an epidemic which might have grown uncontrollable by assembling villagers in thousands at the relief-sheds. It was cheaper to take Government bullocks, work them to death, and leave them to the crows in the wayside sloughs.

That was the time when eight years of clean living and hard condition told, though a man's head were ringing like a bell from the cinchona, and the earth swayed under his feet when he stood and under his bed when he slept. If Hawkins had seen it fit to make him a bullock-driver, that, he thought, was entirely Hawkins's own affair. There were men in the North who would know what he had done; men of thirty years' service in his own Department who would say that it was 'not half bad'; and above, immeasurably above all men of all grades' there was William in the thick of the fight, who would approve because she understood. He had so trained his mind that it would hold fast to the mechanical routine of the day, though his own voice sounded strange in his own ears, and his hands, when he wrote, grew large as pillows or small as peas at the end of his wrists. That steadfastness bore his body to the telegraph-office at the railway-station, and dictated a telegram to Hawkins, saying that the Khanda district was, in his judgment, now safe, and he 'waited further orders'.

The Madrassee telegraph-clerk did not approve of a large, gaunt man falling over him in a dead faint, not so much because of the weight, as because of the names and blows that Faiz Ullah dealt him when he found the body rolled under a bench. Then Faiz Ullah took blankets and quilts and coverlets where he found them, and lay down under them at his master's side, and bound his arms with a tent-rope, and filled him with a horrible stew of herbs, and set the policeman to fight him when he wished to escape from the intolerable heat of his coverings, and shut the door of the telegraph-office to keep out the curious for two nights and one day; and when a light engine came down the line, and Hawkins kicked in the door, Scott hailed him weakly, but in a natural voice, and Faiz Ullah stood back and took all the credit.

'For two nights, Heaven-born, he was *pagal*,' said Faiz Ullah. 'Look at my nose, and consider the eye of the policeman. He beat us with his bound hands; but we sat upon him, Heaven-born, and though his words were *tez*, we sweated him. Heaven-born, never has been such a sweat! He is weaker now than a child; but the fever has gone out of him, by the grace of God. There remains only my nose and the eye of the constabeel. Sahib, shall I ask for my dismissal because my Sahib has beaten me?' And Faiz Ullah laid his long thin hand carefully on Scott's chest to be sure that the fever was all gone, ere he went out to open tinned soups and discourage such as laughed at his swelled nose.

'The District's all right,' Scott whispered. 'It doesn't make any difference. You got my wire? I shall be fit in a week. Can't understand how it happened. I shall be fit in a few days.'

'You're coming into camp with us,' said Hawkins.

'But look here—but—'

'It's all over except the shouting. We shan't need you Punjabis any more. On my honour, we shan't. Martyn goes back in a few weeks; Arbuthnot's returned already; Ellis and Clay are putting the last touches to a new feeder-line the Government's built as relief-work. Morten's dead—he was a Bengal man, though; you wouldn't know him. 'Pon my word, you and Will— Miss Martyn—seem to have come through it as well as anybody.

'Oh, how is she?' The voice went up and down as he spoke.

'She was in great form when I left her. The Roman Catholic Missions are adopting the unclaimed babies to turn them into little priests; the Basel Mission is taking some, and the mothers are taking the rest. You should hear the little beggars howl when they're sent away from William. She's pulled down a bit, but so are we all. Now, when do you suppose you'll be able to move?'

'I can't come into camp in this state. I won't,' he replied pettishly.

'Well, you *are* rather a sight, but from what I gathered there it seemed to me they'd be glad to see you under any conditions. I'll look over your work here, if you like, for a couple of days, and you can pull yourself together while Faiz Ullah feeds you up.'

Scott could walk dizzily by the time Hawkins's inspection was ended, and he flushed all over when Jim said of his work in the District that it was 'not half bad', and volunteered, further, that he had considered Scott his right-hand man through the famine, and would feel it his duty to say as much officially.

So they came back by rail to the old camp; but there were no crowds near it, and the long fires in the trenches were dead and black, and the famine-sheds stood almost empty.

'You see!' said Jim. 'There isn't much more for us to do. Better ride up and see the wife. They've pitched a tent for you. Dinner at seven. I'll see you then.'

Riding at a foot-pace, Faiz Ullah by his stirrup, Scott came to William in the brown-calico riding-habit, sitting at the dinner-tent door, her hands in her lap, white as ashes, thin and worn, with no lustre in her hair. There did not seem to be any Mrs. Jim on the horizon, and all that William could say was: 'My word, how pulled down you look!'

'I've had a touch of fever. You don't look very well yourself.'

'Oh, I'm fit enough. We've stamped it out. I suppose you know?'

Scott nodded. 'We shall all be returned in a few weeks. Hawkins told me.'

'Before Christmas, Mrs. Jim says. Shan't you be glad to go back? I can smell the wood-smoke already'; William sniffed. 'We shall be in time for all the Christmas doings. I don't suppose even the Punjab Government would be base enough to transfer Jack till the new year?'

'It seems hundreds of years ago—the Punjab and all that—doesn't it? Are you glad you came?'

'Now it's all over, yes. It has been ghastly here. You know we had to sit still and do nothing, and Sir Jim was away so much.'

'Do nothing! How did you get on with the milking?'

'I managed it somehow—after you taught me.'

Then the talk stopped with an almost audible jar. Still no

Mrs. Jim.

'That reminds me I owe you fifty rupees for the condensed milk. I thought that perhaps you'd be coming here when you were transferred to the Khanda district, and I could pay you then; but you didn't.'

'I passed within five miles of the camp. It was in the middle of a march, you see, and the carts were breaking down every few minutes, and I couldn't get 'em over the ground till ten o'clock that night. But I wanted to come awfully. You knew I did, didn't you?'

'I—believe—I—did,' said William, facing him with level eyes. She was no longer white.

'Did you understand?'

'Why you didn't ride in? Of course I did.'

'Why?'

'Because you couldn't, of course. I knew that.'

'Did you care?'

'If you had come in—but I knew you wouldn't—but if you *had*, I should have cared a great deal. You know I should.'

'Thank God I didn't! Oh, but I wanted to! I couldn't trust myself to ride in front of the carts, because I kept edging 'em over here, don't you know?'

'I knew you wouldn't,' said William contentedly. 'Here's your fifty.'

Scott bent forward and kissed the hand that held the greasy notes. Its fellow patted him awkwardly but very tenderly on the head.

'And *you* knew, too, didn't you?' said William, in a new voice.

'No, on my honour, I didn't. I hadn't the—the cheek to expect anything of the kind, except . . . I say, were you out riding anywhere the day I passed by to Khanda.'

William nodded, and smiled after the manner of an angel surprised in a good deed.

'Then it was just a speck I saw of your habit in the—'

'Palm-grove on the Southern cart-road. I saw your helmet when you came up from the nullah by the temple—just enough to be sure that you were all right. D'you care?'

This time Scott did not kiss her hand, for they were in the

dusk of the dining-tent, and, because William's knees were trembling under her, she had to sit down in the nearest chair, where she wept long and happily, her head on her arms; and when Scott imagined that it would be well to comfort her, she needing nothing of the kind, she ran to her own tent; and Scott went out into the world, and smiled upon it largely and idiotically. But when Faiz Ullah brought him a drink, he found it necessary to support one hand with the other, or the good whisky and soda would have been spilled abroad. There are fevers and fevers.

But it was worse—much worse—the strained, eye-shirking talk at dinner till the servants had withdrawn, and worst of all when Mrs. Jim, who had been on the edge of weeping from the soup down, kissed Scott and William, and they drank one whole bottle of champagne, hot, because there was no ice, and Scott and William sat outside the tent in the starlight till Mrs. Jim drove them in for fear of more fever. Apropos of these things and some others William said: 'Being engaged is abominable, because, you see, one has no official position. We must be thankful that we've lots of things to do.'

'Things to do!' said Jim, when that was reported to him. 'They're neither of them any good any more. I can't get five hours' work a day out of Scott. He's in the clouds half the time.'

'Oh, but they're so beautiful to watch, Jimmy. It will break my heart when they go. Can't you do anything for him?'

'I've given the Government the impression—at least, I hope I have—that he personally conducted the entire famine. But all he wants is to get on to the Luni Canal Works, and William's just as bad. Have you ever heard 'em talking of barrage and aprons and waste water? It's their style of spooning, I suppose.'

Mrs. Jim smiled tenderly. 'Ah, that's in the intervals—bless 'em.'

And so Love ran about the camp unrebuked in broad daylight, while men picked up the pieces and put them neatly away of the famine in the Eight Districts.

Morning brought the penetrating chill of the Northern December, the layers of wood-smoke, the dusty grey-blue of the tamarisks, the domes of ruined tombs, and all the smell of the white Northern plains, as the mail-train ran on to the mile-long Sutlej Bridge. William, wrapped in a *poshteen*—a silk-

embroidered sheepskin jacket trimmed with rough astrakhan—
looked out with moist eyes and nostrils that dilated joyously.
The South of pagodas and palm-trees, the over-populated Hindu
South, was done with. Here was the land she knew and loved,
and before her lay the good life she understood, among folk of
her own caste and mind.

They were picking them up at almost every station now—
men and women coming in for the Christmas Week, with
racquets, with bundles of polo-sticks, with dear and bruised
cricket-bats, with fox-terriers and saddles. The greater part of
them wore jackets like William's, for the Northern cold is as
little to be trifled with as the Northern heat. And William was
among them and of them, her hands deep in her pockets, her
collar turned up over her ears, stamping her feet on the platforms
as she walked up and down to get warm, visiting from carriage
to carriage. And everywhere being congratulated. Scott was with
the bachelors at the far end of the train, where they chaffed him
mercilessly about feeding babies and milking goats; but from
time to time he would stroll up to William's window, and
murmur: 'Good enough, isn't it?' And William would answer
with sighs of pure delight: 'Good enough, indeed.' The large
open names of the home towns were good to listen to. Umballa,
Ludhiana, Phillour, Jullunder, they rang like the coming
marriage-bells in her ears, and William felt deeply and truly
sorry for all strangers and outsiders—visitors, tourists, and those
fresh-caught for the service of the country.

It was a glorious return, and when the bachelors gave the
Christmas ball, William was, unofficially, you might say, the
chief and honoured guest among the stewards, who could make
things very pleasant for their friends. She and Scott danced nearly
all the dances together, and sat out the rest in the big dark
gallery overlooking the superb teak floor, where the uniforms
blazed, and the spurs clinked, and the new frocks and four
hundred dancers went round and round till the draped flags on
the pillars flapped and bellied to the whirl of it.

About midnight half-a-dozen men who did not care for
dancing came over from the Club to play 'Waits', and—that
was a surprise the stewards had arranged—before anyone knew
what had happened, the band stopped, and hidden voices broke

into 'Good King Wenceslaus', and William in the gallery hummed and beat time with her foot:—

> *'Mark my footsteps well, my page,*
> *Tread thou in them boldly.*
> *Thou shalt find the winter's rage*
> *Freeze thy blood less coldly!'*

'Oh, I hope they are going to give us another! Isn't it pretty, coming out of the dark in that way? Look—look down. There's Mrs. Gregory wiping her eyes!'

'It's like Home, rather,' said Scott. 'I remember—'

'H'sh! Listen!—dear.' And it began again:—

> *'When shepherds watched their flocks by night—'*

'A-h-h!' said William, drawing closer to Scott.

> *'All seated on the ground,*
> *The Angel of the Lord came down,*
> *And glory shone around.*
>
> *"Fear not," said he (for mighty dread*
> *Had seized their troubled mind);*
> *"Glad tidings of great joy I bring*
> *To you and all mankind." '*

This time it was William that wiped her eyes.

MISS YOUGHAL'S SAIS

When Man and Woman are agreed, what can the Kazi do?

                                                    Proverb

SOME PEOPLE SAY that there is no romance in India. Those people are wrong. Our lives hold as much romance as is good for us. Sometimes more.

Strickland was in the Police, and people did not understand him. So they said he was a doubtful sort of man and passed by on the other side. Strickland had himself to thank for this. He held the extraordinary theory that a Policeman in India should try to know as much about the natives as the natives themselves. Now, in the whole of Upper India, there is only one man who can pass for Hindu or Mohammedan, hide dresser or priest, as he pleases. He is feared and respected by the natives from the Ghor Kathri to the Jumma Musjid; and he is supposed to have the gift of invisibility and executive control over many devils. But this has done him no good in the eyes of the Indian Government.

Strickland was foolish enough to take that man for his model; and, following out his absurd theory, dabbled in unsavoury places which no respectable man would think of exploring—among the native riffraff. He educated himself in this peculiar way for seven years, and people could not appreciate it. He was perpetually 'going Fantee' among natives, which, of course, no man with any sense believes in. He was initiated into the *Sat Bhai* at Allahabad once, when he was on leave. He knew the Lizard-Song of the Sansis, and the *Halli-Hukk* dance, which is a religious cancan of a startling kind. When a man knows who dance the *Halli-Hukk*, and how, and when, and where, he knows something to be proud of. He has gone deeper than the skin. But Strickland was not proud, though he had helped once, at Kagadhri, at the Painting of the Death Bull, which no Englishman must even look upon; had mastered the thieves'-patter of the *Changars*; had taken a Yusufzai horse-thief alone near Attock; and had stood under the sounding board of a Border mosque and conducted service in the manner of a Sunni Mullah.

His crowning achievement was spending eleven days as a *fakir* or priest in the gardens of Baba Atal at Amritzar, and there picking up the threads of the great Nasiban murder Case. But people said, justly enough, 'Why on earth can't Strickland sit in his office and write up his diary, and recruit, and keep quiet, instead of showing up the incapacity of his seniors?' So the Nasiban Murder Case did him no good Departmentally; but, after his first feeling of wrath, he returned to his outlandish custom of prying into native life. When a man once acquires a taste for this particular amusement, it abides with him all his days. It is the most fascinating thing in the world—Love not excepted. Where other men took ten days to the Hills, Strickland took leave for what he called *shikar*, put on the disguise that appealed to him at the time, stepped down into the brown crowd, and was swallowed up for a while. He was a quiet, dark young fellow—spare, black-eyed—and, when he was not thinking of something else, a very interesting companion. Strickland on Native Progress as he had seen it was worth hearing. Natives hated Strickland, but they were afraid of him. He knew too much.

When the Youghals came into the station, Strickland—very gravely, as he did everything, fell in love with Miss Youghal; and she, after a while, fell in love with him because she could not understand him. Then Strickland told her parents; but Mrs. Youghal said she was not going to throw her daughter into the worst-paid Department in the Empire, and old Youghal said, in so many words, that he mistrusted Strickland's ways and works, and would thank him not to speak or write to his daughter any more. 'Very well,' said Strickland, for he did not wish to make his lady-love's life a burden. After one long talk with Miss Youghal he dropped the business entirely.

The Youghals went up to Simla in April.

In July Strickland secured three months' leave on 'urgent private affairs', He locked up his house—though not a native in the province would wittingly have touched 'Estreekin Sahib's gear for the world—and went down to see a friend of his, an old dyer, at Tarn Taran.

Here all trace of him was lost, until a *sais* or groom met me on the Simla Mall with this extraordinary note:—

DEAR OLD MAN,—Please give bearer a box of cheroots—Supers, No.1, for preference. They are freshest at the Club. I'll repay when I reappear; but at present I'm out of society.—Yours,

E. Strickland.

I ordered two boxes, and handed them over to the *sais* with my love. That *sais* was Strickland, and he was in old Youghal's employ, attached to Miss Youghal's Arab. The poor fellow was suffering for an English smoke, and knew that, whatever happened, I should hold my tongue till the business was over.

Later on, Mrs. Youghal, who was wrapped up in her servants, began talking at houses where she called of her paragon among *saises*—the man who was never too busy to get up in the morning and pick flowers for the breakfast-table, and who blacked—actually *blacked*—the hoofs of his horse like a London coachman. The turn-out of Miss Youghal's Arab was a wonder and a delight. Strickland—Dulloo, I mean—found his reward in the pretty things that Miss Youghal said to him when she went out riding. Her parents were pleased to find she had forgotten all her foolishness for young Strickland, and said she was a good girl.

Strickland vows that the two months of his service were the most rigid mental discipline he has ever gone through. Quite apart from the little fact that the wife of one of his fellow-*saises* fell in love with him and then tried to poison him with arsenic because he would have nothing to do with her, he had to school himself into keeping quiet when Miss Youghal went out riding with some man who tried to flirt with her, and he was forced to trot behind carrying the blanket and hearing every word! Also, he had to keep his temper when he was slanged in the theatre porch by a policeman—especially once when he was abused by a Naik he had himself recruited from Isser Jang village—or, worse still, when a young subaltern called him a pig for not making way quickly enough.

But the life had its compensations. He obtained great insight into the ways and thefts of *saises*—enough, he says, to have summarily convicted half the population of the Punjab if he had been on business. He became one of the leading players at knuckle-bones, which all *jhampanis* and many *saises* play while they are waiting outside the Government House or the Gaiety Theatre of nights; he learned to smoke tobacco that was three-fourths cow-dung; and he heard the wisdom of the grizzled Jemadar of the Government House grooms. Whose words are valuable. He saw many things which amused him; and he states, on honour, that no man can appreciate Simla properly till he has seen it from the *sais*'s point of view. He also says that, if he chose to write all he saw, his head would be broken in several places.

Strickland's account of the agony he endured on wet nights, hearing the music and seeing the lights in Benmore, with his toes tingling for a waltz and his head in a horse-blanket, is rather amusing. One of these days Strickland is going to write a little book on his experiences. That book will be worth buying, and even more worth suppressing.

Thus he served faithfully as Jacob served for Rachel; and his leave was nearly at an end when the explosion came. He had really done his best to keep his temper in the hearing of the flirtations I have mentioned; but he broke down at last. An old and very distinguished General took Miss Youghal for a ride, and began that specially offensive 'you're-only-a-little-girl' sort of flirtation—most difficult for a woman to turn aside deftly, and most maddening to listen to. Miss Youghal was shaking with fear at the things he said in the hearing of her *sais*. Dulloo—Strickland—stood it as long as he could. Then he caught hold of the General' bridle, and, in most fluent English, invited him to step off and be flung over the cliff. Next minute Miss Youghal began to cry, and Strickland saw that he had hopelessly given himself away, and everything was over.

The General nearly had a fit, while Miss Youghal was

sobbing out the story of the disguise and the engagement that was not recognised by her parents. Strickland was furiously angry with himself, and more angry with the General for forcing his hand; so he said nothing, but held the horse's head and prepared to thrash the General as some sort of satisfaction. But when the General had thoroughly grasped the story, and knew who Strickland was, he began to puff and blow in the saddle, and nearly rolled off with laughing. He said Strickland deserved a V.C., if it were only for putting on a *sais*'s blanket. Then he called himself names, and vowed that he deserved a thrashing, but he was too old to take it from Strickland. Then he complimented Miss Youghal on her lover. The scandal of the business never struck him; for he was a nice old man, with a weakness for flirtations. Then he laughed again, and said that old Youghal was a fool. Strickland let go of the cob's head, and suggested that the General had better help them if that was his opinion. Strickland knew Youghal's weakness for men with titles and letters after their names and high official position. 'It's rather like a forty-minute farce,' said the General, 'but, begad, I *will* help, if it's only to escape that tremendous thrashing I deserve. Go along to your home, my *sais*-Policeman, and change into decent kit, and I'll attack Mr. Youghal. Miss Youghal, may I ask you to canter home and wait?'

About seven minutes later there was a wild hurroosh at the Club. A *sais*, with blanket and head-rope, was asking all the men he knew: 'For Heaven's sake, lend me decent clothes!' As the men did not recognise him, there were some peculiar scenes before Strickland could get a hot bath, with soda in it, in one room, a shirt here, a collar there, a pair of trousers elsewhere, and so on. He galloped off, with half the Club wardrobe on his back, and an utter stranger's pony under him, to the house of old Youghal. The General, arrayed in purple and fine linen, was before him. What the General had said Strickland never knew, but Youghal received Strickland with moderate civility; and Mrs. Youghal, touched by the devotion of the transformed Dulloo, was almost kind. The General beamed and chuckled, and Miss Youghal came in, and, almost before old Youghal knew where he was, the parental consent had been wrenched out, and Strickland had departed with Miss Youghal to the telegraph-office to wire for his European kit. The final embarrassment was when a stranger attacked him on the Mall and asked for the stolen pony.

In the end, Strickland and Miss Youghal were married, on the strict understanding that Strickland should drop his old ways, and stick to Departmental routine, which pays best and leads to Simla. Strickland was far too fond of his wife, just then, to break his word, but it was a sore trial to him; for the streets and bazars, and the sounds in them, were full of meaning to Strickland, and these called him to come back and take up his wanderings and his discoveries. Some day I will tell you how he broke his promise to help a friend. That was long since, and he has, by this time, been nearly spoilt for what he would call *shikar*. He is forgetting the slang, and the beggar's cant, and the marks, and the signs, and the drift of the under-currents, which, if a man would master, he must always continue to learn.

But he fills in his Departmental returns beautifully.

THROWN AWAY

And some are sulky, while some will plunge.
(So ho! Steady! Stand still, you!)
Some you must gentle, and some you must lunge.
(There! There! Who wants to kill you?)
Some—there are losses in every trade—
Will break their hearts ere bitted and made,
Will fight like fiends as the rope cuts hard,
And die dumb-mad in the breaking-yard.
                    Toolungala Stockyard Chorus

TO REAR A boy under what parents call the 'sheltered life' system is, if the boy must go into the world and fend for himself, not wise. Unless he be one in a thousand he has certainly to pass through many unnecessary troubles; and may, possible, come to extreme grief simply from ignorance of the proper proportion of things.

Let a puppy eat the soap in the bath-room or chew a newly-blacked boot. He chews and chuckles until, by and by, he finds out that blacking and Old Brown Windsor make him very sick. So he argues that soap and boots are not wholesome. Any old dog about the house will soon show him the unwisdom of biting big dogs' ears. Being young, he remembers, and goes abroad, at six months, a well-mannered little beast with a chastened appetite. If he had been kept away from boots, and soap, and big dogs till he came to the trinity full-grown and with developed teeth, consider how fearfully sick and thrashed he would be! Apply that notion to the 'sheltered life', and see how it works. It does not sound pretty, but it is the better of two evils.

There was a Boy once who had been brought up under the 'sheltered life' theory; and the theory killed him dead. He stayed with his people all his days, from the hour he was born till the hour he went into Sandhurst nearly at the top of the list. He was beautifully taught in all that wins marks by a private tutor, and carried the extra weight of 'never having given his parents an hour's anxiety in his life'. What he learnt at Sandhurst beyond the regular routine is of no great consequence. He looked about him, and he found soap and blacking, so to speak, very good. He ate a little, and came out of Sandhurst not so high as he went in. Then there was an interval and a scene with his people, who expected much from him. Next a year of living unspotted from the world in a third-rate depot battalion where all the juniors were children and all the seniors old women; and lastly, he came out to India, where he was cut off from the support of his parents, and had no one to fall back on in time of trouble except himself.

Now India is a place beyond all others where one must not take things too seriously—the mid-day sun always excepted. Too much work and too much energy kill a man just as effectively as too much assorted vice or too much drink. Flirtation does not matter, because every one is being transferred, and either you or she leave the station and never return. Good work does not matter, because a man is judged by his worst output, and another man takes all the credit of his best as a rule. Bad work does not matter, because other men do worse, and incompetents hang on longer in India than anywhere else. Amusements do not matter, because you must repeat them as soon as you have accomplished them once, and most amusements only mean trying to win another person's money. Sickness does not matter, because it's all in the day's work, and if you die, another man takes over your place and your office in the eight hours between your death and burial. Nothing matters except Home-furlough and acting allowances, and these only because they are scarce. It is a slack country, where all men work with imperfect instruments; and the wisest thing is to escape as soon as ever you can to some place where amusement is amusement and a reputation worth the having.

But this Boy—the tale is as old as the Hills—came out, and took all things seriously. He was pretty and he was petted. He took the pettings seriously, and fretted over women not worth saddling a pony to call upon. He found his new free life in India very good. It *does* look attractive in the beginning, from a subaltern's point of view—all ponies, partners, dancing, and so on. He tasted it as the puppy tastes the soap. Only he came late to the eating, with a grown set of teeth. He had no sense of balance—just like the puppy—and could not understand why he was not treated with the consideration he received under his father's roof. That hurt his feelings.

He quarrelled with other boys and, being sensitive to the marrow, remembered these quarrels, and they excited him. He found whist, and gymkhanas, and things of that kind (meant to amuse one after office) good; but he took them seriously too, just as seriously as he took the 'head' that followed after drink. He lost his money over whist and gymkhana because they were new to him.

He took his losses seriously, and wasted as much energy and interest over a two-goldmohur race for maiden *ekka*-ponies with their manes hogged, as if it had been the Derby. One-half of this came from inexperience—much as the puppy squabbles with the owner of the hearthrug—and the other half from the dizziness bred by stumbling out of his quiet life into the glare and excitement of a livelier one. No one told him about the soap and the blacking, because an average man takes it for granted that an average man is ordinarily careful in regard to them. It was painful to watch The Boy knocking himself to pieces, as an overhandled colt falls down and cuts himself when he gets away from his groom.

This unbridled licence in amusements not worth the trouble of breaking line for, much less rioting over, endured for six months—all through one cold weather—and then we thought that the heat and the knowledge of having lost his money and health and lamed his horses would sober The Boy down, and he would stand steady. In ninety-nine cases out of a hundred this would have happened. You can see the principle working in any Indian station. But this particular case fell through because The Boy was sensitive and took things seriously—as I may have said some seven times before. Of course, we could not tell how his excesses struck him personally. They were nothing very heartbreaking or above the average. He might be crippled for life financially, and want a little nursing. Still, the memory of his performances would wither away in one hot weather, and the bankers would help him to tide over the money-troubles. But he must have taken another view altogether, and have believed himself ruined beyond redemption. His Colonel talked to him severely when the cold weather ended. That made him more wretched than ever; and it was only an ordinary 'Colonel's wigging'!

What follows is a curious instance of the fashion in which we are all linked together and made responsible for one another. *The* thing that kicked the beam in The Boy's mind was a remark that a woman made when he was talking to her. There is no use in repeating it, for it was only a cruel little sentence, rapped out before thinking, that made him flush to the roots of his hair. He kept himself to himself for three days, and then put in for two days' leave to go shooting near a Canal Engineer's Rest House about thirty miles out. He got his leave, and that night at Mess was noisier and more offensive than ever. He said that he was 'going to shoot big game', and left at half-past ten o'clock in an *ekka*. Partridge—which was the only thing a man could get near the Rest House—is not big game; so every one laughed.

Next morning one of the Majors came in from short leave, and heard that The Boy had gone out to shoot 'big game'. The Major had taken an interest in The Boy, and had, more than once, tried to check him. The Major put up his eyebrows when he heard of the expedition, and went to The Boy's rooms, where he rummaged.

Presently he came out and found me leaving cards on the Mess. There was no one else in the ante-room.

He said, 'The Boy has gone out shooting. *Does* a man shoot partridge with a revolver and writing-case?'

I said, 'Nonsense, Major!' for I saw what was in his mind.

He said, 'Nonsense or no nonsense, I'm going to the Canal now—at once. I don't feel easy'.

Then he thought for a minute, and said, 'Can you lie?'

'You know best,' I answered. 'It's my profession.'

'Very well,' said the Major, ' you come out with me now—at once—in an *ekka* to the Canal to shoot black-buck. Go and put on *shikar*-kit—*quick*—and drive here with a gun.'

The Major was a masterful man, and I knew that he would

187

not give orders for nothing. So I obeyed, and on return found the Major packed up in an *ekka*—gun-cases and food slung below—all ready for a shooting-trip.

He dismissed the driver and drove himself. We jogged along quietly while in the station; but, as soon as we got to the dusty road across the plains, he made that pony fly. A country-bred can do nearly anything at a pinch. We covered the thirty miles in under three hours, but the poor brute was nearly dead.

Once I said, 'What's the blazing hurry, Major?'

He said quietly, 'The Boy has been alone, by himself for— one, two, five—fourteen hours now! I tell you, I don't feel easy.'

The uneasiness spread itself to me, and I helped to beat the pony.

When we came to the Canal Engineer's Rest House the Major called for The Boy's servant; but there was no answer. Then we went up to the house, calling for The Boy by name; but there was no answer.

'Oh, he's out shooting,' said I.

Just then I saw through one of the windows a little hurricane-lamp burning. This was at four in the afternoon. We both stopped dead in the veranda, holding our breath to catch every sound; and we heard, inside the room, the '*brr—brr—brr*' of a multitude of flies. The Major said nothing, but he took off his helmet and we entered very softly.

The Boy was dead on the bed in the centre of the bare, lime-washed room. He had shot his head nearly to pieces with his revolver. The gun-cases were still strapped, so was the bedding, and on the table lay The Boy's writing-case with photographs. He had gone away to die like a poisoned rat.

The Major said to himself softly, 'Poor Boy! Poor, *poor* devil!' Then he turned away from the bed and said, 'I want your help in this business.'

Knowing The Boy was dead by his own hand, I saw exactly what that help would be, so I passed over to the table, took a chair, lit a cheroot, and began to go through the writing-case; the Major looking over my shoulder and repeating to himself, 'We came too late!—Like a rat in a hole!—Poor, *poor* devil!'

The Boy must have spent half the night in writing to his people, to his Colonel, and to a girl at Home; and as soon as he had finished, must have shot himself, for he had been dead a long time when we came in.

I read all that he had written, and passed over each sheet to the Major as I finished it.

We saw from his accounts how very seriously he had taken everything. He wrote about 'disgrace which he had been unable to bear'—'indelible shame'—'criminal folly'—'wasted life', and so on; besides a lot of private things to his father and mother much too sacred to put into print. The letter to the girl at Home was the most pitiful of all, and I choked as I read it. The Major made no attempt to keep dry-eyed. I respected him for that. He read and rocked himself to and fro, and simply cried like a woman without caring to hide it. The letters were so dreary and hopeless and touching. We forgot all about The Boy's follies, and only thought of the poor Thing on the bed and the scrawled sheets in our hands. It was utterly impossible to let the letters go Home. They would have broken his father's heart and killed his mother after killing her belief in her son.

At last the Major dried his eyes openly, and said, 'Nice sort of thing to spring on an English family! What shall we do?'

I said, knowing what the Major had brought me out for, 'The Boy died of cholera. We were with him at the time. We can't commit ourselves to half-measures. Come along.'

Then began one of the most grimly comic scenes I have ever taken part in—the concoction of a big, written lie, bolstered with evidence, to soothe The Boy's people at Home. I began the rough draft of the letter, the Major throwing in hints here and there while he gathered up all the stuff that The Boy had written and burnt it in the fireplace. It was a hot, still evening when we began, and the lamp burned very badly. In due course I made the draft to my satisfaction, setting forth how The Boy was the pattern of all virtues, beloved by his Regiment, with every promise of a great career before him, and so on; how we had helped him through the sickness—it was no time for little lies, you will understand—and how he had died without pain. I choked while I was putting down these things and thinking of the poor people who would read them. Then I laughed at the grotesqueness of the affair, and the laughter mixed itself up with the choke—and the Major said that we both wanted drinks.

189

I am afraid to say how much whisky we drank before the letter was finished. It had not the least effect on us. Then we took off The Boy's watch, locket, and ring.

Lastly, the Major said, 'We must send a lock of hair too. A woman values that.'

But there were reasons why we could not find a lock fit to send. The boy was black-haired, and so was the Major, luckily. I cut off a piece of the Major's hair above the temple with a knife, and put it into the packet we were making. The laughing-fit and the chokes got hold of me again, and I had to stop. The Major was nearly as bad; and we both knew that the worst part of the work was to come.

We sealed up the packet, photographs, locket, seals, ring, letter, and lock of hair with The Boy's sealing-wax and The Boy's seal.

Then the Major said, 'For God's sake, let's get outside—away from the room—and think!'

We went outside, and walked on the banks of the Canal for an hour, eating and drinking what we had with us, until the moon rose. I know now exactly how a murderer feels. Finally, we forced ourselves back to the room with the lamp and the Other Thing in it, and began to take up the next piece of work. I am not going to write about this. It was too horrible. We burned the bedstead and dropped the ashes into the Canal; we took up the matting of the room and treated that in the same way. I went off to a village and borrowed two big hoes—I did not want the villagers to help,—while the major arranged—the other matters. It took us four hours' hard work to make the grave. As we worked, we argued out whether it was right to say as much as we remembered of the Burial of the Dead. We compromised things by saying the Lord's Prayer with a private unofficial prayer for the peace of the soul of The Boy. Then we filled in the grave and went into the veranda—not the house—to lie down to sleep. We were dead tired.

When we woke the Major said wearily, 'We can't go back till to-morrow. We must give him a decent time to die in. He died early *this* morning, remember. That seems more natural.' So the major must have been lying awake all the time, thinking.

I said, 'Then why didn't we bring the body back to

Cantonments?'

The major thought for a minute. 'Because the people bolted when they heard of the cholera. And the *ekka* has gone!'

That was strictly true. We had forgotten all about the *ekka*-pony, and he had gone home.

So we were left there alone, all that stifling day, in the Canal Rest House, testing and re-testing our story of The Boy's death to see if it was weak in any point. A native appeared in the afternoon, but we said that a Sahib was dead of cholera, and he ran away. As the dusk gathered, the major told me all his fears about The Boy, and awful stories of suicide or nearly-carried-out suicide—tales that made one's hair crisp. He said that he himself had once gone into the same Valley of the Shadow as The Boy, when he was young and new to the country; so he understood how things fought together in The Boy's poor jumbled head. He also said that youngsters, in their repentant moments, consider their sins much more serious and ineffaceable than they really are. We talked together all through the evening and rehearsed the story of the death of The Boy. As soon as the moon was up, and The Boy, theoretically, just buried, we struck across country for the station. We walked from eight till six o'clock in the morning; but though we were dead tired, we did not forget to go to The Boy's rooms and put away his revolver with the proper amount of cartridges in the pouch. Also to set his writing-case on the table. We found the Colonel and reported the death, feeling more like murderers than ever. Then we went to bed and slept the clock round, for there was no more in us.

The tale had credence as long as was necessary; for every one forgot about The Boy before a fortnight was over. Many people, however, found time to say that the Major had behaved scandalously in not bringing the body for a Regimental funeral. The saddest thing of all was the letter from The Boy's mother to the Major and me—with big inky blisters all over the sheet. She wrote the sweetest possible things about our great kindness, and the obligation she would be under to us as long as she lived.

All things considered, she was under an obligation, but not exactly as she meant.

THE SON OF HIS FATHER

'IT IS A queer name,' Mrs. Strickland admitted, 'and none of our family have ever borne it; but, you see, he *is* the first man to us.'

So he was called Adam, and to that world about him he was the first of men—a man-child alone. Heaven sent him no Eve for a companion, but all earth, horse and foot, was at his feet. As soon as he was old enough to appear in public he held a levee, and Strickland's sixty policemen, with their sixty clanking sabres, bowed to the dust before him. When his fingers closed a little on Imam Din's sword-hilt they rose and roared till Adam roared too, and was withdrawn.

'Now that was no cry of fear,' said Imam Din afterwards, speaking to his companions in the Police lines. 'He was angry— and so young! Brothers, he will make a very young Police officer.'

'Does the Memsahib nurse him?' said a new recruit, the dye-smell not yet out of his yellow cotton uniform.

'Ho!' said an up-country Naik scornfully; 'it has been known for *more* than ten days that my woman nurses him.' He curled his moustaches as lordlily as ever an inspector could afford to do, for he knew that the husband of the foster-mother of the son of the District Superintendent of Police was a man of consideration.

'I am glad,' said Imam Din, loosening his belt. 'Those who drink our milk become of our own blood, and I have seen, in these thirty years, that the sons of Sahibs once being born here return when they are men. Yes, they return after they have been to Belait [Europe].'

'And what do they in Belait?' asked the recruit respectfully.

'Get instruction—which thou hast not,' returned the Naik. 'Also they drink of *belaitee-panee* [soda-water] enough to give them that devil's restlessness which endures for all their lives.

Whence we of Hind have trouble.'

'My father's uncle,' said Imam Din slowly, with importance, 'was Ressaldar of the Long Coat Horse; and the Empress called him to Europe in the year that she had accomplished fifty years of rule. *He* said (and there were also other witnesses) that the Sahibs there drink only common water even as do we; and that the *belaitee-panee* does *not* run in all their rivers.'

'He said that there was a Shish Mahal—a glass palace—half a mile in length, and that the rail-trains ran under roads; and that there are boats bigger than a village. He is a great talker.' The Naik spoke scornfully. 'He had no well-born uncles.'

'*He* is at least a man of good birth,' said Imam Din, and the Naik was silent.

'Ho! Ho!' Imam Din reached out to his pipe, chuckling till his fat sides shook again. 'Strickland Sahib's foster mother was the wife of a gardener in the Ferozepur district. I was a young man then. This child also will be suckled here and he will have double wisdom, and when he is a Police officer it will be very bad for the thieves in this part of the world. Ho! Ho!'

'Strickland Sahib's butler has said,' the Naik went on, 'that they will call him Adam—and no jaw-splitting English name. Udaam. The *padre* will name him at their church in due time.'

'Who can tell the ways of the Sahibs? Now Strickland Sahib knows more of the Faith than ever I had time to learn—prayers, charms, names and stories of the Blessed Ones. Yet he is not a Mussulman,' said Imam Din Thoughtfully.

'For the reason that he knows as much of the Gods of Hindustan, and so he rides with a rein in each hand. Remember that he sat under the Baba Atal, a fakir among fakirs, for ten days; whereby a man came to be hanged for the murder of a dancing-girl on the night of the great earthquake,' the Naik replied.

'True—it is true. And yet—the Sahibs are one day so wise—and another so foolish. But he has named the child well; Adam. Huzrut Adam. Ho! Ho! Father Adam we must call him.'

'And all who minister to the child,' said the Naik quietly, but with meaning, 'will come to great honour.'

Adam throve, being played over before the Gods of at least three creeds, in the garden almost as fair as Eden. There were gigantic clumps of bamboos that talked continually, and enormous plantains, trees on whose soft paper skin he could scratch with his nails; green domes of mango-trees as huge as the dome of St. Paul's, full of parrots as big as cassowaries and grey squirrels the size of foxes. At the end of the garden stood a hedge of flaming poinsettias higher than anything in the world, because, child-like, Adam's eye could not carry to the tops of the mango-trees. Their green went out against the blue sky, but the red poinsettias he could just see. A nurse who talked continually about snakes and pulled him back from the mouth of a fascinating dry well, and a mother who believed that the sun hurt little heads, were the only drawbacks to this loveliness. But, as his legs grew under him, he found that by scaling an enormous rampart—three feet of broken-down mud wall at the end of the garden—he could come into a ready-made kingdom, where every one was his slave. Imam Din showed him the way one evening, and the Police troopers, cooking their supper, received him with rapture, and gave him pieces of very indigestible, but altogether delightful, spiced bread.

Here he sat or sprawled in the horse-feed where the Police were picketed in a double line, and he named them, men and beasts together, according to his ideas and experiences, as his First Father had done before him. In those days everything had a name, from the mud mangers to the heel-ropes, for things were people to Adam exactly as people are things to folk in their second childhood. Through all the conferences—one hand twisted into Imam Din's beard, and the other on his polished belt-buckle—there were two other people who came and went across the talk—Death and Sickness—persons greater than Imam Din, and stronger than the heel-roped horses. There was Mata, the smallpox, a woman in some way connected with pigs; and Heza, the cholera, a black man, according to Adam; and Booka, starvation; and Kismet, who settled all questions, from the untimely choking of a pet mongoose in the kitchen-drain to the absence of a young Policeman who once missed a parade and never came back. It was all very wonderful to Adam, but not worth much thinking over; for a child's mind is bounded by his eyes exactly as a horse's view of the road is limited by his blinkers. Between these objectionable shadowy vagrants stood a ring of kind faces and strong arms, and Mata and Heza could never touch Adam, the First of Men. Kismet might do so, because—and this was a mystery no staring into his looking-glass would solve—Kismet was written, like Police orders for the day, in or on Adam's head. Imam Din could not explain how this might be, and it was from that grey, fat Mussulman that Adam learned through every inflection that *Khuda janta* [God knows] that settles everything in the mind of Asia.

Beyond the fact that 'Khuda' [God] was 'a very good man and kept lions', Adam's theology did not run far. Mrs. Strickland tried to teach him a few facts, but he revolted at the story of Genesis as untrue. A turtle, he said, upheld the world, and one-half the adventures of Huzrut Nu [Father Noah] had never been told. If Mamma wanted to hear them she must ask Imam Din.

'It's awful,' said Mrs. Strickland, half crying, 'to think of his growing up like a little heathen.' Mrs. Strickland had been born and brought up in England, and did not quite understand Eastern things.

'Let him alone,' said Strickland. 'He'll grow out of it all, or it will only come to him in dreams.'

'Are you sure?' said his wife.

'Quite. I was sent home when I was seven, and they flicked it out of me with a wet towel at Harrow. Public schools don't encourage anything that isn't quite English.'

Mrs. Strickland shuddered, for she had been trying not to think of the separation that follows motherhood in India, and makes life there, for all that is written to the contrary, not quite the most desirable thing in the world. Adam trotted out to hear about more miracles, and his nurse must have worried him beyond bounds, for she came back weeping, saying that Adam-*baba* was in danger of being eaten alive by wild horses.

As a matter of fact he had shaken off Juma by bolting between a couple of picketed horses, and lying down under their bellies. That they were old personal friends of his, Juma did not understand, nor Strickland either. Adam was settled at ease when his father arrived, breathless and white, and the stallions put back their ears and squealed.

'If you come here,' said Adam, 'they will hit you kicks. Tell Juma I have eaten my rice, and I wish to be alone.'

'Come out at once,' said Strickland, for the horses were beginning to paw.

'Why should I obey Juma's order? She's afraid of horses.'

'It is not Juma's order. It is mine. Obey!'

'Ho!' said Adam. 'Juma did not tell me that'; and he crawled out on all fours among the shod feet. Mrs. Strickland was crying bitterly with fear and excitement, and as a sacrifice to the home gods Adam had to be whipped. He said with perfect justice:

'There was no order that I should *not* sit with the horses, and they are *my* horses. Why is there this *tamasha* [fuss]?'

Strickland's face showed him that the whipping was coming, and the child turned white. Mother-like, Mrs. Strickland left the room, but Juma, the foster-mother, stayed to see.

'Am I to be whipped here?' he gasped.

'Of course.'

'Before that woman? Father, I am a man—I am not afraid. It is my *izzat*—my honour.'

Strickland only laughed—(to this day I cannot imagine what possessed him), and gave Adam the little tap-tap with a riding-cane that was whipping sufficient for his years.

When it was all over, Adam said quietly, 'I am little and you are big. If I had stayed among my horse-folk I should not have been whipped. *You* are afraid to go there.'

The merest chance led me to Strickland's house that afternoon. When I was half-way down the drive Adam passed me without recognition, at a fast run. I caught one glimpse of his face under his big hat, and it was the face of his father as I had once seen it in the grey of the morning when it bent over a leper. I caught the child by the shoulder.

'Let me go!' he screamed; though he and I were the best of friends, as a rule. 'Let me go!'

'Where to, Father Adam?' He was quivering like a haltered colt.

'To the well. I have been beaten. I have been beaten before a woman! Let me go!' He tried to bite my hand.

'That is a small matter,' I said. 'Men are born to beatings.'

'*Thou* hast never been beaten,' he said savagely (we were talking in the native tongue).

'Indeed I have; times past counting.'

'Before women?'

'My mother and my *ayah* saw. *By* women, too, for that matter. What of it?'

'What didst thou do?' He stared beyond my shoulder up the long drive.

'It is long, and I have forgotten. I was older than thou art; but even then I forgot, and now the thing is only a jest to be talked of.'

Adam drew one big breath and broke down utterly in my arms. Then he raised his head, and his eyes were Strickland's eyes when Strickland gave orders.

'Ho! Imam Din!'

The fat orderly seemed to spring out of the earth at our feet, crashing through the bushes, and standing at attention.

'Hast *thou* ever been beaten?' said Adam.

'Assuredly. By my father when I was thirty years old. He beat me with a plough-beam before all the women of the village.'

'Wherefore?'

'Because I had returned to the village on leave from the Government service, and said to the village elders that they had not seen the world. Therefore he beat me to show that no seeing of the world changes father and son.'

'And thou?'

'I stood up to the beating. He was my father.'

'Good,' said Adam, and turned on his heel without another word.

Imam Din looked after him. 'An elephant breeds but once in a lifetime, but he breeds elephants. Yet I am glad I am no father of tuskers,' said he.

'What is it all?'

'His father beat him with a whip no bigger than a reed. But the child could not have done what he desired to do without leaping through me. And I am of some few pounds weight. Look!'

Imam Din stepped back through the bushes, and the pressed grass showed that he had been lying curled round the mouth of the dry well.

'When there was talk of beating, I knew that one who sat among horses such as ours was not like to kiss his father's hand. He might have done away with himself. So I lay down in this place.' We stood still looking at the well-curb.

Adam came along the garden path to us. 'I have spoken to my father,' he said simply. 'Imam Din, tell thy Naik that his woman is dismissed my service.'

'*Huzoor*! [Your Highness!]' said Imam Din, stooping low.

'For no fault of hers.'

'Protector of the Poor!'

'And to-day.'

'*Khodawund*! [Heaven-born!]'

'It is an order. Go.'

Again the salute, and Imam Din departed, with the same set of the back which he wore when he had taken an order from Strickland. I thought that it would be well to go too, but Strickland beckoned me from the veranda. When I came up he was perfectly white, rocking to and fro in his chair.

'Do you know he was going to chuck himself down the well—because I tapped him just now?' he said helplessly.

'I ought to,' I replied. 'He has just dismissed his nurse—on his own authority, I suppose?'

'He told me just now that he wouldn't have her for a nurse any more. I never supposed he meant it for an instant. I suppose she'll have to go.'

Now Strickland, the Police officer, was feared through the length and breadth of the Punjab by murderers, horse-thieves, and cattle-lifters.

Adam returned, halting outside the veranda.

'I have sent Juma away because she saw that—that which happened. Until she is gone I do not come into the house,' he said.

'But to send away thy foster-mother!' said Strickland with reproach.

'*I* do not send her away. It is *thy* blame,' and the small forefinger was pointed at Strickland. 'I will not obey her. I will not eat from her hand. I will not sleep with her. Send her away!'

Strickland stepped out and lifted the child into the veranda.

'This folly has lasted long enough,' he said. 'Come now and be wise.'

'I am little and you are big,' said Adam between set teeth. 'You can beat me before this man or cut me to pieces. But I will *not* have Juma for my *ayah* any more. She saw me beaten. I will not eat till she goes. I swear it by—my father's head.'

Strickland sent him indoors to his mother, and we could hear sounds of weeping and Adam's voice saying nothing more than 'Send Juma away!' Presently Juma came in and wept too, and Adam repeated, 'It is no fault of thine, but go!'

And the end of it was that Juma went with all her belongings, and Adam fought his own way into his little clothes until the new *ayah* came. His address of welcome to her was rather amazing. In a few words it ran: 'If I do wrong, send me to my father. If you strike me, I will try to kill you. I do not wish my *ayah* to play with me. Go and eat rice!'

From that Adam forswore the society of *ayahs* and small native boys as much as a small boy can, confining himself to Imam Din and his friends of the Police. The Naik, Juma's husband, had been presuming not a little on his position, and when Adam's favour was withdrawn from his wife he thought it best to apply for a transfer to another post. There were too many companions anxious to report his shortcomings to Strickland.

Towards his father Adam kept a guarded neutrality. There was not a touch of sulkiness in it, for the child's temper was as clear as a bell. But the difference and the politeness worried Strickland.

If the Policemen had loved Adam before the affair of the well, they worshipped him now.

'He knows what honour means,' said Imam Din. 'He has justified himself upon a point thereof. He has carried an order through his father's household as a child of the Blood might do. Therefore he is not altogether a child any longer. Wah! He is a tiger's cub.' The next time that Adam made his little unofficial inspection of the lines, Imam Din, and, by consequence, all the others, stood upon their feet with their hands to their sides, instead of calling out from where they lay, 'Salaam, Babajee,' and other disrespectful things.

But Strickland took counsel with his wife, and she with the cheque-book and their lean bank account, and they decided that Adam must go 'home' to his aunts. But England is not home to a child who has been born in India, and it never becomes home-like unless he spends all his youth there. Their bank-book showed that if they economised through the summer by going to a cheap hill-station instead of Simla (where Mrs. Strickland's parents lived, and where Strickland might be noticed by the Government) they could send Adam home in the next spring. It would be hard pinching, but it could be done.

Dalhousie was chosen as being the cheapest of the hill-stations;—Dalhousie and a little five-roomed cottage full of mildew, tucked away among the rhododendrons.

Adam had been to Simla three or four times, and knew by name most of the drivers on the road there, but this new place disquieted him. He came to me for information, his hands deep in his knickerbocker pockets, walking step for step as his father walked.

'There will be none of my *bhai-bund* [brotherhood] up there,' he said disconsolately, 'and they say that I must lie still in a *dooli* [palanquin] for a day and a night, being carried like a sheep. I wish to take some of my mounted men to Dalhousie.'

I told him that there was a small boy, called Victor, at Dalhousie, who had a calf for a pet, and was allowed to play with it on the public roads. After that Adam could not sufficiently hurry the packing.

'First,' said he, 'I shall ask that man Victor to let me play with the cow's child. If he is *muggra* [ill-conditioned], I shall tell my Policemen to take it away.'

'But that is unjust,' said Strickland, 'and there is no order that the Police should do injustice.'

'When the Government pay is not sufficient, and low-caste men are promoted, what *can* an honest man do?' Adam replied, in the very touch and accent of Imam Din; and Strickland's eyebrows went up.

'You talk too much of the Police, my son,' he said.

'Always. About everything,' said Adam promptly. 'They say that when I am an officer I shall know as much as my father.'

'God forbid, little one!'

'They say, too, that you are as clever as Shaitan [the Evil One] to know things.'

'They say that, do they?' and Strickland looked pleased.

His pay was small, but he had his reputation, and it was dear to him.

'They say also—not to me, but to one another when they eat rice behind the wall—that in your own heart you esteem yourself as wise as Suleiman [Solomon], who was cheated by Shaitan.'

This time Strickland did not look so pleased. Adam, in all innocence, launched into a long story about Suleiman-bin-Daoud, who once, out of vanity, pitted his wits against Shaitan, and because God was not on his side Shaitan sent 'a little devil of low caste,' as Adam put it, who cheated him utterly and put him to shame before 'all other kings'.

'By Gum!' said Strickland, when the tale was done, and went away, while Adam took me to task for laughing at Imam Din's stories. I did not wonder that he was called Huzrut Adam, for he looked old as all time in his grave childhood, sitting cross-legged, his battered little helmet far at the back of his head, his forefinger wagging up and down, native-fashion, and the wisdom of serpents on his unconscious lips.

That May he went up to Dalhousie with his mother, and in those days the journey ended in fifty or sixty miles of uphill travel in a palanquin along a road winding through the Himalayas. Adam sat in the *dooli* with his mother, and Strickland rode and tied with me, a spare *dooli* following. The march began after we got out of the train at Pathankot, one wet hot night among the rice and poppy fields.

II

It was all new to Adam, and he had opinions to advance—notably about a fish that jumped in a wayside pond. '*Now* I know,' he shouted, 'how God puts them there! First He makes them up above and then He drops them down. That was a new one.' Then, lifting his head to the stars, he cried: 'Oh, God, do it again, but slowly, so that I, Adam, may see.'

But nothing happened, and the *dooli*-bearers lit the noisome, dripping rag-torches, and Adam's eyes shone big in the dancing light, and we smelt the dry dust of the Plains that we were leaving after eleven months' hard work.

At stated times the men ceased their drowsy, grunting tune, and sat down for a smoke. Between the guttering of their water-pipes we could hear the cries of the beasts of the night, and the wind stirring in the folds of the mountain ahead. At the changing-stations the voice of Adam, First of Men, would be lifted to rouse the sleepers in the huts till the fresh relay of bearers shambled from their cots and the relief pony with them.

Then we would re-form and go on, and by the time the moon rose Adam was asleep, and there was no sound in the night except the grunting of the men, the husky murmur of some river a thousand feet down in the valley, and the squeaking of Strickland's saddle. So we went up from date-palm to deodar, till the dawn wind came round a corner all fresh from the snows, and we snuffed it. I heard Strickland say, 'Wife, my overcoat, please,' and Adam, fretfully, 'Where is Dalhousie and the cow's child?' Then I slept till Strickland turned me out of the warm *dooli* at seven o'clock, and I stepped into all the splendour of a cool Hill day, the Plains sweltering twenty miles back and four thousand feet below. Adam waked too, and needs must ride in front of me to ask a million questions, and shout at the monkeys and clap his hands when the painted pheasants bolted across our road, and hail every wood-cutter and drover and pilgrim within sight, till we halted for breakfast at a resthouse. After that, being a child, he went out to play with a train of bullock-drivers halted by the roadside, and we had to chase him out of a native liquor-shop, where he was bargaining with a native seven-year-old for a parrot in a bamboo cage.

Said he, wriggling on my pommel as we went on again, 'There were four men *behosh* [insensible] at the back of that house. Wherefore do men grow *behosh* from drinking?'

'It is the nature of the waters,' I said, and, calling back, 'Strick, what's that grog-shop doing so close to the road? It's a temptation to any one's servants.'

'Dunno,' said a sleepy voice in the *dooli*. 'This is Kennedy's District. 'Twasn't here in *my* time.'

'Truly the waters smell bad,' Adam went on. 'I smelt them, but I did not get the parrot even for six annas. The woman of the house gave me a love-gift that I found playing near the veranda.'

'And what was the gift, Father Adam?'

'A nose-ring for the *ayah*. Ohe! Ohe! Look at that camel with the muzzle on his nose!'

A string of loaded camels came cruising round the corner as a fleet rounds a cape.

'Ho, Malik! Why does not a camel salaam like an elephant? His neck is long enough,' Adam cried.

'The Angel Jibrail made him a fool at the beginning,' said the driver, as he swayed on the top of the leading beast, and laughter ran all along the line of red-bearded men.

'That is true,' said Adam solemnly, and they laughed again.

At last, in the late afternoon, we came to Dalhousie, the loveliest of the hill-stations, and separated, Adam hardly able to be restrained from setting out at once to find Victor and the 'cow's child'. I found them both, something to my trouble, next morning. The two young sinners had a calf on a tight rope just at a sharp turn in the Mall, and were pretending that he was a Rajah's elephant who had gone mad; and they shouted with delight. Then we began to talk, and Adam, by way of crushing Victor's repeated reminders to me that he and not 'the other' was the owner of the calf, said, 'It is true I have no cow's child; but a great *dacoity* [robbery] has been done on my father.'

'We came up together yesterday. There could have been nothing,' I said.

'It was my mother's horse. She has been *dacoited* with beating and blows, and now is *so* thin.' He held his hands an inch apart. 'My father is at the telegraph-house sending telegrams. Imam Din will cut off *all* their heads. I desire your saddle-cloth for a howdah for my elephant. Give it me!'

This was exciting, but not lucid. I went to the telegraph-office and found Strickland in a black temper among many telegraph forms. A dishevelled, one-eyed groom stood in a corner whimpering at intervals. He was a man whom Adam invariably addressed as 'Be-*shukl*, be-*ukl*, be-*ank*' [ugly, stupid, eyeless]. It seemed that Strickland had sent his wife's horse up to Dalhousie by road, a fortnight's march, in the groom's charge. This is the custom in Upper India. Among the foothills, near Dhunnera or Dhar, horse and man had been violently set upon in the night by four men, who had beaten the groom (his leg was bandaged from knee to ankle in proof), had incidentally beaten the horse, and had robbed the groom of the bucket and blanket, and all his money—eleven rupees, nine annas. Last, they had left him for dead by the wayside, where some woodcutters had found and nursed him. Then the one-eyed man howled with anguish, thinking over his bruises. 'They asked me if I was Strickland Sahib's servant, and I, thinking the Protection of the Name would be sufficient, spoke the truth. Then they beat me grievously.'

'H'm!' said Strickland. 'I thought they wouldn't dacoit as a business on the Dalhousie road. This is meant for me personally— sheer *badmashi* [impudence]. All right!'

In justice to a hard-working class it must be said that the thieves of Upper India have the keenest sense of humour. The last compliment that they can pay a Police officer is to rob him, and if, as once they did, they can loot a Deputy Inspector-General of Police, on the eve of his retirement, of everything except the clothes on his back, their joy is complete. They cause letters of derision and telegrams of condolence to be sent to the victim; for of all men thieves are most compelled to keep abreast of progress.

Strickland was a man of few words where his business was concerned. I had never seen a Police officer robbed before, and I expected some excitement, but Strickland held his tongue. He took the groom's deposition, and then retired into himself for a time. Then he sent Kennedy, of the Pathankot District, an official letter and an unofficial note. Kennedy's reply was purely unofficial, and it ran thus: 'This seems a compliment solely intended for you. My wonder is you didn't get it before. The men are probably back in your District by now. My Dhunnera and foot-hill people are highly respectable cultivators, and, seeing my Assistant is an unlicked pup, and I can't trust my Inspector out of sight, I'm not going to turn their harvest upside down with Police investigations. I'm run off my feet with vaccination Police work. You'd better look at home. The Shubkudder Gang were through here a fortnight back. They laid up at the Amritzar Serai, and worked down. No cases against them in my charge; but, remember, you imprisoned their head-man for receiving stolen goods in the Prub Dyal burglary. They owe you one.'

'Exactly what I thought,' said Strickland. 'I had a notion it *was* the Subkudder Gang from the first. We must make it pleasant for them at Peshawur, and in my district, too. They're just the kind that would lie up under Imam Din's shadow.'

From this point onward the wires began to be worked heavily. Strickland had a very fair knowledge of the Shubkudder Gang, gathered at first hand.

They were the same syndicate that had once stolen a Deputy-Commissioner's cow, put horse-shoes on her, and taken her forty miles into the jungle before they lost interest in the joke. They added insult to insult by writing that the Deputy-Commissioner's cows and horses were so much alike that it took them two days to find out the difference and they would not lift the like of such cattle any more.

The District Superintendent at Peshawur replied to Strickland that he was expecting the Gang, and Strickland's Assistant, in his own District, being young and full of zeal, sent up the most amazing clues.

'Now that's just what I want the young fool not to do,' said Strickland. 'He is an English boy, born and bred, and his father before him. He has about as much tact as a bull, and he won't work quietly under my Inspector. I wish the Government would keep our service for country-born men. Those first five or six years in India give a man a pull that lasts him all his life. Adam, if only you were old enough to be my Assistant!' He looked down at the little fellow in the veranda. Adam was deeply interested in the dacoity, and, unlike a child, did not lose interest after the first week. On the contrary, he would ask his father every evening what had been done, and Strickland had drawn him a map on the white wall of the veranda, showing the different towns in which Policemen were on the look-out for thieves. They were Amritzar, Jullunder, Phillour, Gurgaon, Rawal Pindi, Peshawur, and Multan. Adam looked up at it as he answered:

'There has been a great *dikh* [trouble] in this case?'

'Very great trouble. I wish that thou wert a young man and my Assistant to help me.'

'Dost thou need help, my father?' Adam asked curiously, with his head on one side.

'Very much.'

'Leave it all alone. It is bad. Let loose everything.'

'That must not be. Those beginning a business continue to the end.'

'Thou wilt continue to the end? Dost thou not *know* who did the dacoity?'

Strickland shook his head. Adam turned to me with the same question, and I answered it in the same way.

'What foolish people!' he said, and turned his back on us.

He showed plainly in all our dealings afterwards how we had fallen in his opinion. Strickland told me that he would sit at the door of his father's workroom and stare at him for half an hour at a time as he went through his papers. Strickland seemed to work harder over the case than if he had been in office in the Plains.

'And sometimes I look up and I fancy the little chap's laughing at me. It's an awful thing to have a son. You see, he's your own and *his* own, and between the two you don't quite know how to handle him,' said Strickland. 'I wonder what in the world he thinks about.'

I asked Adam this later on, quietly. He put his head on one side for a moment and replied: 'In these days I think about great things. I do not play with Victor and cow's child any more. Victor is only a *baba*.'

At the end of the third week of Strickland's leave, the result of Strickland's labours—labours that had made Mrs. Strickland more indignant against the dacoits than any one else—came to hand. The Police at Peshawur reported that half of the Shubkudder Gang were held at Peshawur to account for the possession of some blankets and a horse-bucket. Strickland's Assistant had also four men under suspicion in his charge; and Imam Din must have stirred up Strickland's Inspector to investigations on his own account, for a string of incoherent telegrams came in from the Club Secretary in which he entreated, exhorted and commanded Strickland to take his 'mangy Policemen' off the Club premises. 'Your men, in servants' quarters here, examining cook. Billiard-marker indignant. Steward threatens resignation. Members furious. Grooms stopped on roads. Shut up, or my resignation goes to the Committee.'

'Now I shouldn't in the least wonder,' said Strickland

thoughtfully to his wife, 'if the Club were not just *the* place where men would lie up. Billy Watson isn't at all pleased, though. I think I shall have to cut my leave by a week and go down to take charge. If there's anything to be told, the men will tell me.'

Mrs. Strickland's eyes filled with tears. 'I shall try to steal ten days if I can in the autumn,' he said soothingly, 'but I must go now. It will never do for the gang to think that they can burgle *my* belongings.'

That was in the forenoon, and Strickland asked me to lunch to leave me some instructions about his dog, with authority to rebuke those who did not attend to her. Tietjens was growing too old and too fat to live in the Plains in the summer. When I came, Adam had climbed into his high chair at table, and Mrs. Strickland seemed ready to weep at any moment over the general misery of things.

'I go down to the Plains to-morrow, my son,' said Strickland.

'Wherefore?' said Adam, reaching out for a ripe mango and burying his head in it.

'Imam Din has caught the men who did the dacoity, and there are also others at Peshawur under suspicion. I must go to see.'

'*Bus*! [Enough],' said Adam, between sucks at his mango, as Mrs. Strickland tucked the napkin round his neck. 'Imam Din speaks lies. Do not go.'

'It is necessary. There has been great *dikh-dari* [trouble-giving].'

Adam came out of the fruit for a minute and laughed. Then, returning he spoke between slow and deliberate mouthfuls.

'The dacoits live in Beshakl's head. They will never be caught. All people know that. The cook knows, and the scullion, and Rahim Baksh here.'

'Nay,' said the butler behind his chair hastily. 'What should *I* know? Nothing at all does the Servant of the Presence know.'

'*Achcha*! [Good],' said Adam, and sucked on. 'Only it *is* known.'

'Speak, then, son,' said Strickland to him. 'What dost thou know? Remember my groom was beaten insensible.'

'That was in the bad-water shop where I played when we came up here. The boy who would not sell me the parrot for six

207

annas told me that a one-eyed man had come there and drunk the bad waters and gone mad. He broke bedsteads. They hit him with a bamboo till he was senseless, and fearing he was dead, they nursed him on milk—like a little *baba*. When I was playing first with the cow's child, I asked Beshakl if he were that man, and he said no. But *I* knew, because many woodcutters in Dalhousie asked him whether his head were whole now.'

'But why,' I interrupted, 'did Beshakl tell lies?'

'Oh! He is a low-caste man, and desired to get consideration. Now he is a witness in a great law-case, and men will go to the jail on his account. It was to give trouble and obtain notice that he did it.'

'Was it all lies?' said Strickland.

'Ask him,' said Adam, through the mango-pulp.

Strickland passed through the door. There was a howl of despair in the servants' quarters up the hill, and he returned with the one-eyed groom.

'Now,' said Strickland, 'it is known. Declare!'

'Beshakl,' said Adam, while the man gasped. 'Imam Din has caught four men, and there are some more at Peshawur. *Bus*! *Bus*! *Bus*! [Enough].'

'Thou didst get drunk by the wayside, and didst make a false case to cover it. Speak!'

Like a good many other men, Strickland, in possession of a few facts, was irresistible. The groom groaned.

'I—I did not get drunk till—till—Protector of the Poor, the mare rolled.'

'*All* horses roll at Dhunnera. The road is too narrow before that, and they smell where the other horses have rolled. This the bullock-drivers told me when we camp up here,' said Adam.

'She rolled. So her saddle was cut and the curb-chain lost.'

'See!' said Adam, tugging a curb-chain from his pocket. 'That woman in the shop gave it to me for a love-gift. Beshakl said it was not his when I showed it. But I knew.'

'Then they at the grog-shop, knowing that I was the Servant of the Presence, said that unless I drank and spent money they would tell.'

'A lie! A lie!' said Strickland. 'Son of an owl, speak the truth now at least.'

'Then I was afraid because I had lost the curb-chain, so I cut the saddle across and about.'

'She did *not* roll, then?' said Strickland, bewildered and angry.

'It was only the curb-chain that was lost. Then I cut the saddle and went to drink in the shop. I drank and there was a fray. The rest I have forgotten till I recovered.'

'And the mare the while? What of the mare?'

The man looked at Strickland and collapsed.

'She bore faggots for a week,' he said.

'Oh, poor Diamond!' said Mrs. Strickland.

'And Beshakl was paid four annas for her hire three days ago by the woodcutter's brother, who is the left-hand man of our rikshaw-men here,' said Adam, in a loud and joyful voice. 'We *all* knew. We all knew. I and the servants.'

Strickland was silent. His wife stared helplessly at the child; the soul out of Nowhere that went its own way alone.

'Did no man help thee with the lies?' I asked of the groom.

'None, Protector of the Poor—not one.'

'They grew, then?'

'As a tale grows in telling. Alas! I am a very bad man!' and he blinked his one eye dolefully.

'Now four men are held at my Police-station on thy account, and God knows how many more at Peshawur, besides the questions at Multan, and my honour is lost, and my mare has been pack-pony to a wood-cutter. Son of Devils, what canst thou do to make amends?'

There was just a little break in Strickland's voice, and the man caught it. Bending low, he answered, in the abject fawning whine that confounds right and wrong more surely than most modern creeds, 'Protector of the Poor, is the Police Service shut to—an honest man?'

'Out!' cried Strickland, and swiftly as the groom departed he must have heard our shouts of laughter behind him.

'If you dismiss that man, Strick, I shall engage him. He's a genius,' I said. 'It will take you months to put this mess right, and Billy Watson won't give you a minute's peace.'

'You aren't going to tell him?' said Strickland appealingly.

'I couldn't keep this to myself if you were my own brother.

Four men arrested with you—four or forty at Peshawur—and what was that you said about Multan?'

'Oh, nothing. Only some camel-men there have been——'

'And a tribe of camel-men at Multan! All on account of a lost curb-chain. Oh, my Aunt!'

'And whose Memsahib [lady] was thy aunt?' said Adam, with the mango-stone in his fist. We began to laugh again.

'But here,' said Strickland, pulling his face together, 'is a very bad child who has caused his father to lose his honour before all the Policemen of the Punjab.'

'Oh, *they* know,' said Adam. 'It was only for the sake of show that they caught people. Assuredly they all knew it was *benowti* [make-up].'

'And since when hast thou known?' said the first Policeman in India to his son.

'Four days after we came here, after the woodcutter had asked Beshakl after the health of his head. Beshakl all but slew one of them at the bad-water place.'

'If thou hadst spoken then, time and money and trouble to me and others had all been spared. *Baba*, thou hast done a wrong greater than thy knowledge, and thou hast put me to shame, and set me out upon false words, and broken my honour. Thou hast done *very* wrong. But perhaps thou didst not think?'

'Nay, but I *did* think. My father, *my* honour was lost when that beating of me happened in Juma's presence. Now it is made whole again.'

And with the most enchanting smile in the world Adam climbed up on to his father's lap.

INTERCHAPTER

PAGETT, M.P.

PAGETT, M.P., was a liar, and a fluent liar therewith,—
He spoke of the heat of India as the "Asian Solar Myth";
Came on a four months' visit, to "study the East", in
November,
And I got him to sign an agreement vowing to stay till
September.

March came in with the *koil*. Pagett was cool and gay,
Called me a "bloated Brahmin," talked of my "princely pay".
March went out with the roses. "Where is your heat?" said
he.
"Coming," said I to Pagett. "Skittles!" said Pagett, M.P.

April began with the punkah, coolies, and prickly heat,—
Pagett was dear to mosquitoes, sandflies found him a treat.
He grew speckled and lumpy—hammered, I grieve to say,
Aryan brothers who fanned him, in an illiberal way.

May set in with a dust-storm,—Pagett went down with the
sun.
All the delights of the season tickled him one by one.
Imprimis—ten days' "liver"—due to drinking beer;
Later, a dose of fever—slight, but he called it severe.

Dysent'ry touched him in June, after the *Chota Bursat*—
Lowered his portly person—made him yearn to depart.
He didn't call me a "Brahmin", or "bloated", or "overpaid",
But seemed to think it a wonder that any one stayed.

July was a trifle unhealthy,—Pagett was ill with fear,
'Called it the "Cholera Morbus", hinted that life was dear.
He babbled of "Eastern Exile", and mentioned his home with tears;
But I hadn't seen *my* children for close upon seven years.

We reached a hundred and twenty once in the Court at noon,
(I've mentioned Pagett was portly) Pagett went off in a swoon.
That was an end to the business: Pagett, the perjured, fled
With a practical, working knowledge of "Solar Myths" in his head.

And I laughed as I drove from the station, but the mirth died out on my lips
As I thought of the fools like Pagett who write of their "Eastern trips",
And the sneers of the travelled idiots who duly misgovern the land,
And I prayed to the Lord to deliver another one into my hand.

[From *Barrackroom Ballads*, etc.]

THE ENLIGHTENMENTS OF PAGETT, M.P.

Because half-a-dozen grasshoppers under a fern make the field ring with their importunate chink while thousands of great cattle, reposed beneath the shadow of the British oak, chew the cud and are silent, pray do not imagine that those who make the noise are the only inhabitants of the field—that, of course, they are many in number—or that, after all, they are other than the little, shrivelled, meagre, hopping, though loud and troublesome insects of the hour.
—Burke, 'Reflections on the Revolution in France'

THEY WERE SITTING in the veranda of 'the splendid palace of an Indian Pro-Consul', surrounded by all the glory and mystery of the immemorial East. In plain English it was a one-storeyed, ten-roomed, white-washed, mud-roofed bungalow, set in a dry garden of dusty tamarisk trees and divided from the road by a low mud wall. The green parrots screamed overhead as they flew in battalions to the river for their morning drink. Beyond the wall, clouds of fine dust showed where the cattle and goats of the city were passing afield to graze. The remorseless white light of the winter sunshine of Northern India lay upon everything and improved nothing, from the whining Persian-wheel by the lawn-tennis court to the long perspective of level road and blue, domed tombs of Mohammedan saints just visible above the trees.

'A Happy New Year,' said Orde to his guest. 'It's the first you've ever spent out of England, isn't it?'

'Yes. Happy New Year,' said Pagett, smiling at the sunshine. 'What a divine climate you have here! Just think of the brown, cold fog hanging over London now!' And he rubbed his hands.

It was more than twenty years since he had last seen Orde, his schoolmate, and their paths in the world had divided early. The one had quitted college to become a cog-wheel in the machinery of the great Indian Government; the other, more blessed with goods, had been whirled into a similar position in the English scheme. Three successive elections had not affected Pagett's position with a loyal constituency, and he had grown insensibly to regard himself in some sort as a pillar of the Empire whose real worth would be known later on. After a few years of conscientious attendance at many divisions, after newspaper battles innumerable, and the publication of interminable correspondence, and more hasty oratory than in his calmer moments he cared to think upon, it occurred to him, as it had occurred to many of his fellows in Parliament, that a tour to India would enable him to sweep a larger lyre and address himself to the problem of Imperial administration with a firmer hand.

Accepting, therefore, a general invitation extended to him by Orde some years before, Pagett had taken ship to Karachi, and only overnight had been received with joy by the Deputy-Commissioner of Amara. They had sat late, discussing the changes and chances of twenty years, recalling the names of the dead, and weighing the futures of the living, as is the custom of men meeting after intervals of action.

Next morning they smoked the after-breakfast pipe in the veranda, still regarding each other curiously, Pagett in a light grey frock-coat and garments much too thin for the time of the year, and a *pagri*ed sun-hat carefully and wonderfully made; Orde in a shooting-coat, riding-breeches, brown cowhide boots with spurs, and a battered flax helmet. He had ridden some miles in the early morning to inspect a doubtful river-dam. The men's faces differed as much as their attire. Orde's, worn and wrinkled about the eyes and grizzled at the temples, was the harder and more square of the two, and it was with something like envy that the owner looked at the comfortable outlines of Pagett's blandly receptive countenance, the clear skin, the untroubled eye, and the mobile, clean-shaved lips.

'And this is India!' said Pagett for the twentieth time, staring long and intently at the grey feathering of the tamarisks.

'One portion of India only. It's very much like this for three hundred miles in every direction. By the way, now that you have rested a little—I wouldn't ask the old question before—what d'you think of the country?'

"Tis the most pervasive country that ever yet was seen, I acquired several pounds of your country coming up from Karachi. The air is heavy with it, and for miles and miles along that distressful eternity of rail there's no horizon to show where air and earth separate.'

'Yes. It isn't easy to see truly or far in India. But you had a decent passage out, hadn't you?'

'Very good on the whole. Your Anglo-Indian may be unsympathetic about one's political views; but he has reduced ship life to a science.'

'The Anglo-Indian is a political orphan, and if he's wise he won't be in a hurry to be adopted by your party grandmothers. But how were your companions unsympathetic?'

'Well, there was a man called Dawlishe, a judge somewhere in this country, it seems, and a capital partner at whist, by the way, and when I wanted to talk to him about the progress of India in a political sense' (Orde hid a grin which might or might not have been sympathetic), 'the National Congress movement, and other things in which, as a Member of Parliament, I'm of course interested, he shifted the subject, and when I once cornered him, he looked me calmly in the eye, and said: "That's all Tommy Rot. Come and have a game at Bull." You may laugh, but that isn't the way to treat a great and important question; and, knowing who I was, well, I thought it rather rude, don't you know; and yet Dawlishe is a thoroughly good fellow.'

'Yes; he's a friend of mine, and one of the straightest men I know. I suppose, like many Anglo-Indians, he felt it was hopeless to give you any just idea of any Indian question without the documents before you, and in this case the documents you want are the country and the people.'

'Precisely. That was why I came straight to you, bringing an open mind to bear on things. I'm anxious to know what popular feeling in India is really like, y'know, now that it has wakened into political life. The National Congress, in spite of Dawlishe, must have caused great excitement among the masses?'

'On the contrary, nothing could be more tranquil than the

state of popular feeling; and as to excitement, the people would as soon be excited over the "Rule of Three" as over the Congress.'

'Excuse me, Orde, but do you think you are a fair judge? Isn't the official Anglo-Indian naturally jealous of any external influences that might move the masses, and so much opposed to liberal ideas, truly liberal ideas, that he can scarcely be expected to regard a popular movement with fairness?'

'What did Dawlishe say about Tommy Rot? Think a moment, old man. You and I were brought up together; taught by the same tutors, read the same books, lived the same life, and thought, as you may remember, in parallel lines. I come out here, learn new languages, and work among new races; while you, more fortunate, remain at home. Why should I change my mind—our mind—because I change my sky? Why should I and the few hundred Englishmen in my Service become unreasonable, prejudiced fossils, while you and your newer friends alone remain bright and open-minded? You don't fancy Civilians are members of a Primrose League?'

'Of course not, but the mere position of an English official gives him a point of view which cannot but bias his mind on this question,' Pagett moved his knee up and down a little uneasily as he spoke.

'That sounds plausible enough, but, like more plausible notions on Indian matters, I believe it's a mistake. You'll find when you come to consult the unofficial Briton that our fault, as a class,—I speak of the civilian now—is rather to magnify the progress that has been made towards liberal institutions. It is of English origin, such as it is, and the stress of our work since the Mutiny—only thirty years ago—has been in that direction. No, I think you will get no fairer or more dispassionate view of the Congress business than such men as I can give you. But I may as well say at once that those who know most of India, from the inside, are inclined to wonder at the noise our scarcely-begun experiment makes in England.'

'But surely the gathering together of Congress delegates is of itself a new thing.'

'There's nothing new under the sun. When Europe was a jungle half Asia flocked to the canonical conferences of Buddhism; and for centuries people have gathered at Puri,

216

Hardwar, Trimbak, and Benares in immense numbers. A great meeting, what you call a mass meeting, is really one of the oldest and most popular of Indian institutions. In the case of the Congress meetings, the only notable fact is that the priests of the altar are British, not Buddhists, Jain, or Brahminical, and that the whole thing is a British contrivance kept alive by the efforts of Messrs. Hume, Eardley Norton, and Digby.'

'You mean to say, then, it's not a spontaneous movement?'

'What movement was ever spontaneous in any true sense of the word? This seems to be more factitious than usual. You seem to know a great deal about it; try it by the touchstone of subscriptions, a coarse but fairly trustworthy criterion, and there is scarcely the colour of money in it. The delegates write from England that they are out of pocket for working expenses, railway fares, and stationery—the mere pasteboard and scaffolding of their show. It is, in fact, collapsing from mere financial inanition.'

'But you cannot deny that the people of India, who are, perhaps, too poor to subscribe, are mentally and morally moved by the agitation,' Pagett insisted.

'That is precisely what I *do* deny. The native side of the movement is the work of a limited class, a microscopic minority, as Lord Dufferin described it, when compared with the people proper, but still a very interesting class, seeing that it is of our own creation. It is composed almost entirely of those of the literary or clerkly castes who have received an English education.'

'Surely that's a very important class. Its members must be the ordained leaders of popular thought.'

'Anywhere else they might be leaders, but they have no social weight in this topsy-turvy land, and though they have been employed in clerical work for generations, they have no practical knowledge of affairs. A ship's clerk is a useful person, but he is scarcely the captain; and an Orderly-Room writer, however smart he may be, is not the Colonel. You see, the writer class in India has never till now aspired to anything like command. It wasn't allowed to. The Indian gentleman, for thousands of years past, has resembled Victor Hugo's noble:—

> "*Un vrai sire
> Chatelain
> Laisse ecrire
> Le vilain.*
>
> *Sa main digne
> Quand il signe
> Egratigne
> Le velin.*"

And the little *egratigneures* he most likes to make have been scored pretty deeply by the sword.'

'But this is childish and mediaeval nonsense!'

'Precisely; and from your, or rather our, point of view the pen *is* mightier than the sword. In this country it is otherwise. The fault lies in our Indian balances, not yet adjusted to civilised weights and measures.'

'Well, at all events, this literary class represents the natural aspirations and wishes of the people at large, though it may not exactly lead them, and, in spite of all you say, Orde, I defy you to find a really sound English Radical who would not sympathise with those aspirations.'

Pagett spoke with some warmth, and he had scarcely ceased when a well-appointed dog-cart turned into the compound gates, and Orde rose, saying:—

'Here is Edwards, the Master of the Lodge I neglect so diligently. Come to talk about accounts, I suppose.'

As the vehicle drove up under the porch Pagett also rose, saying with the trained effusion born of much practice:—

'But this is also my friend, my old and valued friend, Edwards. I'm delighted to see you. I knew you were in India, but not exactly where.'

'Then it isn't accounts, Mr. Edwards,' said Orde cheerily.

'Why, no, sir. I heard Mr. Pagett was coming, and as our works were closed for the New Year I thought I would drive over and meet him.'

'A very happy thought. Mr. Edwards, you may not know, Orde, was a leading member of our Radical Club at Switchston, when I was beginning political life, and I owe much to his exertions. There's no pleasure like meeting an old friend, except, perhaps, making a new one. I suppose, Mr. Edwards, you stick to the good old cause?'

'Well, you see, sir, things are different out here. There's precious little one can find to say against the government, which was the main of our talk at Home, and them that do say things are not the sort o' people a man who respects himself would like to be mixed up with. There are no politics, in a manner of speaking, in India. It's all work.'

'Surely you are mistaken, my good friend. Why, I have come all the way from England just to see the working of this great National movement.'

'I don't know where you're going to find the nation as moves, to begin with, and then you'll be hard put to it to find what they are moving about. It's like this, sir,' said Edwards, who had not quite relished being called 'my good friend'. 'They haven't got any grievance—nothing to hit with, don't you see, sir; and then there's not much to hit against, because the Government is more like a kind of general Providence, directing an old-fashioned state of things, than that at Home, where there's something new thrown down for us to fight about every three months.'

'You are probably, in your workshops, full of English mechanics, out of the way of learning what the masses think.'

'I don't know so much about that. There are four of us English foremen, and between seven and eight hundred native fitters, smiths, carpenters, painters, and such-like.'

'And they are full of the Congress, of course?'

'Never hear a word of it from year's end to year's end, and I speak the talk, too. But I wanted to ask how things are going on at Home—old Tyler and Brown and the rest?'

'We will speak of them presently, but your account of the indifference of your men surprises me almost as much as your own. I fear you are a backslider from the good old doctrine, Edwards.' Pagett spoke as one who mourned the death of a near relative.

'Not a bit, sir, but I should be if I took up with a parcel of Babus, pleaders, and schoolboys, as never did a day's work in their lives, and couldn't if they tried. And if you was to poll us English railwaymen, mechanics, tradespeople, and the like of that all up and down the country from Peshawur to Calcutta, you would find us mostly in a tale together. And yet you know we're the same English you pay some respect to at Home at 'lection time, and we have the pull o' knowing something about it.'

'This is very curious, but you will let me come and see you, and perhaps you will kindly show me the railway works, and we will talk things over at leisure. And about all old friends and old times,' added Pagett, detecting with quick insight a look of disappointment in the mechanic's face.

Nodding briefly to Orde, Edwards mounted his dog-cart and drove off.

'It's very disappointing,' said the member to Orde, who, while his friend discoursed with Edwards, had been looking over a bundle of sketches drawn on grey paper in purple ink, brought to him by a *chaprassi*.

'Don't let it trouble you, old chap,' said Orde sympathetically. 'Look here a moment; here are some sketches by the man who made the carved-wood screen you admired so much in the dining-room, and wanted a copy of, and the artist himself is here too.'

'A native?' said Pagett.

'Of course,' was the reply. 'Bishen Singh is his name, and he has two brothers to help him. When there is an important job to do, the three go into partnership, but they spend most of their time and all their money in litigation over an inheritance, and I'm afraid they are getting involved. Thorough-bred Sikhs of the old rock, obstinate, touchy, bigoted, and cunning, but good men for all that. Here is Bishen Singh—shall we ask him about the Congress?'

But Bishen Singh, who approached with a respectful salaam, had never heard of it, and he listened with a puzzled face and obviously feigned interest to Orde's account of its aims and objects, finally shaking his vast white turban with great significance when he learned that it was promoted by certain pleaders named by Orde, and by educated natives. He began with laboured respect to explain how he was a poor man with no concern in such matters, which were all under the control of God, but presently broke out of Urdu into familiar Punjabi, the mere sound of which had a rustic smack of village smoke-reek and plough-tail, as he denounced the wearers of white coats, the jugglers with words who filched his field from him, the men whose backs were never bowed in honest work; and poured ironical scorn on the Bengali. He and one of his brothers had seen Calcutta, and being at work there, had Bengali carpenters given them as assistants.

'Those carpenters!' said Bishen Singh. 'Black apes were more efficient workmates, and as for the Bengali Babu—tchick!' The guttural click needed no interpretation, but Orde translated the rest, while Pagett gazed with interest at the wood-carver.

'He seems to have a most illiberal prejudice against the Bengali,' said the M. P.

'Yes, it's very sad that for ages outside Bengal there should be so bitter a prejudice. Pride of race, which also means race-hatred, is the plague and curse of India and it spreads far.' Orde pointed with his riding-whip to the large map of India on the veranda wall.

'See! I begin with the North,' said he. 'There's the Afghan, and, as a highlander, he despises all the dwellers in Hindustan—with the exception of the Sikh, whom he hates as cordially as the Sikh hates him. The Hindu loathes Sikh and Afghan, and the Rajput—that's a little lower down across this yellow bit of desert—has a strong objection, to put it mildly, to the Maratha, who, by the way, poisonously hates the Afghan. Let's go North a minute. The Sindhi hates everybody I've mentioned. Very good, we'll take less warlike races. The cultivator of Northern India domineers over the man in the next province, and the Behari of the North-West ridicules the Bengali. They are all at one on that point. I'm giving you merely the roughest possible outlines of the facts, of course.'

Bishen Singh, his clean-cut nostrils still quivering, watched the large sweep of the whip as it travelled from the Frontier, through Sind, the Punjab, and Rajputana, till it rested by the valley of the Jumna.

'Hate—eternal and inextinguishable hate,' concluded Orde, flicking the lash of the whip across the map from east to west as he sat down. 'Remember Canning's advice to Lord Granville: "Never write or speak Indian things without looking at a map".'

Pagett opened his eyes. Orde resumed. 'And the race-hatred is only a part of it. What's really the matter with Bishen Singh is class hatred, which, unfortunately, is even more intense and more widely spread. That's one of the little drawbacks of caste, which some of your recent English writers find an impeccable system.'

The wood-carver was glad to be recalled to the business of his craft, and his eyes shone as he received instructions for a carved wooden doorway for Pagett, which he promised should be splendidly executed and despatched to England in six months. It is an irrelevant detail, but in spite of Orde's reminders, fourteen months elapsed before the work was finished. Business over, Bishen Singh hung about, reluctant to take his leave, and at last joining his hands and approaching Orde with bated breath and whispering humbleness, said he had a petition to make; Orde's face suddenly lost all trace of expression. 'Speak on, Bishen Singh,' said he, and the carver in a whining tone explained that his case against his brothers was fixed for hearing before a native judge, and—here he dropped his voice still lower till he was summarily stopped by Orde, who sternly pointed to the gate with an emphatic 'Begone!'

Bishen Singh, showing but little sign of discomposure, salaamed respectfully to the friends and departed.

Pagett looked inquiry. Orde, with complete recovery of his usual urbanity, replied, 'It's nothing. Only the old story. He wants his case to be tried by an English judge—they all do that—, but when he began to hint that the other side were in improper relations with the native judge I had to shut him up. Gunga Ram, the man he wanted to make insinuations about, may not be very bright; but he's as honest as daylight on the bench. But that's just what one can't get a native to believe.'

'Do you really mean to say these people prefer to have their cases tried by English judges?'

'Why, certainly.'

Pagett drew a long breath. 'I didn't know that before.' At this point a phaeton entered the compound, and Orde rose with 'Confound it, there's old Rasul Ali Khan come to pay one of his tiresome duty-calls. I'm afraid we shall never get through our little Congress discussion.'

Pagett was an almost silent spectator of the grave formalities of a visit paid by a punctilious old Mohammedan gentleman to an Indian official; and was much impressed by the distinction of manner and fine appearance of the Mohammedan landholder. When the exchange of polite banalities came to a pause, he expressed a wish to learn the courtly visitor's opinion of the National Congress.

Orde reluctantly interpreted, and with a smile which even Mohammedan politeness could not save from bitter scorn, Rasul Ali Khan intimated that he knew nothing about it and cared still less. It was a kind of talk encouraged by the Government for some mysterious purpose of its own, and for his own part he wondered and held his peace.

Pagett was far from satisfied with this, and wished to have the old gentleman's opinion on the propriety of managing all Indian affairs on the basis of an elective system.

Orde did his best to explain, but it was plain the visitor was bored and bewildered. Frankly, he didn't think much of committees; they had a Municipal Committee at Lahore and had elected a menial servant, an orderly, as a member. He had been informed of this on good authority, and after that committees had ceased to interest him. But all was according to the rule of the Government, and, please God, it was all for the best.

'What an old fossil it is!' cried Pagett, as Orde returned from seeing his guest to the door; 'Just like some old blue-blooded hidalgo of Spain. What does he really think of the Congress after all, and of the elective system?'

'Hates it all like poison. When you are sure of a majority, election is a fine system; but you can scarcely expect the Mohammedans, the most masterful and powerful minority in the country, to contemplate their own extinction with joy. The worst of it is that he and his co-religionists, who are many, and the landed proprietors, also of Hindu race, are frightened and put out by this election business and the importance we have bestowed on lawyers, pleaders, writers, and the like, who have, up to now, been in abject submission to them. They say little, but after all they are the most important faggots in the great bundle of communities, and all the glib bunkum in the world

223

would not pay for their estrangement. They have controlled the land.'

'But I am assured that experience of local self-government in your municipalities has been most satisfactory, and when once the principle is accepted in your centres, don't you know, it is bound to spread, and these important—ah'm—people of yours would learn it like the rest. I see no difficulty at all,' and the smooth lips closed with the complacent snap habitual to Pagett, M.P., the "man of cheerful yesterdays and confident to-morrows".

Orde looked at him with a dreary smile.

'The privilege of election has been most reluctantly withdrawn from scores of municipalities, others have had to be summarily suppressed, and, outside the Presidency towns, the actual work done has been badly performed. This is of less moment, perhaps—it only sends up the local death-rates—than the fact that the public interest in municipal elections, never very strong, has waned, and is waning, in spite of careful nursing on the part of Government servants.'

'Can you explain this lack of interest?' said Pagett, putting aside the rest of Orde's remarks.

'You may find a ward of the key in the fact that only one in every thousand of our population can spell. Then they are infinitely more interested in religion and caste questions than in any sort of politics. When the business of mere existence is over, their minds are occupied by a series of interests, pleasures, rituals, superstitions, and the like, based on centuries of tradition and usage. You, perhaps, find it hard to conceive of people absolutely devoid of curiosity, to whom the book, the daily paper, and the printed speech are unknown, and you would describe their life as blank. That's a profound mistake. You are in another land, another century, down on the bed-rock of society, where the family merely, and not the community, is all-important. The average Oriental cannot be brought to look beyond his clan. His life, too, is more complete and self-sufficing and less sordid and low-thoughted than you might imagine. It is bovine and slow in some respects, but it is never empty. You and I are inclined to put the cart before the horse, and forget that it is the man that is elemental, not the book.

224

> *"The corn and the cattle are all my care,*
> *And the rest is the will of God."*

Why should such folk look up from their immemorially appointed round of duty and interests to meddle with the unknown and fuss with voting-papers? How would you, atop of all your interests, care to conduct even one-tenth of your life according to the manners and customs of the Papuans, let's say? That's what it comes to.'

'But if they won't take the trouble to vote, why do you anticipate that Mohammedans, proprietors, and the rest would be crushed by majorities of them?'

Again Pagett disregarded the closing sentence.

'Because, though the landholders would not move a finger on any purely political question, they could be raised in dangerous excitement by religious hatreds. Already the first note of this has been sounded by the people who are trying to get up an agitation on the cow-killing question, and every year there is trouble over the Mohammedan Mohurrum processions.'

'But who looks after the popular rights, being thus unrepresented?'

'The Government of Her Majesty the Queen, Empress of India, in which, if the Congress promoters are to be believed, the people have an implicit trust; for the Congress circular, specially prepared for rustic comprehension, says the movement is *"for the remission of tax, the advancement of Hindustan, and the strengthening of the British Government"*. This paper is headed in large letters—"MAY THE PROSPERITY OF THE EMPRESS OF INDIA ENDURE".'

'Really!' said Pagett. 'That shows some cleverness. But there are things better worth imitation in our English methods of— er—political statement than this sort of amiable fraud.'

'Anyhow,' resumed Orde, 'you perceive that not a word is said about elections and the elective principle, and the reticence of the Congress promoters here shows they are wise in their generation.'

'But the elective principle must triumph in the end, and the little difficulties you seem to anticipate would give way on the introduction of a well-balanced scheme capable of definite extension.'

'But is it possible to devise a scheme which, always assuming that the people took any interest in it, without enormous expense, ruinous dislocation of the Administration, and danger to the public peace, can satisfy the aspirations of Mr. Hume and his following, and yet safeguard the interests of the Mohammedans, the landed and wealthy classes, the conservative Hindus, the Eurasians, Parsees, Sikhs, Rajputs, native Christians, domiciled Europeans, and others, who are each important and powerful in their way?'

Pagett's attention, however, was diverted to the gate, where a group of cultivators stood in apparent hesitation.

'Here are the twelve Apostles, by Jove!—come straight out of Raphael's cartoons,' said the M. P., with the fresh appreciation of a newcomer.

Orde, loath to be interrupted, turned impatiently towards the villagers, and their leader, handing his long staff to one of his companions, advanced to the house.

'It is old Jelloo, the Lumberdar or head-man of Pind Sharkot, and a very intelligent man for a villager.'

The Jat farmer had removed his shoes and stood smiling on the edge of the veranda. His strongly marked features glowed with russet bronze, and his bright eyes gleamed under deeply set brows, contracted by lifelong exposure to sunshine. His beard and moustache, streaked with grey, swept from bold cliffs of brow and cheek in the large sweeps one sees drawn by Michael Angelo, and strands of long, black hair mingled with the irregularly piled wreaths and folds of his turban. The drapery of stout blue cotton cloth thrown over his broad shoulders and girt round his narrow loins, hung from his tall form in broadly-sculptured folds, and he would have made a superb model for an artist in search of a patriarch.

Orde greeted him cordially, and after a polite pause the countryman started off with a long story told with impressive earnestness. Orde listened and smiled, interrupting the speaker at times to argue and reason with him in a tone which Pagett could hear was kindly, and, finally checking the flux of words, was about to dismiss him when Pagett suggested that he should be asked about the National Congress.

226

But Jelloo had never heard of it. He was a poor man, and such things, by the favour of His Honour, did not concern him.

'What's the matter with your big friend that he was so terribly in earnest?' asked Pagett, when he had left.

'Nothing much. He wants the blood of the people in the next village, who have had smallpox and cattle plague pretty badly, and by the help of a wizard, a currier, and several pigs have passed it on to his own village. 'Wants to know if they can't be run in for this awful crime. It seems they made a dreadful charivari at the village boundary, threw a quantity of spell-bearing objects over the border, a buffalo's skull and other things; then branded a *chamar*—what you would call a currier—on his hinder parts and drove him and a number of pigs over into Jelloo's village. Jelloo says he can bring evidence to prove that the wizard directing these proceedings, who is a Sansi, has been guilty of theft, arson, cattle-killing, perjury, and murder, but would prefer to have him punished for bewitching them and inflicting smallpox.'

'And how on earth did you answer such a lunatic?'

'Lunatic! The old fellow is as sane as you or I; and he has some ground of complaint against those Sansis. I asked if he would like a native superintendent of police with some men to make inquiries, but he objected on the grounds that the police were rather worse than smallpox and criminal tribes put together.'

'Criminal tribes—er—I don't quite understand,' said Pagett.

'We have in India many tribes of people who in the slack ante-British days became robbers, in various kind, and preyed on the people. They are being restrained and reclaimed little by little, and in time will become useful citizens, but they still cherish hereditary traditions of crime, and are a difficult lot to deal with. By the way, what about the political rights of these folk under your schemes? The country people call them vermin, but I suppose they would be electors with the rest.'

'Nonsense—special provision would be made for them in a well-considered electoral scheme, and they would doubtless be treated with fitting severity,' said Pagett with a magisterial air.

'Severity, yes—but whether it would be fitting is doubtful. Even those poor devils have rights, and, after all, they only practise what they have been taught.'

'But criminals, Orde!'

'Yes, criminals with codes and rituals of crime, gods and godlings of crime, and a hundred songs and sayings in praise of it. Puzzling, isn't it?'

'It's simply dreadful. They ought to be put down at once. Are there many of them?'

'Not more than about sixty thousand in this province, for many of the tribes broadly described as criminal are really vagabond and criminal only on occasion, while others are being settled and reclaimed. They are of great antiquity, a legacy from the past, the golden, glorious Aryan past of Max Muller, Birdwood, and the rest of your spindrift philosophers.'

An orderly brought a card to Orde, who took it with a movement of irritation at the interruption, and handed it to Pagett: a large card with a ruled border in red ink, and in the centre in schoolboy copperplate, *Mr. Dina Nath*. 'Give salaam,' said the Civilian, and there entered in haste a slender youth, clad in a closely-fitting coat of grey homespun, tight trousers, patent-leather shoes, and a small black velvet cap. His thin cheek twitched, and his eyes wandered restlessly, for the young man was evidently nervous and uncomfortable, though striving to assume a free-and-easy air.

'Your Honour may perhaps remember me,' he said in English, and Orde scanned him keenly.

'I know your face, somehow. You belonged to the Shershah district, I think, when I was in charge there?'

'Yes, sir, my father is writer at Shershah, and Your Honour gave me a prize when I was first in the Middle School examination five years ago. Since then I have prosecuted my studies and I am now second year's student in the Mission College.'

'Of course. You are Kedar Nath's son—the boy who said he liked geography better than play or sugar-cakes, and I didn't believe you. How is your father getting on?'

'He is well, and he sends his salaam, but his circumstances are depressed, and he is also down on his luck.'

'You learn English diction at the Mission College, it seems.'

'Yes, sir, they are the best idioms, and my father ordered

me to ask Your Honour to say a word for him to the present incumbent of Your Honour's shoes, the latchet of which he is not worthy to open, and who knows not Joseph; for things are different at Shershah now, and my father wants promotion .'

'Your father is a good man, and I will do what I can for him.'

At this point a telegram was handed to Orde, who, after glancing at it, said he must leave his young friend, whom he introduced to Pagett, 'a member of the English House of Commons who wishes to learn about India'.

Orde had scarcely retired with his telegram when Pagett began:

'Perhaps you can tell me something of the National Congress movement?'

'Sir, it is *the* greatest movement of modern times, and one in which *all* educated men like us *must* join. *All* our students are for the Congress.'

'Excepting, I suppose, Mohammedans, and the Christians?' said Pagett, quick to use his recent instruction.

'These are some *mere* exceptions to the universal rule.'

'But the people outside the College, the working classes, the agriculturists; your father and mother, for instance.'

'My mother,' said the young man, with a visible effort to bring himself to pronounce the word, 'has no ideas, and my father is not agriculturist, nor working class. He is of the Kayeth caste. But he had not the advantage of a collegiate education, and he does not know much of the Congress. It is a movement for the educated-young-man'—connecting adjective and noun in a sort of vocal hyphen.

'Ah, yes,' said Pagett, feeling he was a little off the rails. 'And what are the benefits you expect to gain by it?'

'Oh, sir, everything. England owes its greatness to Parliamentary institutions and we should *at once* gain the same high position in scale of nations. Sir, we wish to have *the* sciences, the arts, the manufactures, the industrial factories, with steam-engines and other motive powers and public meetings and debates. Already we have a debating club in connection with the College and elect a Mr. Speaker. Sir, the progress *must* come. You also are a Member of Parliament and worship the great Lord Ripon,' said the youth, breathlessly, and his black eyes flashed as he finished his commaless sentences.

'Well,' said Pagett drily, 'it has not yet occurred to me to worship his lordship, although I believe he is a very worthy man, and I am not sure that England owes quite all things you name to the House of Commons. You see, my young friend, the growth of a nation like ours is slow, subject to many influences, and if you have read your history aright—'

'Sir, I know it all—*all*! Norman Conquest, Magna Charta, Runnymede, Reformation, Tudors, Stuarts, Mr. Milton, and Mr. Burke, and I have read something of Mr. Herbert Spencer and Gibbon's *Decline and Fall*, Reynolds' *Mysteries of the Court*, and—'

Pagett felt like one who had pulled the string of a shower-bath unawares, and hastened to stop the torrent with a question as to which particular grievances of the people of India the attention of an elected assembly should be first directed to. But young Mr. Dina Nath was slow to particularise. There were many, very many demanding considerations. Mr. Pagett would like to hear one or two typical examples. The Repeal of the Arms Act was at last named, and the student learned for the first time that a licence was necessary before an Englishman could carry a gun in England. Then natives of India ought to be allowed to become Volunteer Riflemen if they chose, and the absolute equality of the Oriental with his European fellow-subject in civil status should be proclaimed on principle, and the Indian Army should be considerably reduced. The student was not, however, prepared with answers to Mr. Pagett's mildest questions on these points, and he returned to vague generalities, leaving the M.P. so much impressed with the crudity of his views that he was glad on Orde's return to say good-bye to his 'very interesting' young friend.

'What do you think of young India?' asked Orde.

'Curious, very curious—and callow.'

'And yet,' the Civilian replied, 'one can scarcely help sympathising with him for his mere youth's sake. The young orators of the Oxford Union arrived at the same conclusions and showed doubtless just the same enthusiasm. If there were any political analogy between India and England, if the thousand races of this Empire were one, if there were any chance even of their learning to speak one language, if, in short, India were a Utopia of the debating-room, and not a real land, this kind of talk might be worth listening to; but it is all based on false analogy and ignorance of the facts.'

'But he is a native and knows the facts.'

'He is a sort of English schoolboy, but married three years, and the father of two weaklings, and knows less than most English schoolboys. You saw all he is and knows, and such ideas as he has acquired are directly hostile to the most cherished convictions of the vast majority of the people.'

'But what does he mean by saying he is a student of a Mission College? Is he a Christian?'

'He meant just what he said; and he is not a Christian, nor ever will he be. Good people in America, Scotland, and England, most of whom would never dream of collegiate education for their own sons, are pinching themselves to bestow it in pure waste on Indian youths. Their scheme is an oblique, subterranean attack on heathenism; the theory being that with the jam of secular education, leading to a University degree, the pill of moral or religious instruction may be coaxed down the heathen gullet.'

'But does it succeed; do they make converts?'

'They make no converts, for the subtle Oriental swallows the jam and rejects the pill. But the mere example of the sober, righteous, and godly lives of the principals and professors, who are most excellent and devoted men, must have a certain moral value. Yet, as Lord Lansdowne pointed out the other day, the market is dangerously overstocked with graduates of our Universities who look for employment in the Administration. An immense number are employed, but year by year the college mills grind out increasing lists of youths foredoomed to failure and disappointment, and meanwhile trade, manufactures, and the industrial arts are neglected and in fact regarded with contempt by our new literary mandarins *in posse*.'

'But our young friend said he wanted steam-engines and factories,' said Pagett.

'Yes, he would like to direct such concerns. He wants to begin at the top, for manual labour is held to be discreditable, and he would never defile his hands by the apprenticeship which the architects, engineers, and manufacturers of England cheerfully undergo; and he would be aghast to learn that the leading names of industrial enterprise in England belonged a generation or two since, or now belong, to men who wrought with their own hands. And, though he talks glibly of manufacturers, he refuses to see that the Indian manufacturer of the future will be the despised workman of the present. It was proposed, for example, a few weeks ago, that a certain municipality in this province should establish an elementary technical school for the sons of workmen. The stress of the opposition to the plan came from a pleader who owed all he had to a college education bestowed on him gratis by Government and missions. You would have fancied some fine old crusted Tory squire of the last generation was speaking. These people, he said, want no education, for they learn their trades from their fathers, and to teach a workman's son the elements of mathematics and physical science would give him ideas above his business. They must be kept in their place, and it was idle to imagine that there was any science in wood or iron work. And he carried his point. But the Indian workman will rise in the social scale in spite of the new literary caste.'

'In England we have scarcely begun to realise that there is an industrial class in this country, yet, I suppose, the example of men like Edwards, for instance, must tell,' said Pagett thoughtfully.

'That you shouldn't know much about it is natural enough, for there are but few sources of information. India in this, as in other respects, is like a badly kept ledger—not written up to date. And men like Edwards are, in reality, missionaries who by precept and example are teaching more lessons than they know. Only a few, however, of their crowds of subordinates seem to care to try to emulate them, and aim at individual advancement. The rest drop into the ancient Indian caste groove.'

'How do you mean?' asked Pagett.

'Well, it is found that the railway and factory workmen, the fitter, the engine-driver, and the rest are already forming separate hereditary castes. You may notice this down at Jamalpur in Bengal, one of the oldest railway centres. And at other places, and in other industries, they are following the same inexorable Indian law.'

'Which means—?' queried Pagett.

'It means that the rooted habit of the people is to gather in small self-contained, self-sufficing family groups with no thought or care for any interests but their own—a habit which is scarcely compatible with the right acceptation of the elective principle.'

'Yet you must admit, Orde, that though our young friend was not able to expound the faith that is in him, your Indian Army is too big.'

'Not nearly big enough for its main purpose. And, as a side issue, there are certain powerful minorities of fighting folk whose interests an Asiatic Government is bound to consider. Arms is as much a means of livelihood as civil employ under Government and law. And it would be a heavy strain on British bayonets to hold down Sikhs, Jats, Baluchis, Rohillas, Rajputs, Bhils, Dogras, Pathans, and Gurkhas to abide by the decisions of a numerical majority opposed to their interests. Leave the "numerical majority" to itself without the British bayonets—a flock of sheep might as reasonably hope to manage a troop of collies.'

'This complaint about excessive growth of the Army is akin to another contention of the Congress party. They protest against the malversation of the whole of the moneys raised by additional taxes as a Famine Insurance Fund to other purposes. You must be aware that this special Famine Fund has all been spent on Frontier roads and defences and strategic railway schemes as a protection against Russia.'

'But there was never a special Famine Fund raised by special taxation and put by in a box. No sane administrator would dream of such a thing. In a time of prosperity a Finance Minister, rejoicing in a margin, proposed to annually apply a million and a half to the construction of railways and canals for the protection of districts liable to scarcity, and to the reduction of the annual loans for public works. But times were not always prosperous, and the Finance Minister had to choose whether he would hang up the insurance scheme for a year or impose fresh taxation. When a farmer hasn't got the little surplus he hoped to have for buying a new wagon and draining a low-lying field corner, you don't accuse him of malversation if he spends what he has on the necessary work of the rest of the farm.'

A clatter of hoofs was heard, and Orde looked up with vexation, but his brow cleared as a horseman halted under the porch.

'Hello, Orde! Just looked in to ask if you are coming to polo on Tuesday: we want you badly to help crumple up the Krab Bokhar team.'

Orde explained that he had to go out into the District, and the visitor complained that though good men wouldn't play, duffers were always keen, and that his side would probably be beaten. Pagett rose to look at his mount, a red, lathered Baluch mare, with a curious lyre-like incurving of the ears. 'Quite a little thoroughbred in all other respects,' said the M.P., and Orde presented Mr. Reginald Burke, Manager of the Sind and Sialkot Bank, to his friend.

'Yes, she's as good as they make 'em, and she is all the female I possess, and spoilt in consequence, aren't you, old girl?' said Burke, patting the mare's glossy neck as she backed and plunged.

'Mr. Pagett,' said Orde, 'has been asking me about the Congress. What is your opinion?'

Burke turned to the M.P. with a frank smile.

'Well, if it's all the same to you, sir, I should say, Damn the Congress, but I'm no politician, but only a business man.'

'You find it a tiresome subject?'

'Yes, it's all that, and worse than that, for this kind of agitation is anything but wholesome for the country.'

'How do you mean?'

'It would be a long job to explain, and Sara here won't stand, but you know how sensitive capital is, and how timid investors are. All this sort of rot is likely to frighten them, and we can't afford to frighten them. The passengers aboard an ocean steamer don't feel reassured when the ship's way is stopped and they hear the workmen's hammers tinkering at the engines down below. The old Ark's going on all right as she is, and only wants quiet and room to move. Them's my sentiments, and those of some other people who have to do with money and business.'

'Then you are a thick-and-thin supporter of the Government

as it is.'

'Why, no! The Indian Government is much too timid with its money—like an old maiden aunt of mine—always in a funk about her investments. They don't spend half enough on railways, for instance, and they are slow in a general way, and ought to be made to sit up in all that concerns the encouragement of private enterprise, and coaxing out into use the millions of capital that lie dormant in the country.'

The mare was dancing with impatience, and Burke was evidently anxious to be off, so the men wished him goodbye.

'Who is your genial friend who condemns both Congress and Government in one breath?' asked Pagett, with an amused smile.

'Just now he is Reggie Burke, keener on polo than on anything else, but if you went to the Sind and Sialkot Bank tomorrow you would find Mr. Reginald Burke a very capable man of business, known and liked by an immense constituency north and south of this.'

'Do you think he is right about the Government's want of enterprise?'

'I should hesitate to say. Better consult the merchants and Chambers of Commerce in Cawnpore, Madras, Bombay, and Calcutta. But though these bodies would like, as Reggie puts it, to make Government sit up, it is an elementary consideration in governing a country like India, which must be administered for the benefit of the people at large, that the counsels of those who resort to it for the sake of making money should be judiciously weighed and not allowed to overpower the rest. They are welcome guests here, as a matter of course, but it has been found best to restrain their influence. Thus the rights of plantation labourers, factory operatives, and the like, have been protected, and the capitalist, eager to get on, has not always regarded Government action with favour. It is quite conceivable that under an elective system the commercial communities of the great towns might find means to secure majorities on labour questions and on financial matters.'

'They would act at least with intelligence and consideration.'

'Intelligence, yes; but as to consideration, who at the present moment most bitterly resents the tender solicitude of Lancashire for the welfare and protection of the Indian factory operative? English and native capitalists running cotton mills and factories.'

'But is the solicitude of Lancashire in this matter entirely disinterested?'

'It is no business of mine to say. I merely indicate an example of how a powerful commercial interest might hamper a Government intent in the first place on the larger interests of humanity.'

Orde broke off to listen a moment. 'There's Dr Lathrop talking to my wife in the drawing-room,' said he.

'Surely not. That's a lady's voice, and if my ears don't deceive me, an American.'

'Exactly. Dr Eva McCreery Lathrop, chief of the new Women's Hospital here, and a very good fellow forbye. Good morning, Doctor,' he said, as a graceful figure came out on the veranda; 'you seem to be in trouble. I hope Mrs. Orde was able to help you.'

'Your wife is real kind and good; I always come to her when I'm in a fix, but I fear it's more than comforting I want.'

'You work too hard and wear yourself out,' said Orde kindly. 'Let me introduce my friend, Mr. Pagett, just fresh from Home, and anxious to learn his India. You could tell him something of that more important half of which a mere man knows so little.'

'Perhaps I could if I'd any heart to do it, but I'm in trouble. I've lost a case, a case that was doing well, through nothing in the world but inattention on the part of a nurse I had begun to trust. And when I spoke only a small piece of my mind, she collapsed in a whining heap on the floor. It's hopeless!'

The men were silent, for the blue eyes of the lady doctor were dim. Recovering herself, she looked up with a smile half sad, half humorous. 'And I am in a whining heap too; but what phase of Indian life are you particularly interested in, sir?'

'Mr. Pagett intends to study the political aspect of things and the possibility of bestowing electoral institutions on the people.'

'Wouldn't it be as much to the purpose to bestow point-lace collars on them? They need many things more urgently than votes. Why, it's like giving a bread-pill for a broken leg.'

236

'Er—I don't quite follow,' said Pagett uneasily.

'Well, what's the matter with this country is not in the least political, but an all-round entanglement of physical, social, and moral evils and corruptions, all more or less due to the unnatural treatment of women. You can't gather figs from thistles, and so long as the system of infant marriage, the prohibition of remarriage of widows, the lifelong imprisonment of wives and mothers in a worse than penal confinement, and the withholding from them of any kind of education or treatment as rational beings continues, the country can't advance a step. Half of it is morally dead, and worse than dead, and that's just the half from which we have a right to look for the best impulses. It's right here where the trouble is, and not in any political considerations whatsoever.'

'But do they marry so early?' said Pagett vaguely.

'The average age is seven, but thousands are married still earlier. One result is that girls of twelve and thirteen have to bear the burden of wifehood and motherhood, and, as might be expected, the rate of mortality both for mothers and children is terrible. Pauperism, domestic unhappiness, and a low state of health are only a few of the consequences of this. Then, when, as frequently happens, the boy-husband dies prematurely, his widow is condemned to worse than death. She may not remarry, must live a secluded and despised life, a life so unnatural that she sometimes prefers suicide. More often she goes astray. You don't know in England what such words as "infant-marriage, baby-wife, girl-mother, and virgin-widow" mean; but they mean unspeakable horrors here.'

'Well, but the advanced political party here will surely make it their business to advocate social reforms as well as political ones,' said Pagett.

'Very surely they will do no such thing,' said the lady doctor emphatically. 'I *wish* I could make you understand. Why, even of the funds devoted to the Marchioness of Dufferin's organisation for medical aid to the women of India, it was said in print and in speech that they would be better spent on more college scholarships for men. And in all the advanced parties' talk—God forgive them!—and in all their programmes, they carefully avoid all such subjects. They will talk about the protection of a cow, for that's an ancient superstition—they can all understand that; but the protection of the women is a new and dangerous idea.' She turned to Pagett rather impulsively:

'You are a member of the English Parliament. Can you do nothing? The foundations of their life are rotten—utterly and bestially rotten. I could tell your wife things that I couldn't tell you. I know the life—the inner life that belongs to the native, and I know nothing else; and, believe me, you might as well try to grow golden-rod in a mushroom-pit as to make anything of a people that are born and reared as these—these things are. The men talk of their rights and privileges. I have seen the women that bear these very men, and again—may God forgive the men!'

Pagett's eyes opened with a large wonder. Dr Lathrop rose tempestuously.

'I must be off to lecture,' said she, 'and I am sorry that I can't show you my hospitals; but you had better believe, sir, that it's more necessary for India than all the elections in creation.'

'That's a woman with a mission, and no mistake,' said Pagett, after a pause.

'Yes; she believes in her work, and so do I,' said Orde. 'I've a notion that in the end it will be found that the most helpful work done for India in this generation was wrought by Lady Dufferin in drawing attention—what work that was, by the way, even with her husband's great name to back it!—to the needs of women here. In effect, native habits and beliefs are an organised conspiracy against the laws of health and happy life—but there is some dawning of hope now.'

'How do you account for the general indifference, then?'

'I suppose it's due in part to their fatalism and their utter indifference to all human suffering. How much do you imagine the great province of Punjab, with over two million people and half a score of rich towns, has contributed to the maintenance of civil dispensaries last year? About seven thousand rupees.'

'That's seven hundred pounds,' said Pagett quickly.

'I wish it was,' replied Orde; 'but anyway, it's an absurdly inadequate sum, and shows one of the blank sides of Oriental character.'

Pagett was silent for a long time. The question of direct and personal pain did not lie within his researches. He preferred to discuss the weightier matters of the law, and contented himself with murmuring: 'They'll do better later on.' Then, with a rush, returning to his first thought:—

'But, my dear Orde, if it's merely a class movement of a local and temporary character, how d'you account for Bradlaugh, who is at least a man of sense, taking it up?'

'I know nothing of the champion of the New Brahmins but what I see in the papers. I suppose there is something tempting in being hailed by a large assemblage as the representative of the aspirations of two hundred and fifty millions of people. Such a man "looks through all the roaring and the wreaths", and does not reflect that it is a false perspective, which, as a matter of fact, hides the real complex and manifold India from his gaze. He can scarcely be expected to distinguish between the ambitions of the new oligarchy and the real wants of the people of whom he knows nothing. But it's strange that a professed radical should come to be the chosen advocate of a movement which has for its aim the revival of an ancient tyranny. Shows how even Radicalism can fall into academic grooves and miss the essential truths of its own creed. Believe me, Pagett, to deal with India you want first-hand knowledge and experience. I wish he would come and live here for a couple of years or so.'

'Is not this rather an *ad hominem* style of argument?'

'Can't help it in a case like this. Indeed, I am not sure you ought not to go further and weigh the whole character and quality and upbringing of the man. You must admit that the monumental complacency with which he trotted out his ingenious little Constitution for India showed a strange want of imagination and the sense of humour.'

'No, I don't quite admit it,' said Pagett.

'Well, you know him and I don't, but that's how it strikes a stranger.'

He turned on his heel and paced the veranda thoughtfully. 'And, after all, the burden of the actual, daily unromantic toil falls on the shoulders of the men out here, and not on his own. He enjoys all the privileges of recommendation without responsibility, and we—well, perhaps when you've seen a little more of India you'll understand. To begin with, our death-rate's five times higher than yours—I speak now of the brutal bureaucrat—and we work on the refuse of worked-out cities and exhausted civilisations, among the bones of the dead.'

Pagett laughed. 'That's an epigrammatic way of putting it, Orde.'

'Is it? Let's see,' said the Deputy-Commissioner of Amara, striding into the sunshine towards a half-naked gardener potting roses. He took the man's hoe, and went to a rain-scarped bank at the bottom of the garden.

'Come here, Pagett,' he said, and cut at the sun-baked soil. After three strokes there rolled from under the blade of the hoe the half of a clanking skeleton that settled at Pagett's feet in an unseemly jumble of bones. The M.P. drew back.

'Our houses are built on cemeteries,' said Orde. 'There are scores of thousands of graves within ten miles.'

Pagett was contemplating the skull with the awed fascination of a man who has but little to do with the dead. 'India's a very curious place,' said he, after a pause.

'Ah? You'll know all about it in three months. Come in to lunch,' said Orde.

GEORGIE PORGIE

Georgie Porgie, pudding and pie,
Kissed the girls and made them cry.
When the girls came out to play
Georgie Porgie ran away.

IF YOU WILL admit that a man has no right to enter his drawing-room early in the morning, when the housemaid is setting things right and clearing away the dust, you will concede that civilised people who eat out of china and own card-cases have no right to apply their standards of right and wrong to an unsettled land. When the place is made fit for their reception, by those men who are told off to the work, they can come up, bringing in their trunks their own society and the Decalogue, and all the other apparatus. Where the Queen's Law does not carry, it is irrational to expect an observance of other and weaker rules. The men who run ahead of the cars of Decency and Propriety, and make the jungle ways straight, cannot be judged in the same manner as the stay-at-home folk of the ranks of the Regular *Tchin*.

Not many months ago the Queen's Law stopped a few miles north of Thayetmyo on the Irrawaddy. There was no very strong Public Opinion up to that limit, but it existed to keep men in order. When the Government said that the Queen's Law must carry up to Bhamo and the Chinese border and the order was given, and some men whose desire was to be ever a little in advance of the rush of Respectability flocked forward with the troops. These were the men who could never pass examinations, and would have been too pronounced in their ideas for the administration of bureau-worked Provinces. The Supreme Government stepped in as soon as might be, with codes and regulations, and all but reduced New Burma to the dead Indian level; but there was a short time during which strong men were necessary and ploughed a field for themselves.

Among the forerunners of Civilisation was Georgie Porgie, reckoned by all who knew him a strong man. He held an appointment in Lower Burma when the order came to break the Frontier, and his friends called him Georgie Porgie because of the singularly Burmese-like manner in which he sang a song whose first line is something like the words 'Georgie Porgie'. Most men who have been in Burma will know the song. It means: 'Puff, puff, puff, puff, great steamboat!' Georgie sang it to his banjo, and his friends shouted with delight, so that you could hear them far away in the teak-forest.

When he went to Upper Burma he had no special regard for God or Man, but he knew how to make himself respected, and to carry out the mixed Military-Civil duties that fell to most men's share in those months. He did his office work and entertained, now and again, the detachments of fever-shaken soldiers who blundered through his part of the world in search of a flying party of dacoits. Sometimes he turned out and dressed down dacoits on his own account; for the country was still smouldering and would blaze when least expected. He enjoyed these charivaris, but the dacoits were not so amused. All the officials who came in contact with him departed with the idea that Georgie Porgie was a valuable person, well able to take care of himself, and, on that belief, he was left to his own devices.

At the end of a few months he wearied of his solitude, and cast about for company and refinement. The Queen's Law had hardly begun to be felt in the country, and Public Opinion, which is more powerful than the Queen's Law, had yet to come. Also, there was a custom in the country which allowed a white man to take to himself a wife of the Daughters of Heth upon due payment. The marriage was not quite so binding as is the *nikkah* among Mohammedans, but the wife was very pleasant.

When all our troops are back from Burma there will be a proverb in their mouths, 'As thrifty as a Burmese wife', and pretty English ladies will wonder what in the world it means.

The headman of the village next to Georgie Porgie's post had a fair daughter who had seen Georgie Porgie and loved him from afar. When news went abroad that the Englishman with

242

the heavy hand who lived in the stockade was looking for a housekeeper, the headman came in and explained that, for five hundred rupees down, he would entrust his daughter to Georgie Porgie's keeping, to be maintained in all honour, respect, and comfort, with pretty dresses, according to the custom of the country. This thing was done, and Georgie Porgie never repented it.

He found his rough-and-tumble house put straight and made comfortable, his hitherto unchecked expenses cut down by one-half, and himself petted and made much of by his new acquisition, who sat at the head of his table and sang songs to him and ordered his Madrassee servants about, and was in every way as sweet and merry and honest and winning a little woman as the most exacting of bachelors could have desired. No race, men say who know, produces such good wives and heads of households as the Burmese. When the next detachment tramped by on the warpath the Subaltern in command found at Georgie Porgie's table a hostess to be deferential to, a woman to be treated in every way as one occupying an assured position. When he gathered his men together next dawn and replunged into the jungle he thought regretfully of the nice little dinner and the pretty face, and envied Georgie Porgie from the bottom of his heart. Yet *he* was engaged to a girl at Home, and that is how some men are constructed.

The Burmese girl's name was not a pretty one; but as she was promptly christened Georgina by Georgie Porgie, the blemish did not matter. Georgie Porgie thought well of the petting and the general comfort, and vowed that he had never spent five hundred rupees to a better end.

After three months of domestic life a great idea struck him. Matrimony—English matrimony—could not be such a bad thing after all. If he were so thoroughly comfortable at the Back of Beyond with this Burmese girl who smoked cheroots, how much more comfortable would he be with a sweet English maiden who would not smoke cheroots, and would play upon a piano instead of a banjo? Also he had a desire to return to his kind, to hear a Band once more, and to feel how it felt to wear a dress-suit again. Decidedly, matrimony would be a very good thing. He thought the matter out at length of evenings, while Georgina sang to him, or asked him why he was so silent, and whether she had done anything to offend him. As he thought, he smoked, and as he smoked he looked at Georgina, and in his fancy turned her into a fair, thrifty, amusing, merry little English girl, with hair coming low down on her forehead, and perhaps a cigarette between her lips. Certainly not a big, thick Burma cheroot, of the brand that Georgina smoked. He would wed a girl with Georgina's eyes and most of her ways. But not all. She could be improved upon. Then he blew thick smoke-wreaths through his nostrils and stretched himself. He would taste marriage. Georgina had helped to save money, and there were six months' of leave due to him.

'See here, little woman,' he said, 'we must put by more money for these next three months. I want it.' That was a direct slur on Georgina's housekeeping, for she prided herself on her thrift; but since her God wanted money she would do her best.

'You want money?' she said with a little laugh. 'I *have* money. Look!' She ran to her own room and fetched out a small bag of rupees. 'Of all that you give me, I keep back some. See! One hundred and seven rupees. Can you want more money than that? Take it. It is my pleasure if you use it.' She spread out the money on the table and pushed it towards him with her quick little pale-yellow fingers.

Georgie Porgie never referred to economy in the household again.

Three months later, after the despatch and receipt of several mysterious letters which Georgina could not understand, and hated for that reason, Georgie Porgie said that he was going away, and she must return to her father's house and stay there.

Georgina wept. She would go with her God from the world's end to the world's end. Why should she leave him? She loved him.

'I am going to Rangoon,' said Georgie Porgie. 'I shall be back in a month, but it is safer for you to stay with your father. I will leave you two hundred rupees.'

'If you go for a month, what need of two hundred? Fifty are more than enough. There is some evil here. Do not go, or at least let me go with you.'

Georgie Porgie does not like to remember the scene even at

this date. In the end he got rid of Georgina by a compromise of seventy-five rupees. She would not take more. Then he went by steamer and rail to Rangoon.

The mysterious letters had granted him six months' leave. The actual flight and an idea that he might have been treacherous hurt severely at the time, but as soon as the big steamer was well out into the blue, things were easier, and Georgina's face, and the queer little stockaded house, and the memory of the rushes of shouting dacoits at night, the cry and struggle of the first man that he had ever killed with his own hand, and a hundred other more intimate things, faded and faded out of Georgie Porgie's heart, and the vision of approaching England took its place. The steamer was full of men on leave, all rampantly jovial souls who had shaken off the dust and sweat of Upper Burma and were merry as schoolboys. They helped Georgie Porgie to forget.

Then came England with its luxuries and decencies and comforts, and Georgie Porgie walked in a pleasant dream upon pavements of which he had nearly forgotten the ring, wondering why men in their senses left Town. He accepted his keen delight in his furlough as the reward for his services. Providence further arranged for him another and greater delight—all the pleasures of a quiet English wooing, quite different from the brazen business of the East, when half the community stand back and bet on the result, and the other half wonder what Mrs. So-and-So will say to it.

It was a pleasant girl and a perfect summer, and a big country-house near Petworth where there are acres and acres of purple heather and high-grassed water-meadows to wander through. Georgie Porgie felt that he had at last found something worth the living for, and naturally assumed that the next thing to do was to ask the girl to share his life in India. She, in her ignorance, was willing to go. On this occasion there was no bartering with a village headman. There was a fine middle-class wedding in the country, with a stout Papa and a weeping Mamma, and a best man in purple and fine linen, and six snub-nosed girls from the Sunday School to throw roses on the path between the tombstones up to the church door. The local paper described the affair at great length, even down to giving the hymns in full. But that was because the Direction were starving for want of material.

Then came a honeymoon at Arundel, and the Mamma wept copiously before she allowed her one daughter to sail away to India under the care of Georgie Porgie the Bridegroom. Beyond any question, Georgie Porgie was immensely fond of his wife, and she was devoted to him as the best and greatest man in the world. When he reported himself at Bombay he felt justified in demanding a good station for his wife's sake; and, because he had made a little mark in Burma and was beginning to be appreciated, they allowed him nearly all that he asked for, and posted him to a station which we will call Sutrain. It stood upon several hills, and was styled officially a 'Sanitarium', for the good reason that the drainage was utterly neglected. Here Georgie Porgie settled down, and found married life come very naturally to him. He did not rave, as do many bridegrooms, over the strangeness and delight of seeing his own true love sitting down to breakfast with him every morning 'as though it were the most natural thing in the world'. 'He had been there before', as the Americans say, and, checking the merits of his own present Grace by those of Georgina, he was more and more inclined to think that he had done well.

But there was no peace or comfort across the Bay of Bengal, under the teak-trees where Georgina lived with her father, waiting for Georgie Porgie to return. The headman was old, and remembered the war of '51. He had been to Rangoon, and knew something of the ways of the *Kullahs*. Sitting in front of his door in the evenings, he taught Georgina a dry philosophy which did not console her in the least.

The trouble was that she loved Georgie Porgie just as much as the French girl in the English History books loved the priest whose head was broken by the King's bullies. One day she disappeared from the village, with all the rupees that Georgie Porgie had given her, and a very small smattering of English— also gained from Georgie Porgie.

The headman was angry at first, but lit a fresh cheroot and said something uncomplimentary about the sex in general. Georgina had started on a search for Georgie Porgie, who might be in Rangoon, or across the Black Water, or dead, for aught that she knew. Chance favoured her. An old Sikh policeman told her that Georgie Porgie had crossed the Black Water. She took steerage-passage from Rangoon and went to Calcutta, keeping the secret of her search to herself.

In India every trace of her was lost for six weeks, and no one knows what trouble of heart she must have undergone.

She reappeared, four hundred miles north of Calcutta, steadily heading northwards, very worn and haggard, but very fixed in her determination to find Georgie Porgie. She could not understand the language of the people; but India is infinitely charitable, and the women-folk along the Grand Trunk gave her food. Something made her believe that Georgie Porgie was to be found at the end of that pitiless road. She may have seen a sepoy who knew him in Burma, but of this no one can be certain. At last, she found a regiment on the line of the march, and met there one of the many subalterns whom Georgie Porgie had invited to dinner in the far-off days of the dacoit-hunting. There was a certain amount of amusement among the tents when Georgina threw herself at the man's feet and began to cry. There was no amusement when her story was told; but a collection was made, and that was more to the point. One of the subalterns knew of Georgie Porgie's whereabouts, but not of his marriage, so he told Georgina and she went her way joyfully to the North, in a railway carriage where there was rest for tired feet and shade for a dusty little head. The marches from the train through the hills into Sutrain were trying, but Georgina had money, and families journeying in bullock-carts gave her help. It was an almost miraculous journey, and Georgina felt sure that the good spirits of Burma were looking after her. The hill-road to Sutrain is a chilly stretch, and Georgina caught a bad cold. Still there was Georgie Porgie at the end of all the trouble to take her up in his arms and pet her, as he used to do in the old days when the stockade was shut for the night and he had approved of the evening meal. Georgina went forward as fast as she could; and her good spirits did her one last favour.

An Englishman stopped her, in the twilight, just as the turn of the road into Sutrain, saying, 'Good Heavens! What are you doing here?'

He was Gillis, the man who had been Georgie Porgie's

assistant in Upper Burma, and who occupied the next post to Georgie Porgie's in the jungle. Georgie Porgie had applied to have him work with at Sutrain because he liked him.

'I have come,' said Georgina simply. 'It was such a long way, and I have been months in coming. Where is his house?'

Gillis gasped. He had seen enough of Georgina in the old times to know that explanations would be useless. You cannot explain things to the Oriental. You must show.

'I'll take you there,' said Gillis, and he led Georgina off the road, up the cliff, by a little pathway, to the back of a house set on a platform cut into the hillside.

The lamps were just lit, but the curtains were not drawn. 'Now look,' said Gillis, stopping in front of the drawing-room window. Georgina looked and saw Georgie Porgie and the Bride.

She put her hand up to her hair, which had come out of its top-knot and was straggling about her face. She tried to set her ragged dress in order, but the dress was past pulling straight, and she coughed a queer little cough, for she really had taken a very bad cold. Gillis looked, too, but while Georgina only looked at the Bride once, turning her eyes always on Georgie Porgie, Gillis looked at the Bride all the time.

'What are you going to do?' said Gillis, who held Georgina by the wrist, in case of any unexpected rush into the lamplight. 'Will you go in and tell that English woman that you lived with her husband?'

'No,' said Georgina faintly. 'Let me go. I am going away. I swear that I am going away.' She twisted herself free and ran off into the dark.

'Poor little beast!' said Gillis, dropping on to the main road. 'I'd ha' given her something to get back to Burma with. What a narrow shave though! And that Angel would never have forgiven it.'

This seems to prove that the devotion of Gillis was not entirely due to his affection for Georgie Porgie.

The Bride and the Bridegroom came out into the veranda after dinner, in order that the smoke of Georgie Porgie's cheroots might not hang in the drawing-room curtains.

'What is the noise down there?' said the Bride. Both listened.

'Oh,' said Georgie Porgie. 'I suppose some brute of a hillman

248

has been beating his wife.'

'Beating—his—wife! How ghastly!' said the Bride. 'Fancy *your* beating *me*!' She slipped an arm round her husband's waist, and, leaning her head against his shoulder, looked out across the cloud-filled valley in deep content and security.

But it was Georgina crying, all by herself, down the hillside, among the stones of the watercourse where the washermen wash the clothes.

IN THE PRIDE OF HIS YOUTH

'Stopped in the straight when the race was his own!
Look at him cutting it—cur to the bone!'
Ask, ere the youngster be rated and chidden,
What did he carry and how was he ridden?
Maybe they used him too much at the start;
Maybe Fate's weight-cloths are breaking his heart.

Life's Handicap

WHEN I WAS telling you of the joke that The Worm played off on the Senior Subaltern, I promised a somewhat similar tale, but with all the jest left out. This is that tale.

Dicky Hatt was kidnapped in his early, early youth—neither by landlady's daughter, housemaid, barmaid, nor cook, but by a girl so nearly of his own caste that only a woman could have seen she was just the least little bit in the world below it. This happened a month before he came out to India, and five days after his one-and-twentieth birthday. The girl was nineteen— six years older than Dicky in the things of this world, that is to say—and, for the time, twice as foolish as he.

Excepting, always, falling off a horse there is nothing more fatally easy than marriage before the Registrar. The ceremony costs less than fifty shillings, and is remarkably like walking into a pawn-shop. After the declarations of residence have been put in, four minutes will cover the rest of the proceedings—fees, attestation, and all. Then the Registrar slides the blotting-pad over the names, and says grimly, with his pen between his teeth, 'Now you're man and wife'; and the couple walk out into the street feeling as if something were horribly illegal somewhere.

But that ceremony holds and can drag a man to his undoing just as thoroughly as the 'long as ye both shall live' curse from the altar-rails, with the bridesmaids giggling behind, and 'The

Voice that breathed o'er Eden' lifting the roof off. In this manner was Dicky Hatt kidnapped, and he considered it vastly fine, for he had received an appointment in India which carried a magnificent salary from the Home point of view. The marriage was to be kept secret for a year. Then Mrs. Dicky Hatt was to come out, and the rest of life was to be a glorious golden mist. That was how they sketched it under the Addison Road Station lamps; and, after one short month, came Gravesend and Dicky steaming out to his new life, and the girl crying in a thirty-shillings-a-week bed-and-living-room, in a back-street off Montpelier Square near the Knightsbridge Barracks.

But the country that Dicky came to was a hard land where men of twenty-one were reckoned very small boys indeed, and life was expensive. The salary that looked so large six thousand miles away did not go far. Particularly when Dicky divided it by two, and remitted more than the fair half, at 1-6 7/8, to Montpelier Square. One hundred and thirty-five rupees out of three hundred and thirty is not much to live on; but it was absurd to suppose that Mrs. Hatt could exist for ever on the 20 pounds held back by Dicky from his outfit allowance. Dicky saw this and remitted at once; always remembering that Rs.700 were to be paid, twelve months later, for a first-class passage out for a lady. When you add to these trifling details the natural instincts of a boy beginning a new life in a new country and longing to go about and enjoy himself, and the necessity for grappling with strange work—which, properly speaking, should take up a boy's undivided attention—you will see that Dicky started handicapped. He saw it himself for a breath or two; but then he did not guess the full beauty of his future.

As the hot weather began, the shackles settled on him and ate into his flesh. First would come letters—big, crossed, seven-sheet letters—from his wife, telling him how she longed to see him, and what a Heaven on earth would be their property when they met. Then somebody of the chummery wherein Dicky lodged would pound on the door of his bare little room, and tell him to come out to look at a pony—the very thing to suit him. Dicky could not afford ponies. He had to explain this. Dicky could not afford living in the chummery, modest as it was. He had to explain this before he moved to a single room next the office

251

where he worked all day. He kept house on a green oil-cloth table-cover, one chair, one bedstead, one photograph, one tooth-glass, very strong and thick, a seven-rupee eight-anna filter, and messing by contract at thirty-seven rupees a month. Which last item was extortion. He had no punkah, for a punkah costs fifteen rupees a month; but he slept on the roof of the office with all his wife's letters under his pillow. Now and again he was asked out to dinner, where he got both a punkah and an iced drink. But this was seldom, for people objected to recognising a boy who had evidently the instincts of a Scotch tallow-chandler, and who lived in such a nasty fashion. Dicky could not subscribe to any amusement, so he found no amusement except the pleasure of turning over his Bank-book and reading what it said about 'loans on approved security'. That cost nothing. He remitted through a Bombay bank, by the way, and the station knew nothing of his private affairs.

Every month he sent Home all he could possibly spare for his wife and for another reason which was expected to explain itself shortly, and would require more money.

About this time Dicky was overtaken with the nervous, haunting fear that besets married men when they are out of sorts. He had no pension to look to. What if he should die suddenly, and leave his wife unprovided for? The thought used to lay hold of him in the still, hot nights on the roof, till the shaking of his heart made him think that he was going to die then and there of heart-disease. Now this is a frame of mind which no boy has a right to know. It is a strong man's trouble; but, coming when it did, it nearly drove poor punkah-less, perspiring Dicky Hatt mad. He could tell no one about it.

A certain amount of 'screw' is as necessary for a man as for a billiard-ball. It makes them both do wonderful things. Dicky needed money badly, and he worked for it like a horse. But, naturally, the men who owned him knew that a boy can live very comfortably on a certain income—pay in India is a matter of age, not merit, you see, and, if their particular boy wished to work like two boys, Business forbid that they should stop him. But Business forbid that they should give him an increase of pay at his present ridiculously immature age. So Dicky won certain rises of salary—ample for a boy—not enough for a wife and a child—certainly too little for the seven-hundred-rupee passage that he and Mrs. Hatt had discussed so lightly once upon a time. And with this he was forced to be content.

Somehow, all this money seemed to fade away in Home drafts and the crushing Exchange, and the tone of the Home letters changed and grew querulous. Why wouldn't Dicky have his wife and the baby out? Surely he had a salary—a fine salary—and it was too bad of him to enjoy himself in India. But would he—could he—make the next draft a little more elastic? Here followed a list of baby's kit, as long as a Parsee's bill. Then Dicky, whose heart yearned to his wife and the little son he had never seen—which, again, is a feeling no boy is entitled to—enlarged the draft, and wrote queer half-boy, half-man letters, saying that life was not so enjoyable after all, and would the little wife wait yet a little longer? But the little wife, however much she approved of the money, objected to waiting, and there was a strange, hard sort of ring in her letters that Dicky didn't understand. How could he?

Later on still—just as Dickey had been told—apropos of another youngster who had 'made a fool of himself' as the saying is—that matrimony would not only ruin his further chance of advancement, but would lose him his present appointment—came the news that the baby, his own little, little son, had died and, behind this, forty lines of an angry woman's scrawl, saying the death might have been averted if certain things, all costing money, had been done, or if the mother and the baby had been with Dicky. The letter struck at Dicky's naked heart; but, not being officially entitled to a baby, he could show no sign of trouble.

How Dicky won through the next four months, and what hope kept alight to force him into his work, no one dare say. He pounded on, the seven-hundred-rupee passage as far away as ever, and his style of living unchanged, except when he launched into a new filter. There was the strain of his office work, and the strain of his remittances, and the knowledge of his son's death, which touched the boy more, perhaps, than it would have touched a man; and, beyond all, the enduring strain of his daily life. Grey-headed seniors, who approved of his thrift and his fashion of denying himself everything pleasant, reminded him of the old saw that says:—

> '*If a youth would be distinguished in his art, art, art,*
> *He must keep the girls away from his heart, heart, heart.*'

And Dicky, who fancied he had been through every trouble that a man is permitted to know, had to laugh and agree; with the last line of his balanced Bank-book jingling in his head day and night.

But he had one more sorrow to digest before the end. There arrived a letter from the little wife—the natural sequence of the others if Dicky had only known it—and the burden of that letter was 'gone with a handsomer man than you'. It was a rather curious production, without stops, something like this—She was not going to wait for ever and the baby was dead and Dicky was only a boy and he would never set eyes on her again and why hadn't he waved his handkerchief to her when he left Gravesend and God was her judge she was a wicked woman but Dicky was worse enjoying himself in India and this other man loved the ground she trod on and would Dicky ever forgive her for she would never forgive Dicky; and there was no address to write to.

Instead of thanking his stars that he was free, Dicky discovered exactly how an injured husband feels—again, not at all the knowledge to which a boy is entitled—for his mind went back to his wife as he remembered her in the thirty-shilling 'suite' in Montpelier Square, when the dawn of his last morning in England was breaking, and she was crying in the bed. Whereat he rolled about on his bed and bit his fingers. He never stopped to think whether, if he had met Mrs. Hatt after those two years, he would have discovered that he and she had grown quite different and new persons. This, theoretically, he ought to have done. He spent the night after the English Mail came in rather severe pain.

Next morning, Dicky Hatt felt disinclined to work. He argued that he had missed the pleasure of youth. He was tired, and he had tasted all the sorrow in life before three-and-twenty. His honour was gone—that was the man; and now he, too, would go to the Devil—that was the boy in him. So he put his head down on the green oil-cloth table-cover, and wept before resigning his post and all it offered.

But the reward of his services came. He was given three days to reconsider himself, and the Head of the establishment, after some telegraphings, said that it was a most unusual step, but in view of the ability that Mr. Hatt had displayed at such-and-such a time, at such-and-such junctures, he was in a position to offer him an infinitely superior post—first on probation and later, in the natural course of things, on confirmation. 'And how much does the post carry?' said Dicky. 'Six hundred and fifty rupees,' said the Head slowly, expecting to see the young man sink with gratitude and joy.

And it came then! The seven-hundred-rupee passage, and enough to have saved the wife and the little son, and to have allowed of assured and open marriage, came then. Dicky burst into a roar of laughter—laughter he could not check—nasty, jangling merriment that seemed as if it would go on for ever. When he had recovered himself he said, quite seriously, 'I'm tired of work. I'm an old man now. It's about time I retired. And I will.'

'The boy's mad!' said the Head.

I think he was right; but Dicky Hatt never reappeared to settle the question.

THE ARREST OF LIEUTENANT
GOLIGHTLY

'I've forgotten the countersign,' sez 'e.
'Oh! You 'ave, 'ave you?' sez I.
'But I'm the Colonel,' sez 'e.
'Oh! You are, are you?' sez I. 'Colonel nor no Colonel,
you waits 'ere till I'm relieved, an' the Sarjint reports on
your ugly old mug. Choop!' sez I . . . .

An 'swelp me soul, 'twas the Colonel after all! But I was
a recruity then.
      The Unedited Autobiography of Private Ortheris

IF THERE WAS one thing on which Golightly prided himself
more than another, it was looking like 'an Officer and a
Gentleman'. He said it was for the honour of the Service that he
attired himself so elaborately; but those who knew him best
said that it was just personal vanity. There was no harm about
Golightly—not an ounce. He recognised a horse when he saw
one, and could do more than fill a saddle. He played a very fair
game at billiards, and was a sound man at the whist-table. Every
one liked him; and nobody ever dreamed of seeing him
handcuffed on a station platform as a deserter. But this sad thing
happened.

He was going down from Dalhousie, at the end of his
leave—riding down. He had run his leave as fine as he dared,
and wanted to come down in a hurry.

It was fairly warm at Dalhousie, and, knowing what to
expect below, he descended in a new khaki suit—tight-fitting—
of a delicate olive-green; a peacock-blue tie, white collar, and a
snowy white *solah* helmet. He prided himself on looking neat

even when he was riding post. He *did* look neat, and he was so deeply concerned about appearance before he started that he quite forgot to take anything but some small change with him. He left all his notes at the hotel. His servants had gone down the road before him, to be ready waiting at Pathankot with a change of gear. That was what he called travelling in 'light marching-order'. He was proud of his faculty of organisation—what we call *bundobust*.

Twenty-two miles out of Dalhousie it began to rain—not a mere Hill-shower, but a good, tepid, monsoonish downpour. Golightly bustled on, wishing that he had brought an umbrella. The dust on the roads turned into mud, and the pony mired a good deal. So did Golightly's khaki gaiters. But he kept on steadily and tried to think how pleasant the coolth was.

His next pony was rather a brute at starting, and, Golightly's hands being slippery with the rain, contrived to get rid of Golightly at a corner. He chased the animal, caught it, and went ahead briskly. The spill had not improved his clothes or his temper, and he had lost one spur. He kept the other one employed. By the time that stage was ended the pony had had as much exercise as he wanted, and, in spite of the rain, Golightly was sweating freely. At the end of another miserable half-hour Golightly found the world disappear before his eyes in clammy pulp. The rain had turned the pith of his huge and snowy *solah-topee* into an evil-smelling dough, and it had closed on his head like a half-opened mushroom. Also, the green lining was beginning to run.

Golightly did not say anything worth recording here. He tore off and squeezed up as much of the brim as was in his eyes and ploughed on. The back of the helmet was flapping on his neck, and the sides stuck to his ears, but the leather band and green lining kept things roughly together, so that the hat did not actually melt away where it flapped.

Presently, the pulp and the green stuff made a sort of slimy mildew which ran over Golightly in several directions—down his back and bosom for choice. The khaki colour ran too—it was really shocking bad dye—and sections of Golightly were ochre, and streaks were brick-red, and blotches were nearly white, according to the nature and peculiarities of the dye. When he took out his handkerchief to wipe his face, and the green of the hat-lining and the purple stuff that had soaked through on to his neck from the tie became thoroughly mixed, the effect was amazing.

Near Dhar the rain stopped and the evening sun came out and dried him up slightly. It fixed the colours, too. Three miles from Pathankot the last pony fell dead lame, and Golightly was forced to walk. He pushed on into Pathankot to find his servants. He did not know that his *khitmutgar* had stopped by the roadside to get drunk, and would come on the next day saying that he had sprained his ankle. When he got into Pathankot he couldn't find his servants, his boots were stiff and ropy with mud, and there were large quantities of dust about his body. The blue tie had run as much as the khaki. So he took it off with the collar and threw it away. Then he said something about servants generally and tried to get a peg. He paid eight annas for the drink, and this revealed to him that he had only six annas more in his pocket—or in the world as he stood at that hour.

He went to the Stationmaster to negotiate for a first-class ticket to Khasa, where he was stationed. The booking-clerk said something to the Stationmaster, the Stationmaster said something to the telegraph-clerk, and the three looked at him with curiosity. They asked him to wait for half an hour, while they telegraphed to Amritzar for authority. So he waited, and four constables came and grouped themselves picturesquely round him. Just as he was preparing to ask them to go away, the Stationmaster said that he would give the Sahib the ticket to Amritzar, if the Sahib would kindly come inside the booking-office. Golightly stepped inside, and the next thing he knew was that a constable was attached to each of his legs and arms, while the Stationmaster was trying to cram a mail-bag over his head.

There was a very fair scuffle all round the booking-office, and Golightly took a nasty cut over his eye through falling against a table. But the constables were too much for him, and they and the Stationmaster handcuffed him securely. As soon as the mail-bag was slipped, he began expressing his opinions, and the head constable said, 'Without doubt this is the soldier-Englishman we required. Listen to the abuse!' Then Golightly asked the Stationmaster what the this and the that the proceedings meant.

258

The Stationmaster told him he was 'Private John Binkle of the —— Regiment, 5 ft. 9 in., fair hair, grey eyes, and a dissipated appearance, no marks on the body', who had deserted a fortnight ago. Golightly began explaining at great length; and the more he explained the less the Stationmaster believed him. He said that no Lieutenant could look such a ruffian as did Golightly, and that his instructions were to send his capture under proper escort to Amritzar. Golightly was feeling very damp and uncomfortable, and the language he used was not fit for publication, even in an expurgated form. The four constables saw him safe to Amritzar in an 'intermediate' compartment, and he spent the four-hour journey in abusing them as fluently as his knowledge of the vernaculars allowed.

At Amritzar he was bundled out on the platform into the arms of a Corporal and two men of the —— Regiment. Golightly drew himself up and tried to carry off matters jauntily. He did not feel too jaunty in handcuffs, with four constables behind him, and the blood from the cut on his forehead stiffening on his left cheek. The Corporal was not jocular either. Golightly got as far as: 'This is a very absurd mistake, my men,' when the Corporal told him to 'stow his lip' and come along. Golightly did not want to come along. He desired to stop and explain. He explained very well indeed, until the Corporal cut in with" 'You a orficer! It's the like o' you as brings disgrace on the likes of us. Bloomin' fine orficer you are! I know your regiment. The Rogue's March is the quickstep where you come from. You're a black shame to the Service.'

Golightly kept his temper, and began explaining all over again from the beginning. Then he was marched out of the rain into the refreshment-room, and told not to make a qualified fool of himself. The men were going to run him up to Fort Govindghar. And 'running up' is a performance almost as undignified as the Frog March.

Golightly was nearly hysterical with rage and the chill and the mistake and the handcuffs and the headache that the cut on his forehead had given him. He really laid himself out to express what was in his mind. When he had quite finished and his throat was feeling dry, one of the men said, 'I've 'eard a few beggars in Clink blind, stiff, and crack on a bit; but I've never 'eard any one to touch this 'ere orficer".' They were not angry with him. They rather admired him. They had some beer at the refreshment-room, and offered Golightly some too, because he had 'swore won'erful'. They asked him to tell them all about the adventures of Private John Binkle while he was loose on the countryside; and that made Golightly wilder than ever. If he had kept his wits about him he would have been quiet until an officer came; but he attempted to run.

Now the butt of a Martini in the small of your back hurts a great deal, and rotten, rain-soaked khaki tears easily when two men are yanking at your collar.

Golightly rose from the floor feeling very sick and giddy, with his shirt ripped open all down his breast and nearly all down his back. He yielded to his luck, and at that point the down-train from Lahore came in, carrying one of Golightly's Majors.

This is the Major's evidence in full:—

'There was the sound of a scuffle in the second-class refreshment-room, so I went in and saw the most villainous loafer that I ever set eyes on. His boots and breeches were plastered with mud and beer-stains. He wore a muddy-white dunghill sort of thing on his head, and it hung down in slips on his shoulders, which were a good deal scratched. He was half in and half out of a shirt as nearly in two pieces as it could be, and he was begging the guard to look at the name on the tail of it. As he had rucked the shirt all over his head, I couldn't at first see who he was, but I fancied that he was a man in the first stages of D.T. from the way he swore while he wrestled with his rags. When he turned round, and I had made allowances for a lump as big as a pork-pie over one eye, and some green war-paint on the face, and some violet stripes round the neck, I saw that it was Golightly. He was very glad to see me,' said the Major, 'and he hoped I would not tell the Mess about it. I didn't, but you can, if you like, now that Golightly has gone home.'

Golightly spent the greater part of that summer in trying to get the Corporal and the two soldiers tried by Court-Martial for arresting an 'Officer and a gentleman'. They were, of course, very sorry for their error. But the tale leaked into the regimental Canteen, and thence ran about the province.

THE STORY OF MUHAMMAD DIN

> *Who is the happy man? He that sees his own house at home, little children crowned with dust, leaping and falling and crying.*
>
> Munichandra (translated by Professor Peterson)

THE POLO-BALL WAS an old one, scarred, chipped, and dinted. It stood on the mantelpiece among the pipe-stems which Imam Din, *khitmatgar*, was cleaning for me.

'Does the Heaven-born wan this ball?' said Imam Din deferentially.

The Heaven-born set no particular store by it; but of what use was a polo-ball to a *khitmatgar*?

'By Your Honour's favour, I have a little son. He has seen this ball, and desires it to play with. I do not want it for myself.'

No one would for an instant accuse portly old Imam Din of wanting to play with polo-balls. He carried out the battered thing into the verandah; and there followed a hurricane of joyful squeaks, a patter of small feet, and the *thud-thud-thud* of the ball rolling along the ground. Evidently the little son had been waiting outside the door to secure his treasure. But how had he managed to see that polo-ball?

Next day, coming back from office half an hour earlier than usual, I was aware of a small figure in the dining-room— a tiny, plump figure in a ridiculously inadequate shirt which came, perhaps, halfway down the tubby stomach. It wandered round the room, thumb in mouth, crooning to itself as it took stock of the pictures. Undoubtedly this was the 'little son'.

He had no business in my room, of course; but was so deeply

absorbed in the discoveries that he never noticed me in the doorway. I stepped into the room and startled him nearly into a fit. He sat down on the ground with a gasp. His eyes opened, and his mouth followed suit. I knew what was coming, and fled, followed by a long, dry howl which reached the servants' quarters far more quickly than any command of mine had ever done. In ten seconds Imam Din was in the dining-room.

Then despairing sobs arose, and I returned to find Imam Din admonishing the small sinner who was using most of his shirt as a handkerchief.

'This boy,' said Imam Din judicially, 'is a *budmash*—a big *budmash*. He will, no doubt, go to the *jail-khana* for his behaviour.' Renewed yells from the penitent, and an elaborate apology to myself from Imam Din.

'Tell the baby,' said I, 'that the *Sahib* is not angry, and take him away.' Imam Din conveyed my forgiveness to the offender, who had now gathered all his shirt round his neck, stringwise, and the yell subsided into a sob. The two set off for the door. 'His name,' said Imam Din, as though the name were part of the crime, 'is Muhammad Din, and he is a *budmash*.' Freed from present danger, Muhammad Din turned round in his father's arms, and said gravely, 'It is true that my name is Muhammad Din, *Tahib*, but I am not a *budmash*. I am a *man*!'

From that day dated my acquaintance with Muhammad Din. Never again did he come into my dining-room, but on the neutral ground of the garden we greeted each other with much state, though our conversation was confined to '*Talaam, Tahib*' from his side, and '*Salaam, Muhammad Din*' from mine. Daily on my return from office, the little white shirt and the fat little body used to rise from the shade of the creeper-covered trellis where they had been hid; and daily I checked my horse here, that my salutation might not be slurred over or given unseemly.

Muhammad Din never had any companions. He used to trot about the compound, in and out of the castor-oil bushes, on mysterious errands of his own. One day I stumbled upon some of his handiwork far down the grounds. He had half buried the polo-ball in dust, and stuck six shrivelled old marigold flowers in a circle round it. Outside that circle again was a rude square, traced out in bits of red brick alternating with fragments of broken china; the whole bounded by a little bank of dust. The water-man from the well-kerb put in a plea for the small architect, saying that it was only the play of a baby and did not much disfigure my garden.

Heaven knows that I had no intention of touching the child's work then or later; but, that evening, a stroll through the garden brought me unawares full on it; so that I trampled, before I knew, marigold-heads, dust-bank, and fragments of broken soap-dish into confusion past all hope of mending. Next morning, I came upon Muhammad Din crying softly to himself over the ruin I had wrought. Some one had cruelly told him that the *Sahib* was very angry with him for spoiling the garden, and had scattered his rubbish, using bad language the while. Muhammad Din laboured for an hour at effacing every trace of the dust-bank and pottery fragments, and it was with a tearful and apologetic face that he said, '*Talaam Tahib,*' when I came home from office. A hasty inquiry resulted in Imam Din informing Muhammad Din that, by my singular favour, he was permitted to disport himself as he pleased. Whereat the child took heart and fell to tracing the ground-plan of an edifice which was to eclipse the marigold-polo-ball creation.

For some months the chubby little eccentricity revolved in his humble orbit among the castor-oil bushes and in the dust; always fashioning magnificent palaces from stale flowers thrown away by the bearer, smooth water-worn pebbles, bits of broken glass, and feathers pulled, I fancy, from my fowls—always alone, and always crooning to himself.

A gaily-spotted sea-shell was dropped one day close to the last of his little buildings; and I looked that Muhammad Din should build something more than ordinarily splendid on the strength of it. Nor was I disappointed. He meditated for the better part of an hour, and his crooning rose to a jubilant song. Then he began tracing in the dust. It would certainly be a wondrous place, this one, for it was two yards long and a yard broad in ground-plan. But the palace was never completed.

Next day there was no Muhammad Din at the head of the carriage-drive, and no '*Talaam, Tahib*' to welcome my return. I had grown accustomed to the greeting, and its omission troubled me. Next day Imam Din told me the child was suffering from fever and needed quinine. He got the medicine, and an English Doctor.

'They have no stamina, these brats,' said the Doctor, as he left Imam Din's quarters.

A week later, though I would have given much to have avoided it, I met on the road to the Mussulman burying-ground Imam Din, accompanied by one other friend, carrying in his arms, wrapped in a white cloth, all that was left of little Muhammad Din.

THE MIRACLE OF PURUN BHAGAT

The night we felt the Earth move
We stole and plucked him by the hand,
Because we loved him with the love
That knows but cannot understand.

And when the roaring hillside broke,
And all our world fell down in rain,
We saved him, we the Little-Folk;
But lo! He will not come again!

Mourn now, we saved him for the sake
Of such poor love as wild ones may.
Mourn ye! Our brother does not wake
And his own kind drive us away!

Dirge of the Langurs

THERE WAS ONCE a man in India who was Prime Minister of one of the semi-independent native states in the north-western part of the country. He was a Brahmin, so high-caste that caste ceased to have any particular meaning for him, and his father had been an important official in the gay-coloured tag-rag and bob-tail of an old-fashioned Hindu Court. But as Purun Dass grew up he realised that the ancient order of things was changing, and that if any one wished to get on he must stand well with the English, and imitate all the English believed to be good. At the same time a native official must keep his own master's favour. This was a difficult game, but the quiet, close-mouthed young Brahmin, helped by a good English education at a Bombay university, played it coolly, and rose, step by step, to be Prime

Minister of the kingdom. That is to say, he held more real power than his master, the Maharajah.

When the old king—who was suspicious of the English, their railways and telegraphs—died, Purun Dass stood high with his young successor, who had been tutored by an Englishman. And between them, though he always took care that his master should have the credit, they established schools for little girls, made roads, and started State dispensaries and shows of agricultural implements, and published a yearly blue-book on the "Moral and Material Progress of the State", and the Foreign Office and the Government of India were delighted. Very few native states take up English progress without reservations, for they will not believe, as Purun Dass showed he did, that what is good for the Englishman must be twice as good for the Asiatic. The Prime Minister became the honoured friend of viceroys and governors, and lieutenant-governors, and medical missionaries, and common missionaries, and hard-riding English officers who came to shoot in the State preserves, as well as of whole hosts of tourists who travelled up and down India in the cold weather, showing how things ought to be managed. In his spare time he would endow scholarships for the study of medicine and manufactures on strictly English lines, and write letters to the *Pioneer*, the greatest Indian daily paper, explaining his master's aims and objects.

At last he went to England on a visit, and had to pay enormous sums to the priests when he came back, for even so high-caste a Brahmin as Purun Dass lost caste by crossing the black sea. In London he met and talked with every one worth knowing—men whose names go all over the world—and saw a great deal more than he said. He was given honorary degrees by learned universities, and he made speeches and talked of Hindu social reform to English ladies in evening dress, till all London cried, 'This is the most fascinating man we have ever met at dinner since cloths were first laid!'

When he returned to India there was a blaze of glory, for the Viceroy himself made a special visit to confer upon the Maharajah the Grand Cross of the Star of India—all diamonds and ribbons and enamel. And at the same ceremony, while the cannon boomed, Purun Dass was made a Knight Commander of the Order of the Indian Empire, so that his name stood Sir Purun Dass, K.C.I.E.

That evening at dinner in the big Viceregal tent he stood up with the badge and the collar of the order on his breast, and replying to the toast of his master's health, made a speech that few Englishmen could have surpassed.

Next month, when the city had returned to its sunbaked quiet, he did a thing no Englishman would have dreamed of doing, for, so far as the world's affairs went, he died. The jewelled order of his knighthood returned to the Indian Government, and a new Prime Minister was appointed to the charge of affairs, and a great game of General Post began in all the subordinate appointments. The priests knew what had happened and the people guessed, but India is the one place in the world where a man can do as he pleases and nobody asks why. And the fact that Dewan Sir Purun Dass, K.C.I.E., had resigned position, palace, and power, and taken up the begging bowl and ochre-coloured dress of a Sannyasi or holy man, was considered nothing extraordinary. He had been, as the Old Law recommends, twenty years a youth, twenty years a fighter—though he had never carried a weapon in his life—and twenty years head of a household. He had used his wealth and his power for what he knew both to be worth; he had taken honour when it came his way; and he had seen men and cities far and near, and men and cities had stood up and honoured him. Now he would let these things go, as a man drops the cloak he needs no longer.

Behind him, as he walked through the city gates, an antelope skin and brass-handled crutch under his arm, and a begging bowl of polished brown *coco-de-mer* in his hand, barefoot, alone, with eyes cast on the ground—behind him they were firing salutes from the bastions in honour of his happy successor. Purun Dass nodded. All that life was ended, and he bore it no more ill-will or good-will than a man bears to a colourless dream of the night. He was a Sannyasi—a houseless, wandering mendicant, depending on his neighbours for his daily bread, and so long as there is a morsel to divide in India neither priest nor beggar starves. He had never in his life tasted meat, and very seldom eaten even fish. A five-pound-note would have covered his personal expenses for food through any one of the many years

267

in which he had been absolute master of millions of money. Even when he was being lionised in London he had held before him his dream of peace and quiet—the long, white, dusty Indian road, printed all over with bare feet, the incessant, slow-moving traffic, and the sharp-smelling wood-smoke curling up under the fig-trees in the twilight, where the wayfarers sat at their evening meal.

When the time came to make that dream true the Prime Minister took the proper steps, and in three days you might more easily found a bubble in the trough of the long Atlantic seas than Purun Dass among the roving, gathering, separating millions of India.

At night his antelope skin was spread where the darkness overtook him—sometimes in a Sannyasi monastery by the roadside; sometimes by a mud pillar shrine of Kala Pir, where the Yogis, who are another misty division of holy men, would receive him as they do those who know what castes and divisions are worth; sometimes on the outskirts of a little Hindu village, where the children would steal up with the food their parents had prepared; sometimes on the pitch of the bare grazing-grounds where the flame of his stick fire waked the drowsy camels. It was all one to Purun Dass—or Purun Bhagat, as he called himself now. Earth, people, and food were all one. But, unconsciously, his feet drew him away northwards and eastwards; from the south to Rohtak; from Rohtak to Kurnool; from Kurnool to ruined Samanah, and then up-stream along the dried bed of the Gugger River that fills only when the rain falls in the hills, till, one day, he saw the far line of the great Himalayas.

Then Purun Bhagat smiled, for he remembered that his mother was of Rajput Brahmin birth, from Kulu way—a hill-woman, always homesick for the snows—and that the least touch of the hill blood draws a man in the end back to where he belongs.

'Yonder,' said Purun Bhagat, breasting the lower slopes of the Siwaliks, where the cacti stand up like seven-branched candlesticks, 'yonder I shall sit down and get knowledge.' And the cool wind of the Himalayas whistled about his ears as he trod the road that led to Simla.

The last time he had come that way it had been in state,

with a clattering cavalry escort, to visit the gentlest and most affable of Viceroys, and the two had talked for an hour together about mutual friends in London, and what the Indian common folk really thought of things. This time Purun Bhagat paid no calls, but leaned on the rail of the mall, watching the glorious view of the plains spread out fifty miles below, till a native Mohammedan policeman told him he was obstructing traffic. And Purun Bhagat salaamed reverently to the Law, because he knew the value of it, and was seeking for a Law of his own. Then he moved on, and slept that night in an empty hut in Chota Simla, which looks like the very last end of the earth, but it was only the beginning of his journey. He followed the Himalaya-Tibet Road, the little ten-foot track that is blasted out of solid rock, or strutted out on timbers over gulfs a thousand feet deep; that dips into warm, wet, shut-in valleys, and climbs across bare, grassy hill-shoulders where the sun strikes like a burning-glass; or turns through dripping, dark forests where the tree-ferns dress the trunks from head to heel, and the pheasant calls to his mate. And he met Tibetan herdsmen with their dogs and flocks of sheep, each sheep with a little bag of borax on his back, and wandering woodcutters, and cloaked and blanketed lamas from Tibet, coming into India on pilgrimage, and envoys of little solitary hill-states, posting furiously on ring-streaked and piebald ponies, or the cavalcade of a rajah paying a visit. Or else for a long, clear day he would see nothing more than a black bear grunting and rooting down below in the valley. When he first started, the roar of the world he had left still rang in his ears, as the roar of a tunnel rings a little after the train has passed through. But when he had put the Mutteeanee Pass behind him that was all done, and Purun Bhagat was alone with himself, walking, wondering, and thinking, his eyes on the ground, and his thoughts with the clouds.

One evening he crossed the highest pass he had met till then—it had been a two days' climb—and came out on a line of snow-peaks that belted all the horizon—mountains from fifteen to twenty thousand feet high, looking almost near enough to hit with a stone, though they were fifty or sixty miles away. The pass was crowned with dense, dark forest—deodar, walnut, wild cherry, wild olive, and wild pear, but mostly deodar, which is the Himalayan cedar; and under the shadow of the deodars stood a deserted shrine to Kali—who is Durga, who is Sitala, who is sometimes worshipped against the smallpox.

Purun Dass swept the stone floor clean, smiled at the grinning statue, made himself a little mud fireplace at the back of the shrine, spread his antelope skin on a bed of fresh pine needles, tucked his *bairagi*—his brass-handled crutch—under his armpit, and sat down to rest.

Immediately below him the hillside fell away, clean and cleared for fifteen hundred feet, to where a little village of stone-walled houses, with roofs of beaten earth, clung to the steep tilt. All round it tiny terraced fields lay out like aprons of patchwork on the knees of the mountain, and cows no bigger than beetles grazed between the smooth stone circles of the threshing-floors. Looking across the valley the eye was deceived by the size of things, and could not at first realise that what seemed to be low scrub, on the opposite mountain-flank, was in truth a forest of hundred-foot pines. Purun Bhagat saw an eagle swoop across the enormous hollow, but the great bird dwindled to dot ere it was half-way over. A few bands of scattered clouds strung up and down the valley, catching on a shoulder of the hills, or rising up and dying out when they were level with the head of the pass. And, 'Here shall I find peace,' said Purun Bhagat.

Now, a hill-man makes nothing of a few hundred feet up or down, and as soon as the villagers saw the smoke in the deserted shrine, the village priest climbed up the terraced hillside to welcome the stranger.

When he met Purun Bhagat's eyes—the eyes of a man used to control thousands—he bowed to the earth, took the begging bowl without a word, and returned to the village, saying: 'We have at last a holy man. Never have I seen such a man. He is of the plains—but pale coloured—a Brahmin of the Brahmins.' Then all the housewives of the village said: 'Think you he will stay with us?' And each did her best to cook the most savoury meal for the Bhagat. Hill-food is very simple, but with the buckwheat and Indian corn, and rice and red pepper, and little fish out of the stream in the little valley, and honey from the flue-like hives built in the stone walls, and dried apricots, and turmeric, and wild ginger, and bannocks of flour, a devout woman can make good things. And it was a full bowl that the priest carried to the Bhagat. Was he going to stay? Asked the priest. Would he need a *chela*—a disciple—to beg for him? Had he a blanket against the cold weather? Was the food good?

Purun Bhagat ate, and thanked the giver. It was in his mind to stay. That was sufficient, said the priest. Let the begging-bowl be placed outside the shrine, in the hollow made by those two twisted roots, and daily should the Bhagat be fed, for the village felt honoured that such a man—he looked timidly into the Bhagat's face—should tarry among them.

That day saw the end of Purun Bhagat's wanderings. He had come to the place appointed for him—the silence and the space. After this, time stopped, and he, sitting at the mouth of the shrine, could not tell whether he were alive or dead: a man with control of his limbs, or a part of the hills, and the clouds, and the shifting rain, and sunlight. He would repeat a Name softly to himself a hundred hundred times, till, at each repetition, he seemed to move more and more out of his body, sweeping up to the doors of some tremendous discovery. But, just as the door was opening, his body would drag him back, and, with grief, he felt he was locked up again in the flesh and bones of Purun Bhagat.

Every morning the gilled begging-bowl was laid silently in the crotch of the roots outside the shrine. Sometimes the priest brought it; sometimes a Ladakhi trader, lodging in the village, and anxious to get merit, trudged up the path. But, more often, it was the woman who had cooked the meal overnight, and she would murmur, hardly above her breath: 'Speak for me before the gods, Bhagat. Speak for such a one, the wife of so-and-so!' Now and then some bold child would be allowed the honour, and Purun Bhagat would hear him drop the bowl and run as fast as his little legs could carry him, but the Bhagat never came down to the village. It was laid out like a map at his feet. He could see the evening gatherings held on the circle of the threshing floors, because that was the only level ground; could see the wonderful unnamed green of the young rice, the indigo blues of the Indian corn; the dock-like patches of buckwheat, and, in its season, the red bloom of the amaranth, whose tiny seeds, being neither grain nor pulse, made a food that can be lawfully eaten by Hindus in time of fasts.

When the year turned, the roofs of the huts were all little squares of purest gold, for it was on the roofs that they laid out their cobs of the corn to dry. Hiving and harvest, rice-sowing and husking, passed before his eyes, all embroidered down there on the many-sided fields, and he thought of them all, and wondered what they all led to at the long last.

Even in populated India a man cannot a day sit still before the wild things run over him as though he were a rock. And in that wilderness very soon the wild things, who knew Kali's shrine well, came back to look at the intruder. The langurs, the big, grey-whiskered monkeys of the Himalayas, were, naturally, the first, for they are alive with curiosity. And when they had upset the begging bowl, and rolled it round the floor, and tried their teeth on the brass-handled crutch, and made faces at the antelope skin, they decided that the human being who sat so still was harmless. At evening, they would leap down from the pines, and beg with their hands for things to eat, and then swing off in graceful curves. They liked the warmth of the fire, too, and huddled round it till Purun Bhagat had to push them aside to throw on more fuel, and in the morning, as often as not, he would find a furry ape sharing his blanket. All day long, one or the other of the tribe would sit by his side, staring out at the snows, crooning and looking unspeakably wise and sorrowful.

After the monkeys came the barasingha, that big deer which is like our red deer, but stronger. He wished to rub off the velvet of his horns against the cold stones of Kali's statue, and stamped his feet when he saw the man at the shrine. But Purun Bhagat never moved, and, little by little, the royal stag edged up and nuzzled his shoulder. Purun Bhagat slid one cool hand along the hot antlers, and the touch soothed the fretted beast, who bowed his head, and Purun Bhagat very softly rubbed and ravelled off the velvet. Afterwards, the barasingha brought his doe and fawn— gentle things that mumbled on the holy man's blanket—or would come alone at night, his eyes green in the fire-flicker, to take his share of fresh walnuts. At last, the musk-deer, the shyest and almost the smallest of the deerlets, came, too, her big, rabbity ears erect; even brindled, silent *muschick-nabha* must needs find out what the light in the shrine meant, and drop her moose-like ·

nose into Purun Bhagat's lap, coming and going with the shadows of the fire. Purun Bhagat called them all "my brothers", and his low call of "*Bhai! Bhai!*" would draw them from the forest at noon if they were within earshot. The Himalayan black bear, moody and suspicious—Sona, who has the V–shaped white mark under his chin—passed that way more than once. And since the Bhagat showed no fear, Sona showed no anger, but watched him, and came closer, and begged a share of the caresses, and a dole of bread or wild berries. Often, in the still dawns, when the Bhagat would climb to the very crest of the notched pass to watch the red day walking along the peaks of the snows, he would find Sona shuffling and grunting at his heels, thrusting a curious fore paw under fallen trunks, and bringing it away with a *whoof* of impatience. Or his early steps would wake Sona where he lay curled up, and the great brute, rising erect, would think to fight, till he heard the Bhagat's voice and knew his best friend.

Nearly all hermits and holy men who live apart from the big cities have the reputation of being able to work miracles with the wild things, but all the miracle lies in keeping still, in never making a hasty movement, and, for a long time, at least, in never looking directly at a visitor. The villagers saw the outlines of the barasingha stalking like a shadow through the dark forest behind the shrine; saw the minaul, the Himalayan pheasant, blazing in her best colours before Kali's statue, and the langurs on their haunches, inside, playing with the walnut shells. Some of the children, too, had heard Sona singing to himself, bear-fashion, behind the fallen rocks, and the Bhagat's reputation as miracle-worker stood firm.

Yet nothing was farther from his mind than miracles. He believed that all things were one big Miracle, and when a man knows that much he knows something to go upon. He knew for a certainty that there was nothing great and nothing little in this world, and day and night he strove to think out his way into the heart of things, back to the place whence his soul had come.

So thinking, his untrimmed hair fell down about his shoulders, the stone slab at the side of the antelope skin was dented into a little hole by the foot of his brass-handled crutch, and the place between the tree-trunks, where the begging-bowl rested day after day, sank and wore into a hollow almost as smooth as the brown shell itself, and each beast knew his exact place at the fire. The fields changed their colours with the seasons; the threshing-floors filled and emptied, and filled again and again; the langurs frisked among the branches feathered with light snow, till the mother monkeys brought their sad-eyed little babies up from the warmer valleys with the spring. There were few changes in the village. The priest was older, and many of the little children who used to come with the begging-dish sent their own children now. And when you asked of the villagers how long their holy man had lived in Kali's shrine at the head of the pass, they answered: 'Always.'

Then came such summer rains as had not been known in the hills for many seasons. Through three good months the valley was wrapped in cloud and soaking mist—steady, unrelenting downfall, breaking off into thunder-shower after thunder-shower. Kali's shrine stood above the clouds, for the most part, and there was a whole month in which the Bhagat never caught a glimpse of his village. It was packed away under a white floor of cloud that swayed and shifted and rolled on itself and bulged upwards, but never broke from its piers—the streaming flanks of the valley.

At that time he heard nothing but the sound of a million little waters, overhead from the trees, and underfoot along the ground, soaking through the pine-needles, dripping from the tongues of draggled fern, and spouting in newly torn muddy channels down the slopes. Then the sun came out, and drew forth the good incense of the deodars and the rhododendrons, and that far-off clean smell the Hill-People call "the smell of the snows". The hot sunshine lasted for a week, and then the rains gathered together for their last downpour, and the water fell in sheets that flayed off the skin of the ground and leaped back in mud. Purun Bhagat heaped his fire high that night, for he was sure his brothers would need warmth, but never a beast came to the shrine, though he called and called till he dropped asleep, wondering what had happened in the woods.

It was in the black heart of the night, the rain drumming like a thousand drums, that he was roused by a plucking at his blanket, and, stretching out, felt the little hand of a langur. 'It is better here than in the trees,' he said sleepily, loosening a fold of the blanket. 'Take it and be warm.' The monkey caught his hand and pulled hard. 'Is it food, then?' said Purun Bhagat. 'Wait a while, and I will prepare some.' As he kneeled to throw fuel on the fire the langur ran to the door of the shrine, crooned, and ran back again, plucking at the man's knee.

'What is it? What is thy trouble, Brother?' said Purun Bhagat, for the langur's eyes were full of things that he could not tell. 'Unless one of thy caste be in a trap—and none sets traps here—I will not go into that weather. Look, Brother, even the barasingha comes for shelter.'

The deer's antlers clashed as he strode into the shrine, clashed against the grinning statue of Kali. He lowered them in Purun Bhagat's direction and stamped uneasily, hissing through his half-shut nostrils.

'*Hai! Hai! Hai!*' said the Bhagat, snapping his fingers. 'Is *this* payment for a night's lodging?' But the deer pushed him towards the door, and as he did so Purun Bhagat heard the sound of something opening with a sigh, and saw two slabs of the floor draw away from each other, while the sticky earth below smacked its lips.

'Now I see,' said Purun Bhagat. 'No blame to my brothers that they did not sit by the fire to-night. The mountain is falling. And yet—why should I go?' His eye fell on the empty begging-bowl, and his face changed. 'They have given me good food daily since—since I came, and, if I am not swift, to-morrow there will not be one mouth in the valley. Indeed, I must go and warn them below. Back there, Brother! Let me get to the fire.'

The barasingha backed unwillingly as Purun Bhagat drove a torch deep into the flame, twirling it till it was well lit. 'Ah! Ye came to warn me,' he said, rising. 'Better than that we shall do, better than that. Out, now, and lend me thy neck, Brother, for I have but two feet.'

He clutched the bristling withers of the barasingha with his right hand, held the torch away with his left, and stepped out of the shrine into the desperate night. There was no breath of wind, but the rain nearly drowned the torch as the great deer hurried down the slope, sliding on his haunches. As soon as they were clear of the forest more of the Bhagat's brothers joined them.

He heard, though he could not see, the langurs pressing about him, and behind them the *uhh*! *uhh*! of Sona. The rain matted his long white hair into ropes; the water splashed beneath his bare feet, and his yellow robe clung to his frail old body, but he stepped down steadily, leaning against the barasingha. He was no longer a holy man, but Sir Purun Dass, K.C.I.E., Prime Minister of no small State, a man accustomed to command, going out to save life. Down the steep plashy path they poured all together, the Bhagat and his brothers, down and down till the deer clicked and stumbled on the wall of a threshing-floor, and snorted because he smelled Man. Now they were at the head of the one crooked village street, and the Bhagat beat with his crutch at the barred windows of the blacksmith's house as his torch blazed up in the shelter of the eaves. 'Up and out!' cried Purun Bhagat, and he did not know his own voice, for it was years since he had spoken aloud to a man. 'The hill falls! The hill is falling! Up and out, oh, you within!'

'It is our Bhagat,' said the blacksmith's wife. 'He stands among his beasts. Gather the little ones and give the call.'

It ran from house to house, while the beasts, cramped in the narrow way, surged and huddled round the Bhagat, and Sona puffed impatiently.

The people hurried into the street—they were no more than seventy souls all told—and in the glare of their torches they saw their Bhagat holding back the terrified barasingha, while the monkeys plucked piteously at his skirts, and Sona sat on his haunches and roared.

'Across the valley and up the next hill!' shouted Purun Bhagat. 'Leave none behind! We follow!'

Then the people ran as only Hill-Folk can run, for they knew that in a landslip you must climb for the highest ground across the valley. They fled, splashing through the little river at the bottom, and panted up the terraced fields on the far side, while the Bhagat and his brethren followed. Up and up the opposite mountain they climbed, calling to each other by name—the roll-call of the village—and at their heels toiled the big barasingha, weighted by the falling strength of Purun Bhagat. At last the deer stopped in the shadow of a deep pine-wood, five hundred feet up the hillside. His instinct, that had warned him of the coming slide, told him he would be safe here.

Purun Bhagat dropped fainting by his side, for the chill of the rain and that fierce climb were killing him. But first he called to the scattered torches ahead: 'Stay and count your numbers.' Then, whispering to the deer as he saw the lights gather in a cluster: 'Stay with me, Brother. Stay—till—I—go!'

There was a sigh in the air that grew to a mutter, and a mutter that grew to a roar, and a roar that passed all sense of hearing, and the hillside on which the villagers stood was hit in the darkness, and rocked to the blow. Then a note as steady, deep, and true as the deep C of the organ drowned everything for perhaps five minutes, while the very roots of the pines quivered to it. It died away, and the sound of the rain falling on miles of hard ground and grass changed to the muffled drums of water on soft earth. That told its own tale.

Never a villager—not even the priest—was bold enough to speak to the Bhagat who had saved their lives. They crouched under the pines and waited till the day. When it came they looked across the valley, and saw that what had been forest, and terraced field, and track-threaded grazing-ground was one raw, red, fan-shaped smear, with a few trees flung head-down on the scarp. That red ran high up the hill of their refuge, damming back the little river, which had begun to spread into a brick-coloured lake. Of the village, of the road to the shrine, of the shrine itself, and the forest behind, there was no trace. For one mile in width and two thousand feet in sheer depth the mountain-side had come away bodily, planed clean from head to heel.

And the villagers, one by one, crept through the wood to pray before their Bhagat. They saw the barasingha standing over him, who fled when they came near, and they heard the langurs wailing in the branches, and Sona moaning up the hill. But their Bhagat was dead, sitting cross-legged, his back against a tree, his crutch under his armpit, and his face turned to the north-east.

The priest said: 'Behold a miracle after a miracle, for in this very attitude must all Sannyasis be buried! Therefore, where he now is we will build the temple of our holy man.'

They built the temple before a year was ended, a little stone and earth shrine, and they called the hill the Bhagat's Hill, and they worship there with lights and flowers and offerings to this day. But they do not know that the saint of their worship is the late Sir Purun Dass, K.C.I.E., D.C.L., Ph.D., etc., once Prime Minister of the progressive and enlightened state of Mohiniwala, and honorary or corresponding member of more learned and scientific societies than will ever do any good in this world or the next.